THE SEPARATION

BY
DOUG WHITE

Airleaf Publishing

airleaf.com

© Copyright 2006, 2007 Doug White

Second Printing

All Rights Reserved.

No part of this book may be reproduced, stored in a retrieval system, or transmitted by any means, electronic, mechanical, photocopying, recording, or otherwise, without written permission from the author.

ISBN: 978-1-60002-042-1

CREDITS

In *The Separation,* Peter runs into his first black bear, face to face. Jake, always looking for reasons to teach something new to Peter, took advantage of the opportunity. Although I've had more than one run-in with black bears while canoeing in Northern Ontario, Jake's knowledge is far beyond mine, or at least it was. I'd like to thank Bear World in Rexburg, Idaho for furthering my knowledge on both black and grizzly bears.

I would like to thank Doug Denbow and Shelly Sellepack, my editor and proofreader respectfully.

Hank Hamilton is a driver loved by Peter more than any other driver other than Jake, The series character holds pretty true to the real Henry "Hank" Helton, a retired driver and a good friend. Thanks Hank.

Cathy Hardy, living in Little Rock, Arkansas mans my website and email and has been a big help over the years in many other ways, too. Thanks, Cathy.

Although it has never been identified by name, when home, Jake and Peter along with Betty and Jerry, attend the Orchard Park Community Church. I would like to thank my church for allowing me to use their baptism so Peter could be baptized officially into the Christian faith..

Jake, Peter and the Jake Winters Series are developing a solid base of followers including students. As a result, I'm receiving more email and phone calls than ever. Thank you very much.

Finally, I'd like to thank my family and friends for their love, encouragement and support.

DEDICATION

In memory of Beth Friedman

Beth was born in pre-second World War Germany living there throughout the war. At the end of the war she married an American GI and moved to the United States.

She taught middle school English and history. In her fifties, she was still challenged to arm wrestling occasionally by an eight-grade boy and seldom lost. In her early sixties she retired due to a toboggan accident.

When I started writing, she was one of my biggest supporters and assisted in the editing of my first book, *The Load*.

In July, 2005 she lost her battle with cancer. Thanks Beth, for your support, help and love.

INTRODUCTION

In June 2001, life for Jake Winters—soon to be 58—was going just as he always knew it would someday. He'd been driving a big truck cross-country for eleven years—solo. For years he'd been asked to become a trainer for his company, but he always refused saying he didn't want to be slowed down by somebody else's periodic bodily needs.

Several friends had expressed an interest in riding with him for a week or two, but he told them passengers weren't allowed. They all knew that wasn't true; but they understood. Jake was a people person, yet at times he loved his solitude. He was one of the few people his friends knew who was totally comfortable with himself.

Jake loved to read. He often read a book a week even though he averaged 3000 miles a week. He figured someday he'd write a book; maybe just to prove to himself he could. After all, he was a storyteller and always had been. He figured that if he put his mind to it, he could come up with a good long story or maybe even a book. But he was never in the mood. Maybe someday!

He loved the West and Western history. When able, he visited such places as Fort Bridger, Wyoming; Dead Wood, South Dakota; Tombstone, Arizona; Virginia City, Nevada and Bannack, Montana. There were so many other places he wanted to see firsthand, but he either couldn't with the big truck or he didn't have the time. Maybe someday, he dreamed.

Jake was fiercely independent and loved it. He had neither cares nor worries, nor financial nor personal responsibilities.

His favorite musical was *Paint Your Wagon* from the 1960's. His favorite song in the musical was *I Was Born*

Under A Wandering Star. He felt he was born to wander...and to do it alone.

His only responsibilities were to his company and its customers. While he never married, he never wrote it out of his mind either. Maybe someday!

He had nothing to trouble his mind except what book he would read next and when he'd retire. Little did he know when he delivered a load of paper to a company in Butte, Montana on the morning of June 29, 2001, that his life would change forever.

Jake considered himself a convenient Christian; when he needed God's help, Jake called on him but when the emergency passed, Jake neglected any thought of a personal God until the next crisis.

It never dawned on him that God might need Jake for a crucial assignment.

Jake was dispatched to Slippery Gulch, Montana from Butte to pick up a small crusher: a two-ton piece of equipment used in small mining operations. He would load his trailer at the J. and J. Mines and transport it to a company in Reno, Nevada. But according to the map and the glossary of Montana, Slippery Gulch didn't exist. So his company, QZX, had neither directions to the town nor a phone number for the mine.

He found his way to the town of Basin where Jake met George Swansen, a local amateur historian and half-owner of the Silver Dollar Saloon. He also met Jane Dowdy, George's strikingly beautiful sister and owner of the other half of the saloon. Jane's husband, Mike, gladly escorted Jake to the proper turn-off for Slippery Gulch. After a hair-raising drive along the edge of a cliff, Jake arrived in a quaint tiny nineteenth-century town, typical of so many in this part of the West.

While in town, Jake met Jeremiah Peabody, the owner of the J. and J. Mines. He also met his real assignment from Heaven: a six-year-old, severely neglected boy named Peter Stevenson. Of course, Jake had no idea that God had something special in store for him.

After loading the crusher into his trailer, Jake took several pictures of Peter before departing town.

Jake was a burned-out schoolteacher. He lost his patience with kids many years ago and no longer wanted to have anything to do with them. But as a compassionate human being, he was naturally concerned about Peter's condition. He was determined to get him some help if possible. Before leaving the area, he informed his newfound friends in Basin of Peter's situation. They promised to help however they could.

Relieved, Jake left for Reno, convinced he'd never see Slippery Gulch or Peter again. He really didn't care now. People were constantly stepping into his life for an hour or two; then he'd move on, never to hear from them again. That is the life of the long-haul trucker. In a way, it was a defensive measure; Jake never broke any hearts and he never had his broken…again. And that's the way he planned to keep his life, at least until he retired in a few years. Then, maybe someday…

When Jake arrived in Reno, he learned that the company that ordered the crusher had gone out of business one hundred years ago. Worse yet, it was discovered that the crusher had mysteriously disappeared from his trailer. The FBI was going to charge him with theft. He could be arrested for the theft of interstate freight.

A week after he picked up the crusher, Jake was back in Slippery Gulch, compliments of the FBI, and with his quickly found attorney, Frank Krandell, and his three new friends from Basin.

At that time, Jake learned that not only had Peter been severely neglected, he had also been terribly abused by his father and other citizens of Slippery Gulch. Worse yet, he learned Peter was brutally murdered by his father in 1901. Peter was a ghost.

Because Peter disclosed the whereabouts of the missing crusher, Jake was off the hook with the Feds. Once again, Jake left Slippery Gulch relieved that he would never see Peter or the town again. But he would learn that God was projecting a better plan. Less than a week later, Jake was back. A significant editorial had been discovered in the archives of Jefferson County, one written by the owner of the *Slippery Gulch Gazette* four days after Peter's death, and depicting the life and death of the lad. Seconds before his death, Peter had looked to the heavens and prayed for a friend. Although nobody saw that prayer answered at the time, several near to Jake knew he was now that friend. Peter's prayer was about to be answered.

Jake disagreed; after all, he was only a cross-country trucker just passing through as they always do. He had places to go and things to do and see. But when Jake spent the day with Peter in Slippery Gulch, he came to realize he *was* the answer to a little boy's prayer spoken one hundred years before. Now came the questions, such as "why me?" and "what say do I have in this?" Jake wasn't able to answer the first question but the answer to the second one seemed to be "not much!" He was under a load going to Spokane. He didn't have the time to sit around for days or weeks nursemaiding a one hundred six-year-old ghost. Actually, he didn't have the necessary interest or heart either.

Based on the editorial, Peter's funeral was a Christian disgrace. So Jane, George, Mike and Jake decided to have a proper funeral for Peter on June 30, 2002; exactly 101 years after his first one. It would be a Christian funeral. During the year a beautiful, granite stone would be purchased and engraved and Peter's bones would be interred in a modern casket. But in the meantime, what about Peter?

Peter was a neat little kid...or ghost...or whatever he was. Jake was not sure which. But like always, it was time to move on. The next morning, Jake would be in his truck heading for Spokane—alone. But that did not fit into God's plan.

Peter was filthy dirty and asked if Jake could make him clean. Jake had none of the necessary items for a bath. He reluctantly agreed to come back the next day to bathe Peter. Since Peter was six, Jake figured all he'd have to do is supervise. Much to Jake's surprise, this was to be Peter's first bath of his life. He didn't know what soap was or how to handle it. For the first time, Jake saw the extent of the neglect and it sickened him. As a bachelor he had never bathed a child before, but now he had no choice.

The night before Peter's bath, Jane came up with a great idea—as far as everybody was concerned except Jake. Jane suggested rather strongly that Jake take Peter with him when he continued on his way; after all, Jake was the answer to Peter's prayer. Thinking of his lost independence and freedom from responsibility, Jake came up with every excuse in the book why he couldn't do that. Jane systematically shot them all down. When Jake left for Spokane, he had his first passenger ever.

Peter was six and therefore had a lot of questions. But he was also a product of the Nineteenth Century. Everything he saw and heard was new and exciting but at times, frightening. As a result, he had tons more questions beyond those of a normal six-year-old. At times, Jake's brain was swimming, yet he marveled at himself for the patience he was displaying toward Peter—a patience he hadn't displayed toward children since the mid-1980s.

Their second day together Jake happened to look over at Peter to find him looking back at him. What Jake saw touched his heart like nothing else ever had. A typical six-year-old toothless grin greeted Jake, an expression he had always cherished in children. But it was Peter's eyes that touched him even more. Less than two weeks ago these same eyes had reflected sorrow, loneliness, fear and desperation. Now they reflected friendship, gratitude and love. Suddenly Jake realized his independence was gone and his responsibilities were greatly increased. He found he was teaching again, and he loved it. He also realized his love for Peter was increasing by the day.

The first three weeks were rough on both of them, but they worked together and cooperated as a team. They both came out stronger for their efforts.

During the year, Peter had so many new and wonderful experiences it would be impossible to keep track of them all. It seemed God was providing Peter with the nurturing childhood he'd missed. Jake began to thank God every day for the opportunity.

But Peter's funeral was rapidly approaching. What would happen to Peter? Would he be forced to return to the grave, or would he be allowed to stay with Jake? Jake prayed every day for the later. If Peter was forced to return to the grave, could Jake go on without him, or would he even want to?

Peter took care of that. Before the funeral, Peter made Jake promise that if he were to return to the grave, Jake would carry on for the sake of the team.

When the funeral service came to an end, everybody sat there as if waiting for something to happen. Finally it did. Peter stood, kissed Jake on the forehead and started to walk away. As he walked his body became partially transparent. Forty feet beyond stood a beautiful and also partially transparent woman visible only to Jake. Peter stood before the female apparition for fifteen minutes, leaving everybody in the dark, including Jake. Finally, Peter called Jake over and introduced him to the woman, as his mother. Jake was shocked. After all, Mrs. Stevenson died shortly after Peter was born. What did this mean? For Peter and Jake, was this the beginning of a long future together, or was this the end of a wonderful yearlong experience? Was Jake about to be thrust back under his lonely "wandering star" and a solitude that he no longer desired?

CHAPTER ONE

I stood with my mouth open, attempting to force my brain into overdrive. Before me stood the mother of the little boy that has been living with me for the past year, yet she's been dead for 107 years. I looked at Peter. He's been dead for 101 years. I was standing before two dead people that were talking to me. This funeral and burial was getting crazier by the second.

I looked back at Peter's mother dressed in late nineteenth-century clothes. She was one of the most beautiful women I'd ever seen. It was obvious where Peter got his good looks. She smiled slightly with Peter's same smile and said, "Mr. Winters, it's very nice to meet you." I bit my lip hard. I tasted blood. Mrs. Stevenson was still there. Being partially transparent, she did not offer me her hand. "Thank you so much for taking care of my son for the past year. He had a wonderful time and learned so much. His prayer has been answered."

My heart sank. It sounded like our experience was over. I could almost hear the tears form in Peter's eyes. After clearing my throat and swallowing hard a couple of times, I finally found my voice.

"Mrs. Stevenson, it's an honor to meet you. Your son is a wonderful child. I have thoroughly enjoyed his company. Everyone who meets him loves him. Not only has he enriched my life, he has enriched the lives of everyone he came in contact with."

She smiled and thanked me. "The one thing I wanted and prayed to God for was that Peter have a good childhood. Not only could I not do that, I couldn't even protect him. Now because of you, he has had a far better childhood than I could ever have hoped for. He's happy and in better health than I ever saw him in. He loves you very much, Mr. Winters. And for what all you have done for him, I do too."

"Thank you, but what about his future? Is it time for Peter to move on to heaven?"

Both Peter and I stood anxiously awaiting her answer. "You may not realize it, Mr. Winters, but Peter has been in a heaven on earth for the last year. It is his choice and of course yours, as to whether he stays in this heaven with you or moves on to be in mine with me."

My heart leaped. So maybe this wasn't over! Just a week ago, Peter told me he was already in heaven. Apparently he was right. He has been in a heaven on earth for the past year. But how could he have been in heaven with me, when I, as a living, breathing person, am not anywhere near there? I turned and looked at the people standing around Peter's gravestone. I was certain they were all alive too. One more thing I would probably never understand.

I didn't look at Peter, but knew he was looking at me. "Mrs. Stevenson, we work, play and live well together. But more importantly we love each other. We understand each other and we watch out for and take care of each other. We're a team—a loving team. But what I want is what's best for Peter."

She studied me for a long time; then looked at Peter, and back at me. "Can you get along without him?"

"I got along just fine without him for a good many years." I still didn't look at Peter, but could feel his heart sink and almost hear his tears form again. Mrs. Stevenson studied her son with disappointment, but I suspected she wasn't surprised at his reaction. "But to be perfectly honest, I don't know what I'd do without him anymore. I love him, Mrs. Stevenson. He's like my grandson." Peter's disappointment vanished.

She looked at me, and then gave her son a knowing smile. "For all practical purposes, he is your grandson. He may love me, but only because I'm his mother. He doesn't know me. You mean everything to him, Mr. Winters. And for that reason, if you're willing, I think it best for Peter to remain with you."

"Yippee," Peter yelled and went to jump into my arms, but he passed through me and landed on the ground. "Oops," he said giggling, as he stood wiping off his pants and the front of his suit. "I forgot." His mother and I laughed, but her laughter was shallow. Disappointment was everywhere. Peter saw it too. "Mommy, I'll go with you if you really want me to."

My heart skipped a beat. What would her answer be? It was obvious Peter wanted to stay with me, but was it fair to keep him from his mother? We both waited.

Finally she spoke. "More than anything, I want Peter to live to his full potential. With your love, guidance and encouragement, he's doing that. Mr. Winters, you are a Godsend. You are what Peter needed from his birth. I think Peter should remain with you."

Mrs. Stevenson was now demonstrating the person she was, and I saw where Peter got his character. She was also showing true love for her son. Here was where Peter got his capacity for love. I was choked up. This woman was as good as her husband was bad. "Mrs. Stevenson, I'm honored; but I feel sorry for you. I can only imagine how deep a mother's love is for her child. Will you ever have a chance to see him again?"

"Yes. If you come back here at the same time next year, that will be possible."

"We will be here. But that will mean you'll go a year without seeing him."

"My time is different than yours."

I knew that was true. One hundred years from Peter's death till when I met him passed for him in three days. "May I ask a few more questions?" She nodded. "The first day I drove into Slippery Gulch last year, the road had already been washed out by the spring melt. Yet what I saw and drove across was something else. How did that happen?"

She paused in thought. "As you know, what Peter saw when you were in town was different from what was factual. Peter saw a wagon and a team of horses. He wasn't ready to see your truck yet. What you saw was what you had to see. It was essential for Peter and their plans that you get into Slippery Gulch and out again safely. Although you were concerned about driving along the edge of the cliff, your worries were unnecessary. You were protected."

I found this all fascinating. So only half my truck was on solid ground both in and out. Sure glad I didn't know that then! "Who called my company to request a truck to come in to pick up the crusher in the first place?"

She looked skyward. "He was one of them."

I looked skyward, too, then back at her alarmed. "You don't mean some kind of a space alien do you?"

She chuckled. "Oh no, Mr. Winters. He was a God-appointed angel."

I was startled with her answer. "You mean a real angel, like what's in the Bible? With wings and halos and all of that stuff?"

She started laughing. "Yes, sort of. I love your excitement and enthusiasm. It matches Peter's. You two make a good pair."

I had to chuckle too. "And you have Peter's contagious laugh. How long ago was I picked for this…assignment?"

"Many years ago; but the final decision was not made until last Christmas."

"If I was picked to be Peter's mortal guardian years ago, when…"

"At his birth. My death was a consideration. Peter contracted leprosy in his first year. And that played into it. Peter was born to suffer, Mr. Winters. He was being tested. I was allowed to watch him grow, but I could not interfere. I knew what was ahead for him after his death. I was happy for him. But watching the life he had to endure for six-and-a half years…do you have any idea how hard that is for a mother?"

I was as confused as ever. My admiration for this woman was growing by leaps and bounds. It had been extremely hard on me listening to Peter relate the many terrible experiences he suffered throughout his childhood. I can't imagine a mother watching those horrible things happening and not being allowed to intervene. "Mrs. Stevenson, I feel so sorry for you."

"Thank you, but please don't. After all, my son is an angel." She gave a little giggle.

I changed gears: "Peter once told me you and your parents came West on a wagon train, but that your parents were killed during an Indian attack. Is that true?"

"Yes. I was less than a year old, so I remember none of it. After my parents were killed in the attack, some nice folks on the train took me in. They were friends of my parents. Years later they told me about it. We came across the Bozeman Trail in 1868. From what they said, we were the last train to cross it before the army closed the trail."

"Did you have any brothers or sisters?"

"I was the first child, but I was told my mother was pregnant at the time of her death."

"I'm so sorry. Did you have relatives back east?"

"From what I was told, both my parents were orphans. From what my husband told me, once his father was killed at the Little Bighorn, he was orphaned too."

Peter had told me about his paternal grandfather's death at the Little Bighorn, but I wasn't sure how accurate he was. Who could blame me for questioning that; after all, how many living six-year-old children do you know who claim to be the grandchild of a soldier killed with Custer in 1876? "So at your death, Peter was on his own, except for an insane father."

She put her head down in Peter's characteristic way. Then she looked up at me. "Yes. I'm sorry for you. Peter received none of the training normally associated with infancy and early childhood—his father simply tolerated his infant son. As you know, his father didn't teach Peter a thing as a child. So you were forced to deal with situations that you as a bachelor never had to deal with before. It was hard on you and uncomfortable for you at times. You could have responded the way his father did, but you rose to the occasion. You fathered Peter with concern and love. You have been so good for Peter, Mr. Winters."

Enough compliments. I decided to move on. "Can he return here any time and see you if he wants to?"

"Yes. However, if he comes back here without you, he can never go back to you again." Peter and I looked at each other. Both of us instantly knew he'd never come back here alone.

"Peter is very small for a six-year-old child. Children in 2002 are several inches taller than their counterparts one hundred years ago. Was he small for his age then too?"

"Yes, his father was only five-feet-four and you can see my size. You know he was not a healthy child when he lived." I nodded. (I'd never told Peter about his leprosy.)

"One more question. Can you sing?"

"Excuse me?"

"Were either you or your husband good singers?"

"I didn't sing much myself, and I never heard my husband sing. Why do you ask?"

I suspected she knew. "Peter has a beautiful, soprano voice. He sings like an angel, and I suspected one or both of you had a tremendous voice."

She paused for what seemed to be several minutes. "As you know, you are the answer to his prayer; but you are far more than just a friend. I'm sorry. I assumed you knew. Not only is my son an angel, he's your guardian angel. But brace yourself: While in his mortal body, which is most of the time, you are his mortal guardian."

I looked at her sharply. "Wa...wait! What did you say?"

She giggled. "You heard me correctly, Mr. Winters. Peter is an angel."

"Wait a minute! You mean, he's an actual angel? Like the type you were talking about before? Like that guy or the angel that was chosen to call my company? Like the type they talk about in the Bible?" She smiled and nodded.

Peter appeared to be as shocked as I was.

"So when you said a few minutes ago that your son is an angel, you didn't mean he is just a sweet kid. You see, some people during the course of the past year speculated he is an angel, but I didn't accept it. Now it is confirmed."

"I know," she said.

"Has he been an angel since the first day we met?"

"Not quite. From the time you met, he was on what you would call probation. He sang in your church Christmas Eve, correct?" I nodded. "He received his wings, figuratively speaking, that very night."

Well, I'll be! The minister thought he saw a halo of sorts around Peter's head. Apparently he did. I thought back to the movie *It's A Wonderful Life.* When Clarence got his wings, everybody heard a bell ring. That must have been a Hollywood invention. I didn't hear a thing when Peter got his. "What would have happened if Peter refused to sing that night?"

"His dying prayer had been answered. But he would have failed the final obedience test. He would have been sent back to Slippery Gulch and his grave. You would never have seen him again." Peter and I looked at each other, stunned speechless.

"You said that was the final test. There were others then?"

"The entire six months was a test. For both of you!" I looked at her without comprehending. "The dreams were critical tests. He had many fears to overcome, and he required your involvement—your coaching and your patience. The dreams were a test as much for you as for Peter. He was terribly embarrassed, for you were forced to deal with something you'd never dealt with before—dirty diapers. Had you given up on him, you would have failed. It was close, wasn't it?"

Thinking back, I nodded.

"But you both rose to the occasion. His fears were soon conquered and your ability to change diapers drastically improved." We both laughed together on that one, but Peter was frowning in embarrassment.

"The point is, Mr. Winters, without deep love and understanding between the two of you, the bestowing of his angelic status would not have happened. Their choice in you for the appointment of Peter's guardian was confirmed to be a good one."

"I'm honored to be Peter's guardian while he's in his mortal body, though I don't understand why. There are millions of men out there, many of them better qualified than me. Why me?"

"You're right. There are millions of men who are wonderful fathers. But Peter needed a man's undivided attention. He needed a man who could give one hundred percent of himself, to one little person only. A non-family man. But a tested educator. And someone with the patience of Job who could understand a little boy in need of the love he had missed. Unconditional love! You were someone who could give him strong guidance and discipline, mixed with love. You'd proven that as a teacher and a camp counselor and director."

I thought about this. "I *was* an experienced educator many years ago. I *had* the patience of Job, but I had lost it in the meantime. At the time I left Basin with Peter in my truck, I wasn't the least bit sure that I was capable of the task that lay ahead."

"You were far more capable than what you were giving yourself credit for. You may have lost your patience with a group of children, but with an individual child you were always patient and loving. And you could tease kids in love. You could discipline and correct him with love and understanding. You were exactly who was needed for the job.

"As a child living in Slippery Gulch, my son was an intelligent, inquisitive child...but I don't think I have to tell you that. He had hundreds of questions about the simple world around him, but he had no one to turn to for answers. Then moving into your far more complex world, his questions multiplied into the thousands, and he had you. And you handled them just right. You always gave him the answer that he could grasp and emotionally handle. When you didn't know the answer, you never deceived him. Nor did you deny him answers to his questions, no matter how uncomfortable they were for you." She chuckled. "Be prepared, Mr. Winters. Because he is a six-year-old boy, there are more uncomfortable questions coming."

I looked at Peter. He appeared to be puzzled by what she was saying.

"You allowed him to learn by exploring and by making mistakes. You tried steering him toward the good and guiding him away from the bad. Sometimes he doesn't listen." She giggled. "That earned him the nickname, Funny Tummy." Peter looked up with a smile. "The point is Mr. Winters, because of his past, and because of his young age, there will still be times when he won't listen. Sometimes he will have to learn the hard way, but don't lose your patience with him. Continue to guide him and punish him appropriately and out of love. You two are a perfect match."

Where had I heard that before? "How do you know all of this? Have you been with us the entire time?"

"No. I was not with you at all, but I was kept informed."

CHAPTER TWO

"Last December, Peter and I stopped in a mall in Topeka, Kansas, so Peter could talk to Santa Claus." I looked at Peter, realizing I was going to have to be careful the way I handled this. I wished I could send him back to the group while I talked to Mrs. Stevenson alone, but I couldn't. "I sensed he was more than just a helper. Who or what was he?"

"He was an angel sent from God."

I looked at Peter. He appeared to be in a stupor. Mrs. Stevenson looked at me in an understanding way. "Don't worry. Peter has been removed from this part of the conversation."

What did that mean? I waved my hand in front of his face with no reaction. "Are you aware of the note Peter received Christmas morning?" She smiled and nodded. "I assume then you're aware of the gift he got in his stocking at the same time?" Again she nodded. "Was the person…or individual who wrote the note the same one who gave him the angel?" Once again, a nod. I hesitated. "That wasn't from Santa Claus, was it?"

She smiled. "No, Mr. Winters, Santa Claus exists only in the hearts and minds of the young and the young at heart like you. The note and the angel came from God. The night before, Peter had received his wings in your church. It was God's way of saying congratulations. Mortals do not understand much of what God does.

"Since we're talking about Christmas, the way you handled Christmas and Santa Claus was perfectly suited for Peter. He was so excited and so thrilled to think that Santa had visited him. It did my heart good." Chuckling, she added, "I'm not sure who was excited more, you or Peter."

I chuckled. "I know. It was the best Christmas I've had since I was Peter's age."

I decided to move on. I noticed Peter shuffle his feet. I could tell in his eyes that he was back. "When Peter suffers an injury or wound, he's able to repair himself. But he can't do it without me. Why?"

"As a mortal he depends on you. He needs your love and care for everything. Without that love and care you provide, he's helpless." Peter smiled up at me.

"There's another thing I don't understand, Mrs. Stevenson. Peter suffered through a horrible life. He was terribly neglected and abused by his father and finally killed by him. Peter showed me the condition his body was in after that beating. I was sickened. I don't even know how he had the strength to crawl back into the woods. He had no one to take care of his cuts and bruises or to care for him when he was sick. He didn't even have anybody to go to for his emotional pains. Yet for six-and-a-half years he survived. I don't understand how."

"As you know, Peter is exceptionally strong for his size. Emotionally he was also strong. I say *was*; because of you, he doesn't have to be as strong emotionally as he was. Then too, Peter was watched. He could not die until it was time."

Time? Time for what? "Peter says he saw my face in the clouds a short time before he was beaten by the boys in the alley. That was forty-two years before I was even born. How can that be?"

"It was time. Although he didn't know it then, his life was coming to an end. Your face was meant to give him hope."

I thought about this. "Does that mean I was chosen for this assignment before I was born?"

"The choice was providential."

Once again I was stunned—and lost. "Mrs. Stevenson, I don't understand any of this. Am I to assume it's not necessary for me to understand?"

She smiled her understanding. "All of this behind the scenes is not meant to be understood by mortals, nor is it necessary. The important thing is the way you're raising Peter. Everyone is more than satisfied."

So I would remain lost! That was okay. I'd spent most of the year lost, but now many of my questions were answered. Time to move on. "Why did his life end after only six-and-a-half years?"

"He had to be beyond infancy so he could learn and communicate. At age six they felt he was prepared adequately for his life with you. What he wasn't prepared for they knew you could handle."

"Was his final prayer planted in his head?"

"That prayer was his and came right from his heart and soul. I think if he had not stated that prayer, we would not be talking now." She looked at her son fondly. "Even though he was not allowed in the church in Slippery Gulch, he stood under a window every Sunday when the windows were open. Peter learned what prayer was but didn't understand its power. He didn't know God, but God knew him. He never had a prayer answered during his life, as far as he knew, but God was with him always. However, Peter was giving up hope. That's another reason time was running out."

Suddenly the light went on. "So that's what the line in the note left Christmas Morning meant: 'I was with you always'."

She smiled and nodded. This reminded me of the poem "Footprints." I don't remember exactly how the entire poem goes, but it's about a man walking through life. When things are going well the man sees two sets of prints in the sand behind him, his own and God's. But when things are going bad, he sees only one set. He asked God why he abandons him during his greatest time of need. God responds that it's during those times that God carries him. So Peter didn't realize it, but he had been carried by God his entire life. Suddenly, I realized I'd been carried by God much of the last year. Or was it *my* whole life, too?

Mrs. Stevenson brought me back to the present. "When he first ran into you, he was terrified and desperate. That encounter I saw. I saw terror in his eyes." I remembered back one year ago. Those eyes hit me hard. "Later that day when you were preparing to leave, you tickled him, forcing him to laugh. I can't tell you, Mr. Winters, how good that laugh sounded to me—actually to everyone. Perhaps more important to him was your hug. He didn't recognize it for what it was. All he knew was it felt good. Although you saw sadness and loneliness in his eyes, you also saw hope. It was the first time since before his death that those beautiful little eyes reflected hope. You restored that hope, Mr. Winters.

"His final prayer was not for life but for something he saw as more important—a friend. After seeing your face in the clouds the day before his death, he knew who he was praying for. When he looked up into your eyes from the ground after bumping into you, he was scared. He desperately wanted to trust you, but his memory wouldn't allow him to. Who could blame him? It was only three days earlier in his time that he had been murdered by his father."

I understood. "So he's an angel instead of a ghost! What does that mean to both of us?"

"He is now free to stay with you forever, or as long as both of you want." Peter and I looked at each other and smiled.

"You mentioned he is exceptionally strong for his age. He's also exceptionally well coordinated. He has the strength and coordination of a ten-year-old and he's as fast as most ten-year-olds. You and your husband must have been athletes."

"As a child I was always the fastest and strongest. I was told that my husband was too. Peter had to be fast and strong, or he never would have lived to age six."

She paused and went on. "I think you would agree, Peter is a handsome child. But, if you had seen him as a living six-year-old, you would have seen an ugly child because of the terrible wounds he suffered at the hands of his father and others in the town. Since you first met, his body has been free of all physical scars." She looked up again. "They took care of that. His soul was terribly wounded too, but they left the hard work for you."

"Wait a minute! I thought his soul had been repaired by the time we first met."

"Not at all. When he ran out from the alley, bumped into you and fell to the ground...You do realize that was no accident?"

"Yes. He admitted that to me early in our travels."

"All he knew was that you were likely the answer to his prayer. He desperately wanted to meet you, but he was terrified. For had he bumped into someone while he was alive, he would have been severely beaten. Can you appreciate the courage it took for him to get your attention in a way that would involve you immediately? Instead of beating or kicking him, you asked him if he was okay. He saw friendship in your eyes and heard concern in your voice.

"Mr. Winters, the repair work started at that moment. He had a reason to hope, but he was still fearful. When you bent over to help him up, he instinctively cowered, remember? He wasn't ready to trust anyone though he desperately wanted to trust you.

"Later you offered him food and water. You held him in your arms to comfort him. That was the first time a human offered him food. It was the first time he felt love and security.

"Before you left town you got him laughing for the first time in his life. And you hugged him. When you left him standing in the street crying, I'm told you thought you were leaving somebody's sad and lonely little boy. In reality, he didn't know why he was crying. He was confused. He was thrilled and excited, but he didn't understand what meeting his answered prayer was to mean to him.

"You never expected to see Peter again, but he knew you'd be back. You see, Mr. Winters, you began his soul's healing on your first visit.

"You hoped you could get help for Peter, but if it didn't work out for him, so be it." I gave her a strange look. Those were my exact thoughts. "That was your mental attitude, but that's not what was in your heart. By the time you left Slippery Gulch, Peter had captured your heart." Her eyes glanced up. "You didn't know it, but they did."

"So others controlled everything right from the beginning?"

"Yes and no. They brought you in here safely, but they did not control your heart just as they did not plant Peter's final prayer. Had Peter not moved your heart, all would have been lost. But they knew your heart and they knew Peter. When you came back the third and final time, that was your choice. You came back on your own. You thought you were being controlled. In a sense, you were. Your heart took control of your selfish thoughts.

"Last year after you gave him his first bath, he wanted to play in the creek. You told him to be careful. No one ever told him to be careful before. Nobody cared. That simple phrase impacted his soul.

"Your wake-up tradition means so much to him as does your quiet time before bed. You taught him how to wash and dry himself. Essentially he's independent. But washing his hair and drying him after a bath is one more special way you demonstrate your love to him.

"You tease him a lot such as telling him he's ugly in the morning. At first Peter didn't understand. To be honest, they didn't either. They weren't sure where it would lead. But you knew exactly what you were doing. When you explained to Peter that you were teasing him, he came to realize it was another form of your love and he came to cherish it.

"The point is you have repaired his damaged soul and put his broken heart back together again. And you did it faster then even they thought possible. The beautiful thing about it is, you didn't realize you were into soul repair work. Everything you did was just being you. It's just exactly what he needed."

I was overwhelmed with her compliments. I felt like Peter—embarrassed. But she was right, it was just me.

"As an angel his halo sits a little crooked at times. Why does he misbehave sometimes?"

She chuckled. "In his mortal body, he's a normal six-year-old boy. Need I say more?"

I'd figured this out, but it was good hearing it from the little devil's mom! "What about Peter's father? Is his soul still around, and if so, is he someone we have to be concerned about?"

"No. He was insane with hate and evil. After killing Peter, he left town and, sad to say, butchered other little boys.

The father of his last victim, along with some friends, caught and hanged him. His soul is being held in another place for the Final Judgment. You have nothing to fear."

Peter and I let out a sigh of relief. "Thank God!"

Then I thought of something else. "One last question: Shortly after we started our trip last year, Peter stole two candy bars in one day, forcing me to spank him." Peter dropped his eyes now. "Was that a test designed by them also?"

"No, that was Peter. They looked on with interest and concern. I'm told you lost your temper and came close to sending him back, but Peter spoke up before you could act. The incident turned out to be beneficial for both of you. You understood Peter's childish reasons and *they* felt relieved. As a result of his test, Peter knew you were honest, fair and trustworthy."

I looked at Peter with admiration. Suddenly I thought of one last question. "I apologize, Mrs. Stevenson, but may I ask you one more?"

"Certainly. I have all the time in the world."

"Why doesn't God protect Peter when he's a mortal? For instance, why didn't he catch Peter when he fell off that log last year?"

"When he's a mortal, his health and well-being are your responsibility as his mortal guardian. You're doing fine. You're not expected to keep him injury-free. Do your best. He's a boy, as you once were."

I started laughing. I can remember sitting in the tub or standing in the shower looking at my own new bruises and scratches, wondering where they had all came from. They just seemed to materialize out of nowhere. By the time I'd take my next bath or shower, a whole new bunch appeared.

After a full day of running, hiking, climbing, tackling and just plain playing, Peter's legs and arms had so many minor abrasions, lacerations and contusions along with the dirt and grass stains on them, he looked as if he were neglected and abused. I never thought of my own legs suggesting the same when I was a kid.

I was still laughing when I realized both Peter and Mrs. Stevenson were staring at me with humor on their faces. I continued laughing. "You're right. I was an active little kid and walked around with bruises, cuts and scratches all the time. No guardian angel could have prevented them." I looked at Mrs. Stevenson then at Peter. "I promise both of you, I will take care of this little body as best as I can." I winked at Mrs. Stevenson.

There were more questions I could have asked, but I couldn't think of any more except one. "Would you like to hear your son sing?" She smiled broadly at her son and nodded.

"Peter, would you sing *I Walked Today Where Jesus Walked* for your mother? And the others?" He nodded enthusiastically. Meanwhile, everyone standing behind me was transfixed. I said loudly so all could hear, "Folks, I have a treat for all of us. Peter has agreed to sing a song." (I found out later, none were able to see Peter's mother, and he was somewhat transparent to them.) It suddenly occurred to me that of the people present only Betty, Jerry and I had ever heard Peter sing. The rest had no idea what a treat was in store for them. (including his mother.)

While he was singing, I looked in all directions. Boot Hill overlooked the gulch and the ghost town of Peter's birth, his terribly tormented life, and his brutal death. The Deer Lodge National Forest and the huge conifers within it surrounded the gulch. The sky was a royal blue. Forgetting the evil that once existed here, it was a beautiful sight. Yet out of this hellhole rose one little angel.

I looked back at Peter. Beyond him I caught a movement on a distant ridge. I looked closer. I observed a small pack of gray wolves, one noticeably larger than the others. All were sitting as if captivated by the music drifting up from below. Suddenly I realized how fitting this song was for Peter. For his entire life, Jesus had walked with him and often carried him. I looked up. Surely, God the father was smiling proudly on his little son.

The women were in tears while most of the men were trying to disguise theirs. I looked back at Peter, as proud as any grandfather could be. I saw how pleased Mrs. Stevenson was, too. Was I seeing or only imagining ghostly tears!

As Peter completed the song, he sensed that I was looking at something important. He looked with me back to the ridge where the wolves had been. But they were gone. It was only then that I remembered the wolf tracks Mike had observed in this exact spot a week earlier. Based on its tracks, the wolf had come from nowhere. Was it there now? Perhaps Mrs. Stevenson would have the answer, but the time for questions had passed. It was time to move on.

His mother said, "Oh, Peter! That was beautiful. You have made the right choice. I must be going now, son. You go back to Mr. Winters. Perhaps I will see you next year."

She looked at me. "Remember, Mr. Winters, Peter is six. His difficult questions and misbehavior are not over and never will be." She smiled. "But none of us are worried." I smiled my acknowledgment to both of them.

With that, Peter ran up and gave his mother the strangest one-sided embrace any of the mortals behind me had ever seen. I felt a collective tingle run up and down everybody's spine. "I love you, Mommy," Peter cried. She kissed Peter and she was gone. Instantly, Peter was in his physical body, turning, wiping tears and coming my way.

I knelt down next to him and put my hand on his shoulder. Solid again! He stood there for several minutes looking at where his mother had been. With tear-filled eyes, he turned to me. "She's pretty isn't she, Jake?"

"She's gorgeous, Kiddo. Now I know where you get your good looks."

"Am I gorgeous?"

"No. Men and boys are handsome, and you are very handsome."

He smiled and leapt into my arms. Everybody behind me gave a collective sigh of relief. Only then did they know the outcome for sure. "I love her, Jake, and I love you too"

I moved my hand over his heart and smiled. I felt the miracle of life within, as I had moments before his funeral service ended. I had prayed then that I would still feel it ten minutes later. I looked up and thanked God for answering my prayer.

We walked back to the others and the gravestone, hand-in-hand. Although the stone had been brought in a week earlier (no easy task) when we'd first arrived at the site, Peter had gazed at it impassively. As a matter of fact, I had too. We now stood before the beautifully polished, gray granite which was taller than Peter. He read aloud, "Peter Stevenson, born December 2, 1894. Number-One Citizen of Slippery Gulch, Montana. Murdered by his father on June 30, 1901. A Very Special Little Boy Who Will Live Forever. I WILL LOVE YOU FOREVER, LITTLE ONE." He traced the letters in the word "SPECIAL" with his small index finger. Then he went to the last sentence and traced his finger over the word "FOREVER." He turned to me and said, "You said that to me a few days ago, Jake."

I looked at Jane as if to say, "How did you know?" But Jane, George and Mike were looking at the stone nonplused.

"Yes, and I promise I always will." He jumped into my arms. "But you're still ugly when you first wake up."

He laughed, punched me lightly then said. "You're so mean to me."

"Peter, it's good to have you back. When we get back to Basin, would you be willing to sing another song for us?"

"Sure! But can I get out of these darn clothes first?"

We all laughed. George said, "I'll drink to that."

"Before we go, we have a decision to make," I said. I looked at George and the minister. "What do we do with the casket?" We all stood there staring dumbly at each other.

George looked at Peter, then me. "Peter doesn't need it now, thank God. I think we should take it with us. Maybe they take returns."

The minister spoke up. "I don't believe you can return a casket. I've never heard of such a thing. But then I've never heard of the deceased deciding he didn't want to occupy it."

"I guess we'd better bury it and forget it," I said, removing my suit jacket. There were no gravediggers. The job of lowering the casket into the hole and filling in the hole was up to the funeral party.

All of the men stepped forward to help. Lowering the casket and filling in the hole on a hot June afternoon while dressed in a suit was not my idea of fun. Suddenly the casket was in place, the hole was filled in and the dirt was evenly spread out over the grave. Everyone looked at the grave in shock. I looked at Peter. He had a big smile on his face. Rubbing his hands together with satisfaction, he said, "Well, that takes care of that."

Everybody looked at him. "You little peanut. Thanks." I started laughing and soon everyone joined in realizing what just happened.

"Jake, I cheated, but I didn't like the looks of it. It was scary. I'm sorry."

I ruffled his hair. "Peter, I think this was one time when cheating was acceptable."

I chuckled. "Well, now that the work's done, I want to take two pictures of the gravestone—one by itself and one with you standing next to it." I looked at the group. "How often do you see a picture of the deceased posed with his gravestone?" Everybody laughed. Peter stood next to the stone and grinned sheepishly. "Do you remember how I got you to smile a year ago?" He laughed. I got the picture I wanted.

As we turned to leave, I went for his hand but he refused it and said, "Don't you remember how we walked out of here the last time?" I nodded and lifted him up on my shoulders.

The path going down the hill from Boot Hill led to one of the two roads in Slippery Gulch. I said to everybody, "This is the infamous Blood Run Road. It runs through town then leads up to the mine. George, why don't you tell them the legend behind the name?"

"I think Peter can testify to the fact that Slippery Gulch was one rough town. According to the stories, there was a shooting almost daily—you know, as in 'fast draw.' The good citizens in the town finally had enough and passed an ordinance. If two men wanted to blow each other's brains out, they could only do it on this road. Supposedly there was so much blood spilt, they renamed it Blood Run Road. I'm sure there's some truth behind the story."

"That's fascinating," Jason said. "Jake, didn't you once tell me that Peter saw a shoot-out?"

"Do you remember where it was, Kiddo?" I asked.

"It was up there in front of that saloon." He pointed from atop my shoulder to a saloon two buildings up on the left. Silence followed. He didn't want to talk about it.

When we got to the intersection of Main Street and Blood Run Road, Hank looked straight beyond Main Street and up a winding, steep hill. "Is that the road to the mine?" he asked. I nodded. Everyone looked on the road with curiosity. "And you drove your truck up that thing and back down again?" They waited for my answer. Again I nodded. "Now we *know* you're crazy," Hank said.

As we approached Jacob's Mercantile, I put Peter down. He looked at the alley between the saloon and Jacob's Mercantile. It was here that three teen-age boys beat Peter to within a hair of his life the day before his father murdered him. This was the spot where he had lost all hope and the will to live.

At his father's house, Peter shuddered. Here is where Peter was hung by his ankles and beaten with a rope until he was senseless. Once cut down, he managed to crawl out of the cabin and into the woods, more dead than alive. A pack of wolves nursed him back to life.

Peter looked away and squeezed my hand. I'd realized shortly after our cross-country trip started that his squeeze symbolized a hug. He interpreted my squeezes the same way.

I suddenly stopped. Sitting next to the far side of the house was the largest gray wolf I'd ever seen—perhaps the same one I'd seen on the ridge as Peter sang. The others were preoccupied with the cabin while Peter led me to the sitting wolf. For some reason, I felt no fear. Peter stood face to face with the large creature. Its ears stood straight up.

Peter said, "I'm okay, Fuzzy. Jake and I are going to be together forever."

I gave Peter a strange look. So it was the same wolf? The wolf's ears went back. He licked Peter's face and Peter gave him a hug. Then the ears went up again. The wolf looked at me piercingly, as if to assess my very soul. As he approached me, I felt no fear. I reached out and patted his head. "I love him, Fuzzy. I promise I will care for Peter the best I can." The wolf sat again as his ears went down. The wolf took my left arm in his mouth, a form of canine affection. As Peter and I patted him, we smiled at each other then back at the wolf. Now all but his tracks were gone. No tracks led away from our meeting place. I shivered as the chills danced on my spine.

We rejoined the others. There were questions in their eyes but I ignored them.

Peter and I walked up the hill, hand-in-hand. The last time we had walked this hill together, our future had been uncertain. Now we were full of confidence. At the top, my guardian angel looked down on the town that never wanted him and squeezed my hand. "Jake, Santa Claus granted me my wish, didn't he?"

I looked at Peter and smiled knowingly. The little boy nobody wanted no longer existed. In the distance came the cry of a wolf.

CHAPTER THREE

Back in Basin, we all changed in to more comfortable clothes. I did not have to help Peter at all. Before the funeral he had been so fearful of having to return to the grave that he was helpless. Now he casually threw on shorts and a pullover shirt. We walked down to the saloon, happy and contented.

Peter was the man of the hour. Everybody wanted him to sing another song. He came up and whispered in my ear what he'd like to sing and why. I looked at the group. "In memory of September 11th, Peter would like to sing, "*God Bless America.*"

Hank said, "Oh, my God! I forgot, but you guys were there, weren't you?" Everybody knew that except Frank, Agent Smith and the minister. They wanted to hear about it, but I said, "Look, it was really traumatic for both of us. We've had enough trauma for one day. It's time for Peter to sing." Peter looked relieved.

His voice generated many tears. When he finished, I went up to Peter and whispered in his ear. He smiled and nodded. "Folks, we'll be back in ten minutes with something special."

On the way out, I asked the bartender if we could borrow his flag.

Heading for the door, we bumped into two men coming in. Moose and Twig were two Montana construction workers I'd met shortly after returning to Basin from my first Slippery Gulch trip last year. Moose was the gentle giant of Basin, standing about six-feet-eight and weighing in at three hundred pounds. Twig was as small as Moose was big. As Peter and I moved aside for them, Moose looked down at me and said, "Hey, I remember you. You're that crazy trucker. Are you on your way in or out of Slippery Gulch?"

I laughed as I watched my hand disappear in his massive paw. "I went in by pick-up this time. Moose, Twig, I'd like you to meet my grandson, Peter."

Moose looked way down at him as Peter looked way up. "Nice meeting you, little man. You sure have a brave Grandpa. You know what he did last year?" Peter shook his head. "He drove that big truck of his into Slippery Gulch."

Peter looked at me as if I were nuts. Then to Moose, he said, "He did?"

I ruffled Peter's hair. "We'll be back in a few minutes." We walked out to the truck.

I had taught Peter two songs a couple of weeks earlier. He had memorized the words and melody quickly, but the syncopation was harder to grasp. He finally got that down too. At the time I wondered if he'd ever have the opportunity to sing them. Now was his chance. Once in the truck, he practiced them as he changed into a white button-down shirt that was striped red and blue. I had stopped someplace during our travels and gotten him a small, white straw hat that I had painted with red and blue stripes. We were ready.

When we walked back into the bar, Moose noticed the way Peter was dressed and came up to me. "Jake, I know you're having a private party back there, but this looks like something special. Both me and Twig are Vets and most of them guys in here are." He looked at an older gentleman obviously without recognition. The man ignored Moose. He just stared at Peter. "Even the gal behind the bar was in the army. You mind if we join you?"

I looked at Peter. He just shrugged his shoulders, giving his okay.

Moose, Twig, ten other patrons, the barmaid, the bartender and the older gentleman wandered into the room. George was immediately on his feet, ready to throw them all out and fire the bartender on the spot. I said, "Cool your jets, George. I gave the okay." Reluctantly he sat back down.

Peter stayed out of sight until I gave him the cue. I asked if he was ready. He was. He came marching into the room singing *You're a Grand Old Flag* with the flag on a pole over his right shoulder. Everybody rose to their feet. His syncopation couldn't have been better. Some tried to join in but their emotions won out. He marched around the room waving the flag with one hand and his hat with the other. I hadn't taught him that.

I looked at the older gentleman. He did not appear to be the least bit surprised by the beauty of Peter's voice, yet the tears were streaming down his cheeks. At one point I saw him nod his head in a knowing way. Did he know Peter, maybe from a previous life? Yet it didn't appear Peter knew him.

After Peter finished the first song, he went into *I'm a Yankee Doodle Dandy*. When he finished, everybody started clapping, cheering and whistling. George lifted Peter up so he stood on George's massive shoulders. This was heaven for Peter. Then someone started shouting, "Sing it again, Peter." Soon everybody joined in. George was marching around the room with Peter standing on his shoulders. Patriotism was alive and well in Basin.

As things quieted down, Moose and Twig came up to Peter, George and me. "Jake, Peter, that was fantastic. You made our day." The big man wiped a small tear from his cheek. "Thanks, George. I owe you." George smiled. I had made the right decision.

After the unexpected guests left, I approached George. "George, did you know everyone that just came in?"

"Yeah, well, for the most part. Why?"

"Did you know the older man?"

"Sort of. I don't know his name but he stops in for a beer, two or three times a summer. Someone told me once he's an author. I understand he's retired now. Why?"

"Oh, I don't know. It's probably nothing, but I noticed him paying close attention to Peter. I was just wondering if you knew him."

"I've heard he's friends with an older lady in Boulder. I'll do a little checking."

"Peter, you don't know him, do you?"

Peter thought for a minute. "He looks kind of familiar, but I don't know why."

"He's not a ghost, is he? He didn't live in Slippery Gulch with you, did he?"

"No. I'd remember him if he did. They were all mean to me. This guy seems nice. Besides, he's not a ghost. I'd know if he was."

When he had a chance, Hank asked, "Peter, that was really great. Who taught you those songs?"

Proudly he answered, "Jake did."

"That figures. You know, he was probably around when they were written."

Everybody cracked up. Hank got up, walked over and shook my hand then turned to the others. "I've known this sorry excuse for a human for ten or eleven years now. I thought he was beyond help." He put his hand on Peter's shoulder. "Then along came this little guy. Jake is still a sorry excuse for a human, but he's improving."

He waited until the laughter diminished to continue. "Almost a year ago, I happened to be in a truck stop in

Spokane when Jake and Peter pulled in. That morning they'd just begun their journey. That night after Peter went to sleep, Jake told me that if nothing else, he wanted to give this little guy the best childhood a child could have. Well, Jake, even though you're as old as dirt, you're doing a darn good job." Everybody stood up, clapped and cheered. I stood up, shook Hank's hand and ruffled Peter's hair.

After things quieted down, Peter said, "George, can I stand on your table for a minute? It's the only way I can see everybody."

"Peter, you're the man. You can do whatever you want on my table." Peter took off his sneakers and dropped them to the floor.

"I know none of you were alive one hundred years ago, except for maybe Hank." Peter giggled at his own joke as everybody roared, including Hank. Peter put his head down for a few seconds. When he raised it again, his giggles were gone.

"A little over one hundred years ago, everybody hated me." Instantly you could have heard a pin drop. Peter described his life in Slippery Gulch. No one in the room except me had heard any of this first person, and it was hitting them hard.

"Sometimes I was so sore in here," he put his hand over his heart, "I wanted to die." He put his head down. "Then, it was over quickly. I died just like I had lived—alone and afraid." Softly he said, "All I ever wanted in life was a friend, just one."

"The day before my daddy killed me, I saw my friend." People looked from Peter to me in disbelief, then back to Peter—uncomprehending. "I was lying in a field outside Slippery Gulch watching the big, fluffy clouds go by. They were pretty and made me smile. I wondered where they came from and where they were going. I wished I could get on one and leave Slippery Gulch forever. Then I saw my friend. His face was in the clouds." He looked down at me and smiled. "The wind from the cloud seemed to say, 'Be patient, Little One. I'll be there soon.' The face was real clear. It was Jake's." The entire group sat in shocked silence.

"Just a few days later, in my time, I met Jake. He's the friend I prayed for. I told him everything that ever happened to me. He listened and cried with me. He wiped my tears and I wiped his just as we did today. He was the first one who ever cared. He called me, 'Little One,' just as the wind did. First, he gave me a bath, then he taught me everything I know. He made me realize I wasn't weird, strange, ugly, stupid or ungodly. He also taught me how to care for and trust others, and how to love and accept love. Those were the hardest things to learn. Jake never gave up, and he wouldn't let me either.

"He showed me there was more to the world than just Slippery Gulch, and he gave me a chance to see that most people in the world are nice. Sometimes it's still hard for me to believe how nice people can be. Jake was always there for me, and he still is.

"Today we were worried we were going to lose each other, but we learned we will be together forever."

He was silent for a moment, then he looked at me and smiled. "Jake teases me a lot. It didn't take me long to realize Jake's teasing is one more way he tells me he loves me."

He giggled. "Every morning Jake tells me I'm ugly, but then he tickles me. As a result, he wakes me up and I'm no longer ugly. But I'm loved—a lot."

To a standing ovation, he came down on my lap.

This has been an expensive day for Jane, George and Mike. So during dinner I slipped around and asked everybody for donations.

Between dinner and dessert, I stood up and said, "Ladies and gentlemen, may I have your attention." I looked at Peter. "Peter, I really appreciate your compliments and will take half the credit for teaching you everything you know. You can lead a horse to water, but you can't force it to drink." Peter looked at me puzzled. "In order to teach anybody anything, that person must want and be eager to learn. He also must be able to learn." I looked back at the group. "Peter wanted to go to school, but the schoolmaster told him he was too stupid. So he started to teach himself to read and write.

"Last July after Peter lead us to the missing crusher, Jane, George and Mike went to Slippery Gulch to look for Peter's grave. They never saw Peter, but he saw them. Upon leaving town they found in the dirt in front of Jacob's Mercantile a message. It said, 'Sa helo to Jak'." I spelled his message for everyone. "Two small knee prints were in the dirt. I was in Salt Lake when Jane called to tell me about the message." I looked at Peter. "It was then I knew how special this little guy is.

"Teaching yourself to read is no small feat for anyone, but in Peter's case, it was a miracle. Most of his time was spent surviving one more day. In order to teach himself, he had to go into town. When he got caught, he often suffered a beating. But he felt it was worth it. The day Peter saw my face in the clouds was the last peace he would experience on earth during his first life." I swallowed hard. "Later that day he paid the ultimate price for his desire to learn. He was beaten unmercifully by some teenagers in the alley next to

Jacob's Mercantile. The next day he was dragged to the center of Main Street more dead than alive and murdered.

"When Peter asked me to teach him to read, write, spell and do math, I was skeptical. I knew he was smart, but I wasn't sure how intelligent he really was. Let me tell you folks, he is highly gifted. Because he is so motivated, he is and has been a dream student. He can now read at the eighth grade level. That's about four grades above you, isn't it Hank?

"I think you all agree with me that today is a happy occasion. We all went to a funeral and were entertained by the deceased." Everybody hooted and clapped. "It was extra-special for Peter. He listened to his funeral and then walked away from it." Again they cheered.

"But that's not all. I know all of you realized something happened after the service, but you aren't sure what. Peter walked away from all of us and as he did, his body began to fade to our eyes. I for one feared that he was gone forever. Obviously that was not the case. But today, both Peter and I had an opportunity to meet his mother." There were gasps from several in the room. "That's right, and I now know where he gets his good looks. He also has her sweet personality, charm, character and courage."

"Yeah, she was gorgeous," Peter added, "and Jake always notices the gorgeous women." This drew laughs.

"Hey, Funny Tummy, this is my speech." This drew Peter's contagious giggle.

"As I was saying, many of you have wondered what happened to his father." That changed the mood quickly. "Peter was only the first little boy he murdered. Suffice it to say, Mr. Stevenson was finally caught and hanged. His soul is forever in…let's say suspended animation, to put it kindly.

Peter never has to worry about him again." Everybody clapped.

"We both learned something else today. Many people have mentioned to me during the year that they thought Peter was an angel and specifically, my guardian angel; after all, he'd saved my life more than once. He even saved yours once, Hank." Hank looked at me blankly. "Remember last February, you were going down Elk Mountain, on I-80 in Wyoming, heading east? You hit that bridge at over 70 MPH realizing too late that it was covered with black ice.

"Your truck started sliding. You knew it was going to take a miracle to get you across that bridge in one piece and you prayed. Well, Hank, I'm holding that miracle right now." Hank was speechless. "We were in Texas at the time, when suddenly Peter told me he'd be back in a few minutes and disappeared. A few minutes later he returned. 'Hank is okay now,' he said. He would never have said anything to you, because as you know, that's not his way." The room was silent. Hank appeared to be in shock.

"As I was saying, we both learned something else today. One hundred plus years ago, a certain minister wouldn't let Peter go to church. Peter was told he wasn't good enough for God. The minister was wrong. It seems Peter was on probation for the last six months of 2001. As some of you know, he sang two songs in my church on Christmas Eve. Our minister mentioned to me after the service, that he witnessed a beautiful light surrounding Peter's head as he sang *Oh Holy Night*." Peter looked at me surprised. He'd never heard this before. "It seems Peter got his wings that night. Peter is now a full-fledged angel and my guardian angel. And I am his guardian father while he is in my care. We can now be together forever." Everybody stood up and cheered.

"As a mortal child, Peter is fun-loving and mischievous. As a little angel, they don't come any better. Now Peter, I've been thinking about all of this for several hours. And I think there should be some changes."

He looked at me with concern. "Like what?"

"Well, Kiddo, over the last year there have been times when I've been quite mean to you: Jumping at you in the morning before you have your eyes open and scaring the living daylights out of you. I don't think a mortal should do that to an angel."

"What!" he yelled, jumping to his feet. Everybody laughed. But before he could say, anything else, I went on. "I've been teasing you an awful lot this past year. An angel should not be teased at all. I'll cut that out too."

"What!" He yelled waving his arms as if to say stop this kind of talk. Everybody but Peter could see where this was going. "But..."

"No angel should be tickled and abused the way I've abused you this past year. I will stop that too."

Peter was beside himself. (Lord, was I being mean.) "But Jake, that's why you're my guardian. That's why you're...I don't want you to stop any of that."

"Wait a minute. You want me to be mean to you?"

"Yes!" He screamed. Everybody was laughing in earnest now.

"Okay. Would you put your sneakers on. Your feet stink."

He started laughing. "They do not."

"And you want me to keep teasing you?"

Again he screamed, "Yes."

"Okay! Man are you ever ugly in the morning." Now he was laughing so hard, he was almost out of control.

"No I'm not."

"And you want me to continue tickling and abusing you?"

"Yes, yes, yes!" And with that, he fell on the floor, laughing hysterically, knowing what was coming.

"Okay." I picked him up and tickled him on the spot. "Kiddo, I'll never stop those things. They're to important too both of us."

Instantly, he stopped laughing. "You really are mean."

"Angel or no angel, I'm going to continue to be as mean as can be."

After we all regained our composure, I got serious. "Folks, you realized that this generous celebration on the part of Jane, George and Mike was expensive so you kicked in $250. This should help with expenses. Thanks from all of us." I handed George the money.

Over the next half-hour, calls came on my cell phone from all across the country: Connie and Randy from Rochester; Bill, Danny and Sue, Grace Pryor and Dr. Bruce, Judy and Carl Rotundo from Buffalo; Cindy and Pat from Phoenix; and other friends from the Buffalo area as well as from Seattle, Flagstaff, Little Rock, New London and Denver. They were all friends of mine who had met Peter. They were worried about Peter's fate. They were thrilled that Peter was allowed to stay with me; whereupon I got congratulations and best wishes!

The last call was a call back. It was Jamie Rotundo, Peter's best little friend. His parents hadn't told him what all hung in the balance until after they called me. Jamie was shaken and upset. He insisted he talk to Peter. I put the cell phone on speaker so I could hear too—with Jamie's permission. "Peter, Little Brother, are you okay?"

"Hi, Jamie. I am now."

"Are you okay, Mr. Winters?"

"I'm fine, Jamie. Thanks for your concern."

There was a pause on the other end, and a sniffle. "Peter: I mean, Mr. Winters, is it true we, you, almost lost Peter today?"

"It was close, Little Guy." I looked at Peter. (He was my Little *One*.) "We were all very worried but everything's okay. Peter and I can stay together forever."

"So I can see both of you again?"

"You sure can. In fact, when we get home, we'll invite you for a sleepover."

"Okay. Great! Peter, did you really go to your own funeral?"

Peter giggled. "Yeah."

"Cool! Well, I have to go. See you when you get home." He paused. "Glad you're coming home, Little Brother."

"Me too, Big Brother! Me too! See you in a few weeks."

After another half-hour, I got everyone's attention. I reminded them of our bedtime tradition. It's eight our time and tonight our talk is going to be special—for both of us. George, could we borrow your office for a while?"

"Be my guest. You know where it is."

Peter and I said our temporary good-byes and walked to George's office. Peter was quickly on my lap. "I sure enjoyed meeting your mother. Now I understand you even better."

"You do?"

"I sure do. She loves you so very much. But, Peter, you could have gone with her. Why didn't you?"

"I love my mother, Jake. I'm sorry I didn't know her." He thought for a minute. "I love my mother because she is my mother, but I love you because I know you and because you're my grandpa. During the year, you've cared for me and been there when I needed you the most. You taught me all kinds of things. You took me everywhere with you when it would have been easier for you to go alone. We've had a lot of fun together. I know we still will. That's why I wanted to stay with you."

"For the last week you've been pretty worried we wouldn't be together anymore, haven't you?" He nodded. "Well, Kiddo, I've been worrying about it since Basin, way last summer."

He looked surprised. "You have?"

"Yeah, I sure have. I brought up the question to Jane, George, Mike and Tasha the night before I removed you from Slippery Gulch. I've been worried about it ever since. That's the same reason everybody's here today. And why so many people called tonight. Today, when you walked away and started to fade out, I tried to stand and go after you, but my legs had no strength. I tried to yell, but I had no voice. I was scared stiff that I was going to lose you. If you had chosen to stay with your mother, I would have understood. But I would have been crushed."

"I'll never leave you, Jake, if I don't have to." He paused. "Jake, I'm sorry about this past week."

I was lost. "What do you mean?"

He was embarrassed. "I felt like a baby most of the week. Except when we went to Bannack. It was so interesting and so much fun that I could forget my funeral was two days away. Except for Bannack, I couldn't do anything for myself. I was so worried and scared. I couldn't think straight. My muscles and brain stopped working."

"I'm not going to pretend I wasn't worried about you; I was. But I was pretty sure I knew what was going on. I'm no longer worried. You're one hundred percent again."

"Jake, since I'm an angel, why do I sometimes poop and pee at the wrong time? Sometimes I don't poop at all. Why do I puke too? Why do I misbehave and get into trouble? Why do I still have nightmares once in a while? Why do I..."

"Peter, cut! You could go on with questions like that for the next half-hour. The answer to all your questions is the same: Most of the time, you're not an angel; you're a normal six-year-old boy. You're going to puke, pee and poop some more at the wrong times and in the wrong place. You're going to have more nightmares, and you're going to get in trouble again. I may have to spank you again, but I hope not. The point is, you're a normal little boy and I love you that way. You're the son I never had because I never went through with a near-wedding that was not to be. I wouldn't want my life today any other way."

"Thanks, Jake but there's something I don't understand. Why me? Why am I an angel?"

"Peter, didn't you hear your mother explain that?" He shook his head no. It was then that I realized this was another part of the conversation that he was not privy to. Now I was confused. There had to be a reason. How much should I tell him? I decided to wing it to see what would come up next.

"In a way, Kiddo, I think you always were a messenger from God—that's what angel means: messenger."

Peter was total focus, total attention. "According to the editor, you never called anybody the terrible names they called you. You always said please and thank you. No matter how terribly you were abused, harassed, humiliated and beaten, you were, as the editor said, 'the perfect little gentleman'."

Peter was now total introspection, his head down and tears dropping down on his feet. "I'm just glad to be your mortal guardian. Peter, you can't imagine how happy I am knowing I well never have to part company."

He smiled through his vanishing tears. "Could I ask you something?" I nodded. "Last year when we were camping, you said I was no angel and if I were, you wouldn't be interested in me. Now that I am an angel, do you feel that way?"

"Yep, I sure do."

Instantly his lower lip began to quivered. "You, you mean you really don't want me?"

"Peter, last year when I said that, you and everybody else thought you were a ghost, yet ninety-nine percent of the time you were a mortal boy. As that little boy, sometimes you misbehaved and disobeyed me. There were times when you were a little peanut, but you certainly were not an angel. There will still be times when, as that little boy, you misbehave, disobey me and get into trouble. You see, as a mortal boy you are not an angel. You're a normal boy. I wouldn't trade you for all the angels in Heaven."

His smile came out like the sun from behind a cloud. "Now I understand. You don't want me to be perfect, just normal, like when I complain about having to take a bath or brush my teeth. You want me to misbehave sometimes, because then I'm just like other little boys?"

"You've got it, Funny Tummy. Just don't over-do it. I'm not worried though. Don't you change and I won't either. You be that little boy I love to tease, tickle and hold. And I'll continue to be your imperfect grandpa and the best friend you could ever pray for."

He threw himself into my arms. We were a happy pair again.

We started to rejoin the others, Peter now in my arms. "Peter, one more thing: This afternoon when you were singing after your funeral, the gray wolf was sitting on a ledge with several other wolves, listening."

"They were?"

"I think they were sitting there enjoying your singing with the rest of us. It was heavenly. But today was not the first time I saw him."

He looked surprised. "When?"

"Last year! The first night you stayed with me in my truck I had a dream. I was driven to your father's cabin in a horse-drawn coach. I looked out the back window and thought I saw a large wolf sitting back in the woods watching the cabin. I tried to clean off the window pane for a better look, but it was gone. Several weeks later, when you told me about the wolves and about the big one, I had chills on my spine. I knew it had to be the one I saw in the dream. Today that was confirmed."

"Wow!" He thought for a few seconds. "Who was the coach driver, Jake?"

"You know, as I think about it now, he must have been a messenger—an angel. Now enough angel talk. Let's go back and celebrate with our friends."

CHAPTER FOUR

As we rejoined the group, Peter climbed onto my lap. He was responsive until 9:30, when he fell asleep.

After a few minutes I stood up to look around the room. In the gathering were my sister and brother-in-law, Betty and Jerry Cummins, who had come all the way from Buffalo, New York. Jason, my driver manager from Salt Lake and Bill Murphy from Richmond, Virginia. Bill was the executive vice president of QZX, the company I drove for. Hank and Margie were next. Both were drivers for QZX. Sitting next to Margie was Frank Krandell, a Federal Attorney from Reno, Nevada who represented me a year ago when the crusher vanished from my trailer. Next to him was Agent Smith, one of the two special agents from the FBI who were trying to prove that I stole the crusher. Next to her was the local parapsychologist, Tasha Milinski. There was the minister, and Jane Dowdy, half owner of the Silver Dollar Saloon in Basin and her husband, Mike. Next came George Swansen, Jane's brother and owner of the other half of the saloon.

The only one I hadn't known very long was the minister. Everybody but he had been concerned about Peter's fate and concerned about how I might lose Peter. I got everybody's attention.

"I want to thank all of you for coming. It means the world to Peter and me." I passed onto them several things I'd learned from Mrs. Stevenson.

George raised his hand. "As we were leaving Slippery Gulch today, you and Peter went over to a small cabin. To the rest of us it looked as if you two were talking to somebody, but nobody was there. What was going on?"

"A year ago, Peter and I spent our first night together right here in Basin in the truck. That night I had a dream." I explained it in detail, including how the wolves saved Peter after his last beating by his father. "At Peter's death, the editorial said the wolves cried. We didn't understand what the editor meant, but we do now. Today, as we were leaving Slippery Gulch, I saw the same wolf sitting next to a cabin. That was the cabin Peter was born in. It's the same wolf who stood watch over Peter one hundred years ago." All were amazed.

"By the way George, this isn't a classroom. You don't have to raise your hand."

"Well, you're a teacher." He looked at Peter. "And a darn good one I'd say."

"Oh, and Jane, George and Mike: I want to thank you for having, 'I'll love you forever, Little One' inscribed on Peter's stone. But how did you know I'd said those exact words to him a few days before?"

The three of them looked confused. Finally Jane spoke. "To be honest—and brace yourself—when we moved the stone to Peter's gravesite last week, it wasn't on there. It was as much a surprise to us as it was to you."

We all sat quietly for a moment contemplating that here was yet another miracle.

Jane asked, "Jake, many of us suspected Peter was an angel most of the year but, you were insistent he wasn't. Why?"

I stood there collecting my thoughts. "Last August while camping, Peter reminded me of a situation I was involved in, in Texas over four years earlier. I had made a snap decision to exit I-30 before my designated exit. Just as I followed through on that decision and moved onto the exit ramp, a west bound big truck jackknifed, bounced across the median and would have nailed me in my cab. Peter recalled the incident exactly as it happened. He said the decision to exit when I did was not mine. I asked if the decision was his. He said no, but he had been informed. After all the person who was to be the answer to his prayer could not be killed." I sensed a chill go over the group.

"I knew at that point I had a guardian angel. But I never dreamed it was Peter."

"Peter mentioned earlier that the day before he died, he saw your face in the clouds and knew you would be his future friend," Jane continued. "But how is that possible?"

"I was informed just today that Providence picked me for this assignment in 1901. If you're looking to me for explanations, I don't have a clue." I turned to the minister. "Sir, perhaps you can enlighten us."

He moved in his chair as if trying to figure out how to frame his reply. "Folks, this has been the most amazing day of my life. Mr. Winters, I haven't yet figured out why I was able to observe the deceased sitting before me during the service." The rest of us chuckled. "I don't have a clue as to why we are observing an angel on a sustained basis. This day has been packed with mysteries. Call them miracles if you wish. They don't exactly match up with things in the Bible. But as with so much in our lives, there are mysteries all about us. I'm sorry, Mr. Winters, but I can't answer your question."

I thanked him and apologized for putting him on the spot. "The questions surrounding Peter, I don't believe we mortals can comprehend. Long ago I accepted Peter for what I thought he was. Now I accept Peter for what I know he is… to me…my special grandson." There were nods. "You mentioned the brevity of angelic visitations in the Bible.

What I am holding in my arms actually is a mortal with angelic interludes.

"While I have sort of an inner circle here, I'll give you something else to ponder. Following Peter's terrible life and brutal, cruel death, he was quickly buried among the rocks and boulders on Boot Hill. But in his time, on his third day he came back."

We few in the room grew silent. No one in the room had known what I had just related. They all had assumed it was one hundred years in Peter's earthly years.

I let them ponder this for a moment. "Many of us thought it amazing Peter was able to live to age six. God was protecting him. He easily could have died at two or four. The wolves played their part."

I explained the timing of Peter's death as his mother explained it to me. "As to why me, Mrs. Stevenson said that Peter and I were considered a perfect match."

I looked at the minister. "Pastor Wilkins, I thank you from both Peter and myself. His funeral one hundred years ago—well, there were no prayers or anything else resembling a Christian burial. The only people in attendance were the undertaker, the owner of the newspaper and two men hired to carry the box of Peter's remains. The only eulogy a pallbearer quoted: 'Well, at least were finally rid of the little bastard.'" Many people in the room shifted their weight, though they had read this in the editorial. "Today he got the Christian funeral he deserved."

"May I?" the minister spoke up. "Several months ago, Jane came to me and asked if I would be willing to preside at a funeral for a young boy who'd been brutally murdered by his father. Sickened, I asked when. When she said June 30, I was curious: that was four months away. But I didn't pry.

"I became skeptical but curious when she said the murder occurred in 1901. And that the deceased would be there! I thought this lovely lady here had lost it completely.

"Then she had me read the editorial. I was sickened. When she said that the boy was currently roaming around the country with a truck driver in his 18-wheeler, I had to see these crazy people firsthand. She assured me that the lad would be back in the area in time for his second funeral. She then leveled an entirely unnecessary request: 'Don't tell anybody about this.' Now I ask you, who would I tell?" At this point we were in stitches.

"As I said earlier, this was the highlight of my career. Jane, thank you so much for calling on me for this service today. As long as I live I will never forget today.

"When I stood before you at the service, I was afraid the whole thing was a hoax: That I was being set up to be the laughingstock. Peter certainly didn't look like any ghost I'd met in fiction. But, Mr. Winters, when you held Peter in your arms and described your traditions, developed between you over the year, Peter's tears told me something was going on beyond my training and experience. Then after the service, Peter walked away, well! I'm still at a loss for words.

"I've never heard *I Walked Today Where Jesus Walked* sung any better by professionals. Such feeling! I knew then, Peter was an angel. There was no other explanation."

"You could make millions by exploiting the boy, Mr. Winters, but I know you won't. Were you that type of person, God would not have placed Peter in your care.

"I'm sorry I wasn't able to answer your question. I think you're right. You've been a party to some miracles; but the biggest and best one is asleep on your lap. The why's and how's are not up to us mortals to figure out. We understand by faith."

I asked if we could conclude on a fun note. They agreed we needed to lighten up. "I took Peter through a fun house once. We got to one scary scene. After he recovered from his fright, I saw something in his eyes while he listened to the others scream. I looked at him and said, 'Don't even think about it.' He gave me his cute, innocent look. Once we were out of the place, I told him I knew what he was entertaining in his imagination: 'Boy could I ever have fun in here.'" Everybody laughed. "He admitted that's exactly what he was thinking, but claimed he would never have done it. I'm sure the only reason he wouldn't have was because he knew he would have been in big trouble with me.

"He knows the only time he can vanish or use his angelic power is when there's an emergency. Or when I give him permission. Any other time he's cheating. That's the rule."

"Does he understand what an emergency is?" Margie asked.

"Yes. He has a good understanding. Today, when he put the casket in the ground and filled in the grave, that open grave scared him; after all, he came close to occupying it.

"As to rules: They say no directions come with children. Well, I can attest to the fact that no directions come with little angels either." Some parental heads nodded in agreement.

"Mr. Winters," Pastor Wilkins interjected, "based on what you've said, I believe his voice is mortal, not angelic."

"You're right. If he used his angelic powers to sing, he'd be cheating. I've heard him sing to himself when he didn't realize I was nearby. It is the same voice."

We talked for a while when suddenly Peter let loose with a blood-curdling scream. The others in the room jumped. Two of the women squealed. Peter started kicking and swinging with his arms. I was picking him up to get a better hold on him, when he let loose. Although he had shorts and underpants on, urine was soon dripping on the floor.

Jane ran to get towels and washcloths. Mike got a bucket of water and a mop. I apologized to George and Jane since it is their floor while Peter continued to scream and cry and fling his limbs.

Betty got his pants off just as Jane came back into the room and put a towel on the table. I laid him on the towel. While I cleaned Peter, Bill and Mike cleaned the floor. As Peter awoke, he looked around confused, trying to get his bearings. He looked at me and said, "It was the same one, Jake. I was hanging in my father's cabin. That same man was coming at me with a knife. I thought they were over. I don't want to go through this again. I'm too much trouble. The people in Slippery Gulch were right; I'm no good. I don't want to go with you. I want to go back to the…"

Before he could get out the word grave, I yanked him off the table, threw him over my lap and spanked him three times. He howled. The others were shocked at this display of violence. Nobody had ever seen me like this before, including my sister. I picked him up by his arms and held him in front of me, shaking him. There were tears in my eyes and terror in his.

"Don't you understand? I don't care what you do or don't do. I love you. We beat this before and if need be, we'll beat it again, but we'll beat it together. You're not going back to the grave."

I pulled him into my arms and hugged him, hard. Peter and I weren't the only ones in tears. I knew my reaction was a result of the extreme emotions of the day. I was sure Peter's nightmare was a result of the same thing; plus being back in that God-forsaken town again.

After a few minutes, he said, "Jake, could you stop hugging me so hard? It hurts!" I started laughing, and put him down. He started rubbing his butt. "Jake, I promise, I'll never talk of going back again." Everybody produced a relieved sigh. Peter gave me a sheepish smile.

I gave Hank the keys to my truck. He returned with clean clothes for Peter. As he slipped into dry shorts, I said, "Good, because if you do, I'll spank you twice as hard the next time. And if I ever hear you say again that those idiots in that rotten town were right about you, I'll spank you for that, too. The editor was right. He said you were sitting on the right hand of God. Well, you are and you have been." I picked him up and put him on my lap. "I'm sorry for scaring you, Kiddo, but you pushed me to it. I don't ever want to lose you."

"I know. I'm sorry, Jake."

Then George said, "What about the rest of us? You scared the hell out of me." He looked at Peter. "Oh, sorry, Little Angel." George looked back to me. "I was afraid you were going to kill him." Laughter eased the group again.

"George, I'm sorry for peeing on your floor." Peter concluded the episode.

George got up and walked over. "Jake, could I take Peter off your hands for a moment?" I handed Peter to George. Peter looked a little worried. "You know what I'm going to do about it?" he asked Peter while holding him in his massive arms. Peter looked more concerned than ever, shaking his head. "I'm going to do what Jake would do. I'm going to tickle you." For the next moment, Peter squirmed, laughed and squealed as George laughed in delight. George finished by saying, "Peter, you can pee on my floor anytime you want. Just don't make it a habit, okay?"

Peter, still out of breath, agreed. He gave George a hug. George passed Peter back to me.

"Do you have to pee again?"

A little embarrassed he said, "No, I think I'm out." We all laughed. He thought for a minute. "You were right again, Jake. I guess I will pee again where and when I'm not supposed to." With that declaration, he went back to sleep in seconds.

Then Jane asked, "Is that what you two went through last summer?"

"Yeah, every night for over two weeks."

"Wow! I don't know how you did it," George said.

"It wasn't easy but I made up my mind we were going to beat it. I was sure we could. Peter never had anybody that cared for him. I'll tell you I think that's what has given him the will to fight on. He finally realized I care for him, and I do love him. He also knew I wasn't going to give up on him. That moved him not to give up on himself."

Mike said, "You deserve a lot of credit, Jake. I would not have had that kind of patience."

"It was tough at times, but when I got discouraged, all I had to do was remember that unbelievably sad face I first met. Everything seemed worth it.

"Well, look folks, I'm physically beat and emotionally drained. I'm going to bed."

Suddenly Peter sat straight up staring off into nothingness. I knew what was coming. "I'll be back in a few minutes, Jake." Then he vanished. Everybody in the room jumped except me.

Hank was the first one to ask what happened. "Somebody that he knows and cares for is in serious trouble. What just happened is exactly the same thing that happened when he helped you, Hank. Without being asked, he won't say much about it."

A few minutes later Peter reappeared. He stood before me, covered in mud. "Bobby's safe now."

The only Bobby he knew was the little boy we had met while camping last summer. Everybody was speechless, except me. "What happened, Kiddo?"

"Bobby got lost in the woods not far from his house. He thought he knew how to get home, but he was walking in the wrong direction. It got dark and he was scared. There was a search party looking for him, but he was turned around and kept walking further away from them. He walked into a marsh and was more scared, and cold. Then he started to sink in quicksand. He was up to his chin and knew he was going to die. He started praying and I heard him. He's okay now." He looked down at himself. "I'm a mess, aren't I?"

I laughed. "You sure are, but don't worry about that. Is he going to be found?"

"I put him down close to his house. He found his way home. He's cold and a mess, but he's safe now." I picked Peter up and put him on my lap. "Jake, you're going to be a mess, too."

"Don't worry about it. I'm very proud of you, Little Angel." ("Little Angel" had become his CB handle, given to him by a women driver in Iowa last spring.) How did you know Bobby was in trouble?"

"I don't know, I just did."

He was too far-gone to think about it, and was soon asleep.

"Well folks, I'm beat. I think I'd better get the angel and myself bathed and in bed." I said goodbye to everybody and thanked them all for coming.

Jane, Mike and I went back to their house. Jane helped me give Peter a bath then put him to bed. She was amazed he didn't wake up. After a shower I joined him. That night, Peter slept with me. I was hoping he'd remain dry for the night. I put a pair of Pull-Ups on him just in case, but that proved unnecessary.

CHAPTER FIVE

The next morning Jane did laundry for Peter and me. While Jane, Mike and I were sitting in the kitchen drinking coffee and waiting for the washing cycle to finish, Peter staggered into the kitchen and collapsed across my lap. Yesterday morning at this time, I wasn't sure if this would ever happen again. I put my hand on his bare back, looked up and thanked God again.

"How goes it this morning, Funny Face?"

Without raising his head, he said, "Not good, Jake. I can't wake up."

Within twenty seconds he was wide-awake and out of breath.

Peter soon noticed he was wearing Pull-Ups. "Jake, why am I wearing these?" he asked, pulling at the waistband.

"Just in case you had another nightmare last night. Better safe than sorry."

"I guess. Can I take them off?"

I gave the okay, so he stood up and started to slide them down. "Hold it, Peter. I didn't mean here. Why don't you go back to our room to change?"

"Okay." He pulled them back up. "Hey, I'm clean."

"Jane and I gave you a bath last night before we put you to bed."

"Oh, okay. Thanks," he said as he dashed off. He was soon dressed and ready for breakfast and the day.

After breakfast Jane, Mike, Peter and I walked back to the truck and loaded our bags. All but Hank and Margie had left the night before. I forgot to have Peter say goodbye to Betty and Jerry, but we'd be home in another three weeks anyway.

As Peter jumped into my arms from the truck, the puzzling older gentleman from the day before approached us. The others followed him around the truck to see what was going on. He looked at Peter. "You're Peter Stevenson, aren't you?"

Peter looked at the man confused. Then he looked up at me, worried. George approached the man. "Buddy, you've been coming into my bar on and off for the past year, yet I don't know a thing about you. I think it's time you explain yourself."

He ignored George while addressing me. "I don't know your name, sir, but I know what you are." I glanced at George who was about ready to lose it. "You're the answer to Peter's prayer."

That just about leveled me. I stared at him, wordless.

"Allow me to introduce myself. I'm Ron Durban. I am an author who wrote one book." For the first time, I noticed two books under his left arm. "It didn't sell very well, but I didn't really expect it to." He handed both George and me a book. We examined the cover's image. A picture was taken from a hill looking down into a ghost town. It was taken from Boot Hill of Slippery Gulch. The book was entitled *The History of Slippery Gulch.* I opened my copy to the copyright: 1956. George was still focused on the man.

"During my research for the book in the mid 1950s, Mr. Winters, I knew that the answer to young Peter's prayer had been born, living somewhere as a young boy himself. I also knew that Peter would not return until the last resident of Slippery Gulch died. That happened in the spring of 2001. That death began my waiting game. I missed all the action last year because I was ill at the time.

"I learned from a local of these parts that a big truck surprisingly entered Slippery Gulch on June 29. Since it was a ghost town of some one hundred years, I understood the truckers presence. The thing I didn't understand was how he got there. I had been in there around Eastertime and found the road washed out at the cliff. I had to walk from that point. I returned August 18, following the tracks of the truck, still visible. It had driven over the road and across the defaced cliff as if the road were still there. I knew then that the miracle I'd been waiting forty years for had occurred. As I walked around town I saw your tracks, Mr. Winters, and I also saw the barefoot tracks of a child. I then walked up to Peter's grave, as I'd done so many times over the past forty-plus years. I placed my hand on the ground over the grave. Don't ask me how but I knew instantly, Peter was gone.

"I sensed that you'd both be back this year about the same time, but I could not imagine why."

"Mr. Durban, I wish you would have identified yourself to George before this. Yesterday was June 30, exactly one hundred one years since Peter was murdered. Yesterday was Peter's second funeral. But this time he got a Christian funeral."

He bowed his head. When he looked up there were tears in his eyes. He looked at Peter. "As I read about your first funeral in the editorial…"

"Wait! You've read the editorial?" I asked Mr. Durban.

"The daughter of the man who wrote it gave me a copy in 1955."

Peter looked at him, surprised. "You know Sadie?"

"I knew Sadie, Peter. She died twenty years ago as an old lady. She was a wonderful person, but she died with a guilty conscience and a sad heart along with the other residents of Slippery Gulch."

"They did?" I put my hand on the back of his head.

"Peter, you and the good Lord were responsible for Slippery Gulch becoming a ghost town. Sadie's father wrote the editorial four days after you died. Everybody in town read it or had it read to them. It caused them to reflect on what they did to you—and had not done for you. It caused them to take stock of their actions—a sort of John the Baptist moment in truth in the wilderness of their sinful hearts. Within a month of your death, Slippery Gulch was a ghost town.

"The morning you were murdered, Sadie was trying to locate you. Her family had decided the night before to bring you into their home to live. When she found you, it was too late. She never got over the grieving.

"Her father told her about your funeral. She cried, even as an old women when she would rehash it to me in every detail."

"She did?"

"Yes, she did. Her parents wanted to leave town as soon as her father wrote the editorial, but Sadie refused. It was she that carved your stone. She refused to leave until it was finished and on your grave. She grew to regret her use of the town's nickname for you, "The Brat," but it was too late. Of course she was only eleven at the time. Once she and her father wheeled the stone to your grave, they left. She never went back. In fact, one by one the residents left, never to return to Slippery Gulch. Apparently they never told anybody where the place was or the events that they were a part of there."

"But you knew! And so did George and Mike," Peter restated.

"I knew because Sadie told me."

"Mike and I knew but thought the town died because the mine shut down," George confessed.

"As a result of the experience he had in Slippery Gulch, Sadie's father moved his family to Helena where he became a pastor. He dedicated his life there to neglected and abused children. He helped hundreds of children through the years and for his efforts eventually received a highly prestigious humanitarian award from the State of Montana. But he could not get the worst child abuse case out of his mind. Nor how he never lifted a finger to help. It was a thorn in his conscience. The weight of his guilt was too heavy. In his old age he took his own life."

"Was that me?" Peter asked.

"Yes, it was, Peter. I don't know how, but Sadie was convinced that your last prayer would be answered. At first I thought she was crazy. She finally convinced me otherwise. She thought you were quite a kid. According to the editorial, her father did too. But not just quite a kid. The older she got the more she thought you as an angel of judgment on the town."

Peter shot a look at me; Mr. Durban caught it. He looked at Peter, and back at me. "He *is* an angel, isn't he!" There was a long silence. "Peter is a genuine heavenly angel...isn't he?" Mr. Durban pressed me for a reply.

I looked at the others contemplating what to say. I looked down and opened his book to thumb through it. He had known about Peter forty-six years before I did! He knew people that had known Peter as a living child. This man knew of Peter's last prayer and was convinced it would be answered. He knew that someone was coming, without knowing it would be me.

"Sir, why did you not speak to George about all of this?"

"I thought he would consider me a senile old man."

"Yes, Mr. Durban, Peter is an angel. But not as you see him standing here."

"I thought so. Peter, were you an angel from the beginning?"

Peter looked at me for help. "No, he wasn't. Peter and I met his mother yesterday at his funeral." Mr. Durban gasped. He was taken aback at the news. "She appeared to me and answered many of my questions. Peter was born to be an angel, but he did not get his wings until last Christmas. But as a mortal, he's anything but an angel. He's just a good little kid."

"Sounds like that's what he was in Slippery Gulch. People were blind to his goodness until after his death."

Peter attempted a smile but was near tears. "So I caused the death of a town?"

At this point I stepped in. I lifted Peter into my arms. "No, Peter, you didn't. When we visited Bannack last week, we talked about this. Bannack had a few evil people, but the town itself was basically good. Slippery Gulch was a thoroughly evil place. The evil infected most everyone who lived there. Sadie saw the good in you. She rose above the evil and eventually her family did too. Her father's editorial brought judgment on the town with such impact that people began leaving immediately. Mercifully, the town itself died, crushed by the weight of its own evil."

"So everybody in town lived on somewhere except me. I died."

Everybody looked at me including Mr. Durban, wondering how I was going to field that one. Suddenly I was reminded of Easter and Durban's previous visit to Slippery Gulch. "Last Easter, Kiddo, you learned that Jesus died for the sins of all mankind. And you thought at the time you died for no one. Remember?" He nodded. "Well, you're not as big as Jesus, are you?"

"No way. Jesus is God's special son."

"Well, Jesus died for the judgment of mankind, but you died to bring judgment on the dark soul of an evil town. Your death broke the back of evil in Slippery Gulch. God used you and the editor to end the hatred that ruled there."

Peter, wide-eyed, said, "Oh!"

"True, you died but have been brought back as an angel. As a result, you're living the life that other little boys could only dream of."

He rested his head against my chest. "And I got to live with the answer to my dying prayer." He paused and then sat up. "But, Jake, why wasn't I infected by the evil?"

"Because God honored and protected your innocent heart." I turned to Mr. Durban. "The minister in Slippery Gulch wouldn't let him come in the church because he said he wasn't good enough for God. So Peter just sat under a side window alone and listened to the worship and the preacher." I could tell this was all new to Mr. Durban. "But you weren't sitting alone."

He looked at me. "I wasn't?"

"No. You were never alone. You thought you were, but you weren't. You thought you died alone, but you didn't. Yesterday before your mother left, you sang the song *I Walked Today Where Jesus Walked.* As always, it was beautiful." I was on a roll. "Hey, do you remember the note that was left for you on Christmas morning?" He nodded again. "At one point in the note it said, 'I was with you always.' That was God who said that, Kiddo. You were never alone. When you sat in the dirt under the church window listening to the word of God, or whatever that minister was talking about, God was sitting next to you like the loving Father he is."

"But, Jake, if God was with me always, why did he allow me to get beaten all the time? Why did he allow those boys to beat me in the alley? Why did he…"

"Peter, you were not allowed to listen in on the conversation your mother and I had about this. Why? I don't know." I told him what she'd said about time. "You see, Little One, during your entire life in Slippery Gulch, God was preparing you to be an angel. The devil was tempting you to fail and God was allowing him to do it. You knew all the bad words. You could have used them against your enemies, against the whole d…darn town, but you never did. The editor realized that. You and I know that you have a very strong and accurate arm. Again, you could have used your arm against your enemies, but never did. Why God was so tough on you, I don't know. That's not up to us to understand. But we now know that whatever his reason was, he was right. You're a fantastic angel and not a bad kid either. Well, most of the time, anyway." Peter flashed his devilish smile at the others and giggled.

"Peter, before you go, would you sing your song for me?" Mr. Durban asked.

Peter looked at me. I nodded. "Okay, but can I sing it inside?" He looked at George.

George gave the okay. Inside he removed his sneakers, and I lifted him onto the table. Even though the setting was not as beautiful as it was yesterday, Peter's voice was. As I looked around the small group, the reactions were the same. Everyone had tears, but Mr. Durban was holding his head raining tears on the table under his elbows.

When Peter finished the song, I stood him on the floor. Mr. Durban went to him and dropped to his knees. He took hold of him by his upper arms and said, "Peter, that was the most beautiful thing I have ever heard." Then Mr. Durban hugged him. Peter looked at me over his shoulder as if to say, "What do I do now?" I winked at him.

Mr. Durban released him and said, "And this one is from Sadie." He hugged him again. When he released him, he said "Peter, the hug from Sadie was from one hundred one years ago, but would have been the same today. You're a beautiful boy, Peter. Sadie saw that in you. Thank you so much for singing for me. I'm sure Sadie is smiling too." As Peter put his sneakers back on, he thanked Mr. Durban for his kind comments and said he wished he'd seen Sadie before she had died.

It was time for the truckers to get moving. We walked outside to the trucks. Before leaving, Hank asked Peter how Peter knew he was in trouble on the bridge last winter.

Peter thought about this for a few seconds, then said, "I'm not really sure. We were going along and all of a sudden I could see everything, like I was watching a movie. I could see you, your truck, the bridge, the ice and even what was going to happen. I knew I had to do something quick or..." his voice trailed off.

Hank was silent for a minute, then got down on his knees and hugged Peter. "Thanks Peter. Now I guess both Jake and I owe you, big time."

"You're a good friend, Hank. I guess that's what I'm here for. To be your friend in need."

After a few seconds of silence I said, "That's okay, Funny Face, but just don't forget whose guardian angel you are. I mean, it's okay to help the Old One here once in a while when he can't manage to keep his rig on the road, but just don't make a habit of it." Peter started laughing.

"Hey, you old goat. Don't call me old. After all, you remember when Niagara Falls was brand new." The two of us went back and forth for the next two or three minutes, much to Mr. Durban and Peter's delight. Just a year earlier at the end of our first day together, Peter and I had run into Hank in a truck stop in Spokane. It was there that Peter learned that teasing could come from friendship, not just hate. As a result, I'd teased Peter a lot ever since. He loved it because he knew it was coming from love.

Finally, Peter stepped between the two of us and yelled, "Hey you two old grandpas, let's hit the road." We both looked down at him; then at each other and mouthed, "Old Grandpas"? At my nod we attacked him. He got a double tickling, much to his delight, followed by rewarding hugs from both of us. Things were back to normal.

"Come on you old coot, the Little Angel has spoken," Hank said.

I turned to Mr. Durban and extended my hand. "I'm so glad Peter and I have met you. I know Peter now has a much healthier view of the devastating events at Slippery Gulch. I will have Peter read your book to me as we drive. I'm sure both of us will find it very interesting."

He handed me his card. 'Ron Durban, attorney-at-law.'

"If you have any questions or concerns about the book, don't hesitate to call." He paused. "I don't mean to sound insulting, but I think you should read it to Peter. It would probably be a little advanced for him."

"Peter is reading at the eighth-grade level."

Ron chuckled. "Why doesn't that surprise me? Peter, read it all you want. It was a thrill to finally meet you." He looked at me. "Jake, may I call you Jake?"

"Certainly."

"Great! Please call me Ron." He looked at the other adults. "Please, all of you." He looked back at me. "Jake, it's a real honor to finally meet the answer to Peter's prayer.

I don't know you that well, but you appear to be quite a guy. Is he Peter?"

"Yeah, he's okay."

"What?" I grabbed Peter and said, "You little peanut," and threw him into the air. Peter was giggling all the while. "Now tell him the truth."

Still laughing, Peter said, "Jake's the greatest, Mr. Durban. He's my first friend and my best friend. I love Jake and he loves me and we'll be together forever." Giggling he added, "I only said that because if I didn't, he'll unbutton my bellybutton."

"You're cruising today aren't you, Funny Tummy?" I said.

Ron, smiling, looked at me. "Jake, I have to admit, I'm envious. It must be great living with a kid like Peter."

"Yeah, it's okay, I guess."

Peter came over and punched me lightly. "Ja-a-a-ke."

"Gotcha, Funny Face. Actually it's wonderful living with Peter. This past year has been the best year of my life. We're a team, a lovin', truckin' team. I wouldn't trade Peter for a brand new Freightliner condo." I thought for a minute. "Although I might think about it, if it was the right color."

Again everybody laughed. Peter giggled. "Now you're the one that's cruising, Grandpa. Come on you guys, we got-to-get-truckin'."

We said good-bye all around and hopped in our trucks. I got on the CB at once. "Hank, Margie, you both in your trucks?"

"Well, now, you got eyes, don't ya?" Margie shot back.

"You forget already?" Hank chimed in.

Peter and I were both laughing. "Ready on the airhorns?" I asked. They both acknowledged. "Okay, on three: one, two, three." We all three blasted at once, pulled out and waved. I'm sure with the air horns of three big trucks blasting at once, the windows in Basin were vibrating.

Jane called me later in the week and said that Ron was there until 10:00 that night, per their invitation to stay that late. They got to know each other and found him a very interesting fellow. And of course they filled him in as best they could on my first trip into Slippery Gulch and everything that happened to us in the past year. Ron had quite a day.

Hank was heading east on I-90 for Chicago and Margie was heading east to the I-25 split; then she would head south for Denver. Hank and Margie would run together to the split. No doubt they had plenty to talk out.

Peter and I were heading west. We all went as far as Butte together. I let Peter do most of the talking on the CB. Once we got to Butte, Peter said, "Good seeing both of you again. Keep it between the lines, you two."

Hank laughed. "You're getting this CB jargon down pretty good, kid. Sure good still having you around, Peter. Keep an eye on the ugly one for me and maybe I'll see you at your birthday party again, if I'm invited."

Then Margie added, "I agree with Hank. It was great seeing you again, Little Angel, and it's great knowing you're still with Jake. Take care of him for me, and Jake, it was great seeing you again, too. We'll see you both again, somewhere out there."

I also said good-bye to them and headed into Butte. We stopped at the World Museum of Mining.

I bought our tickets. As we walked around, it occurred to me: all of the pieces of equipment on display were new at the time Peter was born. Others were produced after his death up through the 1900s. We were both amazed at the size of the biggest crusher on display. After a couple of hours, we grabbed a bite to eat and continued west.

It was raining by the time we got back to I-90. Shortly after the I-90, I-15 split, one of the most beautiful rainbows I'd ever seen materialized before our eyes. Within seconds it became a double rainbow. "Wow, Peter, look at that. Isn't that beautiful?"

Peter looked at the double rainbow, then at me. "Yeah, it is but, Jake, I've seen a lot of rainbows since I've been with you and you must have seen hundreds, maybe even thousands in your life. Why do you always get excited when you see a new one?"

"It's one of the ways God talks to us, Kiddo. Remember? He's keeping his promise to us that he will never flood the earth again. But this one is special. It arches right over I-90. We may drive right under it. And this one is a double. We've seen doubles before, but not like this one. The second rainbow is as bright as the first and both are very bright from one end to the other. I think this one is meant for us. I think it may be God's way of saying he's going to honor the promise he made to us that we can stay together forever."

Peter's eyes enlarged. "Do you think?"

"It's possible."

"Do you think everybody can see it?"

"I don't know. Let's find out." I picked up the mike. "Brake one-nine."

The radio crackled back. "Go ahead brake."

"Thanks for the come-back. Am I seeing things or is that the most beautiful double rainbow ever?"

There was a pause then the driver came back. "I see a single rainbow and it's brilliant on both ends at the ground, but it fades out at the top. And I see only one. What's you're twenty?" [location]

I gave the driver my mile marker. "You're about a mile ahead of me driver. Maybe it appears as a double where you are."

A driver going east and across the median from us responded. "I'm looking in my side mirrors and only see a single rainbow, driver. I think you're seeing things."

"Well, thanks for the comeback. I must be picking up a reflection in the window. Have a good one."

But both Peter and I knew it was not a reflection. We drove mile after mile watching the beauty. We never did go under it. Finally, it began to fade and was soon gone, leaving Peter and me deep in our own thoughts.

Although our load was going to Portland, the first part of our trip was a repeat of our first trip together a year ago. Then we were going to Spokane. As now, the person sitting in the passenger seat was a six-year-old boy and a product of the nineteenth century. Unlike now, everything was new, different and in some cases frightening to him. The questions were endless. He was as uncertain of me as I was of him. All I knew for sure was that he was a ghost. As it turned out, I didn't even get that right.

I didn't know how long he was going to be with me and I wasn't sure how long I wanted him. In some ways I was resentful of Jane and the others because I felt I got roped into taking him in the first place. I was giving up a lot, most importantly my independence. But I was the answer to his last prayer. I could not ignore that.

I looked over at my little boy. I was no longer riding with a ghost or a stranger. I had forfeited my independence and accepted the responsibility God placed on my shoulders, namely—giving this little guy from another time and era the love he never had, but so richly deserved. As a result he was enjoying the childhood he missed out on. For that I'd been rewarded with the greatest year of my life: my very own guardian angel and the greatest little kid you'd ever hope to know. Peter was the happiest he'd ever been and so was I. We were a happy, contented team.

Peter interrupted my pleasant thoughts. "Jake, I hate my father. I always have. When I was alive, I always hoped someone would kill him. Instead, he killed me." He paused for a long time. "It isn't right to hate, is it?"

I had to pull off someplace. This was going to require my full concentration. The opportunity came up out of the blue. It was an exit I'd never noticed before. I pulled off and back on to an entrance ramp and parked. He sat on my lap. "Peter, you're right, it's wrong to hate. But if anybody has a reason, you do. But hate is a very strong emotion. His hatred killed you and destroyed him. Now your hatred of him could destroy you.

"You asked me once if God had a plan for all of us. We know what his plan is for you: to be an angel. But how can you be the angel he wants if you have hate in your heart? I don't think God is finished molding you."

Had he been in his pajamas, he'd have played with them now. Instead, he unbuttoned one of my shirt buttons, then rebuttoned it. He'd do this time and time again. He played with the bottom of his shirt, rolling it up to his chest, letting it fall back into place then starting over. He rediscovered his bellybutton. After several minutes he said, "Jake, I don't think I can stop hating him. I don't think I can ever forgive him."

"I don't think you can either—alone. Maybe that's one of the reasons God brought us together, Kiddo. Maybe I can help. Yesterday you and I met a wonderful woman—your mother. She is loving and understanding. She knows what you've been through since your birth, and she knows what you're capable of. She knows that I love you and will never leave you. She loves you very much, Little One.

"I often wondered during the year where you got you capacity for love after the life you lived. You once said I taught you how to love. I think what I did was to rekindle a spark in your heart and God's spirit for love. The capacity for love was inherited from your mother. Your father may have been a horrible human being, but he did two good things."

"What?" he asked skeptically.

"He married a wonderful woman and sired a peach of a kid."

"But then he killed me."

"That was all part of God's plan, Kiddo. Every previous life has to come to an end. Everything is set. All we do is get surprised by our end. But in your case, you were meant to wait for me to come along."

"You mean God made my daddy do all those bad things to me?"

"No! We are all given choices in life. What we do with those choices is up to us. Last summer when we were camping, I told you to stay off of downed logs because they could be slippery. When you came across a downed log, you had a choice to make: listen to me or have fun. You chose fun and you had fun...until you fell. Your father made choices too: but remember, your father was mentally ill. God allowed his illness and his bad choices to happen. Peter, since your birth, God has been preparing you for your present existence. I don't know why, but you had to suffer as a living child. That was all part of his plan."

"How do you know that?"

"Your mother told me yesterday. But you were not allowed to hear that part of the conversation. Why? I'm not sure. Maybe because you weren't willing to face your hatred of your father yet. Before we left Slippery Gulch a year ago, we peed on a circle that I drew in the dirt in front of the mercantile. You added two lines like arms to it and said that was your father. At that time you told me you hated him. You never mentioned that again until now. At that time, I knew he murdered you, but I didn't know about the beatings. Talking now about your hatred for your father, I believe, is a sign that you're ready to find forgiveness in your heart."

"But, Jake, he hurt me so bad. And not just my body. It hurts so bad in here." He put his hand on his chest. "It still does." He started crying. "All I ever wanted was a daddy that loved me and was proud of me. I wanted my daddy to be my friend—my best friend. I even prayed to God for that, but it didn't help. The day before daddy killed me, I prayed someone would kill him. I felt guilty for doing that. I knew it was wrong, but I couldn't help it, Jake." He paused as the tears increased. "How can I ever forgive him?"

"Peter, that prayer for his killing may have changed everything. Just as your final prayer did. God may have realized your capacity for love was dwindling. After being beaten so severely in the alley by the teenage boys, Fuzzy could have come and rescued you again, but he didn't, did he? And you didn't care, did you?" He shook his head. "You had suffered enough. You no longer wanted to live. Your time on earth as a mortal was coming to a close. But God needed someone to rekindle that spark within you. That's where I came in."

He played with a button on my shirt again. Finally he said, "I love you, Jake. I love everybody, but I can never love my father. I can never forgive him."

I knew I was going to need God's help with this. A year ago, Peter had told me in graphic detail of the terrible abuses and torturous beatings he suffered at the hands of his monster father. I was quickly reduced to tears as I pictured in my mind the brutality Peter suffered. As a result, I understood the severity of his nightmares. I could now understand the magnitude of his hatred he felt for his father.

"Peter, the Indians have a saying: 'Never judge a man until you've walked a mile in his moccasins.' He looked at me puzzled. "In other words, don't judge another individual until you have experienced what he has experienced. Well, Kiddo, I can never physically experience what you have experienced; but emotionally, I suffered as you suffered. During the year there were many times I felt I walked many miles in your sneakers with you."

A year ago when I learned of the abuses he'd suffered at the hands of his father, I grew to hate the man myself. While Peter suffered emotionally as he relayed the abuse to me, I suffered emotionally with him as I was there in our parked truck. I walked a mile more than once in his tiny sneakers. My tears were close to the surface now.

"Peter, you remember the note you received last Christmas morning? It said, 'I'm sorry you didn't think I was with you in Slippery Gulch, but I never left your side.' You thought that note came from Santa Claus. But as I told you yesterday, it came from God. You remember the little angel you received in your stocking, right?" He nodded. "Do you know who it was from?"

"Santa Claus, wasn't it?"

I smiled. "Actually, that gift was from God. It was his way of congratulating you for getting your wings Christmas Eve in church. Santa Claus probably delivered them, but they were from God. You see, Little One, God has never left your side, and he's in this truck right now." Peter looked around. "He's never left my side either. He's been with me long before I started driving. He can help both of us out on this hate business.

"I don't expect you to feel love for your father, and I don't think God does either. But loving and forgiving are two different things." I paused. "Peter, I told you once, if I had been there the last time your father beat you, I would have killed him. Confession time, Kiddo! For what he did to the little boy I love, I hate him too." He looked at me amazed. "I've never hated anybody before, but I hate your father. I have to find a way to forgive him myself. Remember, Kiddo, we're a team. Together we've overcome your worst fears. With God's help, together we'll overcome this too."

"Jake, what will happen if I can't forgive him? I'll never be able to forget what he did to me."

"Forgiving is not the same as forgetting. I don't expect you ever to forget, and I don't think God does either. Remember, if it wasn't for your father, I wouldn't have you now."

He wiped away my tears as I wiped his. "I know. You really are the father I always wanted. You're my daddy and grandpa all wrapped into one." He paused in thought. "Maybe I should forgive him and maybe you should too. After all, if it wasn't for him, I wouldn't have you either." Again he paused. "Jake, I don't think I hate him anymore… but is it okay if I still don't like him very much?"

I smiled. "I think that's fine. And you know what? I don't hate him anymore either. I just feel sorry for him. His hate never allowed him to know his son. His own hatred was his own punishment."

We both smiled. "Let's head west, Funny Face."

After mutual hugs, he went back to his seat. As he crawled away from me, I said a prayer of thanks. I shifted the Babes into second gear and released the brakes. As I approached I-90, I checked my left mirror to make sure the lane was clear. After pulling onto the interstate, I looked into the right mirror out of habit. The ramp we had just used had vanished. "Peter, quick, look in your mirror. The ramp we were just on is gone."

Without looking, he smiled slightly. "I know."

CHAPTER SIX

Late that afternoon we stopped at a small truck stop for dinner and to spend the night. While eating, Peter noticed several people smoking. He looked at them with interest. "Jake, why do people smoke?"

"Nicotine is very addictive, Kiddo. People start smoking as teenagers and get hooked. Once they start, it's very hard to quit."

"Just about all the men in Slippery Gulch smoked, and most of the boys did too. You don't smoke, do you?"

"I don't anymore. I quit the day I went into Slippery Gulch to pick up the crusher. I don't know why. After I met you that first time, I never wanted another cigarette."

After eating we went out to the truck. That evening we were both on my bunk reading, watching television and in general relaxing when out of the blue, Peter asked, "Jake, are those dreams going to start over again?"

"I don't think so. I think your nightmare was just a result of the stress of your funeral. And being back in Slippery Gulch. To be on the safe side though, why don't you sleep in your Pull-Ups and next to me." Moving his sleeping bag to my bunk was a treat, but sleeping in the Pull-Ups was disappointing. But he didn't complain though he seemed troubled.

After collecting his thoughts, he said, "Jake, I'm confused. Now that I'm a real angel, how am I supposed to behave?"

I thought about my response while he studied me. "Peter, you've been an angel since the day we met, but we didn't know it. Knowing it now shouldn't change anything."

"Did you know I was an angel?"

"No, but many people we met believed you were. After you saved that little girl in New Mexico last year, Jason, Jane and Margie suggested it. George and Mike did too. Even Danny believed it. So did the minister and Cindy. Even Jamie suspected it. The only one that didn't was me."

He looked at me disappointed. "Why didn't you?"

"I knew you better than they did. During the year, you did things I just couldn't believe an angel would do: You'd disobey me, got hurt, and got into trouble, right? You stole candy bars twice and lied to me about it. As it turned out, you had a darn good reason for doing that, and it was valuable to both of us, yet it was hard to believe an angel would do those things."

He put his head down. I lifted his head. "Peter, I'm not saying these things to embarrass you. I'm just explaining why I didn't believe it.

"I completely forgot that most of the time you're as mortal as I am. As a result you're going to get sick, misbehave and disobey me at times.

"Your final prayer was to have a friend, but the good Lord knew you needed more than just a friend. You needed someone who could hold your hand and ruffle your hair. You needed someone to remind you to be careful and to tend to your cuts and scrapes when you weren't. You needed someone to tell you how to behave and punish you with love when you didn't. You needed someone who could tickle and roughhouse with you, but at the same time could caress you and be tender when needed. You needed a lap to sit on. You needed someone who could give you hugs and kisses.

"In order to experience all that, you had to have a mortal body. So the Lord in his wisdom, returned to you your own repaired body and your own personality, disposition, sense of humor, intelligence and character.

"I bet the Lord is having a blast watching you. I think there are times when he's laughing and other times when he just shakes his head in a knowing and loving way. I think the way you are and have been behaving as a little boy is just what the Lord expects.

"Remember, God has a son too. As you know, his name was Jesus. Once he was six-years-old just like you are. Jesus knew he was the Son of God just as you know you're an angel. I bet there were times when he was wondering how he should behave too. I'm sure he tried to be good and always listen to his parents. But I bet it didn't always work out that way. In fact as a little boy, I bet he was always getting dirty and in trouble at times."

Peter's eyes opened wide. "Do you think so?"

I winked at him. "I'd bet on it."

He seemed satisfied so I changed the subject. "You know Kiddo, in a few weeks we're going home for a month. What do you want to do during our time off?"

"Can we go fishing, camping and canoeing again?" Without waiting for an answer he said, "Do you think Danny and his dad will go with us again? Do you think we'll see Bobby and his dad again? Do you think Darlene and her mom will be there? Can we stay longer?"

I started laughing. "Wait a minute. I haven't even said we can go again."

"I knew what you'd say. You love the same things I do." He paused. "No, I guess I love the same things you do because you taught me everything."

"And I'm glad you do. You bet we can but we can't stay any longer. We have a birthday party to go to in Rochester, remember?"

"Oh yeah, I forgot." He was quiet for a minute. "Jake, am I going to have another birthday party this year?"

"Oh, I don't know. One every hundred years is enough, isn't it?"

He looked at me. "Are you serious?"

I quickly stuck a finger in his ribs. "No, I'm just kidding, Kiddo. Every six-year-old deserves to have a birthday party. As long as you don't turn seven on me, you'll have one."

"Good! I like being six."

"There could be a problem this year though. We made it home last year for your birthday because it was really special, after all it was your first one ever. This year we may not get home. But if we don't, we'll do something special. And don't worry, this year I won't pretend to forget."

Peter smiled, nodded and went to sleep still smiling.

CHAPTER SEVEN

We delivered in Portland, then picked up a load going to Denver. During our drive through Western Oregon, we were singing to music on the radio when the news came on. During the report, we heard about an eight-year-old boy who had become separated from his parents while camping in the Rocky Mountains in Northern Montana. Tonight was his fourth night, wearing only shorts and a short-sleeve cotton shirt. The forecast was below freezing for that region. Officials said it was critical that he be found by nightfall.

I looked over at Peter. He was staring straight out the front window. I knew what was coming. He finally said, "Jake, he's still alive. They're not going to find him until tomorrow afternoon. He's cold, hungry and scared. He's praying for help, Jake, but his help isn't going to find him in time. Tonight he's going to die, alone and afraid. I know where he is. Can I go save him?"

I pulled onto a ramp. "What do you need?"

"Can I take your extra sleeping bag?"

"No. Take yours. It's smaller and lighter but just as warm as mine and plenty big enough for two kids." He agreed. "I'll tell you what. Let me empty out my shoe bag and we'll fill it with goodies. You can put the long strap over your shoulder and carry the sleeping bag under your arm."

We packed a bag of cookies, several peanut butter and jelly sandwiches and water. We also included a pullover hat, a towel, washcloth and a small first aid kit with antibiotic salve and bandages for scratches and cuts. Peter was in his heavy jacket ready to go.

"Peter, when will you be back?"

"Not until tomorrow afternoon when the rescuers get to him."

"You know, you're quite a kid and you know something else?" He shook his head. "Tonight will be the first night we haven't been together in a year."

"I know." He thought for a minute. "Do you want me to stay here?"

"I'd love you to, but that would kill that little boy. Now get your little butt in gear and do what you have to do. Little Angel, be careful."

"I will. You be careful, too." We gave each other a hug. "I love you, Jake" Before I could respond, he was gone.

That evening I pulled into a truck stop in central Oregon. As I backed into a spot, I thought about tonight. What was I going to do? With Peter, my evenings were set and that's the way it's been for a year. But Peter wasn't here tonight. What did I do before Peter? Well, for one thing, I read during my dinner.

After dinner and a few chapters in my book, I noticed a bar across the street. I continued my walk back to the Babes when I remembered I was free. I had no duties or responsibilities. I thought about walking over and having a beer. Then I thought about Peter and wondered how he was making out. If I knew my little angel, he was doing fine and the lost boy was too. I stopped and looked at my truck, then at the bar. Why not?

I walked across the street and into the poorly lit structure. I looked around. I didn't expect to see any recognizable faces, and I didn't. I went to the bar, ordered a beer and went to a corner table.

As I sat there, I couldn't get my mind off Peter and the Northern Montana Mountains. However, I soon found myself reflecting on the last twelve months. 2001 started out as every other year. I left home on December 28, 2000 and drove into 2001 with confidence. I knew by the end of February, I would have traveled to at least forty states.

I was a senior driver for the company and very often could choose my destination. But if the company had a two-dropper [two deliveries], the first in Burlington, Wyoming and the second in Sheridan, Wyoming running across the Big Horn Mountains on US 14 in January, I'd do it. If the company needed a driver to take a load of class A hazmat, in other words, explosives, from Wisconsin to Nevada, I'd do it. Why? It was different and exciting. With the explosive placards all over my truck, I always noticed I had far fewer tailgaters.

I was having fun, I was enjoying life and I was good. I was good from the standpoint I was always polite to the customers and projected a clean, professional image. I was never late to an appointment because of my mistakes. Road conditions and storms not withstanding.

But driving was another matter. Years ago during my third month driving, I decided I was the best driver on the road. That afternoon I backed into another trailer and almost lost my job. I learned my lesson. Never again did I become overconfident in my driving skills—no matter what I was driving.

I was my own man. All my decisions were mine and for me. When I made the wrong one, I admitted it and paid for it. When I made the right decision, I loved life even more.

Although I was nearly fifty-seven, I started thinking of retirement. I planned to buy a small motor home and travel to the places I couldn't get to in the big truck. My big problem was deciding when I'd retire. Would I retire at age sixty, sixty-two or sixty-five? How nice it was to have that as my biggest concern.

I went back for another beer and returned to my table.

I met Peter on June 29, 2001 and my life hasn't been the same since. I no longer make decisions with only me in mind, and sometimes I have them made for me, by Peter. Or sometimes as a result of circumstance!

My time was no longer my own, but ours. I used to read a book a week during meals, loading and unloading time. Now those times were spent communicating and teaching.

In the past when I finished a meal, I cleaned up myself and paid for one. Now I cleaned up two and paid for two.

In some ways this past year has been difficult for me. My independence is a thing of the past and for the first time in my life, I'm responsible for another person (except for the times I was a camp counselor.) But that was different. In the past year I've taken care of more cuts, scratches and bruises than I thought possible. I've been urinated on twice and vomited on once.

For the first time ever, I had a passenger, and this one was year-round. I found I was forced into teaching things I never dreamed I'd have to teach, such as how to brush one's teeth. And I found I had to answer questions I never dreamed I'd have to answer as a bachelor.

I've had more questions thrown at me in the last year than I'd had in all of the twenty-two years I taught school combined.

My breaks in rest areas during my ten-hour driving days were no longer based on my needs, but on the needs of my passenger. And I no longer ran in and out. I would give Peter ten to twenty minutes to burn off some of his energy. As a result my ten-hour days went to twelve. And my exhaustion increased.

When I left Basin a year ago with that little ghost and his mortal body, I had no idea how long he was going to be with me, and I had no idea how long I wanted him.

Now my little ghost was in reality my own heavenly guardian angel. Because of his six-year-old mortal body, I was his mortal guardian. Although he's learned a lot and matured emotionally, his body and internal organs had not grown and never would. Therefore frequent stops were still necessary. The difference was, I now exercised with him. As a result, my physical condition has improved and my energy level has too.

While driving a big truck, my social life went to poor. But now, unbelievably, it's improving again. Indirectly it has to do with Peter. Spending all my time with a six-year-old, I find I have to spend more quality time with adults. When Peter and I are home for three to five days, I spend at least one night out with friends or on a date without Peter. At first it was hard on him, but he adjusted.

In some ways I was not the man I used to be. But then I didn't have a young child to care for. I thought back to my previous career. How often during those many years of teaching and counseling in a camp did I want to smack a father along the side of his head and say, what are you thinking? You have a son or daughter that needs your love, attention and understanding.

For that matter, how many times have I seen a father who had his son or daughter with him in the big truck for a weekend or a week during the summer, and completely ignored them? It would be easier on me to do that with Peter. That way I wouldn't have as many questions to answer.

Then there was my religious conviction. I've always been a Christian, but a convenient Christian. I asked God for help when I needed it, then I would conveniently forget he existed. During Peter's horrible nightmares a year ago, I found myself praying for help, strength, patience and understanding. I also prayed that God would help Peter and be with him.

After Peter overcame his problems, we both prayed together every night before bed. Then I prayed everyday that Peter would be allowed to stay with me after his second funeral. Now I thank God everyday that Peter was allowed to stay with me. Sometimes I wonder if someday God isn't going to say, "Oh, it's you again."

I looked at my shrinking beer and decided to get another. For some reason I felt lonely. Before Peter, I was never lonely. Maybe I was becoming too dependent on Peter and his company. But there wasn't much I could do about it now. After all, he was my guardian angel and we were destined to be together forever.

I looked at my beer. Was this my second one or third? I never use to drink more than one.

How many drivers wouldn't give their right arm to have their guardian angel as their driving partner? Yet I'd given up a lot. Maybe even my manhood!

I took the glass for another sip, but it was gone. I strolled to the bar for another. "It would be cheaper to get a pitcher," the bartender said.

I looked at him not comprehending at first. "Oh, yeah. Okay." I walked back to my depressing table with an empty glass and a full pitcher. I filled up my glass and got back to where I was.

I love Peter and he loves me. And he needs me, but do I need him? All I am anymore is a baby-sitter for a six-year-old when he's not out saving somebody. I thought for a minute. That's it...saving. He has saved my life more than once. But maybe I'd be better off dead. In fact, maybe I am dead like Peter, and just don't know it. Maybe that's why Peter and I were drawn together.

I was sitting there trying to decide whether I was dead or alive when I heard someone say, "It looks like you're carrying all the problems of the world on your shoulders."

I looked up into the blue eyes of a young lady in her mid-thirties. She was attractive but not beautiful. If I were dead, wouldn't she be also? But she didn't look like it. She had a glass of beer in her hand. "I was just thinking of my grandson." I stood and offered her a seat. Her name was Alice.

"Is your grandson okay?"

"Oh sure, he's fine. I was just thinking that when he's with me, I'm no longer in control of my life."

"How old is he?"

"Six." I removed the picture of Peter from my wallet that I had taken of him last summer while he was standing on the dock at the swimming area. As normal, he had a big toothless grin on his face.

She looked at it. "Oh, he's adorable. Does he ride with you often?"

"He was with me last week."

She started laughing. "I remember when my son was six. You're lucky you even *had* a life. He looks like a real sweetheart, but he also looks like he could be a handful at times."

I laughed. "You've got that right. At times he can be an angel. Other times he can be a real pistol. But he's a pretty good little kid." I poured another glass of beer and filled her glass.

I woke up at 8:00. It was light out but that didn't make any sense. I don't remember going to bed. How many beers did I have? What happened to Alice? I looked around but she wasn't there. Why was I concerned about the whereabouts of Alice, but not Peter? Peter! I forgot about him. I had to get moving. I was under a load. And Peter was coming back today.

I started to get up but fell back down hard. My head was throbbing. Was this a hangover? I've never had a hangover before because I've never been a drinker. I had to get a cup of coffee. What happened to Alice? What did I do last night? At least I was still wearing my clothes. How many beers did I have? Who got me into my truck? This is why I never drank. I don't like the feeling of not being in control of things. But wasn't Peter in control of my life now? I had to get a hold on myself. I had to get a cup of coffee.

Standing behind the counter in the truck stop prepared to take my money for my thermos of coffee was April. "Jake, how you doing this morning?"

I rolled my eyes. "I feel like I'm going to die."

She laughed. "Well, that's better than your grandson. He is dead."

I looked at her, shocked. What did I tell her last night? There wasn't anyone else in line. "I don't remember what I told you about Peter."

She laughed. "That doesn't surprise me. You went through a lot of beer last night. You said Peter is an angel. Seeing a picture of him, I can believe it. He rides with you all the time, but he's up in the Northern Montana Mountains trying to rescue the little boy that's lost up there. I hate to tell you this but I heard on the news this morning that it is believed he is...he didn't survive."

I was terribly disturbed by this news, but tried not to show it. "I'm sorry to hear that. Peter is certainly an angel to me, but I'm certain right now, Peter is close to home. Well,

I'm running late. I must get going. Thanks for visiting with me last night."

"I enjoyed it. By the way, Jake, you were a perfect gentleman last night, even though you were drunk."

That didn't help me much. I still didn't know what I did or didn't do. "Thanks. Nice meeting you."

That morning while driving east on I-84 through Oregon, I thought about Peter, me and last night. Seldom do I have more than one beer at a sitting and never more than two. Last night I lost count of how many beers I had before I bought the pitcher. And did I buy just one?

And what about Alice? Was she in my truck last night and if so, what did we do?

Then there's Peter. I love Peter. I couldn't love him more if he was my own biological son or grandson. Sure, I missed my freedom, lack of responsibility—my old lifestyle. But I'm happier than I've ever been. I'm a better Christian than I've ever been and it's all because of Peter. My decisions are no longer made with just me in mind, but don't all good parents face the same thing?

I could reclaim my old lifestyle very easily. All I'd have to do is send Peter back to Slippery Gulch, but that would condemn him to the grave forever. He would have failed and the world would be rid of one beautiful little angel. But I need Peter just as he needs me. I'm a better person because of him and it's not just me. He's touched so many lives in a positive way. Last night it was the beer and the devil speaking. I wondered when Peter would be back. I missed him.

That afternoon about two, I was twenty-five miles east of Mountain Home, Idaho on I-84 when I heard a quiet voice say, "Jake."

"Peter? Is that you?" Suddenly he was there in the truck with me. "Are you okay?"

"Yeah. I'm okay and Stevie is too."

"He is? I heard on the news this morning it was believed the little boy perished in the mountains last night."

"Well, they were wrong."

We had a rest area coming up. "Great! Fill me in."

"I gave him something to eat and water to drink. I cleaned the boy up and treated some scratches. Then we climbed into the sleeping bag together so I could warm him up. I stayed with him until the rescuers were about five minutes away. Then I grabbed all my belongings and ducked behind a large tree and disappeared. Here I am."

"Stevie did see you then?"

"He had to. It was the only way I could give him my body heat. But I wore the hat and let my hair hang out." He wrinkled his nose a little. "I think I looked like a girl. I never told him my name."

I started laughing. "That's great! So you're a hero again. Well, what do you think? Ready to go?"

He wasn't. He turned around, faced me and hesitantly asked, "Jake, did, did you miss me last night?"

I wasn't expecting this question, but I should have. I didn't miss Peter at all because I was too drunk. And once I went to bed (whenever that was) I slept like a baby. But I couldn't tell him any of that. He didn't have a need to know anyway. "Last night, Little One, was one of the longest, loneliest and worst nights I've ever had. I didn't sleep much because I was thinking about you. Man, did I ever miss you." Most of that was true.

THE SEPARATION

Excitedly he said, "You did? You really did?"

"Peter, I can't tell you how great it is to have you back." It was great to have him back. Now I could get back to where I was destined to be. I kissed his forehead then ruffled his hair. "Come on, Little Angel, let's get back on the road, together."

Later that day we heard on the radio that the little boy lost in the mountains was found alive and well. Stevie, lost in the Rocky Mountains for four nights, was found in unbelievably good condition for what he'd been through. However, it asked for the little mystery girl who had assisted him to please come forward. The family was offering a sizable reward. I noted the 800 number to call. We looked at each other and laughed. The network completed its report by stating that Stevie didn't expect the little girl to come forward because he believed her to be an angel.

That evening I came up with an idea. "Peter, if you called the 800 number on my cell phone, could you make it so the call could not be traced to my phone or our location?"

He looked at me puzzled. "I think so. Why?"

I told him of the idea I had. I told him what to say, but in his own words. I handed him the phone and gave him the number. When someone answered he said, "Hi. I'm the one who took care of Stevie." He was asked several questions and gave answers only that he, Stevie, and the rescuers would know. "I would like you to put the reward money toward Stevie's college fund. And Stevie's right. I am an angel. Say hello to him for me." Then he hung up.

As the day wore on, Peter's call caused a sensation all over the West. It turned out the call was taped. Stevie was brought in to listen to it and identified the voice as that of the little girl who took care of him, the voice of an angel.

They tried to trace the call but couldn't. They couldn't even be sure what country the call had come from. Peter must have done a number on their equipment.

The call was played over and over again on news reports, talk shows, religious programs and even a couple of sports programs. During call-in shows, people from all walks of life speculated that the call was a hoax. A few speculated the whole missing child thing was a hoax, dreamed up for publicity. Many ministers called in. Some claimed it was definitely the voice of an angel, while others said angels don't use telephones. Two suspected Stevie hallucinated while lost, and that there never was a little girl. One was certain it was the devil posing as an angel, proof the world would soon come to an end. One real kook suggested the call came from outer space. His proof was the fact that the origination of the call defied analysis. He was certain the child was a space alien.

As Peter and I listened with interest and some chuckling, he said, "Jake, maybe we shouldn't have done that."

"Yeah, I know. I've been thinking the same thing. But you never lied. He asked you twice what your name was, but you ignored the question. He never asked if you were a boy or girl. And he never asked where you were calling from. You told him you were an angel, and that was true. I think we're okay, kid."

We received a phone call from Jane, Jason and even Betty, convinced the voice they heard on the radio was Peter's. We were a little embarrassed the story went nationwide. Finally, the radio shows got tired of the story and moved on. (We did too.)

We finally delivered in Denver and moved into a motel for the rest of the day. It had a large pool where we spent the evening swimming.

One night after reading, I announced I was going to buy Peter something when we got home. "What?" he asked with wonder in his eyes.

"Well, if you're going to be a good canoeist, you should have the right size paddle. That one last year was a foot too long. No promises but we'll try and find the right one."

"You're going to get me my very own paddle? Wow, my very own paddle. That'll be neat. Why are you doing it? It's not my birthday."

"Gee, that's right, it's not. Maybe I'll forget it."

He looked at me. "Really?"

I poked his ribs. "Peter, I'm doing this because I want to. You need the paddle. Let's just call it your funeral present."

"Is there such a thing?"

I chuckled. "There is now."

"I wish I had some money to get you something once in a while."

"You give me everything I could possibly want: your friendship, love and affection. However I'm going to give you an allowance." He had no idea what that was. "I will pay you five dollars a week. You could spend it as you want or save part of it. How much is up to you. But if you misbehave, you could lose it for a week or two."

He thought about this for a minute. "You'd pay me something for doing nothing?"

"Certainly not! You help me all the time here in the truck. And at home. And while we're camping.

"Actually Kiddo, I started it the first week in January. But since I wasn't sure what was going to happen after your funeral, I didn't say anything to you. Right now there's $120 for you. If you don't spend any between now and the time we get home, you'll have $135." His eyes grew in size. "I would suggest you don't touch that and save it for when you really need it."

"Wow, $135!" Then he thought for a minute. "When is your birthday?"

"July 31."

He was quiet for a minute. He was remembering. "Wait a minute! You had a birthday after we got home last year?" I smiled and nodded. "Why didn't you say anything?"

"At that time, you'd only been with me for three weeks and still pretty unsure of yourself. And me. My sister and I decided it best not to take any attention away from you, so we celebrated it quietly one night after you went to sleep."

"Could we have a birthday party for you this year?"

"Well, I'll tell you what. When we get home you can ask Betty about it, okay?"

"Okay," he said excitedly and was asleep in less than a minute.

The next three weeks were uneventful for both of us, an improvement over last year. The severe nightmare Peter had in Basin was his last.

We turned in the truck at the Ohio yard, rented a car and drove home to Orchard Park, New York, looking forward to a month off. Peter became more excited by the day. Part of it was because he was looking forward to the camping trip. But he was also looking forward to my birthday. Every Monday I gave him his five dollar allowance. He spent very little of it.

CHAPTER EIGHT

When we pulled into our driveway, Betty came out to greet us. Jerry was on the road. Peter jumped out of the car and into her arms. "My Lord, Peter, what has gotten into you?"

Pulling her toward the house, he said, "Come inside. We have to talk."

"Has my little brother been mean to you again?"

He chuckled. "Always, but that's not why I have to talk to you." Betty looked at me. I just shrugged my shoulders. They both disappeared into the house leaving me to unload the car.

A few minutes later they were back. I asked what that was all about. "None of your business," Betty said. Peter chuckled. He was a part of a conspiracy again and loved it. The last time was also with Betty last Christmas, for my present.

That night after Peter got into his PJ's, we talked for a while. "Hey, Funny Face, it sounds as if you and Betty are involved in a conspiracy."

"What's a con, conperapy?"

"Conspiracy. A conspiracy is a secret plan between two or more people. You and Betty wouldn't have some kind of a secret would you?"

He giggled a little, but desperately tried to keep a straight face. "No, Jake, we wouldn't do anything like that."

He seemed relieved when I said, "Hey, why don't we go down and join Betty?"

I threw him over my shoulder and bounced down the stairs amid laughs. I sat in "our rocking chair" with Peter on my lap.

"Peter, I can't tell you how great it is to have you home. We were really afraid you two were going to be separated," Betty sighed.

"We'll never be now, Aunt Betty."

Betty smiled. "I hope you're right, Peter."

The next morning after joining us in the kitchen, Peter collapsed over my lap like a rag doll. "Jake, why am I always so tired in the morning when I first get up?"

"Because you're not awake yet."

"Can you do something about that?"

I looked at Betty and winked. "I think I can." I dug into both sides of his ribcage. After a good giggle, I asked, "Are you awake now?"

"Yeah," he said still giggling.

"Great! Do you want to take your bath first or should I take my shower?"

"Ah, Jake, I don't need a bath."

"Oh yes you do. You stink."

He laughed. "I do not."

"Maybe not but you're going to take a bath anyway. Now get moving."

He slipped off my lap and headed for the stairs. In time Peter called.

"Duty calls. It's time to wash his hair and dry him. See you later."

After breakfast, Betty and Peter left me to clean the house while they went out. When I asked them where they were going, the only answer I got was, "none of your business."

They didn't get back until about three. As they both came in I said, "Where have you guys been?"

As they walked through the kitchen to the stairs carrying shopping bags, they both said in unison, "Around." Peter was giggling all the way.

After ten minutes they both came down stairs. "How come I get the feeling I'm missing something?"

He chuckled again. "You ready to go?"

As promised to both Peter and Jamie, we picked Jamie up at 4:00. While Jamie joined Peter, his mother Judy, came up to me. "I knew you wouldn't lose him, Jake?"

"You were right but I was scared stiff."

Once we returned home, Peter asked, "Can we go out and play tag?"

As soon as I said yes, both boys darted from the car and began running. Tag soon turned to tackling. The boys were having the time of their lives because they were reunited again.

That night Jamie never mentioned Peter's funeral. However, after Peter went to sleep, Jamie said, "Peter's an angel isn't he, Grandpa?" It was more a statement than a question.

"Yes he is. You were right. Is this going to change the way you feel about him?"

"No way. He's my little brother. Hey, can we take a bath tomorrow like we did in May?"

That was music to my ears. Jamie saw business as usual. "Are you guys going to get me in trouble again with my sister?" After that bath, water was everywhere. Betty came in, saw the water and pretended she was extremely upset. I got bawled out for not supervising.

He chuckled. "Probably.

"We'll see." I chuckled myself, readjusting the covers and assured him I'd see if we could try it again. "Have a good night sleep."

My peaceful coffee with Betty was broken the next morning when Peter yelled down the stairs. "Jake, can Jamie and I take a bath?"

We looked at each other and suppressed our laughter. I'd told Betty the exchange I'd had with Jamie the evening before. "Sure, go ahead, Kiddo," I shot back.

"Could you come up with us?" He yelled.

"I'll be there in a minute. Start the water."

Betty looked at me. "Oh no you won't."

She stood and marched up the stairs. I followed her but stayed in the hall and out of sight. Peter said nervously, "Where's Jake?"

"He's downstairs. Remember the last time you took a bath together? I told you the next time I was going to supervise. Well, I am. Now, in the tub." After that I didn't hear a sound, as I headed back downstairs. I felt a little sorry for the boys. The whole idea of taking a bath together is to have fun. Well, those are the breaks.

Ten minutes later I heard squeals and screams coming from the bathroom. I went rushing up the stairs. I walked into the bathroom to find it a mess. Water was everywhere and Betty was drenched. No one saw me—they were too busy. I backed out and shut the door laughing. Betty was on her own. Meanwhile the squeals continued.

I walked back poker-faced with my hands on my hips. "What's going on in here?"

Betty jerked around acting embarrassed that I'd caught her. The boys seeing me upset was vexing to them. Betty said, "Jake, I lost to these demons."

I fought to keep my poker face. "Well, get this room cleaned up and now, all three of you." Both boys jumped out of the tub, no smiles on their face. Betty handed both of them a towel as I turned to leave. After a moment I went back in.

Peter was dripping wet standing with the towel in his right hand, a forlorn expression on his face. Jamie was drying himself as Betty moped up water. I took the towel and dried Peter and his hair. "Now get this bathroom cleaned up." All were happy as I walked out. I stood in the hall listening.

"Mr. Winters was pretty mad, wasn't he?" Jamie asked concerned.

"He'll get over it." Betty volunteered. Peter was silent.

Minutes later I walked back in. "Looks pretty good. Peter, Jamie, where are your clothes?"

"We left them in the bedroom. We didn't want to get them wet again."

In May, they'd left their pajamas on the floor next to the tub. They ended up drenched. "You could have left them on the counter here."

They both looked at the dry counter on the other side of the bathroom. "We didn't think of that," Jamie sighed.

"Well, get dressed. We'll see you both downstairs in five minutes. The boys scampered out of the room leaving Betty and me alone.

"So what happened with the supervision, big sister? I thought you were going to show me how to do it."

Hanging up a wet towel, she said, "Jake, those boys are something else. One minute everything was going alone smoothly and the next minute I was involved in a water fight." She started laughing. "At least they had fun."

"They?"

"Okay. We all had fun."

The boys and I spent the day at Green Lake, a small town park with a lake for swimming and a large playground. There was even a small creek that needed exploring by two small boys. The boys were in perpetual motion. At two in the afternoon, I guided them to a grassy area for a break.

After a twenty-minute rest, it was time for another swim before heading back to take Jamie home.

That night Peter was unusually excited. Part had to do with the good day we'd spent with Jamie and his anticipation over our upcoming camping trip; but a larger part was my surprise birthday party.

He climbed onto my lap. "How do you think your bath went this morning?"

"Okay, I guess. When Aunt Betty told us she was going to supervise us, Jamie and I were worried. We tried hard to behave. We didn't even talk. But Betty splashed both Jamie and me. At first we didn't know what to do. Then she splashed some more. So we splashing back. It was fun—until you walked in and stopped it." I was the heavy this morning and I didn't like it.

"So it was Aunt Betty who started it?" I said in mock sternness.

"Yeah! But were you mad at us?"

"Did you think I was?"

"Yeah, at first. After we got out of the tub, you turned and walked out. Then you came back and dried me like you weren't mad."

"Peter, I wasn't mad. When I walked out I was playing the part. Then I suddenly remembered our tradition and came back in. When I saw that sad look on your face, I'm glad I remembered."

"So you weren't disappointed in me."

"Not at all, Kiddo."

Peter was soon asleep with his characteristic contented smile on his face. After a few minutes I put him to bed and went down to join Betty.

Before I had a chance to sit, Betty said, "Jake, the next time those boys take a bath together, you supervise."

"You've had enough?"

She laughed. "I had fun this morning and I think the boys did too, but it wasn't the same. As I've said before, it's a guy thing and that includes the supervisor. Next time you supervise and I'll be the heavy. Just maintain some control, okay." We both laughed.

The next morning after breakfast we headed over to Bill's house, talked to Sue for a few minutes, and headed out for the mall. Peter wanted to try the scaling wall again. As last year, he scaled it like a monkey. Observers' mouths were agape.

I ruffled his hair and said, "I'm very proud of you."

Danny said, "Wow, Peter, you were really fantastic." Peter smiled and thanked him. He was slowly wearing down, but a little food recharged him for our shopping excursion. I knew he'd nap that afternoon.

After shopping, we went our separate ways, agreeing to meet at Bill's house in two days for our camping trip.

At home, Peter lay down on the couch. I rubbed his chest. He was out in thirty seconds.

As I told Betty about his exploits at the mall, I covered him from the waist down with a light blanket. "Betty, feel right here." She put her hand on the left side of his small chest. "What do you feel?"

"His heartbeat."

"I feel a miracle." She agreed. "When I was standing at the podium at Peter's funeral with him in my arms, I hesitated. Maybe you were wondering what was wrong. I was saying a silent prayer, with my hand on his chest, that in another ten minutes, I could still hold Peter in my arms and fell his beating heart. Betty, God answered my prayer again."

"Little Brother, like some of the others there, I was sure Peter is an angel."

I lowered my head. "I know. And as the lone holdout, I feel guilty about that. Yet because of knowing him best is the reason I couldn't buy it." I pulled the blanket up to his shoulders. "But I still could have lost him." Betty looked puzzled. "You see, Mrs. Stevenson gave her son a choice: either stay with me or go with her. He could have chosen to go with his mother."

Betty was shocked. "At the risk of sounding rude, why did he chose you?"

"We had just spent a wonderful year together in which we both grew. Plus, he'd never met his mother and didn't know her. If he had gone with her, we would never have seen each other again. He couldn't separate us."

Betty stood there looking down at the sleeping angel. She bent over and stroked his forehead with affection. She stood troubled. "Jake, didn't you say Peter was born to suffer? His mother's death, his leprosy and his suffering at the hands of his father and the town's hatefulness were all designed by God, correct?"

I nodded not sure where she was going. "Was that all in preparation for his current life?" All I could do was nod in agreement.

"Well, if this was all God's plan feeding into the present, how could his mother afford to—to give Peter a choice? Wouldn't choosing her love gone against God's plan?"

I stood there perplexed. I had not thought through this. Mrs. Stevenson, surely had to realize this. Why did she give Peter a choice? Betty was studying me now. "You think it's possible this could have been Peter's final test? Could that have been a question from God coming through his mother?"

Betty and I looked at Peter. "Jake, during his life in Slippery Gulch and during this past year, Peter had been given many opportunities to fail. You say his final prayer was his; that God didn't plant it. It was his final test as a mortal: that had he not prayed for a friend, he wouldn't be here now. If he hadn't sung in church Christmas Eve, he would have failed. He was given many chances to fail, but so were you—as I see it. There were many times you could have given up on him—and twice you almost did. The only reason Peter sang in church Christmas Eve, by the way, is because you forced him to. Both of you had many decisions to make this year. Fortunately, for all of us, you both made the right ones." She looked down at Peter again. "Looking back at the past year, maybe it's just as well you weren't willing to accept Peter's angelic nature. Maybe it would have kept you from trusting your better judgment."

I thought hard about this. "I guess that is something we'll never know. At any rate, Betty, Mrs. Stevenson is quite a lady. She loves her son dearly, and she wants the best for him. She recognized the tremendous strides he's made during the year. She's very proud of him."

"It's too bad she had to die at his birth."

"Isn't that the truth. Hey, let's change the subject. I have a problem. The last time I was home, a few people in church were asking why Peter hasn't grown any and why his teeth haven't come in. I just said I didn't know. But now a lot more people will be asking. What do I say? Should I just tell the truth about him?"

Betty thought for a moment. "Why don't you talk to the minister."

After a while, Peter woke up and asked, "Jake, what day is it?"

"Today's Tuesday."

"Yeah, but anything else?"

Again I thought for a minute. "Oh yeah. It's two days before we go camping."

He looked a little disappointed but said, "Yep, that's right." Betty was trying to keep from laughing. Tomorrow is my birthday. "Could we ride our bikes for a while?"

"Sure, let's go." We road for the rest of the afternoon. At one point, we lay down on the bank of a creek to listen to the rushing water and the birds. But Peter couldn't relax. He was really excited about tomorrow. "Peter, what are you so excited about?"

"Ah, we go camping in two days."

"Oh yeah, I forgot about that."

"You did not, did you?"

"Actually I did for a minute."

The next morning, he bounded into the kitchen riding sky high on excitement. He fairly launched himself onto my lap. "Good grief, Kiddo, what's gotten into you this morning?"

"Wake me up, Jake."

"You don't need waking up this morning. You're wired!" Immediately he rolled off my lap and onto the floor pretending a deep sleep, except for his smile.

Betty started laughing and said, "Something's never change." I got down to tickle him, but he took off running for the stairs.

"Where are you going so fast?"

"I'm going to take a bath then get dressed."

"Wait a minute. You took one yesterday; and you're going to have one tomorrow morning. You don't mind three baths in three days?" He smiled, shook his head and scampered out of sight up stairs.

Once we heard the water running, Betty said, "You know, I can't believe how excited he is. He hasn't brought up your birthday has he?"

"He hasn't said a word. I think it's pay-back time. You remember how I pretended to forget his last year." Betty smiled and nodded.

"Just about killed me to go on like that."

Just then Peter called down. "Sorry, duty calls."

After washing his hair and drying him, he jumped into my arms and gave me a big hug.

"What was that for?"

"Nothing. I just thought you needed one."

I ruffled his hair in returned. "I can always use a spare hug." He scampered off, leaving me holding his wet towel. Down the stairs I heard Betty say, "Peter, what are you doing down here like that?"

"Ops! Sorry! I knew I forgot something." As I was walking down the stairs, he suddenly rushed past me, giggling. "I forgot my clothes."

As I walked into the kitchen, Jerry had just arrived home from the road. Both he and Betty were laughing hysterically. Betty said, "I've never seen a youngster so excited. Peter came down here after his bath and stark naked." It wasn't long before Peter appeared, clothed and almost in his right mind.

"Sorry about that. Isn't forgetfulness a sign of old age, Jake?"

"It can be."

"Well, I'm one hundred seven. What can you expect?"

We all had a good laugh.

After breakfast, Betty gave Jerry and me a bunch of errands to run. Some seemed rather ridicules to me, but she told me not to argue. "Okay. Come on Peter, let's go."

"I, ah, well, I think I, ah, will stay here, Jake."

I looked at him. "What? You mean you don't want to go with me?"

He put his head down, aware that he was disappointing me. Betty, however, came to his rescue "Sorry, Jake, but I need Peter's help around here. He's going to vacuum clean and a few other things.

He looked to me hoping for some understanding.

"Betty, that's a great idea. Peter, you can have fun today and help Betty at the same time."

He jumped into my arms and gave me a hug. "Thanks."

"What was that for?"

"You know."

"We may not be back until after lunch," Jerry said. Neither Betty nor Peter argued.

We returned at two to a court packed full with cars. Jerry and I walked in with bags in our arms.

"Somebody must be having a party," I stated to no one in particular.

"Maybe our neighbors," Betty volunteered. As I started to put things down, Peter grabbed my arm and ushered me into the family room and the rocking chair. He filled me in on the finer arts of vacuum cleaning. Betty poked her head around the corner, but I pretended not to notice.

Peter said, "Come with me. I want to show you something." He led me into the living room. As we rounded the corner, a crowd yelled out, "Happy Birthday, Jake." Connie, Randy, the girls and at least twenty of my friends including Bill, Danny and Sue were waiting for us. In the crowd were Jamie and his mother, which surprised even Peter. I have to admit, I was genuinely surprised.

I walked around saying hello to everybody and thanking all of them for coming. Then I turned to Peter. I put my hands on my hips as he had done a year before at his surprise birthday party. His smile up to me was fantastic. "Peter, did you know about this?"

"Yeah," he said with an uncontrollable giggle, "Aunt Betty and I planned it." He was very proud of himself. "That's why I couldn't go to the store with you today."

"Why you little pumpkin! Come here." He came charging across the room and leaped into my arms. I threw him almost to the ceiling with him laughing and squealing all the time. If anybody in the group still thought this party was for me, I think they all now knew whom it was really for. Is it the responsibility of a guardian angel to help plan a birthday party for his charge? Well, maybe so if one's guardian angel is a fun-loving six-year-old.

"Folks, I've got several things to say. First, thank you very much for coming. Second, I will not accept any gifts over $10,000." Everybody laughed. "And last but certainly not least, all of you were told last year that Peter was a ghost. Both he and I thought he was, but he's not. As it turns out, he's been on probation since the day we met."

I knew the majority was confused on that statement. I went on. "Peter had a wonderful funeral in June; you know, the type the deceased walks away from." After the laughter stopped, I continued. "The setting was beautiful. Slippery Gulch is located in the Deer Lodge National Forest. The cemetery is on a hill overlooking the town—a true town of the Old West. As you know it was the location of Peter's birth and death. You also know the terrible life Peter lived and the horrible death he suffered." I looked at Peter still in my arms. "For me, standing on that ridge was like standing on the outskirts of heaven looking directly down into hell.

"The service was like no other funeral service you have ever witnessed: Not only because of the setting but because the deceased was sitting among the mourners." Again there was laughter all around except for my two little nieces. They were lost which was just as will. "Peter's new casket is modern, but thank God, he isn't in it. Peter has been given permission to remain with me as long as he wants." To that everyone cheered. "His new stone is attractive too."

I passed around several pictures. As I did, I said, "Notice how in one picture, the deceased is admiring his own stone."

"After the service, both Peter and I were given the opportunity to meet his mother. As all of you know, she died at Peter's birth. She was able to answer many of my questions. If any of you are wondering where Peter got his good looks, I found out. She's gorgeous.

"But more importantly she has a beautiful personally. She is also a lady of character and principle. As we all know, her son is too.

"All of you were concerned about Peter's future after the funeral, as I was." Looking around the group I realized everyone there had called Slippery Gulch the night of the funeral to check on Peter's status. I thanked them for their interest and concern.

"Most of you were aware of the terrible dreams he suffered through our first two weeks together last year. As it turned out, they were far more than nightmares: They were tests designed by the Almighty for both of us. I guess we both passed." An absolute silence came over the room.

"The final test came Christmas Eve, but neither one of us knew it. Peter was set to sing two songs. The poor kid was scared stiff, but I insisted he go through with it. You all know that he did an outstanding job. As a result, he is no longer on probation." Only Jamie and Danny knew where I was going. I winked at Peter still in my arms. "Folks, I'd like to reintroduce you to Peter Stevenson. No, not Peter the ghost! I hold in my arms my very own, full-fledged, Guardian Angel."

At that point, Danny jumped in the air, threw his right arm up and shouted, "Yes! I knew I saw a halo over his head at Christmas. I knew he was an angel."

Jamie joined him. "I did too."

"You were both right. And let me say this, though it has been obvious to all: I am Peter's earthly guardian as long as he is in his mortal form." I looked at Jamie and winked. "And Lord knows, every little boy needs a guardian." Jamie smiled, slightly embarrassed. "I asked his mother; if he is an angel, why does he need disciplining from time to time? Her answer was matter of fact: 'He's a six-year-old boy. Need I say more?'" Both Peter and Jamie demurred at that.

I could see everybody in awe looking at Peter—Peter noticed this too and was looking worried.

"Look folks, 99.9% of the time, Peter is a little boy just as mortal as we are. And that's just the way he wants to be treated. Please, treat us both as you always have. We still need your love and friendship." We all sat there savoring this truth.

Then I got an idea. "Jamie, would you please come here?" I put Peter down then knelt between them. I put my arms around their waists. I looked at Jamie but addressed the group. "For those of you that don't know, this young man is Jamie Rotundo, Peter's best childhood friend. They met last September in school. I am now going to apply the one test that proves mortality." I began tickling both of them. They both dropped to the floor, and squirming. "See! Both pass the tickle test." Laughter broke out again. Things were back to normal.

It was now time for the gifts. Betty had told all our friends, no gifts, which pleased me. But Peter was dying to give me his gift now. He was so excited he had to run to the bathroom.

I had two woods jackets, but both showing their age. So Peter gave me a new jacket. Unlike the others, this one was a four-season with a removable lining. Betty informed me later that it had been marked down four times. Peter got it for over 50% off and paid for it with his own money. This had thrilled him. As Peter handed me his gift, he was busting with pride. "Happy birthday, Grandpa." I looked at him with love burning in my heart. I tried it on, thanked him, and gave him a huge hug and a kiss. "You're a little peanut, you know that?"

Giggling with pride he shot back, "I know," He came back at me with his own little hug and kiss.

Next we all moved to the dining room to lit the candles on my cake. "Wow!" Peter exclaimed. "There's so many candles on your cake, it looks like a Montana forest fire."

I ruffled his hair and looked at Jamie with a nasty smile.

"Jamie, you were over here the other night. Did you know about this party?" He giggled and nodded.

Peter looked at him surprised. "You did?"

Giggling at Peter he replied, "Yeah! Your aunt invited my Mom, Dad and me, but Dad couldn't make it. I had to promise not to tell."

"Why you little turkey!"

Joining in the singing of happy birthday was another first for Peter. As a living little boy, not only was he never invited to someone else's birthday party, he never had one of his own. Of course we took care of that on his birthday last December 2. Now he knew it and sang it proudly.

That night during our nightly talk he wanted to know if I was surprised. I admitted I was. Then he was concerned. "Jake, I lied to you more than once."

"Yes you did, but they were little white lies: like when you tell people I'm your grandpa. You are not telling a lie that will hurt someone or to protect yourself. You were pretending for a fun reason to be explained later."

"Then you're not mad at me?"

"Of course not."

He beamed then turned serious again. "The thing that bothered me the most was when you went out this morning and I didn't go with you."

"I know, but it worked out fine. And you learned how to use the vacuum cleaner. You were a big help to Betty."

"Yeah. That was fun. Do you think she'll let me do that again?"

I smiled. "Well, I'm not sure, but I have a hunch she will. Why don't we go down and join them and you can ask her yourself."

Minutes later I was in the rocking chair with Peter on my lap.

Jerry asked, "Well, Peter, how do you think the day went?"

"It was great! Jake was really surprise and he likes my gift."

"I understand you picked it out. The jacket was your idea, right?" I asked.

"Yeah! It was really expensive, but I didn't have to borrow money from Aunt Betty. It was on sale."

"Aunt Betty is a good one to go shopping with." I mentioned.

"And she's a good teacher of the vacuum cleaner, I hear," Jerry added.

"Yeah! I bet she could even teach you how to use it, Uncle Jerry."

I almost spit out my mouthful of coffee while Jerry was lost for words.

CHAPTER NINE

On the way to the Adirondacks the next morning, we stopped at every rest area between Buffalo and Utica because of Peter's excitable bladder. The same thing had happened the previous year.

We didn't have to take time teaching Peter how to paddle a canoe. He had a new paddle and was eager to put it to use.

After registering, setting up camp and eating dinner, Bill, Danny, Peter and I were all free to paddle out on the lake to fish. Not one got a bite, but we had fun. By eight we were back at the campsite building up the fire in preparation for a story. Peter walked into the tent and emerged a minute late in his infamous pajama bottoms.

After I put him on my lap crossways, he was facing Bill and Danny who were masking their amusement. Bill said, "I guess you haven't worn out those pajamas yet. They're really you. You wouldn't look right in anything else."

Peter pulled out the waistband and let it snap on his belly. Next he reached behind my neck and stretched. "I love 'em. Jake, how about a story."

By the time I finished, Peter was asleep. Bill said, "You know Jake, Danny, Sue and I were so worried about the outcome of Peter's funeral, we couldn't concentrate on anything else for days. We were worried about you too, in case things didn't work out. Both of you were in our prayers for several weeks. When I called Basin that night, we were all on pins and needles."

"I wasn't." Danny corrected his dad. "I knew he'd be okay because I knew what he was. I prayed though just in case I was wrong."

"Well, you were right, Danny. Thanks a lot for your prayers. I needed them back then. Hey, to be honest with you, I'm tuckered out. Let's all turn in for a good sleep under these glorious stars."

We headed for our lake and a good day of fishing and swimming. The action was so bad, we quit fishing and went swimming at 11:00.

The previous year everything was new to Peter, even the sand. This year everything was old hat. After changing into his trunks, Peter became an acrobat anxious to demonstrate his new skills. He was impressive, doing front and back flips and trying hard to walk on his hands. The three of us applauded. Bill remarked how well his muscles were forming all over his body. The skinny, sickly runt from a year ago was now well developed and strong for a six- year-old! Still in all, he remained thirty pounds. Even our doctor could not explain this.

After lunch, we tried the fishing again. Bill caught a four-pounder, and I caught a three pound bass. Bill and I made the most of skunking the boys.

Peter wanted to show Bill he could clean fish. Bill looked at me doubtingly.

Peter and I rounded up a large bucket, soap, washcloth, towel and a can of spray deodorant and returned to the lake. Bill and Danny looked at him and then me, puzzled. "Wait!"

Peter moved through his grisly task tediously. He would sweep his hair from his eyes with his right hand and slick down his hair in back with his left. He itched and scratched everywhere. Although Bill and Danny were amused, they were impressed with Peter's abilities to clean fish. When he had finished, he had four nicely prepared fillets and a body covered with fish blood and scales.

The four of us walked down the shoreline one hundred feet. Peter removed his trunks as I poured a bucket of water over his head. Next came the shampoo and the scrubbing and rising of his hair. He washed his body while I washed his trunks. Then we repeated the process two more times. Once dry, I sprayed both Peter and his trunks with deodorant. I put his trunks in a Ziploc bag and put the bag in the trunk of the car. Now he no longer smelled like fish.

Bill said. "Peter, that was fantastic. Did I teach you how to do that?"

Peter nodded. "I learned last year by watching you, if that's what you mean."

"That's great but I didn't show you how to get blood all over your body."

Peter laughed. "I know. I need a little more practice."

"You're fillets are beautiful," Bill added. "I hope we'll catch some more fish tomorrow."

But it didn't turn out that way. We had no fish for dinner that night. We decided to drive to the public beech in the Hamlet of Blue Mountain the next day, then drive to the ballpark in the Hamlet of Inlet. Peter was hoping Bobby and his dad would be there for an informal practice as they were last year. If there were a practice today, Bill and Danny would see Peter play ball.

Next morning after breakfast, we four headed to the public beach. The four of us spent about an hour in the water before Bill and I came out and joined the adults nearby. The only one that I recognized from the year before was the mother of Jimmy, the fighter, so I introduced her to Bill.

Later Danny joined us while Peter played in the sand with a few other kids. Danny was about to rejoin Peter on the beach when I looked up just in time to see Peter jump Jimmy. He deliver two powerful punches to Jimmy's face. This was so uncharacteristic of Peter that I was stunned, unable to move. Jimmy at ten outweighed Peter by at least thirty-five pounds. As a result, Peter couldn't prevent Jimmy getting on top. He slammed his right knee into Peter's groin and began pounding Peter in the stomach and face. Peter fearfully tried to protect himself with his arms.

The four of us took off running. At that moment Jimmy managed to hold both of Peter's arms down and deliver a severe blow to Peter's face. The blood flew and Jimmy's mother grabbed him before he was able to deliver another blow. Peter was woozy. I kept him lying on the ground. Both boys were bloody, but Peter got the worst of it. I looked at his eyes. They were normal and now tearful. Instead of comforting him, I went on the attack. I was angry and he knew it. "Why did you attack that boy?" Suddenly he was trembling and crying. I was close to trembling myself. We both knew a spanking was coming. "Answer me, Peter." I picked him up by his arms.

Jimmy was crying and wiped his bloody nose. "I don't know what got into him. I was sitting there playing when all of a sudden he jumped me. I didn't do anything."

Through his tears, Peter looked angrily at Jimmy. "That's a lie and you know it."

I knew Peter was telling the truth, but I gave Jimmy the benefit of a doubt.

"It's a lie, Mom. He's just a stupid, little brat." (Little did he know he was talking about an angel.)

Jimmy's mother remembered Peter from last year and knew he wasn't stupid or a brat. She looked at Peter and said, "Let's hear from you, Peter. What happened?"

He stopped crying, got his composure and began. "He started calling me names and said I was stupid. Some of the names were real bad."

"He's lying, Mom. He's just a little creep."

"Why didn't you ignore him?" I piped up.

"I did."

"You couldn't have. I looked up just in time to see you jump him." I was angrier and Peter knew it. "Why did you hit him?" Peter's nose was running blood, his right eye was swelling and his lower lip was split. He needed my loving care, but I was still on the attack.

"He...he...he starting calling you some terrible names, Grandpa. I couldn't take it any more. That's when I jumped him." He swiped his face of blood and tears which made it look worse.

My heart skipped a beat. Of course! That would explain it. Peter being called names he could handle, but not when the rotten names and insults were directed at me. "The little bastard's lying," Jimmy yelled, lunging and punching Peter in the stomach before any of us could react. Peter went down hard. Jimmy tried to kick him in the face, but was yanked away by his mother before he could deliver. She slapped him across the face. That relieved me of punching him myself. Sometimes I could be a real jerk.

My heart was heavy. I knelt down next to Peter, gently leaned him against me and rubbed his stomach to calm him. Danny was running to the store for ice and paper towels. I talked softly to Peter to relax him until Danny returned.

I got ice on Peter's eye and lip and laid him down flat for a few minutes. His nose stopped bleeding. While I wiped the blood from his chest and stomach, Peter looked at me with terribly sad eyes; eyes I hadn't seen in months. My heart was aching. "Grandpa, why didn't you believe me?"

I picked him up and carried him to the grass above the beach and sat down next to him. I wiped away new tears and put my hand on his reddish chest. "Peter, when something happens between you and another kid, I can't automatically take your side. If I take your word for it immediately, it would be like calling the other kid a liar without hearing his side of the story. I have to be fair." Maybe it's the teacher in me. Or the camp counselor.

I let him think about this for a moment, then went on. "When he called you stupid, I sensed he was lying and his mother did too. Then when you said you first ignored him but then attacked him anyway, things didn't add up. We had to know why. You see, Kiddo, it's not that I didn't believe you, I just wanted to understand. But you've explained, I fully understood now.

"Not only am I proud of you, I'm honored. It never occurred to me that you would stick up for me. I guess that's your job as my guardian angel. I'm sorry for coming on so strong, Kiddo, and for not stopping the jerk from punching you that last time."

He put his hand on mine. "You're proud of me?"

"Oh man, am I ever. As I said, I'm honored. After all, it's not everyday somebody stands up for me." That familiar smile was returning. "But, from now on, do me a favor, will you?" He nodded. "When you decide to stand up for me, check out the kid first. If he's twice your size, forget it. It isn't worth it."

He started laughing. "Okay, but you always say I am worth it. Well, so are you, Jake."

The sadness in his eyes was replaced with joy. "You're a little pumpkin, you know that." I dug my fingers into his ribs so he giggled for me.

"Does this mean you're not going to spank me?"

"Oh, I didn't say that." Instantly his smile turned to worry. I lay down, pulling him onto my chest. "Peter, how could I spank a little boy who just got the tar beat out of him for standing up for me? Of course I'm not going to spank you."

He let out with a huge sigh of relief then rested his head on my chest and said, "Jake, you are mean."

"You bet I am." I gave him a huge hug. "Thanks, Kiddo."

He turned serious. "Jake, remember last month when we both decided to forgive my father?" I nodded. "Remember I said I prayed that my daddy would love me and be proud of me?" I did, and nodded as much.

"God couldn't change my daddy, so he changed daddies for me. Now I have what I prayed for. I have a friend and a daddy and grandpa that loves me and is proud of me. I know you get mad at me and even disappointed sometimes. But I know you still love me."

"And I know you sometimes get mad at me and disappointed in me. Like a few minutes ago! But I know also that you still love me. I guess we're a pretty good team, aren't we?"

"The best, Grandpa. Can we go over to the ball diamond now?"

I lay him back on the grass and put my hand on his stomach and ribs probing, but he had no pain. I gently moved a finger over his eye and split lip. The swelling was down on both, but he was going to have a beautiful shiner. He needed a lot of cleaning. "Peter, I saw him knee you between your legs. How do you feel down there?"

He giggled. "Fine. He missed." He turned serious. "Jake, isn't that fighting dirty?"

"You bet it is. You could have pounded the crud out of him if you chose to do so, but you didn't. It would have been cheating. So instead you took the beating for me you knew you'd take instead of cheating. I'm proud of you, kid."

I helped him get on his feet. "You know, you look like you've just cleaned a mess of fish. Except you don't stink. Let's get you cleaned up."

I took his left hand and led him into the small bathhouse. Bill and Danny followed. There wasn't a shower, only a sink. I blotted his face with damp paper towels. While Bill washed his trunks, I cleaned up the rest of him.

There were times in my life with Peter when I had to pinch myself to see if I was not having a dream. This was one of those times.

CHAPTER TEN

On the way down to the diamond, Danny said, "Man, Peter, you really have guts. The way you tore into that kid was something. You landed two solid punches to his face."

"Yeah, Danny, but when that bigger kid tore into Peter, it was sad," Bill said. "But Peter, Jake tells me you were sticking up for Jake. Danny, would you stick up for me like that? Against a kid twice your size?"

"Well, dad," Danny said, "I think he would have called you every name in the book."

"You mean you wouldn't have put your life on the line the way Peter did?"

"Sure I would. When you found out I didn't do anything, you'd kill me."

After we stopped laughing, I asked Peter how his right hand felt. "You really smashed that kid. Sure hope you never get that mad at me."

We pulled into the ballpark. "A little sore but it'll be okay."

As we walked up to the diamond, we heard a kid in the outfield yell, "Hey, there's Peter." It was Bobby. He and a couple of other kids came running over but stopped short as did Fred, his father. "Peter, what happened to you? That's quite a shiner, kid." Fred stated.

I could tell Peter was proud of himself, so I added to it. "He got into a fight with a kid twice his size defending my honor."

"Wow, I'm impressed," Fred said. I shook hands with Fred and Bobby and said, "Take it easy on Peter's right hand. He let loose with a couple of powerful roundhouses, so his hand is tender." They gingerly shook Peter's hand.

After I introduced them to Bill and Danny, I asked, "How do you feel, Peter? Can you play?"

"Sure," he smiled.

I noticed Bobby staring at Peter. "It was you, wasn't it?"

Peter and I knew what he was talking about, but the others were in the dark. Peter smiled a little, then Bobby gave him a hug as if Peter would break.

(I knew how Bobby felt since Peter saved my life more than once.) I mumbled to Bobby that we talk later. The boys trotted back to the field, but Bobby looked upon Peter with a certain reverence or awe.

It appeared Bobby had grown two or three inches and was now towering over Peter even more than last year. Several other boys snickered at Peter's size as they ran onto the field, but neither Peter nor Bobby seemed to notice.

As Bill, Danny and I took seats in the bleachers, I heard one man ask another, "What's the one-eyed shrimp doing out there? This is supposed to be for kids taller than the length of the bat." The other man laughed sarcastically.

I turned and volunteered, "The cute one belongs to me. He's my grandson." Before he could reply the first ball was hit to Peter. It was a fly. He misjudged it badly, probably because of his bad eye, jumped for it anyway and fell on his butt. The two men laughed hysterically as another boy grabbed the ball and threw it in.

The next ball hit to Peter was a grounder. As it approached him, it took a crazy bounce to the right. Peter dove too late and wound up empty-gloved flat on his stomach. The two men fairly howled at this scene.

The next ball hit in Peter's direction was a fly. He had to run up and to his right but made a perfect catch. He made the adjustment for his bad eye. But when he threw the ball back to Fred, it was closer to the unsuspecting kid on third. The two men next to me laughed again. Peter immediately held his right hand as if in pain. The loud-mouth said, "Hey, the shrimp got lucky. To bad he can't throw."

Peter ignored all of this and got ready for the next one. I could see his right hand did bother him. The big mouth looked at me and said, "Hey Gramps! Is that the first one he ever caught?"

"He's caught a few others." They sniggered. A couple minutes later a sharp grounder bounced through the infield. Peter moved left, scooped it up and threw it back to Fred in one easy motion. I could see that his full power wasn't in it.

It was his turn to hit. The loudmouth yelled out, "Oh come on. Don't waste time with him. Next batter!"

"Let him at least try, pitcher. Who knows. He may get lucky," I yelled. That got all kinds of reactions. The big mouth laughed and said, "I doubt it." Fred, Bill and Danny looked at me shocked and Peter looked over with concern. However I smiled and winked at him. He understood, stuck up his left thumb and smiled back.

Peter stepped to the plate, choked up on the bat and waited for the first pitch. Meanwhile Bobby and the other two boys that were there last year moved back, the rest moved up. The pitch was two feet over Peter's head, so he watched it sail by. The next pitch was just below his knees and again he watched it go by. The next was at head level and again he let it go. He leaned on the bat with his left hand and put his right hand on his hip, looked at Fred and said sarcastically, "Well?" Fred laughed, did a mock windup and threw a perfect pitch. Peter swung hard, missed and almost fell. The two men beside me were of course hysterical. Several of the boys in the field laughed too. But Bobby yelled, "Come on, Peter. Hit it over my head again."

The loudmouth put in his two cents: "That'll be the day. Come on pitcher, we're wasting time."

I yelled to Peter, "Keep your eye on the ball, Kiddo."

The other man snickered and said, "Yeah, the other eye he means. Then they'll both be black." Both men continued laughing.

Until that comment I'd been having a little fun with them. But now I was fuming. I was ready to take them both on when Fred threw another perfect pitch. Peter hit a fly. It sailed over a little boy's head by ten feet. He happened to be the son of the loudmouth. I looked at him. "If your kid had been playing his position correctly, he'd have caught it, wouldn't you agree?" Well, if looks could kill, I would have been dead meat.

His next hit sailed over Bobby's head. Fred pitched the next one harder, but Peter nailed it again. It was a grounder to the son of the loudmouth. He missed again. I said rather loudly to no one in particular, "guess he can't catch 'em in the air or on the ground," Fred pitched another hard one. Peter nailed it deep. But a boy got under it and Peter was out.

Suddenly Peter dropped the bat down and doubled over in pain, holding his right hand. Bill, Danny and I ran to him. So did Fred and Bobby. Peter was fighting tears.

As I reached him, it occurred to me: I had rubbed a finger over his eye, nose and lip. And I probed his ribs and stomach for pain, but I never rubbed his right hand. Could that be the problem? I asked myself! For the next few minutes I gently massaged his hand as everyone looked in suspense. After five minutes he announced his hand was fine. He had no problem for the rest of the practice. Bill and Danny were a little surprised at this.

The next boy at bat was none other than the son of the loudmouth. He started cheering his son on. I yelled to Peter,

"Better move up a little, Kiddo." For that I got a nasty hiss. His first hit was a line drive to Peter who caught it easily and threw it back dead on to Fred. The boy missed the next three pitches. The couple he did hit never left the infield. I could have rubbed it in, but I kept my mouth shut. His last hit was a grounder. Peter ran to his right and made a beautiful catch. Then he burned it into Fred. Danny yelled, "Wow! What a play! He's good."

"Not bad for playing hurt," I submitted. The man next to me was silent. In fact he didn't say much for the rest of the afternoon.

After all the boys had a chance to bat several times, the practice drew to an end. Fred ran towards me in the bleachers with Peter and Bobby not far behind. He was obviously upset. "Why did you put Peter down his first time up to bat?" Fred wanted to know. Bill, Danny and Bobby were concerned too, but Peter was chuckling. When they realized that, they all looked at him.

Peter said, "Jake said that but smiled and winked at me. I knew he was having fun with the guy sitting next to him."

"That jerk was ripping Peter apart. And what hurts him hurts me. I knew Peter was going to connect so I was having fun. I knew he would understand the smile and wink."

"Jake, you got mad when that guy made a crack about my one good eye, didn't you?"

"I sure did, Kiddo. I was ready to stand and take them both on. Then you got that hit."

"I'm glad you didn't. They were both bigger and younger than you."

Peter and Bobby moved off with the other boys.

Fred said, "Jake, I thought I'd better talk to you first. I'm putting a game together in three days. Would Peter be interested in playing? The problem is since it's a game, Peter would have to wear a jockstrap. For practice they don't but for a game, they do. Go figure but it's the park rules." He looked at Peter. "I don't know if they even make one that small. If they don't, he wouldn't be able to play."

"I think he'd love it. It would be a good experience for him, but where can I get a child's jock strap?"

"A friend of mine owns a sports store in Old Forge. If anybody would have one, he would. If not, he may be able to order one if they make them that small. I'll call him right now if you'd like."

I told him to go for it and gave him Peter's size.

"Wow! He really is little."

Fred got his friend on the phone. "Harvy, Fred, how you doing?...Great! Hey look, I have a bit of a problem. A friend of mine is camping in the park for a couple of weeks with his grandson. We're going to have a game in three days and the boy needs a jockstrap. The problem is, this boy is six but really little; he wears toddler four. Do they make them that small?...Yeah, I know, but this kid is amazing. He looks like a four-year-old but believe me, he's got the strength and coordination of a nine or ten-year-old. And can he hit!...No, I'm not kidding...Yeah, come on over. You'll love it, but first find me a jockstrap...Okay."

"I'm on hold while he looks. He thinks the smallest they have is child four but that would work." He looked at me. "Yeah, go ahead...You do? Well save it. He'll be over in an hour or so. He's Jake Winters, and his grandson is Peter. Thanks, Harvey! See you at the game."

"That's great, but let's make sure Peter wants to play." I called Peter over. Both Peter and Bobby joined us. "Peter, Bobby has a baseball game in three days and Mr. Thomas wonders if you'd be interested in playing?"

"Me? In a real game?" Bobby was getting excited too.

"I guess that answers your question," I said laughing. "The only problem is he's never played in a game. He doesn't know the rules."

"Do you have some time right now? I can quickly cover them."

I didn't have to look at Peter to know his answer "Bill, Danny, what do you think?"

"Let's do it." Danny said. That took care of that. We walked back to the diamond.

For the next half-hour we went over the basic rules of the game. Some rules would be forgotten but relearned in the course of the game through making mistakes. Fred said that is a given in kids ball games. After all, they are just learning.

Peter was so excited, he could spit. He was going to play in a real game. I took Peter aside for a minute. "Fred, give Peter a pitch. I mean burn it in—overhand."

He looked at me confused but went to the pitchers mound and burned one at Peter. Peter connected and the ball flew far out of the park much farther than any ten-year-old child could ever hit. It finally tipped the top of a large pine tree beyond the center field fence and fell into a canal.

Fred turned around and looked at Peter, his mouth open. "How did you do that?"

I started laughing. "He won't be playing like that in three days. He used his special powers. Actually, if he played using his powers, no ball would get by him in the outfield either, no matter how high it was. But in public he will play as a mortal."

"Good, but that was a hell-of-a demonstration."

"To be perfectly honest, I wasn't sure what would happen. I was curious myself, but I couldn't have him try it when everyone else was here." I paused. "Look Fred and Bobby, before we go, I think we need to have a little talk.

Bill and Danny, I want you two included." All looked at me puzzled except Peter and Bobby.

We sat down on the bleachers. I looked at Fred. "On June 30th of this year, Bobby was lost in the woods near your house." Fred's eyes widened. "A search party was formed, but by nightfall there was no sign of him. You and your wife were frantic. Around 11:00 he showed up muddy, cold and scared but otherwise okay. Bobby, how much did you tell him?"

He looked a little embarrassed. "I just told him I found my own way back. I didn't think anybody would believe me."

Fred was clueless. And this was news to Bill and Danny. "How do you know about this?" Fred asked.

"Fred, on June 30, Peter and I were in Basin, Montana, for Peter's second funeral." At that point, I described the funeral and reminded them why we had it in the first place. This was new to Bobby. He looked at me then at Peter in shock. For the first time he realized that Peter could have been lost to all of us forever. And just as suddenly, I realized that if Peter had returned to his grave, Bobby wouldn't be here either. I described what happened at the party that evening, including Bobby's rescue. You could have knocked Fred, Bill and Danny over with a feather.

Once his father got his voice back, Fred said, "Bobby, why didn't you tell me?"

"Would you have believed me?"

Fred looked at his son for a long moment—then ruffled his hair and said, "No, I guess not. Could you have blamed me?"

"No. I wasn't sure it happened myself, but it really did, didn't it, Peter?" Peter smiled slightly and nodded.

"Look, you two, I have something else to tell you. Last year, I told you Peter was a ghost. We all thought he was, but as it turns out, he's not." Bobby appeared to know what was coming. "As best as I can understand, a ghost doesn't have the freedom to move around the country the way Peter can. Peter also has more powers than a ghost and his powers are to help people in dire situations." I went on to tell them about meeting Peter's mother and to what she told us. "You see, Peter has been an angel all along."

Fred sat in awe, but Bobby smiled and said, "I thought so. The quicksand was just about up to my mouth. I knew I was going to die so at the last minute, I prayed for a miracle. And there was Peter. Well, I couldn't see him because it was pitch dark, but he picked me up and put me on dry ground near our house. He said, 'You're okay now, Bobby.' I knew then who it was."

"My…my God, Bobby. You, you were that close to…to death?"

Bobby began crying. Fred hugged his son, as he addressed Peter. "You *are* an angel."

"Fred, do you remember hearing about the truck that lost its brakes coming down the Blue Mountain Hill last summer?"

"As if it was yesterday. That's all everybody was talking about for weeks around here. I know the family of one of the children that was on that van. Nobody could explain how that truck stopped. Had it hit that van, everyone would have been killed. It was a miracle. The parents of that child were atheists until then. Since then they've become devout Christians."

"It was a miracle, Fred." I ruffled Peter's hair. "Here is the miracle." I explained Peter acted the same then as he did when we were in Basin. "One minute he was there, the next he was gone. Then he was back again."

Again Fred looked at Peter. "How can we ever thank you?"

Peter was embarrassed. (Sometimes he was too modest for his own good.) Peter said, "Well, could Bobby stay over at our campsite some night?"

We all laughed, but Bobby jumped with anticipation. "One thing I have to explain, Peter's a little boy who enjoys having fun and being loved just like every other little boy. And about his injuries. As a mortal, he suffers the same as anybody else. But tomorrow morning, his wounds will be healed.

"Now, Peter, as far as Bobby staying with us one night; that's up to Bobby's dad."

Bobby looked at his dad with pleading eyes. "We'll talk about it," Fred insisted.

"While you're talking about it, I'll give you something else to talk about. Fred, why don't both of you come over to our campsite early and make a day of it? Then leave the next morning."

"Me? The whole day and night? You've got to be kidding?"

"Please, Dad." Bobby pleaded. "You and I would have fun. We did last year and we were only there for a few hours."

"Do you have a canoe or do you have access to one?" I asked.

"Yeah," Bobby said. "The Ackermans have one, remember, Dad? They said we could borrow it anytime."

Fred was cornered. He and his son had a great time when they came up to our campsite the year before. "If you come up for breakfast, we can spend the whole day canoeing, fishing and swimming."

"We go swimming on the second lake," Peter volunteered. "That's where all the fish are. Well, at least they were last year."

"There probably won't be enough room in the tent, will there?" Fred asked hopefully.

"No problem," Bill said. "We have to leave in two days."

"Please, Dad?" Bobby was practically on his knees.

"Okay, you win," he smiled weakly.

Bobby jumped into his dad's arms. "Thanks, Dad." Then he hugged Peter and they danced around. Then Bobby even had a hug for me. "Thanks, Mr. Winters."

"You're welcome, Bobby."

"Thanks, Jake," Peter added.

"We'd better get going. What time do you want us here for the game?"

"Game starts at 11:00."

"We'll be here by 10:30," Peter concluded.

Fred and I laughed. "Look guys. Let's keep what we discussed to ourselves." They agreed and we four drove to the Hamlet of Old Forge ten miles away.

"Fred and Bobby are nice," Bill said. "You guys are going to have a great time. I get the feeling, Fred's not much of a camper."

"No, he's not. I feel a little guilty. We really backed him into it. I hope he has fun."

"Well, at least Peter and Bobby will." Bill said.

"Man Peter, can you ever play ball," Danny said. "I wish we could see your game. I bet you'll be the star even without using your powers. You'll be the smallest kid out there and I bet the other team will grossly underestimate your abilities. You can use that to your advantage."

"He's right, Kiddo. You're probably going to hear a lot of snide comments and wisecracks about your size, but don't let them get to you. Just become more determined the way you did last year and today."

"Don't worry everybody. I now know when people laugh and make fun of me, it's not because they hate me. It's because I'm little. Hey, where are we going?" Peter asked.

Bill and Danny were privy to the conversation earlier so knew what was coming. "We're going to a store in Old Forge to get you something special for the game."

Excitedly Peter asked what.

"A jockstrap?"

Because of his size and weight, Peter was restricted, by law, to a child restraint seat in the back. He looked at me in the rear view mirror. "A what?"

We all laughed. "A jockstrap. It's also called an athletic supporter. You wear it. It gives you a little bit of protection."

He thought about this. "From what?"

"The ball."

"That's what I have a glove for."

"You don't wear it on your hand. You wear it around your waist. It's sort of like underpants."

He looked down at himself. "Oh. You mean my things?"

"Yes. It helps if the ball hits you between your legs. Look Kiddo, wait until we get back to camp. And you can try it on. It'll be easier to explain then."

We were all laughing. He looked at the three of us and in a disgusted tone asked, "Are you guys making fun of me?"

"Yes, in a way." A year ago that answer would have been deadly, but not now.

As we walked into Harvy's Sport Store, a middle-aged man with salt and pepper hair walked up to us, stuck out his hand and said, "You two must be Jake Winters and Peter. I have the supporter right over here." We followed him to a counter where upon he handed me a small box.

I paid as the man looked at Peter and said, "I understand you're quite the ball player. I'll be at the game." Peter was flummoxed but he thanked the man.

We said we'd see him at the game and went out to get some dinner. Peter was dying of curiosity.

Back at the campsite I introduce Peter to a whole new experience. Being a wilderness site, I was not concerned about privacy. Our nearest neighbor was two miles away.

We were struggling to keep a straight face, sure of what was to come. I had Peter remove his shorts and underpants while I removed from its package, the smallest jockstrap I'd ever seen. I then handed it to him and said, "Here, put this on."

He took it turning it one way, then the other and finally said, "What *is* this?"

At that point we could no longer contain our laughter. "This is a jockstrap, Kiddo. Here, I'll help you." I sat him on my lap and got it up to his thighs, and I stood him down so he could pull it up the rest of the way. He wiggled like a woman struggling with a girdle. He pulled the waistband out, then the crotch and finally felt the two straps in back. He looked at me still puzzled. "Jake," he said in a pleading voice.

Laughing I put my fingers in the waistband. The crotch and the two straps in back were the same. I looked at Bill and Danny. "Looks like a perfect fit."

Feeling his bottom he said, "But, Jake, it doesn't cover my butt."

That got Bill and Danny laughing.

"If I get hit in the butt with the ball, it won't help at all."

"If you get hit in the butt, you're facing the wrong way," I chuckled. "Besides you have more padding back there."

He couldn't see his butt, so he felt around. "Well at least I won't have to pull them down to poop." Bill and Danny laughed their sides off.

"Oh yes you do. Look, Funny Tummy, you treat this thing just like it's underwear."

"Then why isn't underwear okay?"

"For one, it's park rules. Number two, it's designed to help protect those little things up front; namely your testicles."

He pulled the waistband out to look down inside of the cup, deep in thought. Something was coming. Bill and Danny realized it too and got quiet. "Jake, if I had been wearing this when those boys beat me in the alley, would it have helped?"

The internal damage was severe and his pelvis was broken. That was confirmed during the x-rays taken a year ago during his physical exam. The doctor suspected several hard punches or kicks caused the fracture.

Peter bringing up the incident now sent me into an empathetic flashback. I fought the tears. Bill and Danny were taken aback. I had told them in general terms of the incident.

Peter came over to be lifted on to my lap. He faced me. "Jake, are you okay?"

"Sorry, Little One. The way you suffered at the hands of those monsters..." I hesitated, to wipe my tears. "Let's get back to your question. The beating you suffered was so severe, you would have needed a cup. But let's not get into that."

"Will Bobby be wearing a jockstrap?"

"Yep, and all the other kids too."

"Do girls have to wear these when they play in the park?"

Oh boy! Peter knew girls were constructed differently. "No Kiddo, and *you* know why."

"Yeah!" With that I pulled the elastic band in front way out and let it smack against his abdomen.

"Ouch!" Peter said giggling. "Can I take this thing off now?"

"Sure, go ahead. And get into your PJ's."

He was soon back in his pajamas. Hey, I've got an idea. It's only 7:00. How about a long story?"

His eyes lit up. "Okay!"

But before I could begin, Peter said, "Jake, I used my special powers at the ball diamond today."

"I know and that hit was really something."

"That's not what I'm talking about. I used them another time."

"You did? When?"

"When that jerk sitting next to you said something about my eye. I knew you were mad. I saw what was going to happen. You would have gotten hurt bad. I couldn't have let that happen. I would have stepped in, but then everybody there would have seen our secret. So I prayed that Mr. Thomson's next pitch would be perfect. And that I would smack it hard."

"I see. To take everybody's attention off what was about to happen."

"Yeah."

I smiled. "You're a little peanut. As a mortal, you prayed. Thanks, Kiddo! You stumbled onto the mortal's special power. Prayer!

"I did?" His face lit up like—well, like an angel face.

CHAPTER ELEVEN

[At this point in the evening I told one of my best camping stories. I'm setting it out on the page as though I'm telling you, my dear reader.]

Bill built up the campfire he'd built earlier. I started the story of Old Man Johnson, a story I had come up with decades earlier. Peter decided to sit on the ground for this one. I wasn't sure why. I put a towel down for him so he wouldn't get his pajamas dirty. "Peter, this story happened a long time ago in 1968, when you were only 72 years old." Bill and Danny laughed.

"Three friends of mine and I went on a canoe trip in Northern Canada. The area that we went to was a lake chain: In other words, there was one main lake twenty-three miles long and fifteen or twenty smaller lakes you could portage into." I explained the term portage as Peter lay back resting his hands under his head. I was certain that posture wouldn't last long.

"The area was huge, covering hundreds of thousands of square acres. In that entire area was one small fishing camp and four private cabins. At the end of a thirty-five mile dirt road, we arrived at the fishing camp located at the extreme southern end of the main lake. From that point on you were on your own when heading north by boat or canoe."

"We drove to the lodge and looked for the owner, Clint Owens. My family and I had been going up there for several years so I knew Clint well. We found him in a shed repairing an outboard motor. His son, Randy, was with him. Randy was a twenty-one-year-old college student studying criminal law. He spent the summer working with his dad as a guide. We spent an hour with them shooting the bull.

"A nineteen-year old Cree Indian boy called Dark Hair or Thomas Hogan, was working as a guide that summer with Randy. We didn't get a chance to meet him since he was guiding.

"We told Clint where we planned to go and how long we planned to stay out. If we weren't back at roughly the time we said, they'd contact the rangers and a search party would be formed. We told them we'd stay at the last island in the narrows tonight and then head over to Bass Lake in the morning.

"That afternoon we paddled up the lake about five miles to the island for the night. We had planned to spend that night on the island and the next four nights on Bass Lake fishing—a lake known for it's bass. However, we'd forgotten about the time of year. It was early June and bass season didn't start until late June. I knew the area well and suggested the next morning we head for Round Lake instead. The pike fishing would be fantastic. The others agreed.

"After dinner we built up the fire to sit around telling jokes and singing. Finally, I told a scary story. We then sat quietly listening to the noises of the Canadian spring in her deep wilderness. We heard the foghorn voices of bull frogs, a variety of birds including an owl and the haunting voice of loons. But then we heard another noise in the far distance."

(At this Peter sat up.)

"The strange noise was so far away, none of us could identify it. So we finally gave up and went to bed."

(Peter lay back down.)

"The next morning we headed for Round Lake in the opposite direction from Bass Lake. We were in the canoes by six and had a campsite set up by nine. Round Lake had been the scene of great logging activity in the early 1900's. So we all decided to do some exploring that morning. Rog and Slim went in one direction and Ned and I went in another.

"While drifting along the bank of a steep hill, Ned and I noticed something protruding from the woods and into the water. We decided to investigate. We walked into the thick undergrowth and discovered a huge log-run full of logs."

(Peter sat up.)

"Many years earlier, when loggers logged the top of a hill, they'd build a slide out of wood. It was like a slide on a playground but it was for logs. After cutting down a lot of trees, they'd put the logs on the slide. The logs would slide down to the water and save the men a lot of time and work. This slide was so big there was room for two huge logs side by side.

"We climbed to the top of the mountain. The slide was full of logs all the way up. At the top we found another fifty to seventy-five massive logs cut and ready to go. All were rotten. It didn't make sense. Why do all that work then walk off and leave them? It was our first mystery.

"Ned and I met Roger and Slim at our campsite for lunch to compare notes. We told them what we found. Interestingly, they had found the remains of the logging camp.

"After lunch they returned to the camp. I took Ned to another part of the lake where an old trappers cabin sat. Obviously it was still used from time to time, probably in the fall. There was a homemade chair, table and bed with a straw-stuffed mattress in it. There were also a couple of pots and an old wood burning stove. We spent the afternoon there and even fished just off shore a little with no luck."

(Peter lay back down.)

"We met Slim and Rog back at the campsite for dinner. They were excited over their afternoon. They'd found the remains of several other buildings, one of which they were certain was the dinning hall. The roof had collapsed. They wanted us to join them the next morning but we had other plans. We wanted to try our luck at more serious fishing.

"That evening we built up the fire, told a few jokes, sang a few songs and told another ghost story—then we listened. Again we heard frogs, birds and loons. We were just ready to go to bed when we heard a scream.

(Peter shot up.)

"We remembered the scream from the night before. It had been too far away and too faint to identify. Tonight it was much louder coming from somewhere on Round Lake, but we still couldn't identify it. It sounded a little like a timber wolf with a few other animal screams thrown in.

"Peter, a timber wolf in the East is about the same as a gray wolf in the West. After waiting for the animal to scream again, we gave up and went to bed. About ten minutes later we heard a large animal moving far back in the woods behind our tent. Figuring it was a bear or moose, we all drifted into sleep.

"The next morning Slim and Rog went back to the logging camp. Ned and I fished near our campsite.

(Peter relaxed and lay down again.)

"At about ten we looked toward the logging camp and saw a lone canoe coming towards us. We knew it was Slim and Rog since we were the only four on the lake. But something was wrong. They were both paddling fast and normally neither one of them did anything fast.

(Peter, Danny and Bill chuckled.)

"We decided to meet them and find out what was going on. We met them halfway. Both looked nervous.

"It seems they had found two small standing cabins. They went into the first and found a table, chair, crude bed and a stove. They walked to the second cabin. In that one they found only a crude table. Resting on the table was an old hatchet.

(Peter once again sat up.)

"There was a brown stain running down part of the wood handle. They speculated it was dried blood left over from the butchering of a small animal forty years before.

"In retracing their steps back to the first cabin, they noticed a poorly defined trail going right off the main trail. They walked only twenty feet and came across a little mound. Protruding from the dirt was a small bone. Both amateur archaeologists, they decided to dig into the grave to discover the type animal buried there.

(Peter now moved a little closer to Danny.)

"After a half hour, they found the skull. They also found a slit in the back of the skull, apparently from a hatchet. It was only then that they realized what they held in their hands. The skull was human…a murdered human. At that point they both had a race to see who could get back to the canoe the fastest.

(Peter stood and went to Danny to be lifted onto his lap.)

"Ned and I thought this all sounded neat and intriguing and asked them to show us the site. They looked at us as if we were nuts.

(Peter looked at me the same way.)

"They didn't want to go back to the place until Ned and I pointed out that the camp had closed down forty years ago. The killer was long gone and probably dead. Hesitantly they agreed.

"They led us through the first cabin on the way to the burial site. It was just as they described, but Ned and I weren't satisfied. We dug a little deeper and came up with two more human skulls, both with slits in the back. We asked Slim to get the hatchet. We wanted to see if the blade matched the slits. Hesitantly, Slim went to the far cabin alone. Shortly we heard a blood-curdling scream from that direction. Slim suddenly ran along the main trail heading for the canoes yelling, 'the hatchet's gone.' The three of us looked at each other then suddenly grasped what he had said. Until that point we had been the only four humans on the lake. Now we knew there was a fifth. Ned, Rog and I suddenly had a race to see who could get to the lake the fastest.

(Peter's eyes were now huge.)

"We went back to the safety of our campsite. It was on the opposite side of the lake from the logging camp. We ate a silent lunch, all deep in thought. That afternoon Ned and I led Rog and Slim to the trappers' cabin. It was on the same side of the lake as our campsite, therefore safe. After walking into the cabin, Slim let out with another scream. The bloody handled hatchet was sitting on the table. Only two hours before it was discovered at the logging camp on the other side of the lake. We all left quickly.

(Peter moved even closer to Danny.)

"We were perplexed. Although it was a fairly large lake, (about five miles long and five miles wide—thus it's name) there were only three campsites on the lake. One was just around the corner from the logging camp, one was on the point where the trappers cabin was and the third was ours. Yet ours was the only one currently occupied. But now we knew beyond a reasonable doubt, there was at least one other person on the lake. We just didn't know who he was, where he was and worse yet, his intentions.

"We knew the lake had been the site of several vicious murders. Clint had told me years earlier the logging camp was abandoned in 1928, but he never said why. I suppose as a businessman in the area, he didn't want to publicize the murders, even though they took place a generation ago.

"But what if the murders had not occurred forty years ago? What if they took place only five or ten years ago? Could the killer still be in the area? Could he be on Round Lake looking for fresh victims? If so, he could be sizing us up right now for his source of fresh blood.

(Peter shivered and put his arm around Danny's neck.)

"I never expressed my thoughts to my companions.

"We continued fishing for the next two hours, but all of us were too distracted. We had other things on our mind. We returned to our campsite, fearful of what we might find. But it was just as we'd left it. After dinner we built up our fire and sang some songs. But that night we elected to tell jokes and sing but skip the ghost story. After the songs we sat listening. The scream came. It sounded louder…and closer. We waited for the animal to scream again but it never did. We quietly crawled into the tent. About ten minutes later we heard a large animal moving through the woods. I stuck my head out the front of the tent and shined the light into the woods. I caught a quick movement. Something large jumped behind a tree. This was no bear.

(Peter quickly got off Danny's lap and move to Bill's.) I chuckled silently.

"Midway through the next morning it occurred to me what could be going on. I recall that Randy told me once how he and another guide scared people. They would wait until a few greenhorns or newcomers to the north woods would go out camping on their own for a night or two. Later that night Randy and his buddy would sneak out to their campsite by canoe, make a few unrecognizable noises and quickly paddle back to the lodge. That's all they had to do. The rest was taken care of by imagination.

"But Randy knew this game wouldn't work with me. I knew the woods too well. Anyway, each night the scream and the creature in the woods came closer. Randy knew when we were to leave. I expected that Randy or whoever would get closer in the woods. They planned to nail us the last night. So I suggested to my friends that we put the shoe on the other foot. Every night we'd do just as we have been doing and give no clue that we were on to him. The others agreed with my plan.

(Peter, feeling safe, went back on the towel.)

"That afternoon we did some serious fishing and I caught a thirteen pound pike. We had a great dinner that night. After dinner we did everything the same. As I predicted, the scream was closer and later the creature in the woods was too. I moved a little slower that night with the flashlight and failed to catch any movement. We knew we had Randy's plan figure right.

"The last night we could hardly wait. The scream was within a few hundred yards of our campsite, as predicted. We waited for a few minutes then crawled into the tent. But instead of getting ready for bed, we got ready for Randy. We all had big knives. I had the Bowie.

"The tent was an old canvas model so it had both a back and a front flap or door. Rog and Slim were at the back and Ned and I were at the front. Soon we heard the creature approach. We waited until he was directly behind the tent. On a signal we all jumped out at once. We were yelling and screaming with our knives slashing through the air and our flashlight beams darting in all different directions. We had the poor guy surrounded. He darn near jumped to the top of a tree.

(Peter, picturing the scene, was rolling on his towel now, laughing hysterically.)

"Suddenly we were no longer screaming, just staring. It wasn't Randy or the Indian guide.

(Peter stopped laughing looking at me with stark fear in his eyes.)

"The man that stood before us was huge. Peter, he was even bigger than Moose out in Basin. He was at least six-foot eight. The stranger before us had long, wild, gray hair and a long unkempt beard.

(Peter began creeping toward me.)

"Worst of all were his eyes. They were barely human. They were more like the eyes of a wild beast or a man that was totally insane.

(Peter wanted to be lifted onto my lap. Only his security blanket would work at a time like this.)

"This frightful creature stared at us as we stared back. Then he turned and bolted into the dense woods out of range of our flashlights.

"We were frozen in shock. Gradually we retreated into the tent, but no one slept that night.

"The next morning we had a hurried breakfast, packed and left. We took turns looking over our shoulders all the way across the portage.

(As night was approaching our little campsite, Peter was looking over his shoulder, too. Just then a loon let lose a crazy cry. Peter shuddered and came closer. He no longer considered the loon's cry neat.)

"As we approached the dock, Clint greeted us. 'How was Bass Lake?' he asked. It was only then that I realized our intruder couldn't have been Randy. He thought we were on Bass Lake. If he went looking for us and found we weren't there, we could have been on any one of fifteen or twenty other lakes. The only way to find us would have been by plane.

"Clint looked at me hard. 'You spent four nights on Round Lake? How'd it go?' His voice carried some concern.

"So we filled him in on what we discovered...and what discovered us.

"Client said, 'In the 1920's there was a large logging camp on Round Lake. That's the one you found. Many of the loggers were French Canadian. One in particular had a hard name to pronounce for the English-speaking loggers so they called him Johnson. Johnson was a hard-working family man from Frenchtown, the nearest community some forty-five miles south.

'Johnson was an orphan so his family meant everything to him. His wife and seven young children lived in a small wood-frame cabin. They were poor, and a wood stove and two kerosene lanterns provided their only heat and light.

'One day Johnson received a letter from a friend in Frenchtown. There had been an accident. A knocked-over lantern caught the cabin on fire and it burned like tissue paper. It burned so fast, no one had a chance. It seems his entire family perished in the time it took him to read that letter. His every reason for living was gone. His future vanished along with his family.

'More importantly his sanity slipped. And it slipped fast. Johnson was a mountain of a man and very powerful. But he was known as the gentle giant. He was a friend to everybody. However, after the devastating news, everything changed. He began to pick fights. Finally he killed a man with his bare hands. After that he fled the camp and moved into the woods. He was a skilled outdoorsman. Then his attacks on the area loggers were just beginning.

'He was excellent at throwing the hatchet and the ax. For years he'd won every contest there was both in accuracy and distance. In his insanity, instead of throwing them at stationary targets, he was now throwing them at men. And he seldom missed. That explains the skulls you found."'

(Peter put his arms around my neck. I suspected I was going to pay for this story in the middle of the night.)

'The loggers went out hunting for Johnson. The only thing it got them was two more murdered men. That's when they decided to abandon the camp. That was in 1928. That explains the abandoned log run you found. Forest rangers came in at different times to try and capture or kill him, but never succeeded.

"Why did we survive the encounter?" I wanted to know.

'Johnson is nothing more than a wild animal. He has the instincts of a wild animal. He was stalking you. It sounds as if he was planning to attack last night, but instead you scared the tar out of him. Since you thought it was only Randy, your fearfulness disarmed him. Of course, I'm speculating. I don't know how his mind works. And nobody else does either.

"How old would he be today?" I asked.

"Client answered me as best he could. 'At the time he learned of his family's demise, he was between thirty-five and forty. That would make him between seventy-five and eighty today'."

"He moves pretty good for a senior citizen," I said. "In fact he moves like he's still a young man."

'Think about it,' Client said. 'He's living a totally natural life. No preservatives in his water or food and he's getting plenty of exercise'."

"Well, guys, that's the end of the story of Old Man Johnson."

"Jake, is that story true?" Peter wanted to know. I smiled. How many times have I been asked that question?

"What do you think?"

Peter looked at me. "I think it is. You're the bravest person I've ever known."

"Remember, Kiddo, we thought it was Randy. It's not that we were brave, we just didn't realize what was really going on. If we would had only known about Old Man Johnson, we would have left Round Lake real quick. Are you okay after that story?"

"Sure, I'm fine. That was great! It was really scary, but I wasn't scared at all." I looked at him raising an eyebrow. "Well, maybe a little. I like scary stories. Could you tell me another one tomorrow?"

"We'll see, but for now how about you taking a pee in the woods there before going to sleep?"

"Okay." He stood and looked at the dark woods in the vanishing light of day. In the distance we heard the mournful cry of a loon. Peter looked at the lake; then looked back at the darkening woods and its many deepening shadows fifteen feet away. I noticed him shiver. "Jake." He turned and looked at me. "Will you come with me?"

I took his hand as we walked to the edge of the woods. "Peter, are you sure you're okay?"

"Yeah, I'm fine." He hesitated. "Jake, you are going to sleep next to me tonight aren't you?" He adjusted his pajamas.

"You bet, Little One. I always sleep next to you." I picked him up.

He hugged me. "Jake, maybe I was a little scared during the story, but it was good."

"It's okay to be scared during a scary story. A scary story is supposed to scare you. I noticed both Danny and Bill were kind of nervous too."

"They were?" He asked amazed.

"Sure! A scary story gets your imagination going. This story was about a crazy logger by the name of Old Man Johnson. He lived in the dark woods of Canada running around killing people. When it was time to take a pee, you looked at the dark woods and thought of Old Man Johnson, didn't you? That's your imagination."

"Do you ever think of Old Man Johnson?"

"Not too much anymore, but I used to. I bet you Bill and Danny will be thinking of him when they go to the woods later on."

"Do you think so?"

"I'll guarantee it." We moved back to the fire. Peter crawled up on my lap again.

I said, "Peter, I have a question I've never asked you before." He turned sideways and looked at me with interest. "When you attacked that kid this morning, you delivered two vicious punches to his face. They were hard and fast, but they were both with your right fist. When you lived in Slippery Gulch, you didn't have a left arm, did you?" Bill and Danny looked at me. Obviously they'd forgotten that fact. Peter nodded.

"Did you get into a lot of fights?"

He put his head down. "A few, when I was in town. I never started one. I never even threw the first punch."

"So did you always wait until you were punched first?"

"No! I was too fast. I moved when they tried to punch me. Then I punched them."

"Were they always bigger than you like teenagers?"

"Not always that big. Sometimes they were like Jimmy and sometimes they were smaller like me."

"Was it always one on one?"

"Hardly ever. I could usually take even a bigger kid if I could stay on my feet. I could have beaten that kid today if I could have gotten up. Usually it was three or more."

"So they ganged up on you?"

"Yeah. They'd surround me. I'd try to get away, and sometimes I did. Once I started running, no one could catch me. I'd run into the woods and hide. They didn't follow me into the woods anyway. They were afraid of the woods because they thought one of the big cats would get them."

"If you didn't get away, what happened?"

"I'd get in one or two good punches. If they were kids my size they would sometimes back off and I could get away; but if they were bigger kids like Jimmy, they wouldn't. Two or three would be in front of me trying to punch me. They usually missed. Another two or three would be behind me. I couldn't keep away from all of them. Sometimes one behind me would punch me in my back." He pointed to his kidney. "That knocked the wind out of me. I still tried to fight, but one in front would punch me in the stomach. When I went down to my knees, I was done. They had me then.

"Other times some kid would tackle me from behind and take me down. Once I was down, they had me. The gang would punch me in my stomach and sometimes in my face. They'd all be yelling and screaming. It was as if they finally beat the monster." Tears formed in his eyes. "I didn't stand a chance. They thought it was funny. When they had their fun, they'd leave me in the street." Peter was sniffling and Danny was too.

"Teenagers would sometimes take your clothes off and make you run through town. Would the younger kids do that?" I asked.

"Once the teenagers started that, the smaller kids thought it was funny. They'd wait until the teenagers punched me in the stomach and left. Then they'd jump on me. I had no time to get up. When I was naked, they punched me everywhere. They thought it was funny to fight dirty when I was naked."

"Were there ever any girls involved?"

"If you mean did any girls ever do anything to me—no. Sometimes a couple of girls would stand around and watch the boys beat me up. They always giggle when I was naked."

Bill and Danny sat there with their mouths open not knowing what to say. Danny wiped his tears. I hugged Peter. "Your fighting days are over, Kiddo. There's no reason for it anymore." We all sat staring into the embers—all but Peter who was asleep now.

Sometime passed. Bill spoke first. "I think the story of Old Man Johnson bothered Peter a lot more than he was willing to admit."

"I know. I think I'd better sleep with a towel tonight to be on the safe side."

"Jake, you never talked to him about the fights he was in as a living boy, did you?" Danny asked.

"Not to that extent. I wasn't aware of the details of his fights. When I saw those two right hooks today, it got my curiosity up. I've never seen a kid with such a powerful punch. With one arm, he became like a blind person who develops exceptional hearing.

The subject was changed. We talked about the day and Peter's massive home run came up. We laughed over the two goons trying to create a stir.

With that, we all went to bed.

That night Peter had a little nightmare. He woke all of us up screaming. Not hysterically though! He apparently outran Old Man Johnson and kept his pants dry.

CHAPTER TWELVE

When Peter joined us at the fire the next morning, I woke him up with our traditional tickles. After Peter regained his breath and the rest of us stopped laughing with him, we talked and decided to spend the day on our lake fishing and swimming.

Morning fishing was slow again, though Danny caught a three pounder. After building a sand castle and swimming, we skipped stones, lay in the sun, and watched Peter tumble and explored.

That afternoon Bill and I got a bass apiece but Peter got skunked. He didn't care, he was happy for us. He was eager to practice his fish-cleaning skills again.

This time we all helped in the cleaning preparation. Just as Peter started on the first fish Tom Casey, the park ranger, pulled up. Upon checking in with him our first day in the park, I told him of Peter's new status. Tom wasn't surprised and very pleased.

As he crawled out of his government-issue 4x4, he asked in alarm, "Peter, what are you doing?"

Peter giggled and said, "I'm cleaning a fish."

Tom watched Peter, as he worked with total focus. Peter would itch and scratch as usual.

Tom waited till Peter was done before going to him. He whistled. "Jake, look at those. My fillets never look that good. Peter, who taught you how to do that?"

"Bill taught me."

"You keep improving and you're going to be able to teach your teacher a thing or two." Peter swelled up with pride.

"Okay, Little Angel, down to our spot."

Peter removed his shorts and I poured a bucket of water over his head. Then I lathered his hair. Danny grabbed his shorts and started scrubbing them. I looked at Tom. "You know, Tom, this is how it all started. I first washed his hair in the creek behind Slippery Gulch. I've been washing it ever since. Of course that day was a tender and emotional time for both of us."

I poured the water over Peter's head and watched the soapy water run down his body. I dried my hands and pulled the first picture I took of Peter from my wallet to show Tom. Tom looked from Peter to his picture and back again. Tom shook his head.

"Peter's an angel. I knew that before you ever left the park last summer. When I called Basin in June and heard you two would be together. I was not surprised."

Peter completed washing himself the second time and waded out of the lake for me to dry him. "Tom, Peter is capable of drying himself now. But to be wrapped in a big, soft towel and dried, hugged and loved is just what he needed then. It still is, isn't it, Little One?" Peter nodded and snuggled.

Then I removed the towel. "This is not part of the original tradition, but with fish-cleaning we've added it." I took the can of deodorant and sprayed Peter up one side and down the other. "Better he smell like Old Spice than fish. Now, Mr. Bare Butt, put your dry shorts on.

"Tom, would you care to stay for dinner? We've got plenty."

"Thanks but my wife is waiting for me. I just wanted to stop in and say good-bye to you two, Bill and Danny. I hope to see you two back here next year."

That evening we went out in our canoes for a while. That night Peter wanted another scary story, but I kept it mild.

As usual, Peter fell asleep as the story ended. Bill, Danny and I reviewed our week: Tom Casey, Peter fishing, Peter at baseball, Peter cleaning fish and Peter. It was a good way to finish out our day.

I stood up with Peter in my arms. "Let's go into the tent."

I lay him on his sleeping bag. Thanking God for Peter, we turned in ourselves.

CHAPTER THIRTEEN

The next morning after Peter woke up, I said, "Peter, we have to help Bill and Danny pack. They have to get going."

"Oh yeah. I forget about that."

But nobody moved. Finally Bill looked at Peter and said. "Meeting you and getting to know you this past year has meant a lot to both of us."

"Knowing that you're an angel is pretty cool too," Danny said.

"That's true, Danny," Bill said.

"But dad," Danny said, "being willing to take a beating for Jake instead of using his super powers to beat the crud out of Jimmy, sure got my respect. You're the greatest, Peter!"

Peter put his head down in his typical way then looked up. "I really love you guys. I was so scared of you last year before I met you Danny, just because you were a teenager. Now you're one of my best friends ever."

Danny was so touched he couldn't speak. He went over, picked Peter up and gave him a big hug. Once reclaiming his voice he said, "Thanks, Little Angel. That means more than you'll ever know."

I was standing at Bill's window of his car and Peter was at Danny's. We were saying our final good-byes when I noticed Peter staring at nothing. Bill told us to have a great week and Danny wished Peter good luck in the game tomorrow. Then Peter said, "Wait!"

He walked directly in front of their car and knelt down. I walked to the front from the left side to see what was going on. Peter was on his hands and knees. Suddenly a small toad appeared. I was certain it wasn't there only seconds before. Peter appeared to catch it then release it several times until he finally held on. He stood up, moved out of the way and said, "Okay, you can go now."

Bill and Danny laughed. "Peter, you're even a guardian angel to toads," Danny chuckled. We all waved as they drove off.

I knelt down and put my hand on Peter's shoulder. "What just happened, Kiddo?"

He looked at me innocently. "What do you mean?"

"Come on, Kiddo. Remember whom you're talking to. I'm your guardian and I'm your best friend. I know you far better than anybody else. I saw you stare at nothing even though it wasn't long. And that toad appeared out of nowhere."

He gave me a half-hearted giggle. "I can't get away with anything with you. There's a car traveling towards Blue Mountain from Inlet. The driver's coming back from an all-night party and he's drunk—real drunk. He's going to hit a curve too fast in a few minutes, cross the double line and go into the ditch on the other side of the road. If Bill and Danny had left when they were planning to, the drunk would have hit them head on at over 70 MPH. Everybody would have been killed. Now they'll be okay. Bill and Danny will be the first on the scene."

I just stared at him for a moment. "You're something else. Will the drunk be okay?"

"Yeah, but he'll be asleep. Bill will call the police."

"Hey, let's go for a ride. They're only a few minutes ahead of us."

We got to the scene a few minutes after they did. The police had gotten there just ahead of us. Bill and Danny were surprised to see us. "We just wanted to make sure the drunk was okay." They were stunned. We both started laughing. However it wasn't a laughing matter. Both Peter and I turned serious, but Peter wasn't about to talk about it. I told them what happened and the reasons for Peter's stall tactic. You could have blown them over with a gentle breeze. The two of them were now recipients of Peter's angelic powers.

Peter got a huge hug from both of them again. Peter assured them they'd reach home safely now. Nevertheless, we reminded them to be careful, then went back to our campsite.

CHAPTER FOURTEEN

Since the big game was tomorrow, as we paddled toward our lake, we went over the rules. Halfway to our lake, Peter announced he had to pee.

"Can you wait until we get to our lake?"

"I can't, Jake. I really have to go bad."

"Okay. I'll run you into shore."

"I can't wait that long. What can I do?"

"Why didn't you go before we left?"

"I didn't have to go then."

"Well, why didn't you tell me five minutes ago?"

"I didn't have to go that bad then. What do I do?"

This is something I will never understand about little kids. How can it be that they don't have to go one minute but have to go real bad five minutes later."

"The only thing you can do is stand there carefully and pee over the side."

"But there's a boat over there," he said, pointing to his right.

I looked at him. This was the little boy that would appear before anybody naked without a second thought? "Pee the other way. But be careful."

He carefully stood and dropped his pants. While he urinated he sighed, "Uh-oh."

I looked at him. "What?"

He suddenly tilted his head far back then came forward with the worst, most powerful sneeze he'd ever produced. As he leaned forward with his sneeze, his body kept going on over into the lake. I started laughing so hard I almost capsized the canoe. When he surfaced and saw me laughing, he got madder than a hornet with no one to sting.

"Jake, it's not funny!" I pulled him into the canoe. "Now I'm drenched and you're doing nothing to help me. All you're doing is laughing."

I finally got self control—sort of. "Sorry, Funny Tummy. You said, 'uh-oh,' and I looked up in time to see your bare little bottom go flying over the side. It was pretty funny."

We paddled silently for five minutes. "Jake, that was the first time I ever fell into the toilet I was peeing in. Do you know how disgusting that is?"

That got both of us going. We laughed so hard we couldn't paddle for a while.

The fish were nonexistent, so we went swimming before noon. We went to our beach where he removed his shorts and underpants. I wrung them out and laid them on a rock while he put his trunks on. We played water tag.

After lunch he spread the towel on the ground, rolled down his trunks and lay down. I lay down next to him. He raised his head so I could put my arm comfortably under it.

We were soaking up the sun when Peter asked, "Jake, do you remember the very first bath you gave me in the creek behind Slippery Gulch?"

"Sure. As if it were yesterday! Why?"

"I feel the love in your arm now like I felt everything in your hands then. I knew you were sad and felt sorry for me. I knew you were concerned. I knew you cared. I never felt anything like it before. I always wondered what love felt like. I was hoping you'd hug me. But you didn't...then anyway. When you finished drying my hair and me, you wrapped that big soft towel around me and hugged me. That was the best thing I ever felt in my life. I wanted to stay in your arms forever."

"Well, now you can."

"I know." He put his hand on mine and kept my thumb moving slowly across his chest with his. I figured he'd soon be asleep. We lay there in silence for a few minutes. Suddenly he rolled away from me and said, "Jake, can we climb that mountain over there this afternoon?"

I looked at Blue Mountain. "Are you sure you want to try that again?"

"Yeah! But this year I'll listen to you. No more walking on old logs."

I chuckled. "That's good! We'll have to hustle. No more swimming or lying in the sun. We'll have to fly back to the campsite."

We changed and made it to our campsite in record time. We took a couple of canteens of water and a small backpack and headed for Blue Mountain.

We were on the trail by two. Peter immediately took off running when I yelled to him. He stopped dead in his tracks. "No more daredevil stunts, kid."

He smiled. "I won't, Jake." He'd disappear around a bend then return. Then off he'd go again. As I came around one bend in the trail, I found him standing in front of the same log he'd taken a bad fall from a year ago. I put my hand on his shoulder.

He looked at me. "I was tempted to try it again, Jake."

"That was the devil talking, Kiddo. I'm glad you resisted. Hey, Little One, let's get to the top of this mountain."

He took my hand as we headed to the top. He squeezed my hand. Smiling down, I returned it. He shot an angelic smile back.

At the top, we were in awe of the spectacular view. Not only could we see Lake Durant, the lake we were camped on and our fishing lake, we could see many other lakes including

THE SEPARATION

Blue Mountain Lake, Raquette Lake and Long Lake. The water was a beautiful blue with silver streaks caused by the wakes of boats. The sky was blue with a few fluffy white clouds. And the north woods were green with pines and silver birch.

Peter motioned to be picked up. He put an arm around my neck. "It's beautiful, Grandpa."

"It sure is, Kiddo. This is God's country."

Suddenly, Peter pointed out a small plane taking off from Long Lake. It was no more than a speck. He started jumping up and down and yelled, "That's Sam, Jake."

"How do you know that?"

"I don't know. I just do." We watched it slowly rise into the air then bank toward Blue Mountain before passing out of our view. "Quick, Jake, put me on your shoulder. He's coming back this way."

I put him on my shoulder knowing the plane may not come back our way. Anyway, the chances of it being Sam's plane were slim. If it was Sam, the chances of him seeing us were slim. But it was fun. Soon we heard the noise of a plane. Seconds later it came into view still below us. It looked like Sam's plane. Peter was insistent. He started yelling and waving, so I did too as the plane flashed by. It was far enough away I could barely make out a pilot, let alone identify him.

The plane headed out over the lake and continued to circle until it was headed back towards us in a climb. It swept by at an altitude barely over our heads and was soon out of sight. Peter was beside himself with excitement. "It was Sam, Jake! I knew it was."

I wasn't convinced. I was about to lift him off my shoulders when we heard the whine of a plane's engine again. Suddenly, there it was, once again coming from our right. As soon as it came into view, we could see the wings rocking back and forth. By golly it was Sam! As it sped by our location, not 200 feet from the mountain, we could clearly see Sam's huge smile on his face while waving. Peter bounced up and down on my shoulders, waving and squealing.

We watched as the plane sailed farther away. "Jake, why is he slowing down?"

"He isn't, Kiddo. It just looks that way the farther away he gets."

"That was really neat, Jake. Can we go up with him again while we're here?"

"I don't see why not. You ready to head back down?"

Before we descended, I took a few pictures, in addition to the one I got of the plane earlier. It was faster going down even for me. But as I walked along, Peter was down and back a couple of times, like a yo-yo on a string.

Finally, at the parking lot, we sat on a bench. I needed a break and Peter had to recoup some of his energy. He slept for fifteen minutes.

We had a home-cooked meal at a restaurant in town that night before returning to camp.

While waiting for dinner to come, Peter reluctantly asked, "What is that family doing over there staring at their table?"

I said they were praying.

"For their meal they are about to eat?"

"Probably."

He looked at them again, then at me. "Jake, do you think they're thanking God for each other the way you and I do?"

"They may very well be, Kiddo."

"Grandpa, sometimes you and I forget, especially when we're in truck stops and camping. Do you think God gets mad at us?"

"I doubt if he gets mad at us, but I'm sure he becomes disappointed in us."

"You mean the way you're disappointed in me when I misbehave?"

"Yeah, something like that."

"But you always forgive me even when you're *real* disappointed in me. Do you think he forgives us?"

"Always, Little One. Always. He didn't make us to be perfect like he did his son, Jesus."

"Jake, can I say a prayer right now?"

"I think this would be the perfect time." We bowed our heads in prayer.

CHAPTER FIFTEEN

The next morning he wandered out to the fire more asleep than awake, crawled onto my lap and curled into a little ball.
"You look tired."
"I am." That was a strong hint, but instead of waking him I rubbed my hand gently over his curved back and his head. It appeared he was going to fall asleep. This wasn't like him.
"What's the matter, Kiddo?"
"How do you know something is wrong?"
"You forgot how well I know you. Now what's wrong?"
He started to whimper. "I'm scared about the game today. What happens if I make a fool of myself?"
That's what I thought. "Peter, I don't think you're going to make a fool of yourself. Sure, you're going to make some mistakes, but when you do, forget it and play on. You're not going to be the only one to make mistakes. Even Bobby will. And when someone else makes a mistake, don't get mad at them. Say something encouraging to them such as, 'Hey, that's okay, Bobby. Don't worry about it. Comes on, let's play.' If you do that, soon other kids will start doing the same to you when you make a mistake. Encouragement makes anyone feel better.
He thought about this. "Jake, how did you get to be so smart?"
I laughed. "It's not that I'm so smart. I've been around for a long time. Life offers a lot of experiences we can learn from."
"Well, you're pretty smart too." He gave me a hug. "Thanks, Jake. Will you wake me up now?"

I laughed and dug in. After wolfing down a good breakfast, I helped him into his jockstrap. Immediately, he started pulling at the cup. "I hate this thing."

I looked at him and fought the laughter. Looking at this tiny boy wearing a tiny jockstrap stretching it in any number of ways while moving his tiny body this way and that in supposed terrible discomfort, was hilarious. "You don't have to play in the game today, you know. We could go over and watch instead."

"I know, but I want to." He pulled on a pair of his long jeans and forgetting his discomfort.

We arrived at the ball field early, so we played catch. Soon a man and his son walked over to us, introducing themselves. The son was nine and said, "Come to watch the game?"

"Yes, I did but my grandson is playing in it."

Both father and son looked Peter up one side and down the other. The father said, "I didn't realize such young kids were being allowed to play."

"I believe it's for six-to ten-year-olds."

He was about to say something when Bobby ran up with Fred. I could see Fred had no idea who the other father was. They walked away smirking when Fred said, "How about if Bobby and I get to your campsite around 7:30 tomorrow morning?"

Peter let out with a yell and jumped into my arms. I smiled. "Look Fred, I know you're not too interested in camping, but I'm sure the boys will have a great time and if you allow it, I'm certain you will too."

"I had a great time with my son at your campsite last year. I'm sure we will this year, too. It's just the roughing it that makes me a little nervous."

"Don't worry about it. Bring an air mattress to sleep on and leave the rest to Peter and me."

"Do you sleep on a mattress?"

"You bet I do. I'm not sure why, but the ground has gotten a lot harder over the last thirty years." We both laughed but the boys looked on not understanding the joke.

"I'll survive and I know the boys will have a good time. Come on, I'll introduce you and Peter to the rest of the team."

Including Peter, there were nine boys. Perfect! He was the youngest and obviously the smallest. The rest were seven to nine and one ten-year-old. Five of the boys knew Peter. The other three boys started laughing at Peter's size, but Bobby stepped up and said, "He may be small, but he's a better player than any of you. If you want to laugh at his size, wait until after the game. Then if you still want to laugh, go ahead." The other four boys that knew Peter, stepped next to Bobby and agreed. The remaining three stopped laughing.

Harvey, from the sports store, walked up to us. He asked if I'd mind if he joined me in the stands. Since I didn't know anybody, I welcomed his company. "How's the jockstrap working out?" Harvey wanted to know.

I laughed. "He hates it. It's the craziest thing he's ever seen or worn. He had a lot of questions about it and his own anatomy, but it's a perfect fit."

He let out with a booming laugh. "Glad I could help."

After a half-hour of warm-ups, the game started. Fred's team was up to bat first. The first boy struck out, one hit a fly ball and was out, two hit singles and were on base when Peter was up. I could see he was extremely nervous, forgot to choke up and was unable to concentrate on the ball. Everybody in the field moved in. Three pitches and he was out. He was close to tears, but I stayed put. Before the game,

I devised a hand signal for 'I love you.' As he ran onto the field, he looked at me, the tears an eyelash away. I gave him the signal. He gave me a smile. He was ready.

Harvy noticed my signal and Peter's reaction. "What did you signal to him, if you don't mind me asking?"

"I told him, 'I love you.' Sometimes that's all kids need to know." Harvey nodded and smiled. The game continued.

Peter played second base. The first ball hit was a line drive to the shortstop, Bobby, and the batter was called out. The second ball was a grounder to Peter. I held my breath. He caught it, but then he forgot what to do with it. The batter was safe on first base. Some of the people in the stands were starting to laugh, along with members of the other team. A couple kids on his team were angry. Bobby went over to Peter, and put his arm around his shoulder like a big brother. Peter smiled a little and the game continued.

The next ball was another grounder to Peter. It took a bad bounce in front of him and went over his head. An average sized six-year-old would have had it, but he was too short. People in the stands and the other team laughed harder. Many kids would have gotten mad at that point; but rather than anger, I saw determination on Peter's face. The runner on first base made it to third, but the batter stopped on first.

The next batter also hit a grounder to Peter. (They had his number.) But this time it didn't work. He caught it, stepped on second and made a perfect throw to first. Both the runner and the batter were out and the side was retired. Peter had made a double play, and suddenly nobody was laughing.

"Wow!" exclaimed Harvey. "What a play! Your grandson may be little, but he sure has an arm." Then he yelled, "Great play, Peter!" As Peter ran off the field, he smiled at both of us and gave me the 'I love you' signal.

Harvey looked at me, smiling. "That's quite a boy you have there, Jake. Of course, I'd say he has a damn good grandpa, too."

Going into the third inning, it was still a scoreless game. Was this normal for a little league game? I didn't know. I hadn't been to a game in thirty years, but these kids on both teams seemed pretty good to me. They made their share of mistakes. Some were preventable. Once, time out was called because a kid running to first base ran out of his right sneaker. Another time, a kid starting out from second tripped over his own untied shoelace. He was on Fred's team and was tagged out. There were kids on both teams with untied sneakers. Peter and Bobby were not among them. Fred once walked toward his team's dugout; but before he got there, Bobby and Peter had taken care of the situation. All sneakers were tied.

Peter was fourth to bat in the third inning. The first two batters were out while the third made it to first base. I excused myself from Harvy and walked over to Peter. "Relax, Funny Face. You've got the other team right where you want them. They know you're up next and they will all move in. Choke up on the bat and keep your eye on the ball. You'll do fine. Now go get 'em, Slugger; and remember, I love you." I stuck a finger into his ribs and he giggled.

The first pitch was high, and the second was low and inside. He let both go by. The third was perfect. He misjudged it and let it go by, also. Strike one! The fourth pitch was high. Ball three! The next pitch was perfect. He swung hard, missed it by several inches and almost fell down in a knotted pile. Strike two! Full count!

People were laughing again. The other team moved in closer. Peter backed away from the plate, frustrated. "Hey, Kiddo, keep your eye on the ball. You can do this. Remember *The Little Drummer Boy?*" He turned around and I wiggled one finger as if it were digging into his ribs. He giggled and stepped up to the plate. Once again he was ready.

The next pitch was a perfect fast ball from a nine-year-old, with Peter's name all over it. Confidence was written over the pitcher's face. Peter stepped into it and connected. It sailed sixty feet over the head of the center fielder who had moved up almost to second base. The ball rolled to the center field fence as Peter took off running. He was so fast he caught up to the kid who had been on first base. He was going to pass him, but we all yelled for him to stay behind the kid. Peter touched home plate one step behind him. The whole team came out, picked him up and threw him in the air, yelling. He ran over to me and jumped into my arms. "Thanks, Jake."

"Hey, you did it. I just reminded you of some things."

I moved back to the bleachers and Harvey. "That was a fantastic hit. His swing is near perfect, but he's so small he's deceiving. What a player you've got there, Jake. But if you don't mind me asking, what did you mean when you said, 'Remember the little drummer boy'?"

"Last Christmas Eve he stood before our church congregation to sing. He was terrified. I told him he could do it. I started singing with him then stopped as he gained more confidence. He finished the song by himself in his beautiful soprano voice."

"I bet he sings like an angel."

"You wouldn't believe." We got back to the game.

That was Peter's first and last home run, and the only legitimate home run of the game; but it was not his last hit. The other team no longer played up on him. His next time up to bat produced a fly ball to left field. The fielder ran back and to his left a few feet and made a good catch. Peter was out, but he started a rally with his home run. By the time the inning was over, the score was five to zero.

In the fifth inning a ball was hit high over Peter's head. He ran back for it. The ten-year-old playing center field ran in for it yelling, 'I've got it.' The two collided and Peter went down hard. It was a home run with two men on base. Meanwhile both boys were down. Peter definitely got the worst of it. Fred, Harvy and I along with the other boy's father ran onto the field. I heard hysterical laughter from some parents of the opposing team. I couldn't believe their rudeness, their uncaring hearts. Both boys were crying, but the ten-year-old was getting up. I looked into Peter's eyes and found them normal. He just had a good shake-up. After a few moments he was up and ready. With tears in his eyes, he said, "That was my fault, wasn't it?"

"Yes it was, Kiddo." He shook hands with the ten-year-old, and apologized. I hoped some were impressed. The game resumed, but his mistake really bothered Peter.

Later that inning with a man on first, a simple fly ball came to Bobby. The ball was ten feet from second base. Peter moved close to Bobby to cover, but didn't interfere. It was an easy catch, but Bobby missed it. He then lost his temper and threw his glove to the ground in disgust. Peter picked up the ball, ran back to second and the runner was out.

Fred walked out to pull Bobby out of the game when Peter went to Bobby's aid with a remark I didn't catch. Soon both boys were ready to play again. It was clear Peter's mistake was behind him.

In the sixth inning, Peter was first up to bat and hit it short to the right fielder who dropped it. He made it to second. The next time up to bat that inning, he made it to third base, primarily because of mistakes in the outfield that let two boys score.

In the seventh and last inning, the pitcher threw a fast ball inside. Peter turned but it still caught him hard in the left kidney. He dropped like a rock. Again there was laughter from the opposing stands. Fred, Harvey and I went to Peter's aid again. I rubbed his back for awhile.

He was soon ready to go and hit a line drive to the pitcher. The boy missed it with his glove and it hit him square in the stomach. The opposing stands booed. Peter ran to first base and turned left toward the mound. He was immediately tagged out by the first baseman. Peter wasn't paying attention to that. "I'm sorry. I didn't mean to do that."

The boy's father was upset at first, but when he saw Peter's genuine concern for his son, he melted. "It's okay, son. He just had the wind knocked out of him. Thanks for your concern."

When I returned to my seat, Harvey looked at me. "Not only is that grandson of yours a great player, Jake, he's a terrific kid." I thanked him again.

The final score was fifteen to eight in favor of Fred's team. The boys on both teams shook hands as they passed. Several congratulated Peter for a good game. Peter had played in his first game and played well. Mistakes not withstanding, we both felt good.

The father of the pitcher and his son, the first man and boy Peter and I met at the field, came up to Peter and me. "I want to apologize for the rude behavior on the part of some of the adults on my son's team. There was no excuse." He looked at Peter. "Peter, right?"

Peter nodded.

"You're a good ball player son, and an even better sportsman."

The boy looked at Peter. "I'm sorry I hit you with that ball, Peter. I didn't mean to but I was afraid of you." Peter's eyes widened. "By then I knew you were the best hitter on the team and I didn't know what to do. I lost control of it."

"Hey, accidents happen. No harm done," Peter said. "Don't worry about it." The father and son shook hands with Peter and me and we rejoined Fred's team.

Afterwards, Fred took the whole team out for pizza. Harvey was invited to join us, but had to get back to the store. He congratulated Peter for a good game then went on his way.

Peter was a little sore both from his collision and from the ball to the kidney, but he was one happy little ball player.

We finally said good-bye to the rest of the team. Fred and Bobby followed us outside, both boys talking about the next day. After some small talk, it was back to the park camp and a warm shower for Peter. He'd begun to itch from his jockstrap.

Once at the shower and out of his clothes, I noticed a distinct rash where the jockstrap was tightest against his skin.

After a hot shower and a thorough drying, he got into a clean pair of shorts. At the campsite he put on his pajama bottoms to allow for plenty of air on the rash. I explained what causes rashes and how the air would help. Then I had him lie down and he napped awhile.

When he awoke, we went fishing for a couple of hours with little success. Peter was improving in the stern but had a long way to go.

After dinner, we talked about the game. He was upset with himself for making a major blunder that allowed three runs to score.

"Hey, Kiddo, this was your first game. I told you, you were going to make mistakes and you did, but you weren't the only one and some of those other kids have been playing for years. Bobby's mistake was worse than yours: Not only did he miss an easy catch, he lost his temper afterwards. If you hadn't moved over to cover, the man on first would have made it to second. You redeemed yourself. What did you say to him?"

"I told him just what you said I should say. It worked."

I smiled. "When you went running out to that downed pitcher, I about busted my buttons with pride. He wasn't your responsibility. He wasn't even your teammate. Do you know you were the only person on your team that went to him?"

"You and Mr. Thomas did."

"I know. I meant of the kids. But speaking of adults. When you were hurt in the outfield and in the batter's box, did any kid or adult for the other team come to you? No, they laughed! You were a bigger person than any of them. You gained a lot of unspoken respect out there, but especially from the pitcher and his father."

"I did?"

"You know it!"

"I didn't do it to get respect."

"I know that. You didn't even do it because you're an angel. You did it because you're a fellow human kid who feels for others." He smiled and cuddled against my chest. "That's another reason I love you so much, Peter. Hey, are you looking forward to tomorrow?"

He sat up excited. "Yeah," he said. "I can hardly wait. Bobby's a neat kid and I like his father too."

"What do you think we should do?"

"Go fishing and swimming! Then we can fish some more and swim some more."

"Sounds good to me. How about if we go into the tent and go to bed?" It was a little after nine. He wouldn't make it much longer.

On the way to the tent, he took my hand. I looked down at him. "You are a little nervous about tomorrow, aren't you?"

"Yeah, I guess so. I want Bobby to like me for other reasons than just because I can throw a ball or because I'm an angel."

"He already does, Kiddo. Tomorrow, just be you. He can't help but like you, okay?"

He nodded. "Jake, I love falling asleep on your lap, but falling asleep next to you in the tent is neat too."

"I like this too." He smiled. And before it left his face, he was asleep. When I took my hand off his chest, he put it back. I said his name softly but he didn't respond.

I was still his deep-down security blanket. He needed me and I needed him, and we both knew it.

CHAPTER SIXTEEN

The next morning at 7:00, Peter came bounding out of the tent unbelievably excited. About five minutes after waking him, Fred and Bobby pulled into our campsite.

Bobby jumped out of the car and ran over to us as excited as Peter. "Hi, Peter. Hi, Mr. Winters. We made it."

"I can certainly see that. Breakfast is just about ready. Peter, why don't you go in and get dressed? Fred, how about a cup of good camp coffee? Then we'll get your car unloaded. Bobby, care for a cup of hot chocolate?" Peter was dressed in a moment and joined the three of us.

After unloading enough for a full regiment on a one-month campaign, I started cooking pancakes over the fire.

After cleanup, we loaded the canoes and headed for the other lake. Fred and Bobby had a problem keeping up with us. Although Peter didn't say a word about it at that time, he noticed they were constantly switching from one side to the other. This is a sure sign the canoeist has no idea what he's doing.

We tried fishing with worms and bobbers but got nowhere fast. We tried various locations and I tried casting, but it was as if fish had left the lake en mass.

We agreed to go swimming. Bobby wanted to know where we changed. "Right here," Peter answered as he removed his clothes. Bobby looked at his suddenly naked friend and then around the lake. He realized we had the lake to ourselves, but he was still nervous. As Bobby slowly removed his underpants, Peter was in his trunks and yelled as he raced across the beach, laughing. When Peter yelled, both Fred and Bobby jumped in surprise. They watched Peter running and screaming, wondering, I'm sure, what was wrong with him. Curiously, Fred stared at his son as if he'd never seen him undressed before. I was puzzled.

"Peter's excited about you two joining us here." As Peter ran back towards us, he did a series of back and front flips.

At Bobby's side he challenged, "Come on. It's fun. Put your trunks on first."

Bobby looked down at himself apparently realizing he forgot something. Once in his trunks, Bobby and Peter tore from one end of the beach to the other. Bobby was limited to somersaults. After about three minutes, I called them back to us. They raced back to me and slid in as if to home plate.

They both lay flat on their backs, out of breath and laughing.

"It's time to swim," I announced.

Peter said, "Jake, can we teach them how to play tag?"

"Sure. It's real simple. When one of the boys is it, all he has to do is touch one of us." Looking at Fred, I added, "but whoever becomes it has to tickle one of them like this." I grabbed Peter and dug in amid squeals and laughter. Bobby started laughing too. "The last one caught is it. What do you think, Bobby? Do you want to play?"

Bobby, still laughing said, "Yeah, that looks like fun. Who's it?"

"I'll be it first. I'll count to ten." Then I charged after the closest one, Bobby, and caught him. I grabbed him and tickled his stomach and ribs as he squirmed, giggled and laughed. I suspected he had never been tickled before. He loved it. I was laughing and looked at Peter. I saw a little disappointment in his eyes, so I put Bobby down and went after Peter who didn't even try to get away. That's all it took. I tickled him a little longer before going after Fred. He was not too competitive, so I soon tagged him.

He was now it. I thought it would be interesting to see how he reacted when he caught his son. He caught me first, then Peter. He tickled him only slightly, not enough to produce a healthy laugh. He then turned to go for his son. When he caught Bobby, he seemed reluctant to tickle him. He tickled him but again it barely produced a laugh.

Bobby was it. He came after me last and I knew why. Before I started again I said, "Fred, both boys love to be tickled. It's fun for them and can be fun for you if you relax and let yourself go. Come on, let's have fun." I deliberately tagged Fred last.

Fred was now it and he went after his son first. Upon catching him he grabbed him from the back and dug his fingers into his ribs. Both laughed like crazy. Then Fred turned him around and hugged him.

Then Fred went after Peter. He responded just as I'd hoped. Fred was learning and both he and the boys loved it.

An hour later the boys had built a castle. They put towels on the ground preparing to lie in the sun. Peter rolled down his trunks to get more sun.

Fred and I headed for the shade. After a minute of silence I said, "You've never tickled your son before have you?"

He said disappointedly, "No, I haven't. You know, he's never even sat on my lap, except last year when you told us Peter's story."

"Well, tonight I'm going to tell another story. Peter's going to be on my lap and I'll guarantee you, Bobby's going to want to be on yours. But you must invite him. If you don't, he probably won't ask. He'll feel funny—you know, kind of out of place."

"How do you know so much about kids?"

"Instinct, I guess." I looked at the boys and said, "Uh-oh, I wonder what that's all about." Fred looked up to see the boys, both with their shorts down in front, comparing each other. Peter looked at Bobby, then at himself and shrugged his shoulders. I watched closely, but soon the shorts were back up and they were both lying back down again.

Fred returned to our conversation. "Jake, do you give Peter baths?"

"Peter washes himself and can wash his hair too, but he always calls me for that. It's one of our many traditions. During shampoos, we talk about anything that comes up or sometimes we have a water fight and laugh. He can also dry himself, but he likes me to. It's tradition. Why do you ask?"

He hesitated. "I've never given Bobby a bath. When Bobby was smaller, my wife always did that."

"That's too bad. You missed a lot."

"I envy the relationship you and Peter have."

I felt sorry for him. "Why don't we eat and go swimming again."

After our swim we dressed and went fishing again, this time with better luck. The boys caught two bass apiece—two to three pounders. They had fun and we had enough for dinner.

"I hope you know how to clean fish," Fred said.

"I'm not very good at it, but Peter is."

Once back at the campsite, Peter removed everything but his underpants and started working. Fred pulled me to one side. "Why does he take most of his clothes off?"

"He gets covered with blood and guts and smells like fish when he's through. So he washes himself several times in the lake. Then I spray him with deodorant to kill the odor. I wash his pants several times too. I put them in a ziploc. The last thing we want is the smell of fish in the tent tonight. That invites a visit from a bear."

Fred looked at me, startled. "Oh! Bears around here?"

"Fred, there are bears all over the park. You never knew that?" He shook his head. "Don't worry. You're becoming a true outdoorsman. As long as you know how to deal with bears, you won't have a problem." Fred looked at me stricken.

When Peter finished, we had eight good fillets. "Wonderful! Where did you learn how to do that?" Fred asked.

"Bill taught me." After washing several times I dried him then sprayed him with deodorant. He put clean clothes on and we were ready to cook. We had a huge dinner of fish, potatoes, baked beans and chocolate pudding for dessert. After dinner we had a terrible cleanup.

When finished it was almost eight, so I had Peter change into his PJ's. Bobby looked at me. "Should I get ready for bed, too?"

"Sure, go ahead."

Just then Peter reemerged from the tent and sat on my lap, clad only in his pajama bottoms. Bobby looked at his dad and Fred nodded. Bobby went into the tent and soon returned to his father's lap, clad in his pajama bottoms. It appeared Fred didn't know quite where to put his hands and looked at me. I had my hands wrapped around Peter with both hands on his stomach, rubbing him gently. Fred did the same. Instantly Bobby put his head back against his father's chest and put his hands on his father's hands. Both father and son looked very satisfied.

"You guys have fun today?" I asked. Both Peter and Bobby smiled broadly and nodded. "What was the best part?"

Playing water tag, they both agreed, but fishing was a close second. Then Bobby added, "But spending the day with my dad was the best part of all." Peter stretched his arms up behind my neck in his traditional way. I knew what he meant and I gently rubbed my hands up and down his ribs. He knew what I meant too.

"I enjoyed it too, son," Fred replied. "Jake and Peter, thanks for inviting us."

"Our pleasure."

"Dad, could we do this again next year?"

"If we're invited, I think so."

It was time to start the story. I decided it might be best to stay with an Indian legend. Peter lasted the entire story, cuddling as soon as it was over.

Both Fred and Bobby looked at him. "Is he asleep already?" Fred asked.

"Oh, yeah. He was basically asleep when I finished the story." I looked down at his peaceful face. I explained what nights were like for him when he was alive. "Now he knows he's safe and with someone who loves him. He goes to sleep fast and he sleeps unbelievably sound."

Bobby looked into the woods then back at his friend. "You mean some mean person could attack him even when he slept?"

"That's right, Bobby. He was never safe, anywhere. But now he's safe everywhere."

Both sat quietly comprehending this. Finally, Fred spoke up, changing the subject. "You know, playing with Peter today...it's just hard to imagine he's an angel. Looking at him now it's a little easier, but..." Fred trailed off.

"I know what you mean. It's much easier for me. I've got a feeling it's easier for Bobby, too." He looked at me and then at Peter and nodded. I rehashed for them the times he rescued me from potentially deadly situations. The assault in the Bronx, they both thought was exciting. I told of several times he rescued other people in addition to Bobby. They wondered how he could have possibly known that Bobby and that Hank were in trouble.

"The best he could explain to me is that out of the blue, he was watching a movie. He could see exactly what was happening and what was going to happen if he didn't act."

Bobby hesitated. "You, you mean he saw me die?"

"That's right, Bobby. He was sitting on my lap and sound asleep, like he is here. Suddenly he was awake and staring at nothing. He said, 'Jake, I'll be right back,' and vanished. Four minutes later he was back, covered in mud and reporting, 'Bobby's, okay now.' He would have left it at that had I not probed. He's not talkative about his exploits."

"He's your guardian angel. Why did he rescue Bobby?" Fred asked.

"He likes both Hank and Bobby a lot. Bobby, you prayed for a miracle when you knew you were about to die. Hank did the same thing. Peter somehow was informed on his built-in screen, saw you were in serious trouble and went to your rescue. Probably the only reason he rescued that little boy in Montana is that we heard of it on the radio. The boy's plight played on Peter's screen. I don't know how else to explain it. Even he can not explain it to his own satisfaction, much less mine."

Fred hugged his son. "I don't understand any of it. But thank God he's here."

"Welcome to the club." I looked at Bobby. "Bobby, you're quite a kid, too. That supposed mistake you made in the game was just what Peter needed to see."

Fred looked at me, confused. "What do you mean, 'supposed mistake'?"

"I was sitting at just the right angle to see everything. Just before the ball came down, Bobby, you glanced at Peter and saw he was coming over to cover. You missed it deliberately, but bumped it towards Peter. He picked it up and easily made the play. Peter, seeing the best player on the team make a mistake, realized mistakes or errors are part of the game—same as they are a part of life. You're okay in my book, kid."

I could see he was embarrassed. "Bobby," Fred said, "I bawled you out for losing your temper. Why didn't you say something?"

He shrugged his shoulders. "I don't know."

Fred hugged Bobby. "I'm sorry, son. I'm proud of you. That was quite a thing you did."

Bobby was still embarrassed but thrilled to receive his father's apology and praise. I could see Bobby was drifting and it wouldn't be long. I studied his face and could tell he was as content as Peter. He was nine and yet it was the first time he would fall asleep on his father's lap. What a shame!

After Bobby was asleep, Fred went on. "You know, seeing Bobby on the beach today—naked—that's the first time I'd seen him naked since he was an infant."

"Yeah?"

"I was uncomfortable at first. I guess I was a little ashamed of myself too. I have always paid attention to Bobby when it comes to sports, even as a little guy. But bathing or cleaning him, I didn't want any part of it." He looked down at his son then at Peter. "Watching these two boys just being little boys on the beach...well, it never occurred to me how free and innocent Bobby is. Today was good for him and it was better for me."

We sat in silence for a minute. "There's something I don't understand. Bobby's a good athlete. He's good at almost all sports. And he's big for his age. Peter is tiny. He's the size of a four-year-old, yet my son can't keep up with him. Peter can hit a ball farther than Bobby. He's got a better arm than Bobby. And he's faster than Bobby."

Fred got specific.

"Last year at the ball diamond, when Peter caught a ball and threw it back to me, I expected him to try and throw it back underhand, like a toddler. When he burned it in overhand, and right on the money, I about fell over. It was easy to understand why the team yesterday grossly underestimated his abilities."

"I know. Think about it, Fred. When Peter was a living child in Slippery Gulch, all he had was enemies. His speed kept him from more than one beating. But his coordination had to be outstanding or his speed wouldn't have helped much. He had no playmates—not one single friend: child or adult. He entertained himself when he wasn't busy trying to stay alive. He'd put up targets in the woods and throw stones at them. He got to the point he'd hit the target almost every time. But he never threw stones at his enemies. Or their properties."

"I wouldn't have been that disciplined. Was he an angel even then?"

"No, he wasn't. Yet from birth he was being prepared for his current existence. His mother told me that. Suffering was an important part of his formation. I don't understand why it had to be so brutal, but it's not up to us to understand."

The next morning Fred and I were out enjoying the peace and quiet of the morning and the camp coffee when Bobby joined us. He appeared to be about half-awake. He headed for a log. Before Bobby had a seat, Fred called him over. Fred had a slight smile on his face, to which Bobby's face brightened into a smile of it's own. Bobby climbed onto his dad's lap. Fred wrapped his arms around his son's girth.

About twenty minutes later, Peter emerged from the tent and staggered towards me. He groaned and seemed to be in agony. Upon reaching me, he said in apparent pain, "Jake, help me," and collapsed across my lap, arms and long hair dangling towards the ground. Both Bobby and his dad were worried. Fred stood up, standing Bobby on his feet, wondering what to do.

I rolled Peter over so his back was bent in an almost impossible position, ribs protruding and said in alarm, "Peter, what's wrong?" Poor Bobby was almost in tears out of concern for his friend.

Struggling to lift his head slightly, he said in a strained voice, "Jake, help me. I can't wake up." He then let his head drop back down. Only then did Fred catch on and he started smiling. Bobby was still in suspense.

"Okay, Peter, I'll help." With that I dug my fingers into his sides producing squeals of joy. I sat him up and continued until he was out of breath. Both Fred and Bobby were now relieved. "You know, Kiddo, you about scared the living daylights out of Bobby and his father."

"I did? I'm sorry."

"Peter and I have developed several traditions over the last year, and one of them is helping him wake up every morning in this fashion. It started that very first morning in Basin. We haven't missed a single day since."

Fred smiled. "Bobby, how would you like to wake up the same way angels do?" It didn't take long for Bobby to get back onto his father's lap. Soon Bobby was sounding much like Peter. Peter and I were laughing with them.

After Bobby regained his breath, he said, "Dad, that was really fun. Could we do that again?"

I smiled and winked at Fred, while he responded, "That was, wasn't it? Yes, we sure can." Fred returned my wink. "Many more times."

Peter smiled over the exchange. He whispered, "Can we talk after they leave?"

"You bet."

After breakfast and clean-up, Peter and I helped them load their gear into their car. I shook hands with Fred. "You know, Jake, Peter—both Bobby and I had a great time. How about two days next year?" Both Bobby and Peter beamed. Peter went up to shake hands with Fred, but Fred picked him up. "Peter, thank you so much for saving my son's life. You gave him back to me, and I never knew I was about to lose him." He then hugged Peter in tears.

Peter walked up to Bobby and shook his hand. Bobby held on and just looked at him. "Thanks, Little Angel. You'll always be my little brother." Bobby gave Peter a big hug.

We were all looking forward to next year together. Thanks to God alerting Peter, Bobby would have a next year.

After they left, it was time to talk. Peter climbed up on my lap and I waited. It didn't take long. "Jake, why doesn't Mr. Thomas love Bobby?"

"What makes you think he doesn't?"

"Well, I guess he does but they're not like you and me. Or at least not until this morning! Did you talk to Mr. Thomas last night?"

"We talked for quite a while. Mr. Thomas never tickled Bobby before yesterday. He hasn't seen Bobby naked since he was a baby until yesterday."

Peter looked at me shocked. "How does he dry Bobby after a bath?"

"He never helped Bobby with a bath or dried him, even when he was a little boy. Bobby's mother did that. Now Bobby is big enough to take care of himself."

"I'm sure glad I'm not that big."

"You are. You can take care of yourself, but neither one of us cares, do we?" Peter smiled but was clearly aghast at hearing all of this.

"Mr. Thomas never did any of the things you do? You're always tickling me or rubbing my back or chest or neck. And we're always laughing and talking. Why do you know how to show your love and Mr. Thomas doesn't; or at least didn't until now?"

"Some men never learned how. Some don't feel comfortable with it."

"I'm sure glad you're not like him. I don't know what I'd do if you were."

"I do. If I were like him, you and I wouldn't be together right now. You need my loving touch. And I need your returned affection and love."

He thought about this. "I guess you're right."

We sat quietly for a couple of minutes. Finally, I picked him up and said, "You know, Kiddo, I like Bobby and his dad a lot, but I sure am glad we aren't like them."

He gave me a hug. "Yeah, me too. Mr. Thomas might love Bobby in his own way, but I like your kind of love" He paused. "I think he's learning how to love Bobby your way now."

"How do you like that? Now you have two big brothers: Bobby and Jamie."

"That's neat."

How about getting dressed? Then we'll get going."

"Okay." He was soon dressed and back at my side. He asked, "Bobby had fun running up and down the beach, didn't he?"

"Did you?"

"Yeah! I always do. I have fun playing in the sand, too."

"I think Bobby had a great time. I think it was good for his father, too, seeing his son playing like a little boy outside of some kind of organized sport."

"I guess." He was deep in thought. "Boy, if you had never seen me naked, I'd be in big trouble."

I chuckled. "Why?"

"Well, just think about it. You taught me how to wash myself in the creek behind Slippery Gulch. And now one of our oldest traditions is you wash my hair and dry me after a bath. After my worst dreams, you washed me. You taught me how to wipe my butt. You taught me how to dress myself and how to put on that dumb jockstrap." I joined him in laughter. "If you'd never seen me naked, I wouldn't know how to do anything."

We both thought about this. Of course, Bobby had a mother where Peter didn't. We agreed it was a shame Fred didn't take as much interest in Bobby as a little boy as he did as an athlete, but maybe now he would.

That morning we went hiking. Well, I was; Peter was running. I covered five miles while he covered more like ten. We were back to the campsite by noon and had lunch before heading over to the public beach. He agreed to ignore Jimmy if he was there.

As it turned out, he was. We went into the bathhouse to change. When we came out we headed for the water. We played for close to an hour, but when we came out, instead of playing in the sand, Peter came up to the adults with me and sat on my lap. He was beat. I told them about my hike and his run. They all laughed but he didn't hear them. He was asleep.

After a half-hour, Peter woke up and of course needed help. I explained our tradition to everybody sitting there and dug in. He squealed, screeched and laughed, to everybody's enjoyment but Jimmy's. Jimmy ignored Peter and wandered off to the beach. His mother then volunteered that Jimmy's father left her when Jimmy was three. Suddenly both Peter and I had a better idea where Jimmy was coming from. She said Jimmy had missed all that Peter and I were enjoying together.

Peter said, "Jake, can we go back in the water and you throw me around?"

"Sure." At the water's edge Peter invited Jimmy to join him in trying to drown me. For the next twenty minutes, I threw both Peter and Jimmy around and tickled them. Both were energized but after twenty minutes, I was beat. On the way back to the adults, Jimmy said, "Mr. Winters, I'm sorry about the other day."

"Thanks, Jimmy. I appreciate your apology." I sat in the chair and Peter was on my lap at once. He sat on my right leg and offered the other to Jimmy. He immediately joined us and soon both boys were leaning back against my chest. My hands resting on their stomachs. It appeared Peter had turned a former enemy into a friend. My six-year-old going on forty was now a gifted child psychologist.

"Hey, Jimmy, let's go back in the lake and swim for a while," Peter said to his new friend. Both boys ran for the lake laughing. I couldn't believe the change in Jimmy. They were two happy boys in the lake having fun. My attention drifted to the adults until I heard Peter yell something. I looked towards the lake to see Jimmy walking out of the lake laughing, while Peter remained in the lake yelling to Jimmy to bring them back. I stood to see Jimmy throw Peter's trunks into a tree laughing, while leaving Peter stranded in the lake. Removing Peter's trunks could have been a little boy prank, but throwing his trunks into the tree was mean.

As I walked toward the lake, towel in hand to rescue Peter, he walked out of the lake toward me. Jimmy's mother, taking in the whole situation, laughed. She was the only adult who saw any humor in the situation.

As I approached Peter, I saw disappointment in his eyes. I wrapped a towel around him, picked him up and walked to the bathhouse. While I did, Jimmy said, "Hey, baby, with the teeny weenie!" Now I saw betrayal in Peter's eyes. He thought he'd made a new friend.

Inside the bathhouse I spotted a broom. I was tempted to break it over Jimmy's head. Peter must have seen it in my eyes because he pleaded, "No, Jake. I'm okay." I exited for the tree and retrieved Peter's trunks. I returned to the bathhouse where Peter put his trunks on.

"Hey, Kiddo, I've got an idea. How would you like to go for some ice cream? Let's go! Just the two of us."

Peter's eyes lit up. "Can we?"

"You bet we can." I took his hand and walked out of the bathhouse. I had told him what to do if Jimmy was still bent on meanness.

Jimmy was waiting for us about twenty feet away. "Hey shrimp, how come your Grandpa's so old and ugly?"

Peter looked at me. "Now?" he asked.

"Now," I said. Peter went over to Jimmy, picked him up with one hand between his legs and the other hand on his chest. He raised him over his head and walked to the shoreline. He threw Jimmy ten feet into the lake, where he landed with a splash and a scream.

Adults cheered while Jimmy's mother jumped up yelling, "What did he do to my Jimmy?"

"He may be little, ma'am, but when he's pushed too far, he's mighty. Lady, you'd better get a big brother to help you with your son, or before long he's going to be doing things a lot worse than picking on little kids." I took Peter's hand. "Come on, Kiddo. Let's go for ice cream."

On the way to the ice cream parlor, Peter said, "Jake, I kind of feel sorry for Jimmy not having a father and all."

"I suppose, but you're in the same boat he is."

He looked at me. "What do you mean?"

"You don't have a father either."

"Yeah, but I have you."

We rode in silence. When he asked why Jimmy acted like that, I said, "I think he's just a mean kid, Peter."

He nodded. "I don't understand it. He seemed so nice when we three played together."

"Yeah, I know. Then jealousy took over. He could have had a real friend in you. He just doesn't know how to behave with self-control long enough to build a friendship. I doubt if he ever had one before."

As we got out of the car at the ice cream shop, he took my hand and said, "I didn't either, but I was never like that."

I squeezed his hand. "I'm sure you weren't, Kiddo. Now you've got so many friends you don't know what to do with them all." I thought for a minute. "You know, Jimmy is the first person you've run into since leaving Slippery Gulch, that has been mean to you."

He nodded. Before we ordered at the outside window, I had him remove his shirt. Ice cream cones, shirts and Peter just didn't mix. Since we were outside, it was okay. Before long, he had a steady stream of melted ice cream running from his chin to his shorts. All I could do was laugh. Some things never change. When finished, I asked the woman for a wet rag. She knew little kids and obliged. Ice cream was now in the band of his shorts and underpants. However, on the way to his shorts, chocolate ice cream collected in his bellybutton. The wet napkin didn't work. It would do until we got back to camp and a Q-Tip.

After pulling into the campsite, I soon had water warming over a freshly lit fire. As I went for my first aid kit, water, towel and washcloth, Peter got out of his sticky clothes. He cleaned the sticky ring on his belly and dried himself. "Put your underpants on and get on the table. It's Q-Tip time."

He started laughing at once. "Time for an operation on your bellybutton, Funny Tummy." The warm, wet Q-Tip did its job quickly.

"Peter, let me ask you something. Do you think I'm too old to be raising you like a son?"

"No, Jake. You're just right. I don't think about age—either yours or mine. We both stay the same, don't we?"

I decided not to continue in that direction at this time, so we went canoeing. I gave Peter a chance to practice the stern. Although he was improving, he decided if we were going down to the far lake, it would be best if I took the stern. The tremendous frustration he suffered a year ago after trying the stern no longer existed.

After dinner we sat by the fire and read for a while, before our nightly talk. He changed into his pajamas and climbed on my lap. We talked about our day and about Jimmy until 8:30 when I said, "Hey, let's go to bed."

He looked at his watch. "Why? It's only 8:30."

"These bugs are killing me." They never bothered him. "I think we'd better turn in together. Is that okay with you?"

"Yeah!" He jumped off my lap, helped me up and then started pulling me toward the tent. I got ready for bed and we crawled into my bag next to his. He rested his head on my arm, and I wrapped my arm around him so I could stroke his chest.

"Jake, when you go out with your friends, do you ever talk about me?"

"Yes. Sometimes! They want to know why you're so ugly in the morning."

He giggled. "They do not."

"Actually most of them ask if I've smacked you around lately."

"They do not...come on, Jake."

"I'm teasing." I looked at my watch. "Hey, Funny Face, it's almost nine. Time for you to go to sleep."

"Okay. Thanks for coming to bed with me tonight."

"Sure! Hey, something just reminded me: tomorrow morning we take showers."

"Oh, Jake, do I have to?"

"Didn't your mother tell you there's nothing worse than a dirty, stinky little angel?" He chuckled, took my hand, squeezed it gently and was soon asleep.

CHAPTER SEVENTEEN

The next morning while enjoying my book and a cup of coffee under a cloudy sky, Peter emerged from the tent and headed for me, more asleep than awake. "Hey, Funny Face, you sure stink this morning." The ray of sunshine I got from his smile was bright enough to cast a shadow. He crawled up on my lap and curled into a little ball. I put one hand on his bare back and the other on his head and rubbed both. "You know, Kiddo, I don't know why I was lucky enough to be chosen as your guardian, but I'm sure glad I was."

"It wasn't luck, Jake. You're the nicest guy in the whole world."

"Ah-uh! You're buttering me up because you don't want to take a shower this morning."

He sat up giggling and said, "How did you know?"

"You're a little stinker!" I dug my fingers into his torso. After giving him time to get his breath back, I had him get dressed. I gathered the stuff we needed for a shower then we went into town for breakfast.

During breakfast, I reminded him we had two days left. "These two days belong to you. What do you want to do?"

"Jake, it seems like we just got here."

"Hey, when you're having fun, time flies."

"I know. Could we go up in the plane with Sam today?"

"We can see if he's available. If not we could go up with someone else."

After warm showers, we drove to Long Lake and to the seaplane company. As we walked into the office, we were instantly recognized. "Well, if it isn't Grandpa and Grandson Peter, I think." Sam's mother was just as pleasant as she was last year.

We both smiled broadly. "Is Sam flying today?" Peter asked.

"I remember you had a good time with him last year." Peter nodded smiling broadly. "Well, honey, you just missed him, but he should be back in fifteen minutes. Would you like to wait or go up with someone else?"

Peter turned to me, but there was no doubt what he wanted to do. "We'll wait," I said. We spent our time talking to Sam's mother. Peter told her some of the things we'd done since we last saw her. He also told her about his first ball game. He never mentioned how well he played or that he hit the only home run of the game. But he told her about his huge mistake.

"We all make mistakes from time to time, but I bet you played pretty good, didn't you?"

"Yeah, okay, I guess."

"Now wait a minute, Kiddo. I've got to step in here for a minute. Peter's not a bragger and I'm proud of him for that, but he played a lot better than just okay. He made that one mistake and a few others too. But he made a lot of darn good plays. And he hit the only legitimate home run of the game."

"Fantastic! I knew I had you pegged right. You're a remarkable child. It's good to tell the facts, but it's not good to brag. Let someone else do that for you. Your grandpa's a good bragger for you. Grandpas get bragging rights." She looked at me. "Maybe I shouldn't ask, but why haven't we got our front teeth yet?"

I thought to myself, "Lady, you got yours, so mind your own business." I decided to give her a truthful answer and see what happened. "Mrs. Silverton, Peter is not my grandson. In fact, he's no relation whatsoever." That perplexed her. She looked at me no doubt wondering if I was a kidnapper. "He's my guardian angel. However, he's in a mortal body because of a final prayer he uttered seconds before his father murdered him in 1901." It was obvious she wasn't expecting this. I went through his abbreviated story, realizing she didn't believe a word of it.

"I see you'd like some proof. Peter, fade out slowly for Mrs. Silverton, then fade back in." I thought she was going to faint. "He may be an angel, but when he's in his mortal body as he is now, he's as mortal as you and I."

"So this explains why he's a perfect child."

"He's not the perfect child. He misbehaves from time to time. Sometime he doesn't always listen. I even spanked him once."

"You spanked an angel?"

Peter smiled. "No," I said. "I spanked the little boy who was misbehaving. And I'll do it again if need be. When he's in his mortal body, as he is now, he's a normal little boy. But, Mrs. Silverton, I'd suggest you keep this to yourself. Nobody would believe you anyway."

"Yes, I can see you're right. It's hard to believe…even though I've seen the proof. There will be no charge today! How can I charge for flying an angel? Of course, if he wanted to, he can fly on his own, right?"

"In a sense, yes. But it's not the same. Also, you're not charging an angel. You're charging a little boy and his grandpa, right?"

"Oh yes, that's right. Somehow it just doesn't seem right."

"How much is it this year?"

"Same as last year, thirty dollars for the two of you," she winked, "for the fifteen minutes."

I took out my wallet and handed her the money. "Here, this is a tip for your kindness."

As she accepted the money she said, "You're both sweethearts."

Just then we heard a man's voice say, "Hey, there's my man, Peter." We turned around to see Sam entering the office with a big smile. "You ready to do some serious flying, little man?"

Peter said, "Yep, I sure am. And this year I won't be scared."

"Ah, you weren't scared that much last year. Just when we took off, as I remember." He looked at me. "I didn't mean to ignore you, Mr. Winters, but it's hard not to ignore others when Peter's around." He shook my hand. "How are you?"

"I know what you mean. Just fine, Sam. And how is everything with you?"

"Couldn't be better. I'm getting married in October."

"Hey, that's great! I hope you've had her up a time or two."

"Sure have, and I told her about Peter. If we have a son, I want him to be like Peter." He ruffled his hair. "Well, what do you think? Let's take off."

"Wait a minute," Peter said, as he went running off to the men's room.

We both laughed. "I guess he made quite an impression on you last year."

"Actually you both did, Mr. Winters. When I'm a father, I hope I can be just half the dad you are to Peter."

"Wow, Sam! I don't know what to say, except thanks."

Peter bounded out the door. "Now I'm ready. The main vein has been drained." The two of us laughed a while over that one.

"Hey, you guys. What's going on?" Sam's mother asked from the office.

"Guy talk, mom. See you later."

As we walked to the plane, I asked, "Same plan as last year?"

"Why not? It worked."

As Peter crawled into the back seat and strapped himself in, he said, "You saw us on the mountain the other day, didn't you Sam?"

"Sure did, little man. At first I thought somebody was in trouble. That's when I buzzed you. I saw you sitting on your grandpa's shoulders as I did a fly by. I thought it was neat, but my passenger wasn't impressed." Peter and I laughed.

Soon we were in the air and Peter moved up to my lap. The flight was to be another long one, but it didn't work out that way. About twenty minutes into it, the engine started sputtering. Both Sam and I exchanged worried looks. Peter calmly stared out the windshield at nothing. One more person was about to realize Peter's secret identity. Smoke began pouring from the engine. Sam was sweating. "It's the oil," he volunteered.

"I'll be right back," Peter said. "Once the pressure comes back, take us down." Sam started to say something, but before he could, Peter was gone. Sam turned cloud white.

"Trust me, Sam. Do as he says." Sam was in near shock. Suddenly the smoke stopped, and the oil pressure returned to normal. Sam looked at me dismayed—then back at the gage. and started down. The landing was a little rough on a lake.

"What is that kid?" Sam finally spouted, turning off the engine.

"He's an angel, Sam. He's my guardian angel." Suddenly Peter was standing on the pontoon outside my door, covered with oil.

I opened my door. "What happened, Kiddo?"

"An oil line disconnected. It's okay now. I'm sorry I got my clothes so oily, Jake."

Sam sat staring with his mouth open.

"Hey, we're down safe. Don't worry about it. Leave your sneakers and socks here, then go down to the bottom of the lake. Get out of them down there and rub dirt over them. You may get most of the oil out." He jumped off the pontoon and vanished. I called after him, "Peter, don't stay too long."

Recovering himself, Sam muttered, "This lake is seventy feet deep here." I smiled that Peter's feats are astonishing at times. Sam said, "Are you sure Peter's okay?" About then, Peter surfaced and handed me his dripping clothes, mostly free of oil. I wrung them out and put them on the dashboard of the plane in the sun. They'd be dry in minutes. Then he climbed up on my lap again as if nothing had happened.

Sam said, "You're serious. He's an angel."

"I'm dead serious. He was last year too, but neither one of us knew it. We thought he was a ghost. But Sam, I wouldn't tell anybody about this. Nobody will believe you and it could hurt your business."

He agreed. "So in his mortal body he's just a boy—a really neat kid," I explained.

Sam, still not quite all there, changed the subject. "When we get back, would both of you be willing to meet my future wife?"

"Can I put some clean clothes on first?"

We both laughed. "I think that would be a good idea, Funny Face."

"Peter, will it start and will it fly?" Sam asked.

"Sure, but when we get back, you better check the oil."

"Oh, by the way, your mother knows about Peter. While we were waiting for you, she wondered why his teeth hadn't grown in, so I told her. Sam, right now he's not an angel.

He's a normal little boy and he loves and needs what all little boys need: love, affection, attention and some tickling. Like this:" Peter squealed and squirmed as we joined him in laughter.

I removed his shorts from the dashboard. They were almost dry. As Peter slipped into them, Sam said, "Well let's give it a try." Soon the engine was humming and the oil pressure was close to normal. Before long we landed on Long Lake.

"Would you stay with Peter for a few minutes while I get him some clean clothes from the car?"

"Only if I can tickle him."

Peter giggled. "I think that was a yes. I'll just be a few minutes." As I walked away from the plane, I heard Peter squeal. Sam was apparently looking forward to fathering a son.

As Peter was getting into clean clothes, Sam checked the engine, and called his mechanic to come over. Sam then told his mother what happened. Her mouth dropped. "Merciful Heavens!" She came out from behind the counter and hugged Peter. "You *are* an angel." She darted behind the counter. She pressed my thirty dollars into my hand and grew insistent.

"Come on you guys. I want you to meet someone else who's special to me." We walked two blocks and entered a small office to be greeted by a very attractive receptionist. As we approached the desk, Sam said, "Jan, I want you to meet Mr. Winters. Remember? The man with his grandson, Peter Stevenson. This is my wife-to-be in eight weeks, Jan Mitchell."

She extended her hand to us. "I've heard so much about you two. But Sam, you never said how cute Peter is."

"I sure did," Sam protested.

"You said he was cute, but he's beautiful. Look, it's lunch time. Would you two be able to join us?"

We went outside and waited for Jan. "Can I tell *her* about Peter?" Sam asked.

"I wouldn't. Maybe someday, but not now." Sam smiled like a happy groom to be.

CHAPTER EIGHTEEN

After lunch and saying good-bye to Sam and Jan, Peter and I walked past the public beach on our way back to the car. Jimmy and his mother weren't there, but Darlene and her mother were. We'd met Darlene and Paula here last year. Darlene was a seven-year-old little beauty in her pink bikini, thanks to her eye-catching mother, Paula, in her early thirty's. Her blond hair complimented her yellow bikini handsomely.

Peter had loved showing off for Darlene by swinging out on the rope and diving in. That evening they had visited our campsite. It was then we discovered that Paula's son, Teddy, a year younger than Darlene, died six months earlier of Leukemia. With Peter's help, Teddy was able to assure his mother and sister that he was in a better place.

"Hey, Kiddo, would you like to say hello to Darlene and her mom?"

He studied them lying in the sun on the dock. So I studied them, too. "Yes, I would. I hope they're doing better than last year. But can we get changed first?"

Soon we were dressed, Peter in his new, flashy trunks. About ten feet from them Peter handed me his towel and started running toward the end of the dock. Passing beside them, he screamed and jumped for the rope. However, he misjudged his speed and missed it, he and his scream vanishing below the deck of the dock.

Paula and Darlene instantly shot up as a screaming little banshee shattered their peace.

I couldn't contain myself. They both turned around. "Jake," Paula said. Now laughing, she asked, "Was that Peter?"

Still laughing, I nodded. "He wanted to surprise you. I guess he did." As I walked past them with a greeting, I said hello to both and at the end of the dock, looked down. Peter was treading water. "I think you missed."

Giggling he said, "I know. Could you help me up?"

I lifted him to the dock, pulled his trunks up the two inches and then dried him. Peter went to Darlene and I went to Paula. They were now on their feet. I gave Paula a hug. "How are you two doing?"

"Much better than last year, thanks. We're both coping pretty well. We're so grateful to you both."

"Happy to help. Hey, how about you two joining Peter and me for dinner tonight at the campsite? Nothing fancy, but we've got plenty of food."

"I have a better idea. How about you two joining us at the restaurant in Blue Mountain? That way there'll be no cooking and clean-up—just uninterrupted conversation."

"That sounds great but I'll treat."

"No you won't. My treat! Take it or leave it."

Paula was a beautiful woman, but young enough to be my daughter, darn it. I enjoyed her beauty and her charm. I laughed. "Okay! You win. But I better check with Peter first." I turned around. "Peter, would you be interested in dining with these two beautiful ladies tonight?"

Both kids displayed radiant smiles. "Sure, but I haven't been in the lake yet. Well, not the way I meant to anyway."

"It's only two o'clock. We have a few hours. Hey, why don't you and I change places for a few minutes? I'd like to talk to that little beauty for a few minutes." Darlene giggled and blushed.

I sat across from Darlene. "Darlene, you're just as cute this year as you were last year...maybe even a little cuter." She flashed me her blushing smile again, missing some teeth other than her front teeth. "So you're eight this year, going into the third grade?" She nodded. "I bet you have lots of boyfriends."

She giggled. "None as sweet as Peter. He's my favorite. He reminds me of Teddy."

"How did the year go for you?"

"Pretty good. But I still miss Teddy." I nodded as she paused. "I think he's still with us, Mr. Winters. Sometimes I can feel him."

I didn't know what to say. I was saved by Peter. "Grandpa, can Darlene and I go off the rope?"

I stood relieved. "Sure, go ahead." Paula and I walked to the edge of the dock to watch. Peter went first. Grabbing the rope, he ran to the end of the dock, swung out and let go a good dive into the lake. Darlene followed and repeated Peter's dive. The two met in the water and swam back to the dock together. Paula and I helped the two kids up.

Paula and I stood talking as the kids got ready to repeat the dive. Darlene went first as Peter patiently waited his turn. He stood with his arms bent at the elbow, his hands in fists under his chin. Darlene went in with a small splash and a perfect dive. "Peter hasn't changed at all since last year. Shouldn't he have his front teeth by now?"

"He has a condition that won't allow him to grow."

"Oh? What condition is that?"

"Paula, maybe we should sit down." As we sat the kids walked by for another run. I decided to call them both over to sit on our laps. Darlene had already asked Peter the same question. So Peter answered it as I would. Darlene accepted it, Paula didn't.

"Ladies, Peter is a mortal right now." Paula looked puzzled. Darlene looked on with interest. "Most of the time he's just like us, but when necessary he changes into something else." Now both females were confused. "In 1901, Peter was murdered by his father. That's why he hasn't grown—he can't. He's dead."

Paula said, "Wait a minute. Are you saying Peter's a ghost?" Suddenly, Darlene looked at Peter with a trace of fear in her eyes.

"We thought he was, but in June we found out he's something else. On June 30, Peter had his second funeral in one hundred one years." I explained the reasons for it. "Except this time he walked away from the grave. Peter is an angel. He's my guardian angel. I'm privileged to be his mortal guardian as long as he's in his body like now."

Darlene relaxed, but Paula was skeptical. She looked from Peter to me. Understandably she couldn't accept what I was saying. "Jake, I admit that Peter is as cute as I would picture an angel to be, but…"

"Last year when Peter let his body convey Teddy's voice, that really was Teddy. Because Peter is a messenger of God —that's what the word angel means—you heard from your son who is more alive than ever with God."

Paula appeared to be in near shock. Darlene, as a typical kid said, "Cool."

"Jake, I don't know whether to believe you or not."

Peter was sitting against my chest with my back to the other swimmers so he could not be seen. "Peter, why don't you fade out slowly then back in again?"

He did as I requested. Paula put her right hand over her mouth as if to stifle a scream. Darlene sat composed and smiled. "I knew all along Peter was different. But I didn't know how. You really are an angel, aren't you?" Peter nodded modestly.

He changed the subject. "Jake, can we go swimming again?" The two kids stood up in anticipation, so Paula and I gave the okay.

"Jake, this isn't some kind of a cruel trick, is it?"

"Paula, believe me. I would never do anything like that. Who am I to make Peter disappear?"

She looked at me hard. "I believe you! But how? How can this happen? If Peter's dead, how can he have a mortal body? Last year when he sat in his pajamas, I noticed he has all the parts that a little boy should have…so I don't understand any of it."

As the kids swam I explained everything to Paula. "Please remember, before anything else, he's a little boy that loves and needs love. He eats and sleeps like everyone else. He can be hurt both physically and emotionally just as we can. Sometimes he misbehaves and has to be punished. As a little boy he has mischief in his eye just as Teddy did at times, I'm sure."

Memories came rushing back to her as she smiled. "Jake, is Teddy an angel, too?"

"As a living child, Peter suffered terribly since his birth. He had to. It was his preparation for what he was to become. It was a test. I don't mean to burst your bubble, but I doubt it. Yet who am I to say? Like you, I'm a mere mortal, but know the angels played a role, especially the night Jesus was born. And at other times, too—throughout the Jewish and Christian Bibles."

"I'm not too familiar with any of that. Christmas I know about. I know about the angels and shepherds and the wise men," Paula said wistfully.

"By the way, Paula, Darlene is a wonderful child. She's well adjusted. You could have mourned Teddy's death all year and completely ignored her, but you didn't. That's obvious. If you had, you may have lost both your children. I have no doubt it was a rough year, but you rose to the occasion. I have a great deal of admiration for you."

She had tears in her eyes. "Thank you, Jake. That means so much to me." She leaned over and kissed my cheek. "Are you an angel, too?"

I laughed. "Oh no. Peter's the only angel around here. Hey, how about if we join them?"

"Wait! One more question. If Peter is dead he will never grow, correct?"

"That's right. It explains why he's just as he was last year. For instance, he's had only one haircut, to balance things out. He'll never have another."

"Oh, I never thought about that."

"He has grown, though not physically. He has matured emotionally and as a student, exceptional student at that. I'm sure you'll notice as we spend more time together."

The four of us spent the next hour romping in the water together. We had a great time.

As we relaxed on the beach, Peter came up on my lap as Darlene came to Paula's. Peter was soon asleep. "Boy that was fast," Paula said.

"He has the strength and coordination of a ten-year-old, but the body of a young four-year-old. Like a four-year-old, almost every day he needs a nap to restore his energy."

Peter awoke in about fifteen minutes. Paula suggested we change and head for Blue Mountain for dinner. So Peter and I followed them.

We enjoyed our dinner and the visit, but during dessert, I noticed both Darlene and Paula's anxiety. While waiting for our bill, Darlene asked Peter if Teddy was with us. Peter shrugged his shoulders.

Once at the campsite, Peter changed into his pajamas while I started a fire. I set up chairs for Paula and myself. Peter came up on my lap as Darlene went to her mother's. Peter soon began fiddling with the right leg of his pajamas bottoms, though Darlene and Paula hardly noticed.

Peter seemed to grow anxious about something. Finally he said, "Teddy is not coming." He was looking up at the stars overhead in a perfectly clear night sky.

"You mentioned Teddy just now," Paula stated with an eager look of anticipation.

Before I could reply, Peter made a prayer aloud: "Please, God, let him come back to say good-bye again."

We all sat in stunned silence for I don't know how long. Peter grew calmer. He stopped playing with his pajamas. Then he spoke in his own voice. "'Be still, and know that I am God.'"

Paula gasped, "Peter is God!"

I waited until she got her composure. "No Paula, God is God. Peter is an angel. However, I think he has just brought us a message from God. If I'm not mistaken, that is a quotation from the Book of Psalms. I'm not mistaken." Paula's expression morphed from one of disappointment to one of anticipation and back to disappointment.

Darlene sat contented that she had just heard a word from God through an angel. Sitting on her mother's lap, she was not in a position to see her mother's facial changes.

Paula asked, "What exactly does that mean, Peter, 'Be still, and know that I am God'?"

Peter replied, "I wanted to help you hear from Teddy again, but God has spoken instead. I guess he wants us to be quiet for awhile.

And we were, for the better part of an awkward fifteen minutes. Well, it was awkward for Paula and me.

Then Darlene spoke. "Mom, I think it means that God doesn't think we need to hear from Teddy to feel better. Instead, He can comfort us himself."

I was glad that Darlene said it, because she said it better than I could have.

"Maybe we need to be still and put our trust in God more than Peter, who's just one of his messengers. Does that make sense, Jake?" Paula asked.

I nodded, and did not put in words what I was thinking: Out of the mouths of babes...

Paula spoke. "I have to admit. I have been angry with God...well, that silence. Somehow in that silence, a peace came over me. I think it was a peace from God. Darlene, when I was your age, my parents had me in church. I got little out of it. I have never wanted to put you through that. I think I have been wrong. Next Sunday we are going to go looking for a good church until we find one that we like. I want to promise that here and now."

"Thank you, Mom. Some of the girls at school began to invite me to their church after Teddy died. But I said we were not into church."

"Peter, thank you for your good intentions. I'm glad God overruled you."

"You are welcome."

CHAPTER NINETEEN

Peter joined me at the fire at 7:15 the next morning. "Good morning, Funny Face. How are you this morning?" He came up on my lap without a word or a smile. Something serious was coming. He pulled at his pajama bottoms. I rubbed his back. Finally he asked, "Jake, do you think God is mad at me?"

"Let me ask you one right back. Do you think I'm mad at you?"

"No. Because when you say no, you always give me a reason. But God just ignored my prayer and didn't give a reason."

"You will find Little Angel, that God has his own reasons. The older I get, the more I find I just take what he dishes out without a lot of questions. Maybe I've learned what my church tried to get into my head when I was a kid."

"What's that?"

"To be quiet and know who's God and who isn't."

"I think Paula learned that last night, don't you?"

"I sure do. And all thanks to you."

"Not really. You know who."

"Hey, what do you want to do today?"

He thought about this. "How long are they going to be here?"

"Another four days. They're going back to the beach today and invited us over, but I told them today is our last day and the day belongs to you."

He thought about that. "They're awful nice. It's fun playing with Darlene. She's like a sister. Let's go back to the beach. Can we go down to our lake this morning then go over in the afternoon?"

"I don't see why not but we'll have to move." After waking him, he dressed then we ate a quick breakfast and left for our lake. The fish were nonexistent so we headed for our beach. As we were both changing into our trunks, I said, "I can see you enjoy playing with Darlene. She's a lot nicer than Jimmy, isn't she?"

"Yeah, that's for sure. I don't have to worry about her beating me up or taking my trunks. And she is fun to play with even though she's a girl."

Once in the lake he jumped on my back and tried to dunk me. It didn't work. Instead, I gave a nasty laugh and dunked him. He came up laughing and the fun began.

After an hour of water fun, we headed back to our campsite to gather a few things and head for the public beach. We found the ladies in their beach chairs on the beach. As soon as they saw us coming, they developed huge smiles and greeted us, but Darlene didn't wait for us to get there. She ran to us giving Peter a big hug.

As I approached Paula, I felt something surge in my heart. Then in Paula's eyes, I saw the same something reflected back to me. It was the look a woman would give her much-missed father. The feeling I had was more of a father greeting a long-absent daughter. So I gave Paula a hug.

"Paula, I said last night that today is our last day. My grandniece's birthday party was to be tomorrow, but my sister called last night. My niece has to work tomorrow and the weekend so the party is postponed. We have six extra days. Tomorrow we're going to move to the campgrounds in Old Forge and stay there until Monday morning. Then we'll leave for the party.

"Wednesday afternoon we'll go over to the Water Park for four hours then return Thursday for the day. I called the campsite last night and made all the arrangements. We've driven past the park several times—Peter all wide-eyed, but he's never asked to go in. He doesn't know a thing about any of this. So tomorrow morning, he's going to think we're heading to Rochester for a birthday party."

"Oh, how neat, Jake."

"He's been in a canoe and a thirty-foot yacht but never on a ship. Friday we're going on a lake cruise. Saturday I'll take Peter on his first train ride."

"Oh, Jake, he's going to be so surprised. You're quite a guy."

"Thank you. Now tell me: Would you two care to join us on Thursday?"

"I don't think we should. For two reasons: Do you have any idea what the cost is for an adult and a child?"

"It's $23.95 for an adult and $19.95 for a child. But for you two it's free."

"Oh, Jake, we can't accept that. But that's so kind of you. Besides, I think you and Peter should enjoy your time together, alone."

"Don't worry about that, Paula. We both enjoy both of you. I'd be glad to pay for Darlene's way if you prefer."

"You're very sweet, Jake, but I can't even allow you to do that."

"It would be my pleasure."

"Thanks again, but I think it best you and Peter spend that time together. Then Friday we're leaving. So how did you spend the morning?"

"The whole day was his choice. We spent all morning at our lake, but I'm glad he chose to spend the afternoon here. I think he has a thing for Darlene."

Paula laughed. "I guess she could not do better than having eyes for an angel." After a laugh, she turned serious. "I'm glad both of you came."

I looked at her, concerned. "Paula, are you going to be okay?"

"Believe me Jake, both of us are fine. Teddy's been gone for eighteen months. There were some real tough valleys during that time. But Darlene and I were there for each other. We're both survivors."

"Paula, if I'm sticking my nose in a place it doesn't belong, tell me. Have you been getting support from your family?"

"I have a sister who's been wonderful through all of this. But she lives in California. So we talk once a week. Mother was killed in an accident five years ago, and I may have told you my father died of cancer when I was young.

"My former husband is completely out of the picture. I made a mistake. When we got married, I was eight months pregnant with Darlene. A year after Teddy was born, my husband left me for another woman. He didn't want anything to do with his children or me and gave up his parental rights at the divorce. He pays child support, because he's forced to.

"He knew Teddy was sick so when he died, I called him." She choked up. I put a hand on her shoulder. "His reply was, 'Oh. Now I can save 50% on my support payments.' I told him when and where the funeral would be then hung up before I could go off on him.

"I called his parents because I doubted he would. Teddy was their only grandson. Their reaction was sort of, 'Well, what do you expect us to do about it?' Again, I hung up and have not had any contact with any of them since."

"So none of them came to the funeral?"

"No, not one. Didn't even send a card." Her tears flowed now. "I don't understand how a father can have such little interest in his own offspring."

My mind flew to Peter's father, but decided not to remind her of it. I suddenly understood the feelings I had when Peter and I first walked up to her. I also understood the look on her face at the same time. I was her father figure.

I smiled then looked away at the kids. They were both lying on towels on their backs. Their legs were facing away from us. Peter was wearing his jockey trunks. While Paula and I were talking, Peter had rolled his trunks down to his traditional low level. On our lake where it was private, that was fine. But on a public beach it was totally inappropriate.

"Peter!" He rolled onto his belly and looked at me. By my tone, he knew there was a problem. "Come here." Darlene sat up with interest. He stood up and I rolled his trunks up two rolls so his trunks were where they were supposed to be. "You should know better than that."

He put his head down and sat back down. After a moment of remorse he asked if he and Darlene could go swimming."

I looked at Paula. She nodded. "Sure, go ahead."

"Can you two come with us?"

"Give us a few minutes." Peter and Darlene were off.

"I thought you might punish him."

"I just did. He realized he disappointed me. That's the one thing he never wants to do."

"That's amazing. Teddy was a very sensitive child, too. And he was not the least bit modest about his body either. Darlene used to be that way, but she's grown out of it. Peter never will, will he?"

"I don't imagine so. He's been six for one hundred two years and always will be. His innocence will always remain.

You know, when he was alive and after he'd escaped from his father, some older boys in Slippery Gulch would force him to run through town naked while hitting him with sticks. His body was terribly scared from rope damage, and leprosy had deformed his body. So as he ran, the entire town would watch, laugh and point at the town freak."

Tears formed in Paula's eyes.

"The first time I bathed him in the creek behind Slippery Gulch, I didn't realize any of this. I learned later he feared I was going to laugh at him. If I would have, I would never have seen him again. Of course I saw nothing to laugh at. After his bath, I dried him. The entire episode was an extremely tender scene for both of us. As a result, washing his hair and drying him after a bath or swimming is a strong and meaningful tradition for both of us. Because of not laughing at his nudity, he's very comfortable with his body—sometimes a little too comfortable."

She laughed. "Jake, at his age and size, there's nothing wrong with innocence. I hope he never changes. Last year when we stopped at your campsite unexpectedly, he was wearing his favorite pajamas. Teddy had a similar pair. They never fit right and were revealing. I was embarrassed and uncomfortable with them, but he loved them. It was Teddy and it is Peter.

"Another similarity between the two boys is both are small for their age." She pulled out several pictures from her purse. I saw a cute, blond-haired boy, the hair covering most of his ears. One picture showed Darlene and Teddy sitting on a couch. Darlene was in a nightgown while Teddy sat in his pajama shorts—no shirt. Someone had tucked in his pajamas. I laughed and a chill shot down my spine. The resemblance between Teddy and Peter was uncanny.

I called Peter over and had him look at a picture. "Peter, do you recognize this little boy?"

He looked at several. "Sure! That's Teddy." I showed him the rest of the pictures. When he saw the picture of Darlene and Teddy, he said, "Hey, he has my pajamas on." He looked at the picture more closely. "No, he doesn't. The red design is airplanes, not trucks. Can you two go in the lake with us?"

I looked at Paula for confirmation. She nodded.

Well, that was that. For the next hour or so we played with them in the water. Then it was time for Peter to rest and recharge. I dried him and sat him on my lap. He was soon asleep.

Darlene had observed all of this in silence. Now she said, "I wish I had a grandpa like you. Peter's lucky."

I looked at her. "Thank you, Darlene. And if I ever have a granddaughter, I'd want her to be as sweet as you."

When Peter awoke he said, "Jake, can Darlene and I go out to the rope now?"

"Not without us." After both kids made several dives, Peter decided it was showoff time again. He attempted a back flip from the highest point of his swing. He didn't make it all the way around. He came down flat on his belly with a sickening smack and started sinking at once.

By the time I got to him he was already two feet under. When I got him to the surface, Paula was next to me. Peter was unresponsive.

"Jake, he can't die again, can he?" Paula panicked.

"No, but with his mortal body, he suffers as much as anyone else. The difference is, no matter what happens, the next morning he'll be as good as new."

Peter started coughing as we swam to the dock. Paula climbed up the ladder and I handed Peter to her. She laid him on a towel. All three of us knelt over him while I put my hand on his beet red stomach. "So even if his heart stopped, he'd be fine tomorrow?" I nodded.

Peter struggled to breathe. He coughed and spit up some water as he opened his eyes. "What happened, Jake?"

"You hit wrong, Funny Tummy. How do you feel?"

The tears hadn't slowed. "I'm sore every place. Did I hit something?"

I laughed as I dried his stomach and chest. "Yeah, you hit the water. You did the best belly flop I've ever seen, and from ten feet high. You hit the water so hard it knocked you out. You were sinking and obviously taking in water."

"Wow! I won't do that again."

"What, a belly flop?" I asked.

"Yeah, but I don't think I'll show off for Darlene anymore!"

We all chuckled at his candor.

"Hey, Funny Face, how do you feel?"

"I'm still a little sore every place. I think I should have been wearing my jockstrap." Paula put her hand to her mouth to stifle a laugh.

"Well, what do you think? You ready to try that flip again?"

All three looked at me. "Jake, I don't think so."

"You want to swing on the rope again—the normal way?" I was expecting a chuckle but instead I got a look of concern.

"Jake, did I almost drown?"

"If you had been a normal child, the answer would be yes."

"Were you worried?"

"Peter, you know me well. Sure I worry. I love you." I looked at him. "Peter, are you suddenly a little afraid of the water?"

He hesitated. "I guess a little."

"I can help you with that if you'd like."

"Okay. How?"

"Like this." I picked him up and ran for the end of the dock. When he realized what I was going to do, he wrapped his arms around my neck and yelled, "No, Jake. Please don't." We went in together, under together and up together. He came up gasping. I got him stretched out on his stomach with my hands under his chest and thighs and said, "You're fine, Little One. Remember, I love you. Now swim." Hesitantly, he began paddling. Within ten or fifteen feet, he was swimming like a fish—confidence restored.

"Come here, Kiddo." He did with a smile on his face. I turned around. "Put your arms around my neck and hang on." I climbed up the ladder with Peter on my back and put him down. I knelt down before him and put my hands on either side of his face. "You okay, Kiddo?"

"Yeah, I'm fine. I'm glad you did that."

"Now why don't you and Darlene team up for some fun?" I twitched each ear enough to produce a giggle. Back in they went as if nothing had happened.

"Jake, only a man who understands boys would handle that like you did."

"I know Peter. Even though he was begging me not to jump in, he knew I wouldn't hurt him or let him get hurt."

After a few minutes, we joined them in the water. After the four of us played together a long while, it was time to go. As Peter and I were changing in the shower house, I asked, "Peter, do you think I should invite the girls back to the campsite for dinner?"

Peter looked at me and smiled. "Sure! That would be neat. Could you tell us a story tonight?" Before I could reply, he went on. "Could you make it really scary?"

"I don't think I should. After all, they're both girls."

"Oh yeah. You're right. I forgot about that."

We soon joined Paula and Darlene outside, and extended our invitation.

Darlene lit up a smile. "Fixing a meal over a fire! Fun!"

I promised that we'd all work together on the meal.

Once at the site, I took charge. "Peter, why don't you and Darlene work on the fire and get that going? You can teach Darlene how to build the right fire and how to start it."

Peter beamed but Paula looked worried. "Don't worry. Peter's an expert now." His smile broadened with importance. "Oh, and Peter, why don't you and Darlene soap the coffee pot and the middle-size pot. And explain why we do it. And resharpen our hot dog sticks."

"No problem, Jake." Peter and Darlene got to work while Paula and I worked on the food. (The kids soon had a fire going.) Paula and I kept an eye on them, but Peter had the situation under control. When he sharpened the sticks, he explained why you always move the knife away from your hand and body, and how you make sure you're a safe distance from other people. Then he watched as Darlene sharpened one. Good teacher!

The more tasks I gave the kids, the better they loved it. Who said little kids can't accept responsibility?

After a dinner of hot dogs and baked beans, followed by chocolate pudding, we headed for the lake to clean up.

Back at the campsite, Paula looked at Darlene. "Honey, will you teach me how to build a fire sometime?"

"Sure!" Darlene said proudly. "Peter taught me how." Now both children beamed from ear to ear.

"Jake, can the four of us take a walk?" Peter asked.

I looked at Paula. She smiled and nodded. "I remember the nature hike you took us on last year, Peter. We'd love to."

We were soon on the small dirt road following Peter. He pointed out several plants and animal sounds he'd identified last year. He proudly showed them many new things he'd learned such as a few mosses, ferns and mushrooms. Pointing out one attractive mushroom, he said, "These are decomposers. They break down dead organisms. By doing that, they enrich the soil."

Darlene wanted to know if we could eat them. "No! Some are poisonous. Jake and I don't know which ones are safe to eat, so we avoid all of them. Don't even touch them."

As we walked along, Peter excitedly announced, "Look, Jake, British Soldiers." He was pointing to a rotting log on the side of the road. I had showed Peter a picture of this particular lichen months earlier, but we'd not seen any in the woods until now. He explained the job of lichen in the ecosystem. He also pointed out the distinctive red tip on the lichen. "It reminded our ancestors of the British Soldiers stationed in North America in the 1700's." Darlene was an attentive student. Paula commented to me later on Peter's ability to verbalize his knowledge. I was as proud a grandpa as you could be. Peter was just being Peter.

Once back at the campsite, it was story time. "Jake, can I put my pajamas on?"

"It's only 7:30, Kiddo. Why don't you wait until after the story? I'm going to keep it short."

The story ran about twenty minutes. Everyone enjoyed it. Peter asked if he could put his PJ's on now. I gave him permission. "Okay. Come on, Darlene. I want to show you something."

"Uh, Peter, why don't you wait to show her until after you've changed?"

"Why?"

"Uh, well because Darlene's a girl and you're a boy."

"So?"

Before I could answer, Paula said, "Darlene, I think that would be a good idea."

"Why?"

"Because Peter's going to be taking his shorts off and putting his pajamas on."

"So? He's the same as Teddy."

"I know he's Teddy's age, but it's not the same thing."

Peter stood there taking this in. I sensed what he was thinking. On top of having two big brothers in Jamie and Bobby, he now had a big sister.

"I don't see what the big deal is," Peter chimed in.

"Peter, you're being difficult." I looked at Darlene. "In fact, you're both being difficult." Paula agreed. "You can call Darlene when you've changed."

"Oh, okay," he said in a disgusted manner as he headed for the tent, not really understanding what the problem was. Less than a minute later he called for Darlene.

While they were in the tent, I looked at Paula. "I'm new to this parenting thing. You've had two children. Why do kids have to make simple situations so difficult?"

She laughed. "It's the nature of the beast. Both Peter and Darlene are totally innocent. I have no doubt Darlene would have been in there checking out the tent and paying no attention to Peter. I'm also certain Peter would have changed into his pajamas as if no one were present."

I laughed. "I guess you're right." I looked at the tent. "It's awful quiet in there. Right now Peter is as mortal as Darlene. He's extremely curious and has asked a lot of question during the year about girls. You don't think there's any hanky-panky going on in there, do you?"

She snapped her head around, then back at me. We both stood and walked for the tent. Peeking in through a screen, we saw Peter and Darlene sitting on my sleeping bag. Peter was reading to her from a new book of his entitled *Stars in Our Sky*. We slipped back to the fire, smiling. About ten minutes later the kids joined us. "What were you two doing in there?" I asked.

"I was reading to Darlene from that new book. The one you got me two weeks ago. You know, the one about the stars."

"Yeah, Mom. You should hear Peter read. He reads better than I do. He's really smart."

"Peter's reading at the ninth grade level," I mumbled, poking at the coals.

"Is that because he's an angel?"

"No! It's because he's very intelligent and because he's been a highly motivated student."

Paula smiled. "He must have had an excellent teacher."

"Well, let's say his teacher was motivated too."

The four of us talked until past nine, but Peter was fading. Neither wanted to miss saying good-bye to Peter. They both stood before us. I lifted him off my lap. He was still awake enough to stand on his own.

Darlene said, "Peter, I had a lot of fun playing with you yesterday and today. You're a neat boy. You remind me so much of Teddy. I love you like a little brother." She hugged Peter and kissed his cheek. Peter looked at me and blushed. He figured that in time some good-natured teasing from me would be coming his way.

"I liked playing with you, too, Darlene."

Paula knelt down before him. "I know you'll be asleep soon. Neither one of us wanted to miss saying good-bye to you. Darlene's right; you're a wonderful boy in addition to being an angel. Jake is very blessed."

She looked at me then back to Peter. "And Peter, you are too. Thank you for teaching us girls so much about camping and Mother Nature. I hope we'll see you next year. Thank you for everything." With that she picked him up and hugged and kissed him.

"Thank you." He looked at me. "I think I'm luckier than you, Jake." He looked back at Paula and Darlene. "I hope we see you next year, too."

I sat Peter on my lap again and as we visited a bit longer, Peter fell asleep. I took him into the tent and laid him down.

I came out and picked up Darlene. "Darlene, you're a sweet girl and strong too. Peter and I both think you're great! You've suffered a terrible loss, but you and your mom are a team, like Peter and me. We work together and play together. We watch out for each other. We take care of each other because we love each other just as you and your mom do.

"Sometimes Peter gets angry at me and believe it or not, sometimes I get angry with Peter. But our love for each other never quits. Remember that this year. Have a good year in school and maybe we'll see you next year." I gave her a hug and she gave me a kiss, then I put her down.

I went to Paula. "Paula, I really enjoyed the last two days. I thoroughly enjoyed watching you and Darlene relate to one another. You two are quite a team. You two are doing fine. But as I said, if you need to talk, call me."

"Thanks, Jake. This has been a good two days for Darlene and me. We got to know you and Peter better. You and Peter have come to mean more to us than you can ever know. Watching you and Peter has encouraged me. We love both of you. Jake, you are like the father I barely remember. To Darlene, you're the grandfather she never had. Thank you very much." We embraced and parted with a mutual kiss.

I gave Darlene another quick kiss on her forehead and looked at Paula. "Stay in touch."

She promised she would through misty eyes and a beautiful smile and drove off.

CHAPTER TWENTY

The next morning I was up by 5:45, got a fire going, had a cup of coffee then started packing.

Peter woke up at 7:15. As last year, Peter awoke to find himself in his sleeping bag on the table. I sat on the bench and watched him wake. "Hey, Funny Face, how you doing this morning?"

He gave me his special ray of sunshine. He stretched his arms over his head, looked around to find the tent gone then said, "Did I sleep long enough to miss most of the work?"

"Most of it, you little stinker." Then I dug in. After he got his breath back, I said, "So now you've got two big brothers and one big sister. What do you think of that?"

He stretched his arms over his head again and turned serious. "It's neat having two big brothers." He paused. "I guess it's okay to have a big sister, even though I never wanted one. If I have to have one, Darlene's okay."

I was fighting a smile. "Yeah. I suppose Tammy would be better though, right?"

He looked at me, "Jake, you're making fun of me again."

I put my hand on his chest. He flinched in anticipation of what was to come, but it didn't. I rubbed my thumb across his skin. He brought his right hand down on mine. "I'm teasing you a little, Kiddo, but seriously, which one do you like the best?"

He thought about this. "Are you going to tease me?"

"Probably, but I'll only do it in private."

He giggled. "Okay. I liked Tammy in school last year and at the parties. I never really played with her much. I've known Darlene longer than Tammy, but not as well until the other day. Now I know her better than Tammy. She's fun to play with. Sometimes she's like a boy."

"She sure doesn't look like one. I bet she's a lot cuter than you when she first wakes up."

He blushed slightly. "Of course she is. She's a girl."

"So you're finally admitting you're ugly when you wake up?"

Again he giggled. "Jake, you're so mean to me."

"I know. Peter, you and Darlene are a cute pair of kids and you play well together."

"You mean I'm not that ugly when I first wake up?"

"Oh, I didn't say that." He laughed, sat up and punched me. "Let's get moving. We'll finish packing, go over and take showers, then return the canoe." I handed him his clothes.

We moved rather slowly that morning, but I didn't care. We couldn't move into our campsite until 1:30 that afternoon. Peter still didn't know about the campground in Old Forge.

Just east of Old Forge was the campground. As I pulled in, Peter asked, "Why are we going in here?"

"I want to introduce myself."

We pulled in and parked in front of an impressive log building. A large porch was in front. There were many kids ranging in age from three or four on up on bikes. Inside the building was a game room, laundry room, a store, the office and the registration counter. Peter and I stood there looking around. "What do you think of this place, Kiddo?"

Not far away was a small playground. Part of a lake could be seen. "Kind of neat."

"Come with me." We walked up to the counter where I lifted him into my arms. Looking at the women behind the counter, I introduced Peter and myself. After getting the usual responses to Peter, I explained I knew we were early, but that we were going into town and would be back around 1:30.

As we walked out the door, Peter said, "Jake, what's going on?"

"Surprise! Betty called last night. The party has been postponed until Monday. We have six extra days so I thought we'd try this place for a few days."

Driving into town we passed the Water Park. Peter looked at it wide-eyed. "Are we going to go to that?"

"We could but we don't have to. It's up to you."

He looked at me and smiled. "It looks like fun."

"Does that mean you'd like to?"

His smile grew. "Yeah."

"Phew. That's good. I already paid for it. Had you said no, I think I'd trade you in for a new guardian angel."

He laughed. "You did?"

"Yeah. When I called last night to reserve a campsite, I bought Water Park tickets at that time."

"I love your kind of surprises, Grandpa."

"Hey, I have to keep my guardian angel happy. Let's stop in and say hello to Harvey." We wandered through the Old Forge Hardware store, a store well-known throughout the Northeast. It's fascinating. You can get just about anything you want there...except perhaps a size toddler four jockstrap.

We were back at the campgrounds at 1:30. Upon walking into the lodge the same young woman said, "Hi, Peter. Hi, Mr. Winters."

Another young lady looked up and said, "Wow, he is cute."

I looked at her and with a big smile said, "Well, thank you."

THE SEPARATION

That got a few laughs, but Peter set the record straight. "She's not talking about you. She talking about me."

I looked at the woman and winked. "Are you sure?"

"Of course I'm sure. You're too old to be cute." That got more laughs. But when Peter twitched and giggled as I tickled him, everybody behind the counter and the customers standing in line joined the laugher.

After checking in we were given a map directing us to our campsite, number 626. We thanked them, walked to the porch, sat down on a bench and studied the map. The camp roads looked like a maze. This huge campground could prove interesting.

We drove to our tent site following our directions carefully, passing a lake about the size of our fishing lake. An impressive beach was just off the road. This place was beautiful. After parking, we scanned the site and set up our tent.

Peter looked around. "Where's the outhouse?"

"No outhouses here, Kiddo."

"What?"

I laughed. "Come on. Let's go look for a bathroom, then we can go exploring. After that, a dip in the lake!"

A search for the bathroom and shower became our exploring time. As we continued walking we found another facility. We decided it was time for a swim, but neither one of us knew how to get back to our site.

"Jake, why don't you look at the map of the campground they gave you when we checked in? We'll be able to find out where we are and how to get back to our tent."

I looked at him sheepishly. "That's a good idea, Kiddo. The problem is, I left it in the tent." I honestly believe Peter tried not to laugh at my stupidity, but was unsuccessful.

After simmering down and trying to be helpful, he said, "We can ask someone for directions."

Being an adult male, I rejected that idea. A half-hour later we found the tent, but I still had no idea which facility was the closest. In fact, neither one of us could remember how we got to them nor even how we got back to our tent from the last one we found.

Peter, trying to conceal a smile said, "Grandpa, later on when we have to pee, maybe we should take a map with us."

I chuckled. "Yeah, I suppose you're right."

Enough humiliation for one day! I moved on to something else. "Well, let's change into our trunks and head for the lake."

As he was removing his shirt he asked sarcastically, "Do you think you can find it?"

I laughed uproariously then attacked him.

Later, we did find out that the nearest facility was about 600 feet away. We found how to get to it and back without getting lost. We also discovered a water spigot thirty feet from our site.

The beach was much like a public beach, crowded. The dock was for fishing but not for jumping from. As we walked to the wide beach, ideal for play, Peter asked if I thought there would be a kid like Jimmy on this beach.

"It's possible, Kiddo; but if there is, avoid him."

We were soon in the lake when I began throwing Peter from here to there. After half an hour I returned to the beach. Setting up my chair near some adults, I was asked by a chubby woman if the little blond-haired boy was my son. "Grandson," I explained.

Before long Peter joined me. Once on my lap I asked, "Well, what do you think?"

"This is neat. The campground is huge. Can we go to the playground?"

"Sure, after we relax for a few minutes."

Within a minute he was asleep. The woman looked at him. "Is he asleep already?"

"Yes. It doesn't take long."

"He certainly speaks clearly for such a young child. Most people can't understand my four-year-old." As if on cue, a grossly overweight girl waddled up to her mother. This youngster had to weigh 90 pounds. I felt sorry for her.

"Peter's six-and-a-half, just small for his age."

She looked skeptically at Peter but didn't challenge me. "Well, whatever. He certainly is a handsome youngster."

"Easy to live with too," I added. I looked at her daughter and almost said, and doesn't eat much either, but caught my tongue.

Fifteen minutes later he woke. "Well, Funny Face, you ready to go to the playground?"

After waking him, we said good-bye to everybody and walked to the playground. The playground didn't have a lot to offer, however it was designed for younger kids—kids the size of Peter. I watched him carefully. There were five little boys and two little girls present between the ages of three and five. Most were bigger than Peter. But he played with them in an age appropriate way.

He lifted the smallest child onto a ladder so she could climb to the top of an enclosed slide and stayed with her until she was safely to the top.

One boy threw some stones up the enclosed slide. When the mother said nothing, Peter stepped in and told the boy he shouldn't throw stones because someone could get hurt. The boy stopped.

On and on it went for the next half-hour...parents paying little or no attention to their children while Peter became the playground supervisor.

Finally Peter came to me. We were both ready to leave and have dinner.

After dinner we took a hike around the lake. The trail was all within the confines of the camp. It was one-mile long.

Peter took the lead. He learned a lot in the past year, not only in the identification of plants, ferns and fungus, but also in how to move though the woods.

On our first hike in the woods behind my house a year ago, he bumped into low-hanging branches, tripped over logs and rocks and was noisy. Now he didn't trip over anything and missed nothing. As a result, we saw several deer, one raccoon and a bear from a distance, plus an assortment of smaller animals such as chipmunks and squirrels.

Once back to the tent, I grabbed a chair then we went to the outdoor movie arcade for a Disney movie. It was a nice way to end the day.

The next morning, Peter joined me at the fire at 7:15. I was going to wake him, but realized we now had neighbors. Some may not be awake yet. I suggested we wait until eight. So we sat there and talked. "What do you think of this place so far?"

"In some ways I like it better than the other place. There are kids around to play with if I want to. There are a lot of places to hike. The bathroom doesn't smell like the outhouse did. The movie was neat last night. But we don't have a good fishing lake. We don't have privacy. Talking about that, I have to pee real bad."

I stood up, took his hand and led him behind our tent. It provided a small amount of privacy if we faced the right way. I pointed this out to Peter. "This can be our own peeing site."

When we returned to the fire, we discussed the day. The campgrounds had canoes but also paddle boats. They were unique to both of us so we decided after breakfast, we'd rent one.

They had pedals for two. Fortunately the seats were adjustable. The lever for the rudder was between the seats so Peter steered the boat. Once away from the dock, we went around in a circle to the right. We soon did another circle to the left. Finally he figured it out and we went straight…sort of. The important thing was we had fun. However, we decided to turn the boat in for a canoe. It was more familiar to both of us.

While paddling around, we had a father and son come up to us. They had been watching us and wondered how we could steer the canoe without switching sides. I spent ten minutes demonstrating the sweep and the J-stroke to the father. Staying with them for another twenty minutes we saw that the father was catching on pretty well.

At that point, Peter and I pulled into shore and changed positions. The father was amazed that Peter could manage the stern as well as he could. The father decided to change positions with his son and let him have a try. His son was ten. At first it was a disaster but Peter worked with the boy as I had with the father, and eventually he started to catch on.

Peter and I were just returning to the lake after moving back to our normal positions when a canoe overturned in the middle of the lake. In it had been a family of six: the two parents and four small children. It had been over-loaded. I pointed it out to Peter earlier for that reason, but also because neither parent nor the two older children were wearing life preservers.

The children were screaming and the mother was near panicking out of concern for her children. The father was yelling trying to calm everybody down, but it had the opposite effect.

Peter looked at me. "Should I, Jake?"

"Are any of them near drowning?"

"Not yet."

"Then put your angelic powers into your strokes and let's get to them quick. But watch them, Kiddo. If any of them go under, do whatever you have to do."

The power Peter generated was phenomenal. All I could do was sit in the stern and rudder. I couldn't keep up with his strength. We made it to the overturned canoe in nothing flat.

When we got to them, the two toddlers were scared but in no fear of drowning. The two parents were tired but okay. The two older children were exhausted and would not have lasted much longer. We had one parent and one toddler hang on to either side of our canoe for balance while Peter effortlessly lifted the two older children into our canoe. Peter and I paddled them back to shore while the other father and son towed the overturned canoe back.

On shore, the parents hugged their children then thanked Peter and me profusely. I pulled the parents aside while Peter stayed with the children. "They have the life preserver law for a reason, you know. You almost lost two of your children and you easily could have gone down with them. Thank God it was a small lake or the outcome could have been a recovery rather than a rescue."

The father gave me a nasty look. "Are you calling us stupid?"

"Is it necessary?"

THE SEPARATION

I don't think he was expecting that kind of a response. He reflected a moment and his expression mellowed. "No, it isn't. I should have known better. Thanks."

It turned out the family was staying in a tent two sites down from us. Peter now had some playmates. Cindy was seven, Jimmy was six, Jon was four and Barb was three. After returning the paddles and life preservers to the store, the Clays, Peter and I decided to return to the beach.

We all had a good time in the water together, but after a while the adults headed for shore and comfortable chairs. The kids played in the sand while the adults talked. "Jake," Walt Clay said, "I saw Peter pull Cindy and Jimmy from the water today. I didn't think about it too much at the time. I was just grateful. But thinking back now, it was amazing. He's smaller than both of them, yet he pulled them out as effortlessly as an adult would. How did he do that?"

"I know what you mean. The doctor said Peter has the strength and coordination of a ten-year-old. But today, Peter was scared one of your kids was going to drown. I'm sure some of that was pure adrenaline." My explanation satisfied them.

After lunch, Peter asked if we could take the Clay family on a nature hike around the lake. They were quite interested but had to be back by three. They were going to the Water Park for four hours that afternoon then would spend all Wednesday. We were going at three on Wednesday then would spend all day there on Thursday.

We started the hike at once. Peter led the entire hike. After we returned, Judy Clay asked, "Peter, where did you learn so much about nature?"

Peter took my hand affectionately, smiled and said, "Grandpa taught me."

"I can't take all the credit. Peter is an excellent reader and has read on his own, too," I added. "He knows more plants than I do now."

We spent the rest of the day alone. Before he fell asleep for his afternoon nap I asked, "Peter, would you want to come here for our entire vacation next year?"

He thought about that. "This is fun, Jake. But there are some problems. There's no place to fish. Would Bill and Danny stay here with us? Could we still fly with Sam? If we stayed here would we ever see Darlene and her mother again?"

I whistled. "That does present a problem, doesn't it?"

Peter blushed. "Jake, you know what I mean."

"I sure do. Darlene's fun to look at, right?" Peter blushed more. I looked at him and recognized the deep feeling he felt for Darlene and Paula. I was ashamed of myself. "Peter, I'm sorry. I'm teasing you. Darlene's a wonderful little girl. She means as much to me as you do to Paula. And Paula's a very special and classy lady. And yes, she's as good looking to me as Darlene is to you."

"She looks pretty good to me too, Jake."

"Careful kid. Remember, you're not supposed to notice things like that." He laughed. "You're right though, there could be some problems. Maybe what we should do is do what we're doing this year. We could split our time between the two places.

"As far as flying with Sam goes, we could drive up there anytime. And who knows, maybe Paula and Darlene would come down here for a couple of days. If they don't or can't, we won't forget them. We will get together with them for a couple of days no matter what. Well look, we've got the whole year to talk about it."

"Hey, maybe they could come down here and stay in our tent with us."

"No, that wouldn't work."

"Why? It would save them money and us too, wouldn't it?"

"Uh, well yes, but…"

"Well, why not then? There's plenty of room in our tent for them. That would be fun."

Oh boy. Peter was doing it to me again. His innocence was a beautiful thing, but at times it drove me nuts. "Peter, Paula and I aren't married. You and Darlene aren't brother and sister."

"So? Darlene wouldn't mind and I betcha Paula wouldn't either."

"Look at it this way, Kiddo. I know it wouldn't bother you to get ready for bed in front of Darlene and Paula, but I don't think Darlene would want to change in front of you and me."

"Why not?"

Oh boy! "It isn't proper. Don't worry about it. It's not going to happen."

"Oh." He thought about this. "Jake, sometimes this proper stuff is a pain."

"I know, but that's the way it is." He let out with a deep breath of disgust, closed his eyes and fell asleep.

That afternoon we decided to explore one of the many gullies in the area. While walking to the gully, we came across two deer—a young buck and a doe. Hesitantly the doe walked up to Peter and nuzzled him in the belly with her nose. Peter giggled and petted her for a few seconds before she wandered off. He wondered why deer every place weren't this friendly.

"Here they know people are not going to hurt them."

Just then two boys went by on their bikes. "Jake, if we come here next year, could we bring our bikes?"

"I don't see why not. That would be fun."

While in the gully exploring a small pool, we heard a crash in the gully ahead of us. We looked up to see a black bear charging through the creek twenty feet away. The bear we saw the day before was much farther away. This was the first bear Peter had seen since leaving Slippery Gulch. There the bears were mostly grizzly bears and presented a good reason to be fearful. Peter crept close to me and wrapped a small arm around my right leg for protection.

I picked him up. He wrapped both arms around my neck as we watched with interest. "It's a black bear, Kiddo. They're not as dangerous as the bears you're used to, but show your respect. In the campgrounds, they're accustomed to people the way the deer are. But we never go up to a bear to pet it."

Peter and I watched the bear effortlessly run up the other side of the gully. "No way! That was neat."

That evening Peter and I decided to stay in the campsite for reading and a story. At eight he went into the tent to change into his pajamas. He emerged from the tent, walked behind it and relieved himself. Suddenly he was yelling and screaming, "Jake, help! A bear! Help!"

I raced to the back of the tent and stopped dead in my tracks. I took in the situation and started laughing. Peter had walked around the tent, his eyes on the forest floor so as not to trip over a stump or rock. Once in the right place, he lowered his pajamas and looked up. Five feet away was a bear watching his every move. At that point, Peter had turned around to run. His pajamas dropped to his ankles and he fell flat on his face. So he yelled for me.

What I found was the bear five feet from Peter, shaking her head slowly back and forth, but not stomping her front feet or slapping the ground. She was not showing any signs of aggression or anger. I felt certain she found humor in the situation as did I. Chuckling, I casually picked up Peter, thanked the bear for not harming my little angel and returned to the front of the tent. I wiped the dirt off his front and pulled up his pajamas as I walked.

Peter's screams brought several families to our tent, the Clay family among them. After explaining the situation, Peter became quite the hero. The Clay family already considered him a hero. Peter forgot how scared he was and played the part convincingly. Although all the adults laughed at the situation, I could tell they were all thankful it was Peter rather than their child, and me rather than them that had to rescue the child.

After the action was over everybody returned, hesitantly, to their own campsites. Peter had one question. "Jake, why did you laugh when you came behind the tent to save my life?"

I couldn't help but laugh all over again. Peter looked hurt. "Peter, you weren't in any real danger. That bear was laughing over the situation as much as I was. If it had been upset it would have been shaking its head harder and stomping its front feet or swinging at the brush.

"That mama bear saw you for what you are—a cub. She probably thought you were as cute as her cubs. She saw you walk behind the tent and she stopped to see your intentions. When you reacted to her the way you did, I'm sure that's when she started laughing."

Still angry over my reaction to the whole situation he said, "But, Jake, she could have eaten me. Did you ever think of that?"

"Black bears don't eat little kids. They taste funny." He looked at me, not sure whether to believe me or not. "Peter, black bears are omnivores: they eat both plants and animal life. The animals they eat are worms like grubs and some insects, not little kids. They also eat roots and berries. The garbage we humans make is a special treat for them. But they don't eat humans. If you leave them alone, they leave you alone."

"I was leaving her alone. I was just standing there peeing when she attacked me."

"Peter, that bear didn't attack you any more than she attacked me. I don't want you saying that to people. It's not true. That's how rumors start. If word gets out that a bear attacked a little boy, the authorities would probably destroy her. That wouldn't be fair."

He looked aghast. "You, you mean kill her?"

"That's exactly what I mean."

He put his head down. "That would be a bad lie, wouldn't it?"

"Let's say it would be a gross exaggeration of the facts. It could cost that bear her life."

When he looked up, he was close to tears. "I wouldn't want to cause the death of any animal. I'm sorry." He thought for a moment. "But she did scare the pee out of me and almost something else."

Again I laughed. "That's okay to say."

"Jake, why weren't you scared?"

"I have a pretty good understanding of black bears, Kiddo. Whether in a campground like this or in the wild, if you leave them alone, they'll leave you alone. Now if you step between a mama bear and her cub, you could be in big trouble. I'll tell you though, Funny Face, if I had been standing there peeing the way you were, looked up and saw a bear five feet away, I think I would have been scared too."

Peter looked at me. "You would?"

"I think so. Perhaps a better word is startled." I thought for a minute. This was an outstanding lesson for Peter. Why drop it here?

"Peter, do you have any idea how big you were when you were born?"

He thought for a moment. "I don't know. Maybe this big." He moved his hands about a foot apart.

"That's probably a pretty close guess. Any idea how much you weighed?"

"I don't know. Maybe three or four pounds?"

"Perhaps, but most humans weigh between five and eight pounds. I weighed seven pounds and two ounces."

"How do you know?"

"I weighed myself before I put my diaper on."

His eyes bulged. In amazement he said, "You did?"

I laughed. "One of my stories, Kiddo. My mother told me how much I weighed as a baby years later. But let me ask you a few more questions. That bear was pretty big, wasn't she?"

"Yeah, you're not kidding. She could have snapped me in two without breaking a sweat."

I chuckled. "Do you remember the bears you saw around Slippery Gulch?"

He thought about this. "A little. I think they were all brown. I didn't get real close to any of them."

"It's probably just as well. Many of them were probably grizzly bears, although some of the brown colored bears could have been black bears…"

He crossed his arms. "Well, if they were black bears, why were they brown?"

"A very logical question. A few black bears in the East are tinted brown, but many of them out West are as brown as the grizzly bears. It may have something to do with their diet.

"At any rate, the bear you saw tonight may have weighed 200 pounds." Peter tried to whistle. (He hadn't mastered that yet.) "Black bears can get up to 500 pounds. Grizzly bears can weigh as much as 1000 pounds. And the Kodiak grizzly can weigh as much as 1500 pounds. Kodiak is an island off the coast of Alaska."

"Wow!" he said as his eyes enlarged.

"But how much do your think a black bear and a grizzly weigh when they're born?"

"Oh man! If I weighed six pounds they must weigh… wow, maybe as much as…gee, I don't know. Maybe eighty or ninety pounds."

I chuckled. "You're way off."

His eyes once again enlarged. "Heavier?"

"Oh, no. A black bear weighs about one-half pound and a grizzly weighs about a pound."

Disbelieving he said, "No way."

"Way!"

"But how can something that big come into the world so tiny?"

The gestation period for a bear is two months, but I decided I didn't want to get into a discussion with Peter on that. "That's just the way God works it, Kiddo."

"Wow! God is really something, isn't he?"

"He sure is. God works one way with cubs and another way with kids. After six years of life, you weigh thirty pounds. After one year a black bear will weigh about one hundred pounds."

"You mean they gain that much in a year with the junk they eat?" I smiled and nodded. "Maybe I should start eating worms and insects. Then maybe I'd gain some weight."

"If you start eating worms, you're not living with me."

Once again he thought for a minute. "Jake, I promise I'll never say anything bad about that bear. But I hope the next time I go behind the tent to pee, she isn't there."

"I doubt if she will be. On the other hand, she has to see you are a pretty neat little human."

"Do you think so?"

"I'd bet on it. But you'd better hope she never sees you when you first wake up. You're so ugly she may attack out of self defense."

He giggled. "Jake, I am not." He punched me lightly, and settled down to cuddle. He was asleep in no time.

Peter joined me at the campfire after sunup. More asleep than awake, he said, "Jake, I have to pee bad."

"Well, run around behind the tent and deal with it."

He looked at the tent, then back at me. "Couldn't I pee here?"

"No way!"

Again he looked at the tent, then back at me. "Can you come with me?"

I took his hand and we walked behind the tent. "Peter, you could probably walk behind this tent every day for the next year and never see another bear. To become a good outdoorsman, you have to get over this fear. But don't lose your healthy respect for bears."

"But what if I walk back here and there she is?"

"Turn around and walk away. Or stand there and talk real nice and gentle to her. But don't look her in the eyes. If she stands up on her hind feet, it doesn't mean she's going to attack you. She either wants a better view of you or a better sniff. Hey, that's a good reason to shower every day."

Disgustedly, he said, "Jake, I don't have to smell that good. But what if she attacks me?"

"She won't. But if she takes a step towards you, walk away; don't run."

"How can you be so brave?"

I laughed. "It's you that we're talking about, not me. Come on. Let's eat and go out in a canoe for a while before we go to the Water Park."

The camp bus leaves the lodge at 2:45 and picks us up at the Water Park at 7:00. The next day we would have from 10:00 to 7:00. Before leaving, I had Peter take a short nap.

We arrived at the park at three. We picked up our map and passes for tomorrow. After receiving the map, Peter looked at me with a wise-guy look. "Jake, maybe you should keep the map today." I gave him a nasty look as he giggled.

Peter made a beeline for a huge statue of Paul Bunyon. He'd read many tall tales about the huge lumberjack over the past year. Peter posed on the blade of the ax for our first picture of him in the park.

After a discussion, we decided to check out the various water slides. Unfortunately, all the higher and longer slides had minimum height limits from forty-two to forty-eight inches. Peter didn't even come close to qualifying.

As we walked along, Peter watched normal-sized six-year-olds enjoying some of them. His face got longer and sadder. I was beginning to think the Water Park was a poor idea.

Fortunately we found a few water slides with no restrictions, but they were designed for toddlers. Peter sensed he was being treated like a baby. I tried to explain liability insurance. He wasn't too interested.

We did find some dry rides he would enjoy and enough other activities to keep us both occupied. We agreed we'd try to have an enjoyable day tomorrow. He tried to muster enthusiasm for the place.

There were huge stones and small boulders stationed throughout the park bordering the pathways. He climbed to the top of some of them to jump off on the other side. His energy level seemed to increase as his enthusiasm for the park revived. Tomorrow would be a good day.

That afternoon, while we rode above the entire park in a two-person cable car, Peter spotted the Clay family. We yelled to them. They looked all around and finally up. We all waved.

We missed a circus that afternoon but Peter got to ride an elephant. He mentioned that the bear of the night before wasn't so big after all.

We found the Clays for the five-minute bus ride back to the lodge that evening. From the bus, we saw a bear. Peter was convinced it was the same one that caught him with his pants down the night before. This got the Clay children all wound up.

I walked back to the campsite with the Clay family while the children ran ahead. I invited them to our campsite for marshmallows and a story. I fetched two chairs from the tent while Peter uncovered our wood supply. Peter took the matches I gave him and had a fire going in no time. Walt Clay watched Peter with interest. Once the fire was going, Walt asked, "How did he do that? I have a devil of a time starting a fire."

"I taught Peter fire safety and how to build a fire last year. Before you start a fire, you have to be well organized. Here's our small supply of birch bark. Next our kindling then medium-sized wood and finally our larger split logs."

Walt understood the logic of being prepared. We enjoyed roasting our marshmallows until it was time for the story. Peter and the Clay children sat on the ground while I stood.

I told a humorous Indian legend, one Peter had heard before and loved. After the story we chatted for a while, but it was soon bedtime for the children. The Clays were leaving the next morning, but there would be time enough for our good-byes then.

The sunrise was outstandingly beautiful promising a perfect day for the water park. Peter joined me shortly after seven and announcing he had to pee and would be peeing all alone. He turned to leave, took two tentative steps, and turned back to me. "Jake, you'll be here, won't you?"

"Right here, Kiddo."

He half-smiled, turned and slowly walked behind the tent. Thirty seconds later he tore around the corner of the tent then quickly slowed to a casual walk to my chair for his morning wake-up. "No bears!" was his report.

On the way to the lodge to catch the bus, we stopped at the Clay's campsite to say good-bye. For them it was emotional. Thanks to Peter, they were returning home with *all* their children. Never in their wildest dreams could they imagine Peter was an angel. But he'd left his mark on the Clay family.

Peter dressed in a white pull-over and his jockey swim trunks under light blue shorts. I wore trunks under shorts too. I brought my small backpack to leave our stuff in when we went on rides. I brought $30 but locked my wallet in the trunk of our car back at our campsite.

Peter stripped to his trunks at the first water slide and that's the way he stayed for the rest of the day. The thirty-foot slide ended in a shallow pool. Though it was in the shadows of a huge slide that Peter would have preferred, he made the most of it.

At another activity, three ropes thirty feet long were suspended across a two foot deep pool of water. The idea was for a child to move hand over hand from one side of the pool to the other without falling in. As we stood watching, one kid after another tried, but none made it all the way.

"That would be easy," Peter said. "Can I try?"

"I suspect it's harder than it looks, Kiddo. The rope is probably wet and hard to hang on to." We walked around to see if they would let Peter try.

The only requirement was knowing how to swim. Once we reached the front of the line, a female employee looked down at Peter and said, "He can't do this."

I looked at her. "Why not?"

"He's too short. He can't reach the rope."

"I'm sorry, but we stood over there watching other kids that were too short to reach the rope. You and the other folks working here lifted them up. Lift Peter up too."

The woman working the next line looked over and asked, "Can he swim?"

"Like a fish! But he won't even get wet."

The woman chuckled and shrugged her shoulders. The woman running Peter's line picked him up so he could grab the rope, and he was off. He never faltered. He was across in no time, leaving both women standing with their mouths open. The nearer woman asked, "How did he do that?"

I laughed. "He's very strong. He has an iron grip and he only weighs thirty pounds."

"Would he be willing try again?"

"I'll ask him when he gets over here."

He was. At the front of the line, he was again lifted to the rope and off he went. Once again he made it comfortably.

We came to a water ride that was slow and looked comfortable. The participant was given a rubber tube. He'd float through a considerable portion of the park in a two-foot-deep "trail" of water. Peter was too small for his own tube, so he rode with me. He climbed onto my legs so he was facing me. He lay back finding a comfortable position. His feet were on either side of my stomach with his head resting comfortably on my ankles. His hands were comfortably under his head and his eyes were closed. Life was treating him well.

As we drifted slowly around a bend, I noticed a waterfall flowing into the left side of the ride. If you chose not to get a shower, you guided your tube to the right side, avoiding the waterfall. But I chose to get wet. I turned the tube so my feet were going first. Peter never saw it coming. It caught him completely by surprise. He rolled to the right to get away from the unexpected shower. As a result, he rolled off my legs and into the water. He had to swim to catch up to the tube and me. After I pulled him back on my legs, we had a good laugh. "Jake, why didn't you warn me that was coming?"

Still laughing, I said, "because I'm mean."

At one point while drifting along he said, "Jake, it's getting boring."

"Yeah, you're right." I flipped my legs up quickly and he landed in the water again, two feet behind the tube. Once again he had to swim to catch up, laughing and gasping for air all the way.

Once off the ride, I looked at him and said, "Hey, how come I'm dry and you're wet?" As I dried him, he was off and running again.

For lunch we stopped at the Yukon Trading Post. On a stage inside the building was a band composed of mechanical animals with musical instruments. It was quite a show. Peter loved it.

After lunch he was off and running again. But by mid-afternoon he was slowing noticeably. I found a bench in the shade and called him over. Resisting, he said, "Ah, Jake. I don't want to take a nap. This is too much fun."

"Kiddo, your energy is running low. Come on." He knew I was right. He came up on my lap and settled in. He slept for thirty-five minutes. When he woke, he was ready for the rest of the day.

While he slept, I spent my time people watching. Because of the temperature, most of the boys, like Peter, were wearing just their trunks. The girls were also in swimwear. As I watched I became aware of the overweight children—both boys and girls. Some were only slightly overweight but many were obese. Toddlers even! Nearly half of the kids were overweight. What happened? Twenty years ago when I taught school and worked in a summer camp, few children were overweight. Seldom did I see an obese child. Then I noticed the parents. About half of them were overweight as well.

I thought back to the three ropes strung across the pond. Come to think of it, a large proportion of those children who were attempting to cross were overweight. Many who weren't were out of shape.

Once awake, Peter and I walked back to the Yukon Trading Post. Outside we watched kids try Zack's shoot-out. Peter wanted to try. The rifles used were about the size of a 22 rifle, but electronic. The targets were electronic too. The rifles were so big for Peter, he had to put the butt in his armpit, but he still couldn't hold it steady. It didn't make a lot of difference, for the target was hard to miss. One target was against a wooden barrel so when it was hit, water would squirt out at the shooter. Peter couldn't get enough of this concession.

We headed to other rides and activities, Peter running and skipping on ahead. He'd climb to the top of the larger rocks and boulders and jump onto the smaller ones. His energy was back. Except for his nap, Peter was in perpetual motion from the time we'd entered the park.

We caught a small train ride around a portion of the park and went to the circus. Both were a good break from his motion, and both were enjoyable.

We walked past the ropes going across the pond. We stopped to watched both boys and girls try and fail. Finally one boy about ten succeeded. Both Peter and I congratulated him for being in good shape.

I told Peter to show his stuff again. I met him at the other side of the ropes. When I got there, a family was talking to him.

The man looked at me. "Are you this boy's father?"

"Grandfather."

"Well, he was something to watch. How does he stay in shape? My own boy tried it twice, but can't make it halfway. And he's nine."

I looked at the overweight boy standing in his trunks. His father was in the same shape. "How do you keep this lad trim?"

"Well, to begin with, no video games. I watch his diet carefully. We seldom eat in fast food joints. Today is an exception. He does push-ups, pull-ups, sit ups, leg lifts and deep knee bends every day. He also has two five-pound weights that he works with. I'm a cross-country truck driver. Peter rides with me. Several times a day we stop at rest areas. I let him have ten minutes to run. You're right. Yes, he's in great shape."

The man looked at his son. "I can't get Timmy to do all that. I can't even get him to cut back on his video games."

"Did you ever think about unplugging them and putting them away?"

"I couldn't do that. Timmy would get mad at me."

I rolled my eyes. "You're the father and the parent. Take back your control." I could see neither child was happy with what I was saying. "When Peter first came with me a year ago, he was in terrible shape. I refused to accept that. When he started working out, I did too. Now we're both happy and have a lot of fun playing and working out together."

He looked at Peter then back to me. "If you don't mind me asking, what do his parents think now?"

"They've joined the Y.M.C.A. and have become body builders. Competitive body builders at that." I winked at Peter who was looking at me like I'd lost my marbles.

After moving away from the family, Peter asked me why I was telling such lies. I explained that I was telling him a made-up story in the hopes of saving his and his kid's lives. I said, "Peter, there's a place for hyperbola. So I let him have some."

Peter said, "What's hi, hiperboles mean?"

I repeated the word several times for him. "It's spinning a story to make a dramatic point."

Peter said, "I think you got to the boy's father."

I doubted it. He didn't appear to have the backbone to take back control of the asylum from the inmates.

We drifted through the park on a rubber tube again for what was supposed to be a quiet ride. I threw Peter in the water so often, it was anything but quiet or dry. He loved it.

We finally made it around to the Enchanted Forest. The Enchanted Forest was a small dry park inside the Water Park for toddlers and small children. It was the home of The

Three Little Bears, The Three Blind Mice, Alice in Wonderland were many scenes of various nursery rhymes. It never occurred to me that Peter would be interested in any of them, since he was now reading at the ninth grade level. But he was interested in all of them. Of course he was still a little boy at heart.

From there we went to the petting zoo with many familiar farm animals that were approachable. That was another hit.

Dinner was the usual: hot dogs, french fries and pop. Finally, it was time to go.

The motion of the five-minute bus ride back to the lodge just about put Peter to sleep. Stepping off the bus, I threw him over my shoulder and started jogging. He was wide-awake again.

At the campsite, he changed into his pajamas while I started a fire, then he climbed onto my lap. I expected him to be asleep within minutes, but he wasn't in the mood yet. He wanted to talk about the day. We'd had a far better day than what I was originally expecting. He was disappointed in that he'd not been allowed on the bigger slides. But he understood.

At 8:30, he slipped off my lap. "I'm going behind the tent for a minute," he announced. "You're going to be here, aren't you?"

He was back in twenty seconds and on my lap again.

"Jake, are you disappointed in me because I'm afraid of bears?"

"I don't see a little boy afraid of bears in this campsite. Walking behind the tent alone when it's almost dark doesn't demonstrate a fear of anything. I think you have developed a healthy respect for them, but that's not fear. I'm very proud of you."

A big smile spread over his face. He cuddled but clearly wasn't ready for sleep. "Jake, you told me how tiny bears are when they're born." I nodded. "Can they walk?"

"No. That takes a few weeks."

"Can they see?"

"No. They can't see for six weeks."

"Do they have teeth?"

"No, they don't have teeth either."

"Well, how do they eat? And what do they eat?"

Uh-oh. I thought, here we go again. He has not asked a sensitive question for a long time. The first few months together he'd asked one a week. As a result, he had a pretty good understanding of the "birds and the bees." But the feeding process was new. It was time to roll up my sleeves and muddle through.

"Peter, all mammal infants feed in the same manner. It doesn't make any difference whether they're cats, dogs, seals, bears or humans. They all nurse. In other words, they suckle on their mother's breasts. Remember, a she-wolf nursed you one time."

He thought about this. Then he examined his own nipples. "So that's what these things are for. Are, well, Darlene's mother's breasts big because they're full of milk?"

"No. Some women are naturally big and some are naturally small. Just like some people are tall and some are short."

"Oh." That seemed to be that. He was satisfied and was soon asleep. I looked down at the little guy on my lap and smiled. This time I'd gotten off the hook easy.

CHAPTER TWENTY-ONE

Friday morning was promising to be a good day. We spent the day in the camp hiking, swimming and canoeing. At 3:30 I said, "Peter, how about a little something to eat?"

"I'm not hungry, Jake."

"How about half a sandwich? You eat one-half and I'll eat the other."

He looked at me. "Why? We're going to eat in another two hours anyway."

"I just think it would be a good idea."

He looked at me suspiciously. "I think you have something up your sleeve."

"You do?"

"Yeah. Come on Jake, what's going on?"

I never divulged my secret. In time I said, "You about ready to go?"

"Where?"

"For a car ride."

"Come on, Jake. Where are we going?" I just winked. "You know, sometimes you can be a real pain."

I chuckled. "I'm getting even."

He sat down and crossed his arms defiantly. "I'm not going anywhere until you tell me what's going on."

I walked over, picked him up and threw him over my shoulder. "That's what you think." As I walked to the car, I stuck my fingers in his ribcage. He squealed. He knew we were going to have fun. I put him in his child seat in the back seat and told him to buckle in. As we left the park, he said, "You know, I really hate it when you pull stuff like this."

Less than a mile from the campsite we pulled into a parking lot. A large white cruise boat was just coming around a bend in the lake and heading in our direction. Peter's eyes lit up. "Are we going to go on that?"

"I don't want to force you. But I know I'm going."

As he unbuckled his seat belt, he said, "I love it when you do stuff like this." He dove over the seat landing upside down, laughing and squealing. Had I told him this morning what we were going to do later in the day, he would have been out of control all day. Doing it my way, I maintained control of the sanity. But I loved his excitability and his zest for anything new. I opened my door and lifted him past me and set him on the parking lot.

I grabbed his hand to walk to the dock to watch the "big ship" come in. It was a sixty-foot replica of the steamboats that used to ply these waters a century ago. Of course the replica was a diesel with false smokestacks for authenticity. This was the kid's cruise. I wasn't sure just what that all entailed, but I was sure Peter would love it.

Once the boat docked, we stood in line for fifteen minutes for our tickets. There were kids from two to twelve everywhere amid Moms, Dads, and Grandparents.

After everyone boarded and the ropes were hauled in, we shoved off. Peter was wide eyed studying everything. This was the experience of a lifetime for him. For Peter this was like the little boy nobody wanted riding the high seas with his grandpa. (I was doing a good job with Peter, and make no bones about it even as I write this account.)

As we picked up speed, Peter was on cloud nine. We walked to the rail and watched the lake flow by. We watched the wake of the boat. We watched smaller and faster boats zipping by. We waved to people on shore. Periodically, Peter took my hand and squeezed it. Every once in a while the captain made an announcement pointing out something of historical significance on shore. As a history buff myself, I was impressed with his knowledge.

Later in the cruise the children were invited into the wheelhouse to take the wheel and steer the boat. Each child sat at the wheel for about a minute. There were fifteen children in line. When Peter reached number five his excitement had reached the boiling point. "Jake, could you hold my place in line? I have to pee."

With Peter's excitable bladder, I was surprised he'd made it this long. He ran for the back of the boat and down the circular stairs. He was back in thirty seconds. "Jake, the toilet is really neat." I chuckled. Only Peter could get excited about a toilet on a boat.

Finally it was Peter's turn. Peter was led into the wheelhouse and hoisted up into the captain's chair. Before him was a huge well varnished wooden wheel suggesting a pirate ship. Peter studied the dials. Pointing at one he said, "That's the RPM's, isn't it?"

The captain looked at him. "Yes it is. Do you know what RPM stands for?"

"Sure. Revolutions per minute."

The captain looked at me. "First child this young to know that!"

"I'm a cross-country truck driver. Peter's been riding with me for a year."

"But now he's my teacher full-time," Peter said proudly.

"Well, good for you. You are a very observant young sailor."

"How would you like to steer this ship?"

Peter's eyes enlarged even more. "Me? Really?" He didn't realize all the kids are given that opportunity.

The captain laughed. "Just put your hands here and here and guide us toward that huge tree on the shoreline down there."

Peter pointed to another instrument with his eyes. "What's that?"

"That's a depth finder. It tells me how deep the…"

Suddenly Peter turned the wheel hard right causing us to sway to the left. "Oh-my," I thought.

The captain was furious. "There's something in the water just below the surface," Peter screamed.

"There's nothing down there. We're in sixty feet of water. I know this lake like the back…"

"There it is," Peter yelled pointing to the left side of the boat.

The captain and I ran to the railing and looked down into the water. There was a huge log drifting a foot below the surface. It was half the length of the boat with a circumference of eight or ten feet. "Good God! It must have drifted free from the bottom. That thing could have sunk us."

"How did it get there?" I inquired as he walked back into the cabin, cut the power then put it in slow reverse.

"It has to be from the logging days on this lake. There must be a huge air pocket in it. Maybe part of the log finally broke off and the air pocket was large enough to bring the rest to the surface." He picked up his cell phone and called the Herkimer County Sheriff, who patrolled the lake. He reported the log and said we'd stay with it until they arrived. Then he turned to Peter. "How did you ever see that, Son?"

"Peter's eyesight is phenomenal, Sir—off the chart."

"Peter, I owe you a debt of gratitude. If you hadn't been behind the wheel, we could be in the midst of a terrible disaster right now. You're a hero."

Just then the sheriff's boat pulled along side with two other powerful looking boats. Several men jumped into the water and wrapped a heavy chain around the log. One end of the chain was attached to one boat and the other end to a second boat. Peter pulled me down to his level. "Jake, as soon as they try and pull it, the water is going to push the air pocket out. It's going to sink like a rock, pulling both boats down with it."

"Captain, once that thing starts moving, is it possible the water could knock the air pocket loose? And if that happens, won't it sink, taking the two boats with it? That thing is huge and must be waterlogged."

The captain looked at the monster log. Suddenly he grasped my point. "Caz, don't move your boats." He repeated my observation to the boat operators.

"I don't think that will happen, Cap."

"But could it?" the captain questioned. "Have you ever done this before?"

Caz looked at the captain then at the sheriff. "It's your call, Sheriff."

The sheriff looked at the monster. "Remove the chains. We'll dynamite that monster." The men had no more then removed the chains when the submerged monster let loose with a huge belch and a monstrous air bubble that surfaced and burst. The splash got everyone wet who was standing on the second deck The monster log dove for the bottom like a rock. Peter was right. The suction was so great it took two men down with it. Other men dove in to help their buddies, who soon came up gasping for breath. They were soon safely on board the boats.

Caz thanked the captain, the captain thanked me and I picked Peter up and hugged him.

The captain looked at us. "Look, I don't believe in coincidence. I believe in God. I also believe in angels. I think God placed both of you in the wheelhouse at just the right time. In my book, you're both angels. Thank you both so very much. I want your address, Sir, before you disembark. I want to formalize my remarks in a letter. I'll never forget this day."

As always, Peter saw the rescue as no big deal, but steering the boat had been huge. Before leaving the wheelhouse, Peter was handed a certificate. At the top it read "Junior Captain License." Peter's eyes about popped out of his head. I handed the captain our address. We thanked the captain for the opportunity and moved off with the rest of the passengers. Some knew we were in the wheelhouse during the near accident, but none realized the whole story.

Once back at the dock the captain and the rest of the crew, which amounted to one college girl, said good-bye to everyone. Peter and I were thanked again by the captain.

Peter and I ate dinner in town that evening, making it back to the campsite about 8:00. After changing into his pajamas he came up on my lap. "Well, Kiddo, how did the day go?"

"It was great! The boat ride was really neat. What are we doing tomorrow?"

"Oh, I don't know. Maybe just stay around the park."

He looked at me. "You have something up your sleeve again, don't you?"

"What makes you think that?"

"I don't know. But whenever you do, it's always fun."

Just then the family camped next to us came over. It was the Oakleys, including their two teenage daughters whom we'd met two days earlier. "How did your boat ride go, Peter?" the mother asked.

Peter looked surprised. "You knew about it too?" They laughed and nodded. "Everybody knows what's going on around here except me." The laughter increased. "We had a great time. It was fun. Look at this." He slipped off my lap and held his certificate for all to see in the dimming daylight. But instead of passing it around he said, "This is for steering the ship today. It says 'Junior Captain License to operate a public vessel on the Fulton Chain of Lakes. This is to certify that Peter Stevenson, having been duly examined and found competent by the undersigned Captain of the Passenger Vessel Clearlake, is licensed to serve as Junior Captain upon the Fulton Chain of Lakes, Old Forge, New York, whenever he or she takes a boat ride.' It's dated 8-13-02 and it's signed Robert P. Shore, captain, P.V. Clearlake."

He stood before us a proud boy. Each family member shook his hand and congratulated him.

Back on my lap, he looked at the family. "Do you know what Jake and I are doing tomorrow?"

They smiled and shrugged their shoulders. "You do, don't you? Well, that's okay. It's kind of funner this way. Hey, Grandpa, how about a bedtime story?"

"You're all welcome to stay if you'd like," I said to the family. They appreciated the invitation.

The next day after an active morning around the campground, I suggested to Peter that we go into town and have lunch at McDonald's. It was 11:00. Peter was agreeable and added, "What are we doing today?"

I smiled. "You'll see, Funny Tummy. Let's go."

As we pulled into the train station in the tiny town of Thendara, Peter squealed. "Jake, we're going for a train ride?" I smiled and nodded. "Grandpa, you're the greatest!"

THE SEPARATION

Walking toward the engine, Peter said, "Wow, look at the size of that sucker." I hoped this was going to be a normal, fun day with no surprise rescues.

In line for tickets, Peter asked, "Are there bathrooms on trains?"

"Do you have to go?"

"No. But it will be neat to pee on a moving train."

He'd enjoyed the restroom yesterday on the boat. I hoped his attraction to bathrooms was not habit forming. Was this common among children Peter's age or was Peter unique? I didn't know.

There were four cars including a baggage car. We got seated in the air-conditioned car behind the baggage car. "Wow, this is neat." I chuckled. We started moving smoothly.

As the speed picked up, the car rocked back and forth. Fortunately, we were able to get up and move around or Peter would have fallen asleep and missed everything.

Peter decided it was time to test the bathroom. I pointed out where it was, but he was soon back. "Jake, can you come with me? The train is rocking so much I can't stand still."

The snack bar on board sold candy bars, so I allowed him one.

We walked to the observation deck on the rear car and watched the ties go by. The conductor joined us and we learned a lot about the cars and the diesel engine.

Soon the train began to slow. "Why are we slowing down?" Peter asked. The conductor winked at me and said he didn't know. The 12:30 run was the train robbery run, but I hadn't told Peter that. When the train came to a stop the conductor yelled, "Oh, no. We're being robbed." He jumped from the train as if to help when several shots rang out. The conductor fell to the ground.

I looked at Peter and realized what was going through his mind. I picked him up—his tense body shook. "Peter, relax. This is all pretend. All these people are actors."

He looked at the prone conductor. "Even him?"

"Even him." If Peter had acted, it's the actors that would have needed rescuing.

Soon the conductor was on his feet heading back to his position in the last car. As he climbed in, he looked at us. "Well, how did that look?"

"I thought it was real." That was the best compliment the actor could have gotten. He was followed by several of the actor-robbers. All were carrying rifles, shotguns or pistols. Two were women. As one of the women walked by Peter and me, she gently squeezed Peter's cheek and said, "How you doing, cutie?"

Without hesitation I said, "Just fine, honey." She turned and looked at me fighting to keep a straight face. After all, these were supposed to be ornery train robbers.

Peter said in a disgusted manner, "Grandpa, she was talking to me."

That took care of her orneriness. She cracked up but got herself under control quickly. "See you both later, sweet things." She ruffled my hair instead of Peter's.

Once we were back at the train station and on the platform, the female train robber came up to us. She knelt down in front of Peter and asked his name. "Peter. You're a good actor."

"Well, thank you, Peter. Are you two in a hurry?"

"Not really. What do you have in mind?" I responded.

She stood up and took Peter's hand. "Come with me." As we walked towards the engine she said, "My cousin's the engineer today. How would you like to check out the engine?"

Peter's eyes about popped out of his head as he looked way up. "Really?"

She yelled, "Cindy." The engineer popped her head out a window. "Cindy, come down here for a minute. Got a couple of friends I want you to meet. Cindy, this is Peter and this is…"

She looked at me through apologetic eyes.

"Jake. I'm Peter's grandfather."

She shook both our hands.

"Peter said I'm a good actor," she reported to her cousin.

"Oh, Oh, Peter. Watch out. The last guy that told her that, she married."

"That's okay. I'm too little to get married."

"Cindy, could you show them around the cab?"

"Sure, in fact I can go one step better than that. You have a couple of hours to blow?"

"Well, I guess. What are you thinking of?"

"My next trip departs in ten minutes. How'd you like to ride along in the engine?"

That did it. I thought Peter would explode.

"I don't know, Peter. That doesn't sound too exciting, does it?"

Peter punched my thigh in fun. "What? Are you crazy?"

The two women laughed. "I believe that means yes."

Cindy looked at me. "I just thought of a problem. I can't take Peter along unless he's been designated a junior engineer."

Peter looked disappointed. "What can we do about that?" I said with concern.

"Peter," Cindy said, "I now appoint you my official junior engineer. That does it."

Peter's eyes lit up. "You mean I can go now?"

"Yep. No problem."

"Yeepie," he shouted as he jumped into my arms. It never ceased to amaze me how intelligent Peter was and yet how gullible he can be.

"Come on. I'll show you two the engine," Cindy said.

I put Peter on the steel steps. The steps were far apart so I had to assist him all the way.

Inside the cab Peter studied the different gages, knobs, switches and dials. "Wow, Jake, this has more stuff than the Babes has."

Cindy looked at Peter. "Who's the Babes?"

"It's more like *what* is the Babes. I'm a cross-country truck driver. The Babes is my name for my truck."

"Oh. So you two don't get to see each other very often?"

"Peter rode with me the past year. I'm a former teacher and now I'm Peter's traveling tutor. Before you ask, his parents are both deceased."

"Oh, I'm sorry to hear that. Now I know I made the right choice in bringing you two along. Well, Peter, you ready to go?"

Excitedly he said, "Yeah. Wait. Do you have a bathroom in here?"

"Oh, no! Do you really?" I asked.

He put his hands to the front of his pants. "Yeah. I have to go bad."

"Do you know where the bathroom is in the terminal?" Cindy asked. He did. "Okay. We'll wait for you. Grandpa, you'd better help him down the stairs."

I got him to ground level and he took off running. Just then a message came through on her walkie-talkie from the conductor at the back of the train. "Cindy, is everything okay up there?"

She chuckled into the radio. "No problem, Luke. Just a miniature bladder to empty. We'll be ready to go in just a minute."

The conductor chuckled. "10-4 on the miniature bladder."

Just then Peter came bounding out of the terminal, his golden locks flying and smile shining. I met him at the bottom step and carried him all the way up.

"Peter, can you reach this lever?"

He tried but it was too high. "Am I allowed to help?" I asked.

"Sure. Grandpas are always allowed to help," Cindy said smiling.

I picked Peter up and he pushed the proper lever counterclockwise. A bell started ringing. Peter's eyes enlarged. "What does that mean?" he asked Cindy.

"That means we're ready to get moving as soon as my junior engineer does one more thing. Grandpa, can you get him a little higher so he can pull that cord?"

I picked him up a little higher. "Just once this time, Peter" Cindy said.

Peter grabbed it. "It's for the air horn, isn't it?" Cindy smiled and nodded. Peter gave it a sharp blast. And jumped in my arms. "Wow, Jake. That's a lot louder than the Babes. Can I do it again?" he asked Cindy, pushing his luck.

"Not yet. On our way out, I'll blow it, but on the way back that will be your job. That is if your grandpa can keep up."

I chuckled, "I'll do my best." Peter smiled.

As we slowly began moving, Peter said, "Why are we backing up?"

"Going out we push; coming back we pull."

Peter watched her every movement. "Where's your gear shift and the clutch?"

"Wow, you really are a trucker. There's no clutch or gear shift in here, just a throttle."

Peter looked at the floor. "Hey, wait a minute. You don't have a brake pedal."

"These are the brake levers." Just then she got a message from the conductor standing at the end of the back car which was now the first or lead car. "Peter, we're coming to a road crossing. Get ready with the bell." I picked him up so he could reach the lever. "Now let it ring until I tell you to turn it off. We're going around a curve. If you look out your side window, you'll see the first car. Get ready. She gave a long blast. As the back car got closer to the crossing she gave it another long blast. Then she gave it a short blast. As the back car got to the crossing, she gave a longer blast as the car crossed the roadway. "The horn has to be blaring as the first unit in line crosses the road. That's the law. On the way back, the engine will be first unit. Then it will be your job." Peter couldn't have been happier if he'd been made the chief engineer.

We crossed several other roads. Peter studied each one and watched Cindy carefully. As we approached the next crossing, Cindy alerted him. He jumped off my lap, pulled my hand and said, "Come on, Grandpa. You have to get me ready for the bell."

Finally, we came to a stop. It was time to head back. The conductor moved from the back car to the engine. Cindy introduced the conductor to us, but when she introduced Peter, she said, "Peter is my junior engineer." Peter's chest was ready to burst.

As we approached the first crossing, Peter slipped off my lap in plenty of time. He took my hand and pulled. "Come on, Grandpa, I have a job to do." I picked him up and he got ready. He looked at Cindy. "Now?"

"Not yet."

After ten seconds he said, "Now?" The answer again was the same.

After another ten seconds he asked, "Now?" The answer was, "Now." Peter proudly threw the switch and the bell rang. He reached for the cord and looked at Cindy. "Now?"

She hesitated for a few seconds then said, "Now."

He gave it a mighty yank and let go a long blast. He was flashing a victorious smile. He waited ten seconds and blew it again. Cindy smiled and nodded. Thirty feet from the road he gave it a short blast. Ten feet from the road he gave it a blast until the engine was across the road. In short order, he turned the bell off grinning.

"Peter," Cindy said, "Your timing was darn good."

Peter was beaming from ear to ear. Still holding Peter in my arms, I said, "Hey, Funny Tummy, your six-year-old ego is about to burst. Time to get it back where it belongs." I pulled his shirt up and played a few ribs to get a giggle and to deflate his swollen pride. He squealed to the delight of the conductor and Cindy.

At the next two crossings he rang the bell and blew the horns without Cindy's prompting. As we were climbing a slight hill to the third crossing, we naturally started slowing. Cindy gave it more power. The engine roared, but the slowing continued to a stop. Cindy tried several different things with the controls, but we didn't budge. At first I thought it was part of the scripted trip like the robbery on the last trip. But we were a mile from the station and we were stuck. This was obviously unplanned.

The conductor called the station on his cell phone and briefed someone on the state of the 1941 diesel engine.

While he was on the phone, Peter quietly said to me, "Jake, I can get us back to the station."

"Peter, I don't think that fits into your job description as junior engineer. This isn't an emergency. Let's let them handle it."

We learned that another engine was coming to pull us back to the station. While we waited for help, the conductor walked through the cars to tell the passengers what was going on. Since this was a tourist ride, the restrictions were much more relaxed than had it been a normal passenger train. So many people left their car to wander around the train.

Within half an hour the other engine was in sight. Many fathers and sons came up to the conductor to watch the proceedings. Peter, Cindy and I stood on the porch, as Cindy called it, outside of the cab and watched the huge engine nudge into us. As the two couplers joined, Peter said, "Wow, look at the size of those things."

The engineer of the rescue engine put it into forward for a second. Peter looked at me. "Jake, he does a tug check just like you do when you hook up to a trailer." Then the conductor connected the cables between the two engines. "Jake, they even have a pigtail, just like trucks."

Cindy was impressed. "Peter, you have the terminology down pretty good."

All business, he responded, "I couldn't be a trucker if I didn't."

Cindy was told to shut down her engine. Before long we were on the move again. I asked Peter, "Wasn't that more fun than using your powers?"

"Yeah! That was really neat."

What a day we had. Once we got back to the terminal, the junior engineer gave the senior engineer a huge hug around her waist. That's all the thanks she needed. She bent over and returned the hug, saying, "Peter, this was the best run I've ever made. Breakdowns are entertaining and break the routine. With a bright little assistant like you, I'd gladly take a pay cut."

I chuckled to myself. Every worker on this tiny railroad was a volunteer. "If you ever want to do this again, just let me know."

Before leaving the platform, over a dozen cameras appeared to take shots of Peter and Cindy beside the engine. I got a few myself.

I asked the good Lord to tickle my ribs to prevent my old ego from busting.

CHAPTER TWENTY-TWO

That night in the campsite we had quite a talk. Peter went on non-stop for ten minutes about the last two days. Then he wanted to know what we were going to do tomorrow. "This time, Kiddo, I really don't have anything up my sleeve. I guess we'll just stay in the park and swim, canoe, hike and relax."

"That's okay with me as long as we're doing it together."

Just then the Oakley family approached our campsite. "Could we join you for a few minutes?" Dorothy Oakley asked. They wanted to know how the train ride went as this was their last night in camp.

He looked at them and laughed. "I thought you guys knew." Peter jumped off my lap as his excitement and animation took over. "It was great. We went forwards and backwards and we walked all over the train and I peed on the train and we got robbed and the conductor got shot, but not really and I got to ring the bell and blow the air horns and now I'm a junior engineer and we broke down and this real big engine came along and…"

"Hold it, Kiddo."

"Oh, was I talking too fast?"

"Just a tad. Start over, but take it easy." With some coaching from me, he made it safely to the end.

"And now I'm a junior engineer and a junior captain," he concluded, like a train coming to a stop.

"Wow," Todd Oakley said. "That was quite an experience." I could tell he wouldn't mind taking a ride in the engine himself.

Peter came back on my lap. After we talked for twenty minutes, one of the girls suggested I write a book. I thought she was cute. Peter did too, but not for the same reason. Actually both Oakley girls were cute.

After the Oakleys left, Peter walked behind the tent alone, the bear no longer an issue. Several more people stopped by to say hello and enjoy our fire. Of course, Peter had to tell them also that he was now a junior captain and a junior engineer.

Our last day was enjoyable, but nothing as exciting as the last two days. But like always, it was active.

That last evening we went to the pavilion to watch the movie, *Chiti, Chiti Bang Bang*. The movie lasted until 9:20, but Peter didn't. It was all uphill to the campsite from the pavilion. Although Peter only weighed thirty pounds, asleep he was dead weight…in more ways than one. Usually I admired the way Peter slept, but not at times like this.

Walking up to our area with us was another family who carried my chair. I put Peter over my shoulder explaining to them that this was easier on me. At one point the man made the comment that Peter looked dead. (Little did he know.)

I dressed Peter for bed and lay him on his sleeping bag. I studied his body before covering him. I thought of my conversation with his mother, and laughed. I'd promised her I would take care of Peter's little body as well as I could. But here were Band-Aids on his right knee and shin and a long scratch on his left arm along with a couple of new bruises; all evidence of a fall he took earlier when not paying attention to where he was running.

The next day it was time to pack and leave. Unlike at the last campsite, I didn't take the tent down while Peter slept. He woke at 7:15 and wandered out of the tent. "You didn't take the tent down yet. Didn't I sleep long enough this morning?"

"You little stinker." I grabbed him and threw him up in the air. "You aren't getting out of all the work this time." I ran my beard across his bare belly as he squealed in delight. "Now let's get this tent down and rolled."

Once the fun was over and it was time to work, he was a better worker than most twelve-year-olds. The tent was soon down, rolled and packed in the car. It was then off to the showers.

On the road to Rochester, I asked, "Well, what did you think of that place?"

He didn't think long. "It was a long way to walk if you had to poop bad, but the bathroom smelled better than the outhouse. The showers were closer than the other place, and we had more than five minutes to take one." In the other place the showers were two miles away and two quarters gave you a stingy five-minute shower.

"We always knew the drinking water was clean, but we had to walk all the way to the bathhouse to wash our dishes. That was a pain.

"The ride on the boat and train were great. Can we do that again next year?"

"I don't see why not." Last year at this time I wasn't sure if there would be a next year.

He went on. "All the trails and roads to walk were neat, and we could do it without getting lost…once you decided to take the map with you."

I looked at him in the mirror. "Careful there, boy. You're treading on thin ice."

He gave me a nasty laugh.

"Now we're like pioneers, right? We both know our way around," I volunteered.

I looked in the mirror and noticed a snide smile. "I don't know, Jake. I think I'm like Jim Bridger, but you're more like a greenhorn."

"Boy, that thin ice you're on is about ready to break."

His laughter increased. "Seriously, Jake, that was really fun. If we take our bikes next year it would be even funner. But I still want to spend a day or two fishing on our lake. I hope that Danny and Bill can go with us. I'd like to spend some time with Darlene and her mom. And I'd like to fly with Sam."

"I agree with everything you just said. We've got the whole year to come up with a plan. Plenty of time to work out the details."

"I know Darlene and her mom can't stay overnight with us in the tent, but maybe they can come over for the day and go to the Water Park with us. Darlene and I have a lot of fun playing together. You could have a lot of fun watching Darlene's mother."

I looked in the mirror again. Peter was fighting a giggle. "Boy, you are cruisin' today. It's a good thing I'm driving." His giggle broke into an all out nasty laugh.

Fifteen minutes later we pulled into my niece's driveway. I had my seat belt unfastened before we came to a stop. I ran around to the other side of the car and opened the door for Peter. He was busy watching the house for signs of Betty and Jerry. As he stepped from the car, I grabbed him and gently threw him into the grass and sat on his legs. Until I grabbed him, he had no idea what was coming. He immediately started laughing. "It's pay-back time, boy."

I pulled up his shirt and got my fingers walking up his left rack of ribs. His squeals of joy brought everybody from inside the house. Betty said, "Jake, get off that poor boy. You're torturing him."

Peter laughed even harder, gasping for breath. He loved it when Betty got upset with me. I stopped laughing for a minute. I looked at Betty. "He was meaner to me than I ever am to him."

Innocently, he looked at Betty and in a sickeningly sweet voice said, "I don't know what he's talking about, Aunt Betty."

Betty started laughing. "Oh brother!" she said.

"Why you little stinker," I said. My fingers started walking up his right rack, to a new wave of squeals.

As my fingers approached his armpit, he said, "Okay, I was mean. I'm sorry."

I stopped the walking, looked at him and said, "No you're not."

Still laughing he said, "I know but it sounds good."

That got everybody laughing hard. I lifted him up into my arms and gave him a quick hug, and put him down. As I looked around the group I said, "Yes, we had a great time." Peter immediately agreed. We all went inside to merge with the party we had disrupted.

This year the party went much better for Peter. Last year's birthday party was foreign to him. He'd not been to anybody's birthday party, let alone his own. Plus, the only people he knew were Betty and Jerry. Now he knew everybody and knew he was loved as part of the family.

He talked about the trip with an enthusiasm we all enjoyed. There was more to talk about than he could cover. He talked about his baseball game. Since he never mentioned his home run, I did.

There were a few other things neither of us mentioned: His rescue of Sam and me in the plane and his lesson on prayer. He didn't mention the fight he had with Jimmy, nor did I. He talked about the train and boat ride, but skipped over our close call on the boat. But we did mention Paula and Darlene. I told everybody how cute Darlene was and how much Peter enjoyed playing with her. He blushed, but managed to pay me back.

He had to acknowledge how attractive Paula was and how well she filled out her string bikini. "Jake spent all his time watching her and totally ignored me. I felt like an orphan again." He looked in mocked sadness, around the room inviting sympathy. "I was so lonely I almost cried."

I became the embarrassed one as everybody roared at my expense. That gave me a chance to think. "Lonely? Baloney! Paula wasn't the only beauty in a string bikini. Darlene wore one too. Peter was so busy chasing her over the beach all afternoon, that by day's end he didn't even know which lake he was on."

Peter turned bright red as everyone laughed at *his* expense. "You're a stinker, Jake." The laughter swelled again.

I called him over to my lap. "Are you okay?"

"Sure! But I'm not finished yet."

I looked at him. What did he mean by that?

We both talked about our stay at the campgrounds in Old Forge and our day-and-a-half at the Water Park. He talked about getting caught by a bear with his pants down behind our tent.

The birthday girl looked at him wide-eyed. "Weren't you scared?"

"Yeah, I was real scared. I turned around to run but tripped over my pajama bottoms and fell on my face. The bear was only five feet from me. I screamed for Jake. He came around to rescue me, but started laughing. He said the bear was laughing too. But I was afraid the bear was going to eat me. But Jake said bears don't eat little kids because we taste funny."

My grandniece looked at me for confirmation as all the adults laughed picturing the entire scene. I nodded. "Kids taste real funny to bears."

Peter continued. "Did you know black bears weigh only one-half pound when they're born and grizzly bears only weigh one pound?"

"No way!" Countered my grandniece.

"Way!" Peter said. "Jake said so." That settled any question over my being the ultimate authority.

In a serious moment, I told how Peter overcame his fear of bears, and how he turned fear into a healthy respect for them.

Neither one of us mentioned the rescue of the Clay family.

He described how we got lost the first day at the campgrounds trying to find the bathrooms. He said the only reason we got lost was because I left the map in our tent. The stinker loved to get my family laughing at me. What could I say? The worst part was, I couldn't figure a way to get him back, this time. He had maneuvered me into this. As well as I knew him, I never saw this one coming.

"You got me, Kiddo. But I love you anyway." He gave me a hug.

CHAPTER TWENTY-THREE

After swimming and the gift giving, Peter and I headed for home, followed by Betty and Jerry. We agreed to meet at a local restaurant in Orchard Park for chicken wings, a repeat of last year. But, things didn't work out that way.

Near Buffalo, Peter and I were driving along talking when suddenly he didn't answer. In the mirror I could see he was staring at nothing. What was coming now? "Peter?" I asked.

"Jake, we have to get to Children's Hostipal in Buffalo, quick." (He's never been able to pronounce hospital correctly.)

"What's going on, Kiddo?"

"It's Jamie." I saw the tears starting. "He's real sick, Jake. He's dying."

I almost swerved as I turned my head to look at him directly. "Why? What happened?"

"They don't know. He's been sick three days. Yesterday his temperature went up near 106 degrees. They rushed him to the hostipal. He's near death. He's in a como. He's waiting for me, Jake."

"Can you help him get better, Kiddo?"

He hesitated. "I'm not sure. Maybe." The tears flowed. "He thinks he's going to die. He wants me to guide him to his grandfather."

I sniffled. "Should you go ahead?"

"No! He wants to see you before he goes." He cried harder. "Jake, I don't want him to die. He's my big brother. I don't want him to become like Teddy."

"Does Jamie know we're coming?" I wiped my tears.

"He knows, Jake."

"He's a great kid! I love his unconditional friendship toward you."

Both Jerry and I had CB's. So I got him at once and told him to take it to channel 30. I filled them in on what was happening. I said we'd be home as soon as possible.

They asked if they should go with us. I suggested they go on home and wait for our call.

Fifteen minutes later, we pulled into the parking lot of the hospital. "I don't know how we're going to do this, Kiddo. Jamie's probably in the intensive care unit. They don't allow kids, and then only close relatives."

"No problem. You're his grandpa and I'll have no problem getting in. You're the only one that can see me now."

Peter told me the room Jamie was in. We went to the nurse's station on the proper floor. I explained I was Jamie Rotundo's "grandfather," just in from out of town. I was led right in.

After the door closed, Judy asked, "Jake, how did you get in here?"

"Jamie called Peter and me. So Peter's here too." Peter suddenly appeared and they both jumped. "We were near Buffalo."

Judy looked at me. "But Jake, he's been in a coma since yesterday. He, he's not expected to recover." Her tears erupted.

"I know." I looked at Peter looking at Jamie. Peter was shocked. Jamie had so many tubes running into and out of his small body, I lost count. Plus monitors to register his heartbeat, respiration rate, temperature and Lord knows what else. "Judy, Carl,—don't give up hope." I put my hand on Peter's head. "Not yet anyway." My tears were clouding the scene from my eyes.

Suddenly Jamie weakly called to Peter. In a voice barely audible he asked, "Little brother, are you here?"

Judy and Carl looked at me then at their son. We all circled his bed. Peter said, "I'm here, Jamie." Peter clasped Jamie's right hand, careful not to disturb the IV. With his other hand he wiped his tears.

"I knew you'd come." He had a trace of a smile. "Is your Grandpa here?"

I stroked his right cheek. "I'm here, Jamie." I fought with my tears, too.

"Thank you for being so nice to me, Mr. Winters. I always had fun at your house." He coughed violently.

"You were a pleasure to have, Jamie."

He looked back at Peter. "I was your guide that first day you came to my school. Are you going to be my guide today and take me to my grandfather?"

Both Rotundo parents were crying openly. "I will if I'm needed, Big Brother." Peter looked up appearing confused, then he looked at me. "Jake, you have to take his other hand." I didn't understand, but I walked around the bed. Judy relinquished her son's hand to mine and took Carl's arm. I squeezed Jamie's cold hand gently. The squeeze I got back was barely detectable.

Jamie closed his eyes then opened them again. It was obvious he was fighting to hold on just a few seconds longer. In his struggle, I saw Peter one hundred years ago fighting to hold on one more day. Peter brought me back to the present with, "Jake, don't release his hand for any reason until I tell you it's okay." We all looked at Peter. I didn't understand but sensed that it was extremely important to Jamie. Jamie's parents did too.

Jamie looked at his parents. Tears came to his eyes. Struggling, he said, "I love you, Mom, Dad. Don't worry about me. I'll be fine with Grandpa and Jesus. Say good-bye to my sisters for me." Our tears were falling on the bed sheets like rain. He looked back to Peter. "I'm ready, Little Brother." He closed his eyes.

His small hand in mine fell limp. The heart monitor went to a solid line, and a wail. "Don't let go, Jake, for any reason," Peter emphasized. Judy screamed, "Noooo!" We heard an alarm in the hall outside Jamie's door. Jamie's parents were convulsing in sobs. Jamie looked comfortable and contented. I fought to keep up with my tears with one hand. I looked at Peter. He was smiling. None of us had to be told what had just happened. Peter's smile enlarged. I was more confused than ever, but I held on to Jamie's hand.

"Peter, I'm baffled!"

"Hold on, Jake."

Suddenly two nurses entered the room and rushed to either side of Jamie's bed. They asked me to get out of the way. "Jake, don't let go or all will be lost," Peter yelled. The nurse next to me looked around the room and backed off. Did she hear him?

Now a doctor rushed into the room followed by another nurse pushing a defibrillator. They went to Peter's side of Jamie's bed. The doctor detached the heart monitors from Jamie's small, nonfunctioning chest as the nurse prepared the defibrillator. The doctor told me to step away from Jamie's bed. "Don't do it, Jake," Peter yelled again. "Hang on. Jamie's almost back."

The doctor and all the nurses looked around the room, uncertain. Suddenly and unexpectedly, Jamie's chest and diaphragm started moving. Confused, the doctor reattached the monitors. The solid line was gone indicating a heartbeat. The beeping was back. Jamie's chest and diaphragm were slowly rising and falling. Peter looked up toward heaven.

"He'll be okay now." He looked at Jamie's parents. Suddenly Jamie squeezed my hand with strength he didn't have only seconds before. I noticed he did the same with Peter's hand. The doctor and nurses noticed also.

Peter looked at me. "You can let go now if you want to." I passed Jamie's hand to his mother.

In tears, Judy looked at Peter. "You saved my son's life, Peter. You truly are an angel."

As I walked to Peter's side of the bed the doctor looked at Judy and said, "Excuse me?"

Ignoring the doctor, I pulled Peter's head to me kissing him. "How did you do that, Peter?"

Now the doctor looked at me questioningly.

"I don't know but it wasn't just me. He needed your touch too, just like I do to heal myself." I was confused. "Remember, Jake, we're a team." I didn't understand any of it, but Jamie was alive.

The medical team looked at the monitors and the doctor checked Jamie's vitals. He looked at the nurses and at each one of us confused. Judy asked how her son was doing.

The doctor looked at her in disbelief. He finally shook his head. "It appears he's sleeping. His heart is strong. His blood pressure is near normal. His pulse is strong and his temperature is below 100 degrees. Thirty minutes ago, he was near death. A couple of minutes ago the monitors indicated he had…Yet now he's fine. I don't understand it, but I'm thrilled." He looked at the monitors then back at Jamie.

He noticed Jamie's right hand. It appeared Jamie was hanging onto something. The doctor turned to Jamie's parents. "A minute ago I thought I heard a child yell, 'Don't do it, Jake. Hang on. Jamie's almost back.' Was I hearing things?" They both turned to me as did the doctor and nurses.

I stuck out my hand. "I'm Jake. What you heard was Peter, my guardian angel. I don't understand how, but Jamie contacted Peter about an hour ago asking for help. Peter instructed me to hold Jamie's hand no matter what, or he would die." The doctor looked doubtful. "I don't understand it either doctor, but I wasn't about to let go. Obviously, Peter was right."

He looked at me as if I were a nut case, yet in the background all of Jamie's monitors were purring sweetly. "Am I to assume we just witnessed an heavenly miracle?"

I looked up, then at Peter and finally to the doctor. "Do you have a better name for it, Doctor?" Peter and I smiled at each other. Judy and Carl were smiling too.

"Who are you?"

"I'm a friend of the family."

"Not a family member?" I shook my head. "I don't know who you think you are, but you're breaking hospital rules. Only close relatives are allowed in ICU. You must leave now."

At that point Carl stepped up. "Doctor, if it weren't for Jake and Peter, my son would be dead now. They can stay as long as they want. The hell with your rules." Suddenly he looked ashamed of himself for losing his cool in front of an angel, looked at Peter and apologized. The doctor followed his gaze but saw nothing.

Just then Jamie woke up, looked at the medical team assembled around his bed then at Peter. "My grandpa said it isn't my time yet. He said to go back to my family and friends. He said my friends are very powerful. Thanks, Little Brother." Jamie squeezed an unseen hand.

The doctor and nurses looked to where Jamie was talking. Suddenly all three nurses gasped. Two of them dropped to their knees and crossed themselves, and the other bowed her head in prayer. I looked at Peter. He shrugged his shoulders. One of the nurses told me later that she saw a beautiful array of colors where Jamie was looking.

Meanwhile, the doctor, apparently unseeing and unable to accept the fact that an angel had guided his little patient to the fringes of heaven and back, left the room quickly.

Jamie spent the rest of the night in the hospital with Judy at his side. She told me the next day that two of the nurses remained at his side the entire night, even though their shift was over at 11:00. Other nurses, doctors and medical assistants of various types stopped in during the night, apparently as the story spread, to see the little boy who'd been aided by an angel.

The next morning Peter was anxious to call the hospital, but I insisted we wait until 9:00. When we called, we learned Jamie had been moved to a private room earlier that morning. I was given his room number and I was transferred to his room. I had Peter pick up the other phone and let him do the talking. Judy answered.

"Hi, Mrs. Rotundo. This is Peter. Is Jamie awake yet?"

"Well, good morning, Peter. He's awake and just brightened considerably. I bet you'd like to talk to him."

"Yeah, I sure would."

Soon Jamie was on the phone. Excitedly he said, "Hi, Peter!"

"Hi, Jamie. It's good to hear your voice. When are you coming home?"

"I don't know. I'm ready to leave right now, but they won't let me," Jamie said in a disappointed tone.

"Why not?" Peter asked sounding as upset as Jamie.

I decided this was a good time to break in. "Hi Jamie. How are you feeling this morning?"

"I feel great, Mr. Winters. But I have to stay in this stupid bed for some reason."

I chuckled. "Hey, Jamie, you were a pretty sick little kid and last night you died. I'm sure they will want to keep you for a day or two for observation."

"What do you mean?" Jamie asked.

"The doctors will want to keep an eye on you for a while just to make sure you don't have a relapse."

"What's that?" Jamie asked with worry in his voice.

"They want to make sure that virus doesn't come back."

"Well, that's pretty stupid," Peter said. "God told me you would be okay."

"Hey, you guys, it's standard procedure. Jamie, would it be okay with you if Peter and I come into visit you this afternoon?"

Peter's eyes lit up and I knew Jamie's did too. "Wow! Would you?"

"Only if you promise to sleep for a while if you get tired."

"I promise."

"Great! We'll be there around 2:00. Let me talk to your mom for a minute."

"Okay. See you both later."

"Hi, Jake." She paused and sniffled. "Peter, are you still on the phone?" Peter answered yes. She sniffled again. "I can't thank the two of you enough for last night. Because of both of you, my son is still alive."

"Judy, Peter has assisted God in another rescue, but this time, not without my help. I have no idea what my hand had to do with it, but I thank God, we made it to the hospital in time. We'll see you this afternoon."

CHAPTER TWENTY-FOUR

At 2:00, Peter and I walked into Jamie's room as promised. Peter raced across the room to Jamie's bed. "Hi, Big Brother. Where are all the tubes?" he asked as he climbed onto the side rail of the hospital bed.

Jamie giggled. "I don't need them anymore. I even had one on my...well, you know so I didn't even have to get out of bed to pee."

"Neat!" Peter looked at me. "I could have used one of them last year when I was having those real bad nightmares." Judy and I laughed. "You want to play checkers?"

That settled it. Judy helped Jamie move to a chair. As she did, Peter studied him strangely. "Jamie, why are you wearing a dress?"

"Peter, it's not a dress," I said chuckling. "It's a hospital gown."

As the boys got settled a nurse entered the room. She walked over to Jamie. "Honey, what are you doing out of bed?"

"Peter and I are going to play checkers. It's easier in the chair. I'm okay."

She looked at Peter and at me. "Aren't you the family friend that was in here last night? And wasn't it your guardian angel that saved Jamie?" She looked at Peter. Suddenly the light went on. "Oh, my Lord! You're Peter, the angel." She crossed herself and bowed to Peter several times repeating over and over again, "Praise the Lord."

I walked up to the nurse and put my hand on her shoulder. "No, ma'am. This is Peter, my grandson. That was Peter, my guardian angel last night, but he isn't here now."

She looked at me skeptically. "But this Peter looks like an angel."

"And sometimes he acts like an angel, but there are other times you'd wish he'd disappear. I assure you ma'am, this boy is no angel."

Peter gave her a devilish smirk. "I see what you mean. But that was quite a night last night. Jamie, if you get cold call me. Do you have to go to the bathroom?"

"No ma'am, I'm okay."

"Well, call me when you do."

After the nurse left, Peter asked, "You have to call her if you have to pee?"

"Yeah. She even gave me a bath this morning…and I was still in bed."

Both Judy and I laughed. "Will you two be okay if Jake and I go down for a cup of coffee?" Judy asked.

"Sure. We'll be fine," Jamie said.

"Peter, if Jamie starts getting tired, make sure he lies down for a while."

"No problem, Jake."

Inside the cafeteria I offered to treat her to a cup of coffee and a roll, but she wouldn't hear of it. "Jake, my family owes you and Peter so much. Peter may be your guardian angel, but you both are Jamie's guardian angels."

We enjoyed our coffee and our conversation until the nurse that was in Jamie's room earlier interrupted us. "Mrs. Rotundo, Mr. Winters, I'm sorry to bother you two, but I'm afraid you're needed upstairs immediately."

Judy jumped out of her chair so fast that she spilt her coffee, startling the nurse. "What's wrong with Jamie? Is he okay?" Judy asked frantically.

"Jamie's fine, but you're right, Mr. Winters. Peter is no angel."

"What did he do?" I asked hesitantly.

"He had Jamie sit in his wheelchair, pushed him into the hall and got into a drag race with another child in the hall," she responded obviously very upset.

Judy was trying to suppress a smile. My poker face came in handy. "Did they win?" I asked relieved. My humor was not appreciated by the hospital staff member. We were escorted back to Jamie's room by the stern-faced nurse.

As we walk into Jamie's room, we found Jamie on his bed covered with a sheet to his chest. Peter was in the chair. Both boys sat solemn-faced. I stood before the two of them with my hands on my hips. "Okay, you guys. What happened after we left?"

Peter put his head down lower. "I'm sorry, Grandpa, but we were bored. It sounded like fun."

"Whose idea was it?"

"Sort of mine," Peter volunteered.

"Sort of?" I asked.

"It was all mine," he admitted.

"But I went along with it," Jamie chimed in.

"Did you win?"

They both smiled a little. "No. But the other kid cut us off at the corner."

"Hey, guys, a hospital hall is the wrong place for drag racing or any kind of racing for that matter."

"We should have known better," Jamie said. "We're sorry."

I looked at Peter. "I am too, Grandpa...but it was fun."

"Hey, guys, it's time for us to go. Is Carl coming in?" I asked Judy.

"He'll be here in about and hour. He's staying the night while I stay home with the girls. Hopefully, Jamie will be released tomorrow afternoon, depending on how the tests go."

Peter said, "We'll say our prayers, Jamie."

"We sure will, Jamie," I added. "We'll call tomorrow morning. If you're still here, we'll stop in again. You be good tonight Jamie, and no more racing."

"I can't. My driver's gone." We all laughed on that one.

We called the hospital the next morning. Jamie was still there but discouraged. He had hoped to go home that morning. They told his dad maybe in the late afternoon. I told Carl we'd be in around 11:00.

When Peter and I arrived, Carl was sitting in the hall. At first I thought he was worried; however, he was just tired. "Good morning, Jake and Peter. Jamie's just finishing up his morning bath."

"Then everything's okay?"

"Everything's fine except he doesn't appreciate sponge baths."

Carl and I both laughed, but Peter didn't understand the humor. "Can we go in?" Peter asked.

"No. We're not allowed in because Jamie's naked."

"So? I take baths with him all the time and Jake see's him naked too."

"I understand where you're coming from, Peter, after all, I'm his father. But it's one of the hospital's rules. Kind of ridiculous, right?"

Peter and I agreed. "What do you think, Carl? Is he going to be allowed to go home this afternoon?"

"I certainly hope so. We all know he's fine, right Peter?"

"Yeah, he's fine."

"Believe it or not, even his sister's miss him."

Just then an attractive young nurse walked out of Jamie's room pushing a cart with the materials on it for a bath. "How come we couldn't come in?" Peter asked. "Jamie and I take baths together all the time."

The nurse gave Peter a charming smile. "I'm sure you do but it's hospital rules. You can go in now."

As we walked in, Jamie was thrilled to see Peter again. Peter had his checkered board again plus a deck of cards. Pretty soon Carl asked if I would be interested in going down for a cup of coffee. I looked at the boys. "Are you two little monsters going to behave while we're gone?"

They both gave me their innocent smiles. "No racing you guys."

"We won't, Jake. I promise," Peter said.

Carl and I walked to the elevator. "I hope they behave today."

He started laughing. "Judy told me about yesterday. Those two are quite a pair. I guess it could have been worse."

As we walked into the cafeteria, we were still laughing. After pouring our coffee, we had a seat at a table. "Jake, I am really indebted to you and Peter. If it hadn't been for the two of you, we'd be putting Jamie in the ground right now instead of drinking coffee." His right hand shook and his eyes were moist.

"Life is so precious, yet so fragile." He clasped his mug with both hands. "Two nights ago, Jamie was not expected to live through the night." (He choked on the word live.) "Then you appeared in Jamie's room. Judy and I didn't understand why or how you were able to get in there. Suddenly Peter appeared out of nowhere. We were shocked but to be perfectly honest, we were annoyed too. After all, that was to be our last private time with our son." A tear hit the table.

"The next five minutes moved so fast. Jamie died and was standing on the threshold of heaven—his grandfather apparently waiting for him. Then the miracle of miracles occurred. Because of you and Peter, he was returned to us. I don't understand any of it, but for the first time in my life, I'm thanking God many times a day for sparing Jamie."

He stared into his coffee in silence. Finally he continued. "Jake, I asked Jamie today if he'd like to invite Peter over to our house for a sleepover some day. He wasn't excited about it. I questioned him on that. He loves his parents and his house. He even admitted he likes his sisters sometimes—sort of. It turns out the reason he doesn't want to invite Peter over is because he knows he can't invite you. He loves you the way he loved his grandpa. And frankly, I can understand. I've been a little—well, I never saw affection as I grew up and I've short-changed Jamie all these years. Jamie has been given a new lease on life, and I feel I have too. So I'm going to try and make some changes. I know Jamie will help."

"Carl, I'm humbled to hear this."

"Well, my late father-in-law played with Jamie the way you do with Peter. I've had it modeled for me. Now that Grandpa's gone, the ball comes to me. I'm not going to short-change Jamie again."

I was speechless. And choked. Finally, I said, "I'll pray for you, Carl!"

"Thanks. That's another thing new to me."

"To be honest, Carl, real prayer is new to me too."

Carl closed with assurance that the day would come when the Rotundos would be hosting Peter overnight.

"Wonderful. There'll be another time."

CHAPTER TWENTY-FIVE

When Jamie was released from the hospital, the boys were hoping for a sleepover before Peter and I went back on the road. But Judy and Carl were given strict rules for Jamie to follow. The most important one: No strenuous activity for at least three weeks. The boys were disappointed but they spent two afternoons together playing quiet games.

Saturday evening we had a church spaghetti dinner to attend. Betty, Jerry, Peter and I walked in a little late. The place was packed which was nice to see since it was a fundraiser for the church. Peter played with some kids while Betty, Jerry and I visited with other members. Of course there were questions pertaining to Peter. He had not grown at all in any way during the year. The minister and I had already talked and decided it best to inform the congregation of Peter's status. Tomorrow morning in church would be an appropriate time. I told members of the congregation, I would explain Peter's situation then. Finally the four of us had a seat and waited for dinner to be served. During grace, I prayed that God would be with me during the service tomorrow morning as I formally introduced his little servant.

My answer didn't do much to satisfy people's curiosity. As a result, many people now suspected something was seriously wrong with Peter. Across the table from me (Peter was sitting between Betty and Jerry for a change), a senior leaned over her appetizer and whispered, "Is something wrong with Peter?" I pacified her with the assurance that I'd explain in the morning. Several people felt Peter must have some kind of a disease, and asked if it was fatal. I was asked if he would outgrow it. Then I felt a tap on my shoulder. I turned around to a mother of two small children, wondering if Peter was okay. And was his "problem" contagious. I assured her it was not. "Will it affect his beautiful singing voice?"

One woman said she suspected Peter "wasn't quite right" from the beginning.

A father of two came up to me at the dessert table. He suspected Peter was different from the beginning; but to him, Peter was "too good." His own son was clumsy, mentally unfocused and generally obnoxious. Suddenly, I realized he was envious of me. I told him that I would update everyone in church tomorrow morning.

Sunday in church was to be special for Peter and me. To begin with, I had the sermon. The minister had given me a week to get my thoughts organized. I had not anticipated all the misplaced "concern" at the previous night's dinner.

I have to add, Peter was special to many people in the church family for godly reasons. At Christmastime, I had talked to the minister about the possibility of Peter being confirmed and baptized. However, being on the road all the time seemed like an insurmountable obstacle. But where there's a will, there's a way, especially when it's God's will. The minister had agreed and gave me workbooks and a study guide to work with Peter. We both agreed that Peter and I could cover the material; after all, with the time we had, we could do it. When you're driving ten hours a day, you have a lot of time to think about and to work on something like this. (Actually, the review of my own confirmation was reviving old convictions I'd let slip over the years.)

The final call was Peter's. After explaining baptism to him, Peter was excited. Betty, Jerry and I were members of the church and now he would be a full-fledged member too.

I had hoped to get Peter ready for confirmation when we were home in May, but after we had spent some time with the minister, he decided Peter wasn't ready. I had to agree with him. I was hoping he could be baptized before his funeral in June, being uncertain what would follow the event. However, with God's help things worked out.

The minister had met with Peter and me for two hours yesterday afternoon. My minister was indeed convinced Peter was ready. Our study time on the road following Peter's funeral went very well since our minds and hearts were at ease.

We discussed having the service in late August, but felt that was up in the air because of my driving schedule. In kicking some other dates around, we all decided to combine my talk in the morning with the baptism.

Normally, family and friends are invited to a baptism. But with such short notice, we could only invite people by telephone. Connie, Randy and the girls were committed to their own church, but the Earlys and the Rotundos were coming. However, Jamie's sisters went to their church with neighbors. A few other friends were able to make it including Mrs. Pryor, Peter's first grade teacher from the previous year.

At the time of my sermon, Peter was in Sunday school with Jamie. Peter would be confirmed and baptized after the sermon. It was such short notice the baptism would not appear in the church program.

When it was time, I walked to the front and stood in the middle instead of at the podium. I had no notes. My sermon was in the program. Since our minister was present, this was highly unusual. Most of the people appeared confused. Many had not been at the dinner the night before. My sermon was entitled, *The Angels Amongst Us*. "Good morning," I said nervously.

"Thank you, Pastor, for inviting me to take the place reserved for your sermon this morning. I must confess, not until I glanced at my bulletin did I realize mine is not a sermon, but rather a testimonial. I am so relieved."

The congregation enjoyed a congenial laugh at my expense over that little ego-slaying insight.

After standing for a minute collecting my thoughts, I said, "Depending on what late-night radio talk show you listen to, you may hear once a week that there are aliens living amongst us." There were many laughs. "They've come from other planets, solar systems, galaxies, constellations, from the center of the earth and other dimensions. Some of them are even time travelers. But it's not very often you hear of the angels that live amongst us. Those that protect us from danger and evil are known as our guardian angels. There are few cross-country truck drivers that don't believe they have a guardian angel.

How many of you believe angels exist?" About 90% raised their hands. (My friends and the minister knew of Peter's status so did not respond.) "How many of you feel you have a guardian angel?" Half the congregation raised their hands. "How many of you believe you've encountered an angel, face to face?" Four people scattered around the church reluctantly raised their hand. Those four received looks of disbelief from the rest of the congregation.

"As a cross-country truck driver, I have been aware for years that I have a guardian angel for over five years. However, in the last year my guardian angel has changed. I have a new one. And I've been privileged to meet my guardian angel, face to face."

Most looked at me skeptically while four looked on with anticipation. You could have heard a pin drop. "As you know, for the past year, I've had temporary custody of Peter Stevenson. I had no idea how long the custody would last. Recently, both of us had the opportunity to meet his mother for the first time.

"His mother did not give up Peter voluntarily. She had no choice. She had died during his birth." There was a lot of chatter in the congregation. "Bear with me, folks; this story gets better. Peter was born in Slippery Gulch, a small mining town deep in the mountains of Montana. His father blamed his wife's death on his infant son, Peter, whom you all know. As a result, the senior Stevenson grew to despise the boy. He abused Peter terribly—both physically and emotionally. Finally he murdered him when Peter was just the tender age of six." There was a collective gasp. "That was in 1901. Peter Stevenson is dead."

There were whispers galore. Neighbors whispered to neighbors. The whispering became chatter. Some leaned over a pew to talk to someone two pews away while others turned around to talk. Some of the chatter certainly concerned my sanity. However, the four who raised their hands earlier talked to no one. They sat anxiously awaiting my next words. I let the chatter go nearly a full minute before a hush settled over the room.

"There is why the question, his lack of growth and his still missing front teeth that have not come in. All this time, I must confess, I thought he was a ghost. However, June 30 we found out otherwise." The four were practically on their feet with excitement. "Last Christmas Eve, our minister can testify that he saw a colorful glow above Peter's head when he sang *Oh Holy Night*. It may have resembled a halo." I looked at the four seated around the church. "Perhaps some of you saw the same glow, but were hesitant to mention it, not trusting your own eyes." The four nodded and smiled. "As it turned out, your eyes did not fool you." Two of the women clasped their hands and threw their heads back as if in praise. The other two had beautiful smiles on their faces. "I submit to you, Peter Stevenson received his proverbial wings that night. Peter, is a full-fledged angel; and my guardian angel." Many sat frozen in shock and disbelief.

"Peter did not have an easy or enjoyable childhood. In fact, Peter's body was terribly scarred as a result of the beatings he took from his father. He also developed leprosy as an infant. How? I don't know. All I can say is it was Gods will. His nose was rotting away and his horribly deformed left arm was amputated when Peter was three.

"After running away from his father at age four, he became the town freak, ridiculed and despised apparently by everyone. You want to talk about the homeless? That and worse was Peter's lot in life. For the last two years of his life, all his clothes and most of his food came from the town dump. He lived homeless, loveless and friendless.

"Every Sunday, Peter watched people walk into the building known as church and exit some time later. He sensed the building was special because the miners and tough women were dressed differently than they were the rest of the week. And everybody was polite to each other; something unheard of in a tough, frontier-mining town.

"One day he decided to walk into the building and learn for himself what went on in there. He was turned away at the door by the minister saying, 'you're not good enough for God.' Peter didn't know who God was, so he sat under an open window during good weather trying to find out. He heard the minister talk to someone by the name of God and refer to his son, Jesus. But Peter didn't know anybody in town by those names.

"One day while sitting under the window, he heard the minister say, 'let the children come to me, and do not hinder them; for to such belongs the kingdom of heaven. And he laid his hands on them.'

"Peter mistakenly thought the minister was talking to him. So he walked to the entrance and entered. As he did the minister yelled out, 'God damn, it's him.'

"Peter quickly turned around to catch a view of this God damn fella, but no one was there. He was quickly chased from the building.

"As weeks passed with Peter sitting under the open window of the church listening, he was beginning to think God wasn't a real person. Maybe he was imaginary like the friend he sometimes dreamed of having. But he heard that this was God's house. He also heard that a person could ask God for help through something called prayer. He listened to the minister say prayers, so Peter tried praying for help. But nothing ever happened.

"When Peter told me of his church experience in Slippery Gulch, he and I had been together for three days. The minister had told him he wasn't good enough for God, and Peter believed him. Peter culminated his experience by saying, 'Jake, could you teach me to be good enough?' Peter was tearing at my heartstrings, but at the same time I wanted to smack that minister around. Then from deep in my memory a verse came to me: 'See to it that you do not despise one of these little ones; For I tell you that in heaven their angels always behold the face of my Father who is in heaven.'

"Seemingly, not one of his prayers was ever answered. But he never gave up hope. Seconds before his father murdered him, he was heard to say, 'Please Lord, give me a friend.'

"One hundred years later, Peter's final prayer was answered. Mind you in his time only three days passed." I looked around the congregation, turned around and looked at the cross on the wall behind me then looked at the congregation. "Some parallels!" A few women rubbed their arms as if trying to rid themselves of the chills.

"I don't fully understand why, but I'm his ordained friend. In order to experience the friendship, love and affection that he prayed for, he had to have a mortal body. That is the reason you can see and touch him. The body he has is his, but totally and completely restored to its original beauty by God. 99.9% of the time he is a normal six-year-old boy enjoying the childhood he never had. And as a boy, a normal little boy is just the way he wants to be treated by all of us.

"I know this is hard to believe, but most of what I've said can be validated. Before I do though, I'd like to ask all of you a favor. I'd like to keep this within the congregation. If you tell anyone, you'd look and sound as crazy as I do right now. In addition, if you tell this around, it is just a matter of time before Peter and I have no peace. Everyone from reporters to devil worshipers will hound us. And please keep it from your children. They really don't need to know.

"Now, may I field a question or two?"

A hand went up. "What do you expect us to tell them when they ask about lack of growth?"

"I would suggest you tell them he has a condition in his system that does not allow him to grow. That is the truth."

"You said Peter is a normal boy. But if he's an angel, he can't die, right?" another one asked.

"Correct. He's already been there, done that, as the saying goes. From that standpoint he is paranormal, not normal. What I meant is that he has all the needs of a small child. He can be hurt both emotionally and physically as mere mortals can. When he falls and scrapes a knee, he bleeds, feels pain and cries. He's a normal child. However, by the next day, he's completely healed.

"Peter was six at the time he was murdered. The size he is now is the size he was at the time of his death. In 2002 he's the size of a young four-year-old. There are two reasons for that. For one thing, his father was five-foot-four and his mother was four-foot-nine. Second: Children one hundred years ago were several inches shorter than their counterparts today. However, he's very athletic. He has the strength and coordination of a ten-year-old. And he's very intelligent."

Another hand went up. "Is his body the same as any other child's?"

"I assume you mean does he have all the anatomical parts, both internally and externally?" She nodded a little self-consciously. "Yes, he does and everything works just the way they're supposed to." There were many chuckles on that one. "I have a trusted doctor friend who has given him a complete physical."

Another hand went up. It was the man with the two children from the night before, but before I had a chance to recognize him, he blurted out. "I have to admit, Peter sings like an angel. But this is just too much to believe. I need proof."

Everybody nodded. At that point the minister entered the sanctuary from the back with Peter and Jamie from Sunday school. Jamie returned to his parents while Peter remained in the open vestibule doorway with the minister. All eyes turned to face him. Suddenly he felt very uncomfortable. I knelt down. "Hey, Funny Face, come here." He bounded down the aisle and into my arms.

"Like some others, Kiddo, these folks need proof of who you really are. Would you vanish then slowly fade in?" He instantly vanished. A collective gasp followed. Slowly he faded back in. "Keep in mind folks, Peter, while in his mortal body, is no angel. He's a little boy. He has a lot of energy and needs to burn it off at times. As an angel, he's in God's service from his heart. But as a little boy he sometimes develops a devilish twinkle in his eyes." There was a knowing laugh at that. "And at times it gets him into trouble. At times he needs disciplining, just as do other little boys. He's a fun-loving little kid as many of you know and that's just the way we both want you to treat him. Please don't treat him as anything special."

The hands went up again. "Peter, you are Jake's guardian angel, right?" He nodded. "Have you ever saved Jake from harm or…death?"

He thought about how to answer that; after all, he wasn't a bragger. "We're a team. Jake's my guardian. He protects and comforts me and I do the same for him."

More hands went up. "Could you give us an example?" another man asked.

"When I'm scared, he comforts me. When I'm hurt, he makes me feel better."

This was not the answer they were looking for. The same man said, "But can you tell us how you have protected Jake in a tough spot—maybe in his truck?"

Peter finally looked to me for help. "Folks, in most little boys, modesty is not in their vocabulary. But when it comes to Peter's exploits, he's modest." I mentioned the several times he helped me to avoid dangerous situations including my loss of brakes on the mountain in Idaho nine months earlier. I described the Miracle Rescue on I-40. "Many of you may recall seeing it covered on national news." People here and there nodded yes. Others seemed persuaded and joined the earlier nodders.

A woman stood and looked at Peter. She had been crying. "Hearing about your previous life reduced me to tears." A new tear broke lose. "But living in Orchard Park with Jake, Betty and Jerry must be like living in heaven for you."

Peter smiled at the three of us. "It is my heaven." The congregation took his answer one way, but I know this is his heaven.

Another man stood to be recognized. "Peter, is Jake ever mean to you?"

He giggled with a smile. "Yeah. He's mean to me all the time."

Laughter broke out, relieving the tension.

"I think you'd better explain that, Kiddo."

He giggled again. He gave several examples while the congregation laughed. Then he put his head down. "When the people in Slippery Gulch were mean to me, they hurt me and made me cry. Jake would never hurt me." He was touching hearts like he'd done at Christmas.

Another asked, "Has Jake ever spanked you?"

Peter again put his head down, with real embarrassment. "Yes. Once and it hurt," he mumbled then he looked up. "But when he finished, he picked me up and hugged me and kissed me. I knew I deserved it, but I knew he still loved me. His kiss made me stop hurting." In a quiet voice he said, "My daddy used to beat me with a rope, but Jake was the first one who ever spanked me and punished me in love. He was the first one ever to hug me. I got my first kiss from Jake." He looked at me, asking with his eyes to be picked up. When I did, he gave me a hug. He looked back at the congregation. "I love Jake and Jake loves me." Then almost in a whisper he added, "Jake is the first one who ever loved me."

If he hadn't touched them by now, he did then. I noticed some women were wiping their eyes, including Grace Pryor and Judy Rotundo.

"Peter, did Jake ever make you mad?" another woman asked.

With his arm around my neck he said, "Jake could never make me mad."

"Have you ever gotten peeved at him?"

"No, but I once peed near a bear."

With that the house went wild. Men were holding their sides, most notably the pastor in the double doors leading out to the front entrance. If any late-comers had opened the door and come in on this scene, they would have shut the door and gone home.

To redeem himself I think, the pastor asked in his podium voice so it would carry, "Peter, have you celebrated a birthday in the past year with Jake?"

A smile broke out. "Aunt Betty and Uncle Jerry had a surprise birthday party for me when we got home and Jake was a part of it."

I decided to expand on that. "Folks, his birthday is December 2. He'd never had a birthday party before. In fact, he'd never had anybody wish him a happy birthday. His father used to remind him it was his birthday by saying things like, 'This is the day you should have died so your mother could live,' and 'This is the day you murdered your mother.'" There were groans.

"The morning of Peter's birthday, I'd pretended to forget about it. That just about killed him, but he never reminded me. If ever there was a time he was peeved at me, that was it.

Betty started working on his birthday party in September. The whole family was involved. She even had my driver manager in Salt Lake involved to make sure we got home for it." He gave me a hug.

An athletic man in his thirties raised his hand. "I've watched Peter play in the back room with some of the kids during the year. I always marveled at his athletic abilities being such a tiny youngster. Now I understand. He has an angelic edge on other kids."

"As an angel he does, but in that state he's invisible to all but me typically. As a mortal he's just a normal little kid who happens to have inherited athletic abilities. He's not permitted to use angelic powers except for emergencies. Those are my rules. But I'm convinced they are God's too. What you witnessed were his own God-given mortal athletic abilities."

A woman in the back rose to be heard better. "Would Peter sing *The Lord's Prayer* for us?" I looked at Peter. He smiled and nodded.

"Before he sings, please remember this. If you see him misbehave someplace, please correct him as you would any other little boy. Then tell me about it later." I knew I was setting someone up for one of Peter's tests.

He hadn't practiced the song in a long time; nevertheless, he sang well. There were few dry eyes.

When Peter had finished, he returned to his seat as the minister came down the center aisle to his podium. From the pulpit he looked at Peter and thanked him.

Looking at the congregation, he said, "Folks, as Jake said, I've suspected since Christmastime Peter is an angel." He glanced at my friends and family. "However, many have suspected for many months. At least one has experienced a miracle through Peter first hand, right Jamie?"

Jamie smiled, and the minister continued. "So Peter can turn into an angel on demand. But most of the time he is Jake's six-year-old boy charge, on loan from Peter's heavenly Father. Is that the picture, Jake?" I nodded.

"Since Christmas, Jake has worked with Peter on our confirmational materials. And during those few short times they were home since Christmas, I have too. Today we have a very special confirmation followed by a very special baptism: Not because Peter can turn angelic; rather, Peter at his young age has a good understanding of the life and Gospel of Jesus Christ. Generally, a person this young is not quite ready for membership. But Peter has experienced more evil than most Americans see in a lifetime. He has experienced a forced maturity as a matter of survival. Furthermore, I have questioned him at length and am satisfied he understands his position in Christ and before God the Father. He understands prayer and the moving of the Holy Spirit of God. Jake, you have been a good mentor. Peter, will you come to me, alone please?"

Peter went to the aisle and walked to the front.

"Thank you. Peter, I asked you to come alone. Normally, one or both parents come to stand with the young person. I asked you to come alone because you always thought you were alone and friendless, Jesus was your unseen, faithful friend. You, standing here apparently alone, remind us that your greater friend, greater than faithful Jake, is God. Peter, do you believe that Jesus the Christ is God's only begotten Son, your Lord and Savior?"

"Yes, I sure do."

The pastor nodded to me and I came toward Peter's priceless smile and took his hand.

"Dear friends, we are gathered here to baptize Peter Stevenson into the Christian faith, because our Savior Jesus

Christ has commanded us..." Peter looked up at me and squeezed my hand.

As the minister completed the statement he turned to me and continued. "Jake, do you promise to be a good and loving grandparent to Peter?"

Peter looked up at me then put his arms up to be lifted. I picked him up and looked at the minister. "You bet I do."

Peter hugged me and looked back to the minister. "Do you also promise to remain faithful to him whatever the future may bring, and to respect him as a separate person wherever he may go, and to remember always that Peter was born of God?"

Peter was searching my eyes for my answer.

I looked Peter in the eyes and ran my hand down the back of his head. "Yes."

Peter looked back to the minister.

"Do you promise to instruct Peter in the Christian faith and life as contained in the Scriptures and the great interpreters of the faith? To pray with him and for him and to bring him up in the nurture and guidance of God?"

Again Peter looked to me.

"Yes, I do."

The minister read through the Commitment of the Congregation, after which the congregation responded, "We do."

At that point the minister took Peter into his own arms. He looked at Peter as if he'd never looked at another child, and paused. What did the minister see? Finally, he dipped his hand in the water from the baptismal font. "I baptize you, Peter Stevenson, in the name of the Father, the Son and the Holy Spirit. Amen."

The minister looked at the congregation. "During my career I have baptized many little angels, but never have I baptized a holy angel." Looking to both Peter and me he said, "Thank you. I am humbled and honored." He held Peter towards the congregation. "Folks, on this blessed Sunday, I present to you the newest member of our church family, Peter Stevenson."

Peter had a huge smile on his face. The congregation, already standing, clapped as one. The minister brought Peter back to his chest and was about to hand him back to me when Peter gave him a prolonged hug.

As the congregation sat, Peter looked at them as he settled himself back in my arms. "Growing up in Slippery Gulch, I knew nothing but hate. I didn't have a family. No one wanted me. No one fed me when I was hungry, or helped me when I was sick or hurt. I was alone and afraid. I died—alone and afraid. Now I know love. I feel it and see it every place I look. And now I have two loving families—this big one and Jake's. Thank you."

He buried his face in my shoulder, not in tears but gratitude. However, many of the women wiped tears from their eyes including Betty, Judy Rotundo, Grace Pryor and Sue Early. Jamie had tears, too along with some of the men.

After the service, almost everyone came up to Peter, Betty, Jerry and me in the sanctuary rather than waiting in the reception line later. Individually, each welcomed Peter to his church family with a handshake, pinching his cheek or ruffling his hair. Peter was overwhelmed.

Later in the reception area, I watched Peter carefully. I knew he was concerned about being treated as someone special, instead of the way all other church children were treated. I was certain one of his special tests was coming, but I had no idea what he had in mind. While talking to a few friends, I watched Peter take two cookies from the goodies table. He walked between two women and dropped one.

Instead of picking it up the way he'd been taught, he deliberately stepped on it and continued on his way. (This was the test.) One of the women grabbed him by the collar of his suit jacket. While in tow on their way to the kitchen, Peter looked at me, shrugging his shoulders. A few seconds later they emerged, Peter with a broom and dustpan in hand. As they walked back toward the smashed cookie, he smiled and gave me a thumbs-up. I returned the thumbs-up. He was being treated as any other child and was thrilled.

Later, I walked up to the woman and said, "Congratulations, Sally. You passed." She was puzzled. "Peter deliberately dropped that cookie and didn't step on it by accident. He wanted to see if he would be treated like every other child. Coming back from the kitchen, he gave me a smile and a thumbs-up."

"Did you tell him to do that?"

"Oh no. You don't know this kid. I didn't have to suggest a thing. That was all him, but let me tell you, you made him very happy."

"Well I'll be. Most children these days would have been angry with me. Like it's none of my business."

"Yes, I know. But you made his day. Now he knows he's just another kid."

"You know me, Jake. I can't let something like that pass. He's quite a kid, isn't he?"

"You said it. Considering his terrible childhood, it's nothing short of amazing how lovable and affectionate he is."

"Jake, how bad was it for him? You know I've taught school so nothing shocks me."

"I hardly described a thing." I further described the beatings he took from his father and from the town.

Her past teaching experience did not prepare her for my revelation. "Oh, my God! How do you know all of this?"

"Peter gave me a tour of the town and showed me where all the beatings took place. His day was spent trying to live until the next."

"Do you think he told you the truth?"

"Do you think he'd be an angel now if he hadn't? Peter showed me his body after the last time his father beat him. He offered to show me his body after his father murdered him, but I declined. I couldn't take it. His father stabbed Peter over thirty times from the lower abdomen to the neck with a hunting knife. I can imagine what his body looked like."

Sally looked at the happy little blond-haired boy ten feet away, and was sickened. Swiping her face with a paper napkin, she said, "How could anyone do such terrible things to a child?"

"His father grew insane with bitterness and hatred. As it turned out, he was caught and hung for butchering several other little boys."

Just then Joe Miller, my dentist, came up to me. "Jake, I've been wondering why Peter's teeth never grew in. In fact, I was going to ask you about it today. Now I don't have to. I'd like to ask you. Do you think Peter would be open to some front teeth?"

I thought about this. He was so darned cute without them. But it would make eating apples and chicken wings easier. "Could you do that?"

"I shook his hand a few minutes ago. He's solid and warm, therefore as mortal as I am. I don't see why not."

"What would happen to his teeth when he changes to an angel?"

He thought about that and asked, "What happens to his clothes?"

"They go with him I guess, and he always comes back wearing them."

"Well then, I'd say his teeth would too."

"Let's talk to Peter. I'll meet you in the pastor's office in a few minutes."

I located him in the back room playing with Jamie and a few other kids. After getting his attention, I took his hand and led him into the office to meet with Joe. "Peter, you know Dr. Miller." He nodded. "He's my dentist. Peter, would you like some front teeth?"

He looked at me. "Sure, but they're gone."

"True, they are. But it's possible for Dr. Miller to fit you with some artificial ones."

"What does ar, artic, articficle mean?"

I smiled, repeated it and gave him a chance to try again. "It means man-made. In other words, Dr. Miller can make two teeth for you that would be almost as good as your own. You could take them out when you want, but it would be easier to eat."

"Could I eat an apple?"

We both laughed. "Without any problem at all," Joe answered.

"Will it hurt?"

"Not really. It may be a little uncomfortable when I fit you for the plate, but I'll be very gentle."

"You're going to put a dish in my mouth?"

"Not a dish, Kiddo, a plate. That's what it's called."

Peter turned to me. "I don't know. What do you think, Jake?"

"I know you're concerned about the pain, Kiddo, but Dr. Miller is gentle. There may be a little pain, but I think it would be worth it. Just think, you can eat chicken wings and cinnamon apples without the juice running all the way down to your bellybutton." I poked him in his bellybutton and he giggled.

"Okay, I'll try it."

I looked at Joe. "Should we go with children's teeth or adult teeth?"

"Peter, did your teeth fall out by themselves, or were they knocked out?" Joe asked.

"One day they got real loose and fell out. I got scared."

"Did you see a doctor?"

He put his head down. I pulled him close. "Joe, when Peter was alive, nobody ever talked to him except to call him a name, humiliate him or tell him to beat it. He never had a friend, much less a dentist." I ruffled his hair.

"I'm sorry, Peter," Joe said. "The way he just described it, it sounds like they fell out on schedule. I'd say adult teeth. But let's wait until I have a chance to examine his mouth."

"Well, you won't have a problem: It's big enough."

Peter giggled and Joe laughed. "It is not," Peter said as he punched me.

Joe laughed. "Peter, is this Jake being mean to you?"

He giggled. "Yeah, he's always mean to me and I love it. Jake, you'll be there with me won't you?"

"No, I'll be out of town that day." Peter looked at me with concern. "Come on Peter, we don't even know when it'll be. Of course, I'll be there with you."

He rested his head against my chest then looked at Joe and said, "See, he's mean!"

Joe laughed. "I'm going to be out of town for a week. Call me a week from tomorrow, and I'll try and work Peter in. In the meantime, Jake, treat the boy a little kinder."

"I'll work on that." I winked at Peter. "But no promises."

THE SEPARATION

That afternoon I received a call from a friend inviting me over to his house that night for a game of poker with a few of the guys. Since our games are for fun rather than to try and improve our financial standing within the community, we keep it at a penny ante. And of course, a beer or two goes well with poker. No kids and no women! It's great fun!

"Gee, thanks for thinking of me, Gus, but with Peter…"

"Jake, when was the last time you made it to one of our games?"

I thought about that. "I don't know."

"Well I do. It was April of 2001. That was two months before you met Peter, and you haven't been to one since. A few of us were talking after church. Peter's an angel—your guardian angel. We were all thrilled for both of you this morning in church. But, Jake, you have three full time jobs: You're a full-time truck driver, a full-time teacher, and you're a full-time grandpa. Peter's a terrific kid, but he's six. You have to take a break once in a while."

I never told anybody about the experience I had while Peter was saving Stevie, but as a result of that, I knew Gus was right. Although I've socialized without Peter many times during the last thirteen months, I haven't had a break from Peter in seven weeks, and then that was a guilt trip. Before that, my last break was last May. I made up my mind. "I'll be there, Gus."

During dinner, I announced my intentions to Peter. I had already cleared it with Betty. She agreed with Gus 100%. "Peter, tonight I'm going to meet with a few of the guys for a game of cards."

Peter looked at me shocked. "You are?" I nodded without a smile. "But I thought we were going to talk about my baptism tonight."

I didn't promise that, but because of our traditional nightly talk, it was assumed. "I'm sorry, Kiddo, but we can talk about it tomorrow night. I really enjoy playing cards with the guys and we haven't played together for sixteen months."

Peter was hurt and I was feeling guilty. I was ready to give in when I became angry with Peter and myself. Before I could respond, Betty intervened. "Peter, don't you think you're being unfair?"

Peter looked at her uncomprehending.

"You are Jake's best friend, just as Jake is your best friend. Jake has other friends just as you do. But Jake is an adult. He needs to spend some time with his adult friends, just as you need to spend some time with Jamie. But Jake hasn't spent any time with his other friends since last May. When he does, it doesn't mean he loves you any less. I know he loves you more than the world, but he doesn't want to ignore his other friends either. How would Jamie feel if you ignored him?"

Suddenly the light went on. "I see what you mean, Aunt Betty. Jamie wouldn't understand. I'm sorry, Jake. You have fun tonight. Is Bill going to be there?" I nodded. "Is Danny?"

"Nope. No kids or women allowed."

Peter giggled. "Not even Aunt Betty?"

We both laughed. "Nope, not even Aunt Betty. Hey, I've got forty-five minutes before I have to leave. Why don't we talk right now?"

It was a great compromise and Betty defused a potentially volatile situation. My only concern was why I was so upset with Peter in the first place?

The next day I received a disturbing phone call.

CHAPTER TWENTY-SIX

Monday was supposed to be hot and humid. I suggested to Peter we go to the park in the morning and then come back home for lunch. In a word, a lazy, leisurely morning.

After lunch, Betty and I sat on the back porch watching Peter run through the sprinkler a while. The phone rang. It was our minister.

"Jake, a woman just called me from Child Protective Services. She was asking a lot of questions about you and Peter." Suddenly I was worried.

"Jake, Peter doesn't have a Social Security Number, does he?" I responded with a no. "Does he have a birth certificate?"

"Not that I'm aware of. Why?"

"And you never adopted Peter, right?"

"Of course not."

"If you can't prove he's legally yours, the state could come in and take him."

"What! They can't do that. He was given to me by divine providence. We are meant to be together."

"Jake, what's going on?" Betty asked. I waved her off.

"We know that, but the state doesn't think in terms of providence. Do you have an attorney?" I said yes. "Does he know about Peter?" The answer was no. "If I were you, I'd get over to see him today. Take Peter with you. But leave your home soon. If the state shows up before you leave, they may take him."

Suddenly I was scared. Was I being punished for last night? I explained the situation, as best I understood it to Betty. I called Peter as I picked up the towel. "Peter, we're going to…"

"Jake, what's wrong." I could mask kidding him, but not serious stuff.

"We're leaving for a while, Kiddo. Let's go up and put on dry shorts."

"Where are we going?"

"We're going to see a friend of mine."

Changing into clean, dry clothes he balked, "Jake, you're scaring me. What's wrong?"

Taking his hand I said, "Come on. I'll tell you in the car."

I told Betty I'd call. We drove out of the court and headed to the back exit of the neighborhood. "Jake, what's going on? Why this way?"

I felt his eyes burning into the back of my head from the back seat. He needed an answer, but the answer I had to give him was not the one he wanted. "Kiddo, we have a possible problem. Your mom said we could be together forever, but the state may not view us that way."

"What do you mean?" he asked as the tears formed.

"I have no legal claim to you. In other words, I have not adopted you. You aren't legally my son. You're not even my real grandson. You're not related to me in any way, so the State of New York may think we shouldn't be together. We're on our way to see my attorney."

"God put us together, Jake. Everybody knows that."

"I know. Even if the State agrees, we have to follow the laws they have on the books."

"They can't take me away from you, can they?" I knew they could and would certainly try. I was fifty-eight and single, Peter was six. "Jake?" He was now in tears and scared. I was scared and close to tears myself.

"Let's wait and see what my attorney says."

I wasn't even sure he was in today. We took the elevator to his office. I said hello to his secretary, Bobbie.

"Hello, Mr. Winters." She looked at Peter. "Well, who is this?"

"This is Peter Stevenson. Is Terry in?" Neither Peter nor I were in very good emotional shape.

"Say, you two look troubled. No, Terry's in court. He should be back soon. He can see you then."

"Fine. We'll wait." After a cup of coffee for me and a can of pop Peter couldn't finish, Terry walked in. We took him by surprise. In his office, I introduced him to Peter. Since Terry and I moved in different circles, he didn't know a thing about Peter. After forty-five minutes he knew enough to share my concern. Of course, Peter had to prove he was an angel the quick way.

"The problem we have Terry, is if the State acts and the media takes note of Peter's angelic status, neither one of us will ever get any peace again. And I mean anywhere in the U.S.!"

He thought about this. "I can understand that, but without demonstrating that aspect of Peter to the State, it will see Peter as a normal little boy living with a man who has no legal claim to him. In that situation, the State has every right to remove Peter. And you could be in big trouble."

"No," Peter screamed. "God said we can be together forever."

"That may be true Peter, but we also have to live within New York State laws. And every state has these rules. What Jake has to do is adopt you. Unfortunately, the State will start investigating where you came from and who authorized Jake to be your unofficial guardian."

Peter lit up. "I know! I'll tell the State I'm assigned to Jake by God to be his guardian. How's that?"

"Good thinking, Peter. You are a very keen young man. But, Jake is too old to adopt a boy your age. Plus, he's single."

Peter was in tears again.

"Is it possible to get a private hearing with a judge where the situation could be explained without public knowledge?"

Again he thought about this. "The state would have to agree. I doubt they would. Even if they did, temporary custody could take weeks to arrange."

"What happens to us in the meantime?" I asked.

"Unfortunately, they would put Peter in a foster home in the interim. Jake, there isn't any way of getting around this. If you run, when you're caught they would arrest you for kidnapping. You'd spend the rest of your life in jail."

"If the State wouldn't agree to a private hearing, what would happen?"

"Peter becomes a ward of the State. Montana has no interest in a Boot Hill corpse one hundred years old."

"Terry, we can't allow that. The only one that can adopt Peter is me. God will preclude anything else."

"Those are the words of faith, not the facts as they stand today. Look, we'll come up with something. In the meantime, you're going to have to give Peter up…for a while anyway. If you don't, you're going to end up in serious trouble and destroy any chance of even seeing him again."

During this entire exchange, Peter was sitting on my lap trembling. "Peter, do you understand everything being said?"

In a trembling voice he said, "Yes. Jake, I'm scared."

"I am too, Kiddo." His eyes were so sad they were killing me. "Peter, we have to do this according to the laws of the state. We don't have a choice. This is all going to work out. I don't know how, but God won't allow it any other way.

We both have to have faith. Trust me Kiddo, and trust God, okay?"

He agreed, but I could tell he wasn't too sure about the trusting business. Actually, I wasn't either.

I borrowed Terry's phone and called Betty. "Betty, has anybody from the state been there?"

"Yes. Her name is Ms. Stockton. She wasn't very happy to find you were gone with my having no knowledge where. Jake, where are you?"

"We're at my attorney's office."

"That's what I thought. How's it going?"

"Not well. I have to give up Peter for a while. If I don't, I could be charged with kidnapping."

"Oh, Lord. How is Peter taking it?"

"We're both in shock."

"Where will he go?"

"I guess to a foster home someplace."

"Jake, this isn't right. Is Peter there?"

"Yeah, just a minute." I handed the phone to Peter.

"Aunt Betty, we…" but that's all he could say. He nodded a couple of times and handed the phone back to me.

"Jake…" Now she was too choked up.

"We're going to win this, Betty. I don't know how, but it's just one more battle for Peter and me. God willing, we will win. See you later."

"Okay, Terry," I had my fist on his desk. "Call Children's whatever."

Shortly Ms. Stockton arrived. She walked in with a purpose and an attitude. She had a job to do and emotions were not involved. I found it hard to believe she had ever worked with frightened children before. "So you're Winters, and this must be Peter Stevenson." She walked over, took an arm and pulled him off my lap. "Come with me."

"Jake!" Peter screamed.

I grabbed him and picked him up. He immediately wrapped his arms around my neck, trembling violently. We were both sobbing. "Promise me, Kiddo, don't go back to Slippery Gulch. If you cave in, we'll never see each other again. Just pray! We'll be back together, I promise you."

In a weak voice he said, "I promise."

I rubbed my hand down the back of his head. "I promise you, we will win this."

"And I promise you, *Mister* Winters," Ms. Stockton snapped, "you'll never see this boy again."

"You have no idea what you're dealing with, Stockton. You're in way over your head." I put Peter down.

She bristled. "Ms. Stockton to you."

As Peter was pulled to the door, I said, "And it's Mr. Winters to you." The look I got was deadly. "Remember, Little One, keep your faith in God, Terry and me. We'll win! God's on our side. And no going back to Slippery Gulch."

"He won't be going anywhere," Ms. Stockton boasted.

I ignored her. "Remember your baptism and the promises I made to you, the church and God." Ms. Stockton rolled her eyes. "Those promises stand no matter what anybody tells you." I looked at Ms. Stockton, then back at Peter. I wiggled a finger and said, "'I will love you forever, Little One'." I got a forced fearful smile as the door closed a little too hard.

I looked at Terry through tears.

"My little angel is gone."

ABOUT THE AUTHOR

Doug White, author of the Jake Winters Series, including *The Load, The Editorial, The Gift, The Funeral,* and now *The Separation,* is a former school teacher and camp counselor. He drove an 18-wheeler cross-country for thirteen years. In 2003 he turned in his big truck and bought an RV. A graduate of Massanutten Military Academy in Woodstock, Virginia, and Ashland College (now Ashland University) in Ashland, Ohio, White U.S. Junior Chamber of Commerce (Jaycees) International Senator #32834. He resides in Orchard Park, New York. In his free time he enjoys camping, canoeing and fishing.